BLOOD EAGLE

BLOOD EAGLE

The Whale Road Chronicles: VI

Tim Hodkinson

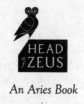

An Aries Book

First published in the UK in 2023 by Head of Zeus Ltd,
part of Bloomsbury Publishing Plc

9 7 5 3 1 2 4 6 8

A catalogue record for this book is available from the British Library.

ISBN (PB): 9781801105422
ISBN (E): 9781801105408

Cover design: Ben Prior
Typeset by Siliconchips Services Ltd UK

Printed and bound in Great Britain by
CPI Group (UK) Ltd, Croydon CR0 4YY

Head of Zeus
First Floor East
5–8 Hardwick Street
London EC1R 4RG
WWW.HEADOFZEUS.COM

To the three wyrd sisters who govern my fate
and the valkyrie who watches over them.
Emily, Clara, Alice and Trudy.

Nú er blóðugr örn
breiðum hjörvi
bana Sigmundar
á baki ristinn

Now with a broad sword
the bloody eagle
is carved on the back
of Sigmund's killer

—*Nornagests þáttr*, an Old Norse legendary saga
(fornaldarsaga)

Part One
936 AD
Jól (Yule)
Northern Norway

Einar Thorfinnsson pulled on his fighting glove. He took a deep breath, trying to calm the nerves that squirmed like serpents in his guts. Soon there would be a fight. Before long the snow would be sprayed red with blood. He prayed none of it would be his own.

Around him the other eight members of Ulrich's crew were preparing for battle. Seven of them were *úlfhéðnar* – Wolf Coats – like Einar, and wore the pelt of a wolf around their shoulders. The other two, the dark-skinned *Serk* called Surt and the Saxon, Wulfhelm, wore heavy wool cloaks. All of them moved without hurrying but with deliberate purpose. They removed their snowshoes and donned shirts made from rings of iron, known as *brynjas*. They buckled on their sword belts and put on visored helmets. All of them were silent. Their usual jokes, jibes and banter were gone, replaced by the serious, quiet and purposeful activity of folk whose job was war and who were preparing to go to work.

The *járngreipr*, Einar's fighting glove, was a standard leather mitten covered with iron rings – the kind that warriors wore in battle to protect their hands. This one, however, had been modified by the greatest craftsman on Middle Earth. Unlike most battle gauntlets, the bottom end of this glove, where the ring and little finger would usually go in, had been replaced by two thick strips of iron that came from where the back of the hand would be and curved around to form hooks that almost touched the palm. These replaced the little finger and part of Einar's palm that he had lost in a duel to the death with his father. The glove allowed Einar to grip a long weapon with all the steadfastness he had before his hand had been maimed.

The snow swirled around him, driven by a gust of cold northern wind. Against all instinct Einar followed his companions' lead, stripping off the bulky, thick furs that kept him warm and alive in the harsh winter landscape. They may have brought comfort but they would restrict his movements when it came to a fight.

'Can we be sure they're following us?' Einar said.

'We're in hostile country, lad,' Ulrich – the small, wiry leader of the Wolf Coat company – said. 'I'm not going to take any chances.'

They had been lucky to spot the group of people coming behind them across the white wilderness. The snowfall had slackened off a little and the blond-haired Sigurd, the Wolf Coat with the sharpest eyes, had noticed a company of folk in heavy furs like themselves, travelling fast on skis in their direction. Even at a distance the shields slung across their backs and the spears they used as ski poles were obvious.

'How do we know they mean us harm?' Wulfhelm said. 'What if they're just a band of farmers out hunting?'

Ulrich cast a black look in Wulfhelm's direction. 'Then this is not their lucky day,' he said, a grim smile on his lips as he drew his sword.

'Think about it, Einar: it's Jól and the weather is filthy,' Skarphedinn – Skar to his friends – the tall, slightly gangling warrior who was Ulrich's prowman, his right-hand man, said. He had the head of his grey wolfskin cloak pulled up over his helmet and flakes of snow caught in the strands of his long, Irish-style moustache. 'Anyone abroad today is either mad or can only be up to mischief.'

Einar was about to point out that they were abroad themselves but then held his tongue. There was little doubt about it. They *were* up to mischief.

It was indeed Jól, the great mid-winter festival, but while the rest of the folk were snuggled up indoors, spending twelve or more days drinking and eating themselves sick, Ulrich's úlfhéðnar were trekking across the snow-covered landscape on a mission that was really just a ruse for their real purpose in being in the folk district: to determine if Jarl Sigurd could trust the local lendermann or not.

After their previous voyage that had taken them to Hedeby at the edge of Denmark and the lair of the notorious viking Asbjorn Hviti – the Bear – they had sailed back to Norway and the employ of Jarl Sigurd of Hlader. The jarl was as powerful as a king himself, but he had thrown his lot in with the young lad Hakon Haraldsson who now held the high seat of Norway. Jarl Sigurd was Hakon's most powerful supporter but the new king was far from secure. The folk may have rebelled and driven Hakon's half-brother, Eirik Bloody Axe, both off the throne and out of the country, but there were many in Norway who had yet to accept Hakon as their new ruler. Some nobles thought they should be king themselves rather than a mere lad of sixteen winters. Their half-hearted support was further eroded by the fact that Hakon had been raised overseas, fostered in the court of Aethelstan of Wessex, the great Christian king who wanted to rule all of Britain and seemed obsessed with meddling in every other land around it as well.

Eirik still lurked, an ever-present brooding menace only a short distance away across the northern seas in his new realm of Orkney: a realm that by rights belonged to Einar.

Ulrich hated Eirik for betraying him and had taken to heart the wisdom imparted by Odin himself – that the enemy of your enemy could be a valuable ally. Hakon thwarted Eirik just by being alive and on the throne of Norway. Jarl Sigurd was keeping Hakon there, so Ulrich and his crew had returned to the cold north and offered their swords in the jarl's service.

Jarl Sigurd had faced opposition himself for his support of Hakon and currently he had his eye on one of his noblemen, a lendermann called Gerpir Halfdansson, who ruled a district to the south of Hlader. He suspected Gerpir of secretly working against him in support of Eirik. Despite it being the festival of Jól, Jarl Sigurd had sent the Wolf Coats to Gerpir's lands, ostensibly with the task of collecting some long-overdue taxes, but really to find out which side Gerpir was on.

Now, if Ulrich and Skar were correct, it looked like Gerpir was indeed working against Jarl Sigurd. Not only that but Gerpir had guessed what the Wolf Coats were really up to, and was about to do something about it.

'I should have known that story about his silver being kept in the back woods was a lie,' Ulrich said, referring to what Gerpir had told them when they arrived at his hall the night before. The lendermann had claimed that all his treasure was held at his brother's hall some way off and, with it being Jól, if the Wolf Coats really wanted it soon they would need to go and get it themselves.

This was how they had found themselves trekking across the empty, white wilderness when everyone else in the district was stuffing themselves with as much roast boar as they could manage.

Einar pulled back on the snowshoes he had taken off to remove his heavy fur britches. Like the others, he kicked snow over the furs he had stripped off to hide them. He was nearly ready.

The Wolf Coats were preparing their trap on top of a hill. When they had spotted the men following them they had been on a trackway that was marked out by occasional tall poles, driven into the ground to stand tall above the snow and show where the path was. Ulrich had ordered them off the track and up the slope of a hill nearby. When they had trudged their way to the summit, they had found it to be a concave bowl. Skar had declared it perfect as the raised lip of the bowl would shield them from the eyes of their pursuers while they made preparations to do something about them.

A natural path led through the bowl on top of the summit, and the Wolf Coats had split in two groups, one on either side of the track. They had planted their round shields into the snow in a line so they formed two short fences opposite each other, then shovelled more snow in front of them into a bank that hid them. From the natural trackway between them, the banked-up snow before the shields merged with the snow behind so they were almost invisible to the casual observer.

Now the trap was ready. Each one of the warriors readied their weapons and crouched behind the line of shields.

Einar was behind the shield wall on the right side of the track. Beside him was Kari. He had black tattooed runes that were visible on the lower part of his cheeks under his helmet visor, making him look a little like a bird had left its footprints there. Next to Kari was Surt. The big, heavily muscled man's black skin contrasted with the snow that surrounded them. Beyond Surt was Starkad, whose blond beard cascaded in a long braid from his chin.

Opposite them on the other side of the track, hidden by the snow banked up on their shields, crouched Ulrich, Skar, Sigurd and the Saxon: Wulfhelm. Somewhere up ahead Einar knew Affreca lurked, her deadly Finnish bow ready to choose who would be slain.

Now he was ready. All they had to do was wait.

Einar drew his sword and grasped it with his járngreipr. A hoop of leather was fastened to the front and back at the base of the metal strips, and Einar looped it over the pommel of his sword, making his grip even more secure.

The cold bit into Einar's flesh everywhere it was exposed. He breathed in, looking at those around him. None of the others appeared to share his apprehension at the coming violence. They were calm and serious, and Einar knew he could not betray his own feelings and invite their derision.

He looked over his shoulder. Behind them the hillside fell in a sharp incline down to a lake. The water was invisible, buried beneath ice and snow, but the wide, flat expanse that filled the valley at the bottom of the hill could be nothing else.

A range of mountains, snow-capped and craggy, bit into the sky beyond the lake. The trees of a wood lined one shore. Everywhere was covered in a deep blanket of white snow. Despite the empty desolation of the landscape, Einar could tell that there must be at least one farm nearby. Cattle moved across the surface of the lake below, probably taken there to drink at holes hacked through the ice. The beasts' breath and sweat rose into the cold air in steamy clouds. Similar pillars of steam rose from the dark piles of shit they had deposited on the ice behind them.

Einar sensed the men beside him tense. He looked around and saw the warriors who had been pursuing them were reaching the summit of the hill.

It was time to spring the trap.

2

The men following the Wolf Coats were no fools. Their view of the summit was hidden by the slope and, when Einar heard the sound of their skis in the snow slow down, he knew they were approaching with caution.

He did not envy them. Climbing a hill in skis was hard work if you were going slowly. You had to bend forward far further than usual and get your body much lower, otherwise the skis did not bite into the snow and you quickly found yourself sliding backwards. It was usually not long before your thighs and calf muscles felt as if they were on fire.

Einar kept as still as the others, though his heart was racing like a frightened rabbit's. Every sense felt strained to the point of breaking. As he listened to the steady swish of the skis getting ever closer, he clenched his teeth, fighting to quell the urge to run forward and attack: to get the fight started and end the insufferable, nerve-shredding anticipation. Despite the cold, he felt a drop of sweat trickle down his cheek.

Then he saw the top of a helmet appearing over the lip of the summit. He ducked his head below his shield. They had to stay hidden now so as not to give their presence away. The Wolf Coats were outnumbered so victory depended on surprise. Affreca would be the one to spring the trap. All the others could do was keep their heads down and wait.

The sound of the skis moved onto the summit of the hill, and Einar guessed they were starting to move between the two snow banks before the shield walls.

'They've gone on over the hill,' Einar heard a man say. He

spoke in the Norse tongue with the heavy accent of northern Norway. 'We should be careful or they'll spot us and know they're being followed.'

At least we know now they were definitely following us, Einar thought. He felt a little relief that he could now be sure they were not about to execute some innocent hunters.

Hunched behind his shield beside him, Einar saw a grin spread across Kari's face. It was an expression more of wolfish delight that their plan was working than one of good humour.

Then the noise of skis stopped.

'Wait,' another man's voice said.

Einar knew then the men on skis had noticed something was wrong.

A flurry of movement at the corner of his eye made him glance to his left. At the far side of the hill summit, Affreca rose from the snow like a geyser, spraying white in every direction. She had her wolf pelt cloak around her shoulders, the head drawn up over her visored helmet so the triangular ears stood up above her head and the snout protruded over her face. She looked every bit like a wolf rearing on its hind legs, except for the drawn bow in her grasp. Even under her helmet Einar could see the cold, flat expression that he knew overcame her beautiful features as her green eyes first sought then locked on to a target.

A moment later she loosed the bowstring. Her arrow streaked across the hilltop, buzzing like an angry hornet. Einar's shield obstructed him from seeing where it hit, but the soft thump it made and the anguished cry that followed told him it had struck one of their pursuers. Cries of consternation burst from the man's companions.

Now it was time for the rest of the Wolf Coats to strike.

They rose as one, the movement practised so many times that they all knew by instinct when to attack. Einar grabbed his shield and powered to his feet, an incoherent bellow thundering from his lips.

Einar had witnessed – even participated in – attacks by the

Wolf Coats when they had moved silent as ghosts, slaughtering men with as much noise as a cat padding over wool. This time, however, Ulrich had given specific orders for the opposite. Each wolf-pelt-clad warrior rose to his feet screaming, shouting or roaring at the top of his lungs.

Einar had once seen a bear attack a sheep. The huge black creature had let out one deafening roar and the sheep had frozen in shock, leaving it an easy victim for the bear. The sudden noise and movement of the Wolf Coats had the same effect on the warriors on skis. They froze. Einar could see the shock and fear on their faces as he charged across the last few paces into them.

There were fifteen of them, travelling two abreast in two columns and outnumbering the Wolf Coats nearly two to one. There had been sixteen but one now lay on his back, dead, feet still in his skis, legs splayed in an awkward tangle, his chest transfixed by Affreca's arrow. His helmet had spilled off his head, his mouth was agape and his tongue protruded, while his sightless eyes stared, fixed on the sky above.

The Wolf Coats piled into the others, four from either side. The man who had been travelling behind the already dead warrior got over his initial shock and tried to turn on his skis to face the oncoming threat. In his panic he blundered into the man beside him. Their skis snagged together and both fell over into the snow. Skar, without breaking stride, brought his axe down on one of the men falling towards him. With a nasty sound the blade dug deep into the warrior's leg, almost severing it just above the knee. Hot blood, bright crimson against the white of the snow, shot out of the wound in a red arc.

Ulrich performed a nimble sidestep to avoid being hit by the second falling skier, then stabbed the man through the throat with his sword as he hit the ground.

The men on skis had their shields slung over their backs so had no time to get them. They went for their weapons but, wrapped up in their heavy furs, their movements were slow and limited.

With the skis strapped to their feet they could not turn to face their assailants in time so had to twist at the waist.

This is almost too easy.

The thought crossed Einar's mind as he swept his shield to the left, batting the spear point of the warrior before him out of the way and opening his chest for attack. He hacked down with his sword and the blade – an *Inglerii*, the best weapon in the known world – sheared through the man's fur jacket and bit deep into his shoulder. His left arm went limp and he dropped his spear, grunting with pain and reaching for the wound with his right hand as a torrent of blood gushed out, matting the fur of his jerkin.

Kari had not even bothered to lift his shield. He had just kicked it over and ran at his enemies, an axe in his left hand and a long seax knife in his right. Two men on skis brought their spears to bear on him but Kari smashed both their shafts with one vicious slash of his axe. He drove the long, broken-backed blade of his seax into the side of the skier to his right. The other warrior drove at Kari with the broken remnant of his spear shaft. Kari arched his back so the thrust missed him, then brought his axe back, burying the blade deep in the other man's chest.

Surt put his big, heavily muscled left shoulder behind his shield and barrelled into the column of skiers. The impact of the big man caused chaos. The two men before Surt collapsed sideways, knocking others around them over. The momentum sent another two of the skiers sliding backwards, out of control, their arms windmilling as they tried to stop themselves toppling over. Then Affreca shot one of them with an arrow and Wulfhelm the Saxon cut the other one down with his sword. Skar, Ulrich, Sigurd and Starkad unleashed a frenzy of strikes, stabbing and hacking the mass of tangled bodies before them. The skiers did their best to defend themselves but it was hopeless. In moments it was all over.

Einar stood, panting, looking at the carnage around him. All sixteen of the men on skis were dead. The white snow was streaked and splattered with crimson. Steam rose into the air from the sweat and breath of the Wolf Coats and the fast-cooling blood of their victims that matted the thick fur clothes of the dead men. For a few moments there was silence, which was all the more stark because of the short burst of screaming that had preceded it.

'Now we know why that bastard Gerpir told us all his skis were being refurbished and he had none to lend us,' Ulrich said at last. He pointed his sword blade at the skis on their pursuers' feet. 'Skis are fast. These snowshoes were meant to keep us slow so this lot could catch up with us.'

'If he wanted to kill us,' Skar said, frowning, 'I'd have thought Gerpir would have sent more men.'

He sounded almost insulted that the lendermann had not seen the Wolf Coats as enough of a threat that his killing company was only twice their number.

'Shit,' Starkad said. 'Maybe he did.' The long-bearded Wolf Coat had walked to the edge of the hill's summit and was looking back in the direction the men on skis had come from.

The others trudged over to join him. Down the hill and back on the track they had been previously following, a big cloud of snow was rising. It was being thrown into the air by the hooves of the horses of a column of riders approaching from the direction of Gerpir's hall. There were a lot of them, most on horses, several on a sledge, way more than the band of skiers and much, much more than the Wolf Coats. They were approaching fast. A flag with the emblem of a blue stag fluttered from a pole above the sledge.

'It looks like Gerpir has come himself,' Skar said, pointing to the flag. 'That's his standard. And he has brought all of his war band with him. The skiers must just have been scouts sent ahead to watch where we went and then lead that lot to us.'

'We could hide up here?' Affreca suggested. 'And let them ride on past.'

Ulrich shook his head. 'They'll know we went this way,' he

said, pointing to the tracks they and the skiers had made in the snow when they turned off the track and climbed the hill.

'We won't be able to outrun them in snowshoes,' Kari said, noting the speed with which the horsemen were already gaining on them.

'Come on,' Ulrich said. 'We need to get out of here. Fast.'

3

'Take their skis,' Ulrich said. 'We can move faster on them.'

'True, but we still won't be able to outrun horses,' Affreca said.

'Perhaps, your high and mightiness,' Ulrich said, 'you'd prefer to stay here and wait for those horsemen?'

Affreca scowled at him and began unstrapping her snowshoes.

'Take any spears that aren't broken too. We can use them as poles. And there's no time to get changed either,' Ulrich said, noticing Wulfhelm had started digging the snow where they had buried their heavy fur over-garments.

'But we'll freeze to death out here without them,' the Saxon said.

'You'll still be putting them on by the time those horsemen get up this hill,' Ulrich said. 'Soon you'll be skiing too hard to worry about the cold anyway.'

As if to reinforce Ulrich's point, the sound of a horse whinnying and the crunch of hooves churning through packed snow came from down the hill. After sheathing his bloodied sword and pulling off his fighting glove, Einar removed his snowshoes then fumbled to undo the fastenings on the skis of one of the dead men. The others did the same.

'We go this way,' Ulrich said. He had skis on and had made his way to the edge of the hilltop on the side that led down to the frozen lake.

'The ice is flat, Ulrich,' Skar said. The big man looked dubious.

Einar could see his point. Once they ran out of the momentum from skiing downhill to the lake, on the flat surface it would not

13

be long before they would slow down to a walking pace. The horsemen would catch up with them before they reached the far shore.

'Trust me: just go down as fast as you can,' Ulrich said. 'Don't stop. Keep going and try to ski as far across the ice as you can.'

The others exchanged glances but no one had a different plan, nor was there time for further discussion. Einar knew they just had to go with their leader's plan. After all, he had not managed to get them killed so far. All of them swapped snowshoes for skis, grabbed a spear each and shuffled over to the edge of the hilltop.

Both Surt and Wulfhelm looked the most concerned of all with Ulrich's plan. Einar knew why. Surt had grown up far to the south in the hot burning lands of the Serks where snow is unheard of, and Wulfhelm was from Britain where there was no need for skis either. Einar, on the other hand, had spent his childhood in Iceland, where learning to ski, skate or slide – anything to get across a frozen landscape – was the first thing children achieved after walking. Since their arrival in Norway he had been teaching Wulfhelm, Surt and Affreca (who had grown up in Ireland) in the art of skiing. Affreca, as was typical of her, had taken it up with ease and was soon far ahead of the other two. Wulfhelm and Surt were still very much finding their feet and the slope down to the lake was long and very steep. Much steeper than the one they had climbed up.

They both looked at Einar as he joined them at the top of the slope.

'Any final advice?' Wulfhelm said. His face was as pale as the snow around them.

'Don't fall,' was all Einar could think of. 'And try not to ski into any of those cows. Get going. I'll be right behind you.'

Surt rolled his eyes.

'Remember: keep going as far as you can across the ice,' Ulrich said. 'Don't even think about slowing down until you're well past the cows.'

Then he turned his skis to the slope and was gone. Skar went

after him, then Affreca, Starkad and Kari. Surt took a deep
breath, then followed. Sigurd had a fierce grin on his face and
Einar realised with a start that despite the dangerous situation
they were in, the Wolf Coat was relishing the prospect of the
rapid downhill ski. As if to confirm this, Sigurd gave a loud
whoop as he hopped over the edge of the summit and began the
descent.

Einar looked over his shoulder. The horsemen were halfway
up the hill already.

'Go!' he shouted to Wulfhelm, who still hesitated, unsure, at
the edge of the summit.

The Saxon nodded, gritted his teeth and drove the spear shaft
into the snow, pushing himself forwards over the edge. The skis
hit the slope and he was away, rushing off down the hillside after
the others.

Einar, now the last one on the hilltop, dug his own spear in and
shoved himself over the edge of the summit and onto the slope
beyond. With the skis pointed straight down the hill, in a moment
Einar went from walking pace to hurtling downhill faster than
a galloping horse. The wind in his ears changed from a mere
whispering to a deafening roar as he plummeted down the slope.

To his surprise, Einar felt a surge of sheer joy in his heart
and all of a sudden he understood Sigurd's pleasure. He was
still aware of the danger they were all in, but at this moment it
was secondary to the sensation of just being alive. He felt like
a falcon, hurtling from high in the sky to snatch prey on the
ground far below.

The cold rush of the air made his eyes stream and he had to
blink so he could still see. The freezing cold air forced its way
through every seam in his clothing and bit into his flesh beneath.
Just ahead he saw Wulfhelm was trying to jump from side to
side to try to control the speed of his descent. Einar knew that
effort was futile and in fact could be more dangerous and result
in a fall. The hill was so steep that there was no choice but to go
with it.

There was no point shouting to Wulfhelm. Einar was behind him and his words would be snatched away by the wind. His only option was to show him what to do.

Einar went into a crouch. At this speed the spear pole was useless so he held it across his body. The snow shot past beneath his skis. His feet shuddered up and down as he picked up even more speed and shot past Wulfhelm. As he did so Einar risked a glance at the Saxon and shouted: 'Like this!' – hoping that somehow Wulfhelm would understand.

Then he turned his attention to keeping his feet in position and staying on his skis. The others were already far ahead, streaking straight down. He was going so fast himself now that he could not take the gamble of looking back. He could only trust Wulfhelm was following.

Before long, his thighs felt like they were on fire but he knew if he changed position at this speed he would fall. The thought of the bone-shattering impact that would result made him grit his teeth and endure the pain.

It seemed as though the frozen lake at the bottom of the slope was rushing up to meet him. Up ahead he heard more whooping and shouting. At first he thought that the others were expressing their delight like Sigurd. Then Einar realised they were shouting at the herd of cows who were dotted around the lake surface, lapping at the water through holes poked in the ice by whatever farmer owned the cattle.

Going at the speed they were, trying to steer around the randomly arranged beasts would be almost impossible. Hearing the shouting, the beasts looked up at the men hurtling downhill towards them. To Einar's relief they began to lumber off. As Ulrich then Skar hit the ice of the lake, shouting and hollering, the cattle got even more spooked and hurried away in all directions, leaving the way ahead clear for the onrushing skiers.

An instant later Einar swooped over the end of the hillside and out onto the flat, snow-covered ice. With the cows out of the way, the most dangerous obstacles to watch out for were their drinking holes and the many steaming piles of dung they had left behind, both of which Einar did his best to avoid.

The swooshing of the skis beneath him was joined by a hollow rumbling as their vibrations echoed across the ice. The fear of falling was augmented in Einar's heart with the dread that the ice beneath him might not be thick enough to bear his weight. If it cracked and he went under, the freezing embrace of the water could well kill him just from the shock of it. Worse, he could end up trapped under the frozen canopy, unable to get back to the air, drowning in the frigid darkness.

The one thing that mitigated this fear was the fact that he was travelling at such a tremendous rate it felt like his skis were hardly touching the ice, never mind resting on it long enough for his weight to push through.

However, the further Einar travelled across the flat ice the more his momentum from the slope waned. As he reached the middle of the lake he was almost down to walking pace. The Wolf Coats ahead were already trekking on their skis. He joined them, using the spear shaft to push himself along as he slid one ski in front of the other.

Einar glanced over his shoulder. Behind him he saw Wulfhelm had made it down the hill, albeit at a slower pace than the rest, and was now on the ice too. His momentum had only taken him about a quarter of the way across the lake, however.

On the slope behind the Saxon, the company of riders were already thundering down, sending up a great cloud of snow as they went. Einar could see that the descent was slowing them as their horses needed to pick their way with care, but even so, as soon as they made it to the lake it would not be long before they caught up with the Wolf Coats.

4

Einar turned around and began to redouble his efforts. Soon he was sweating again, despite the lack of furs, and compared to the rush of the downhill ski, his progress now felt like he was hardly moving at all.

He sensed a vibration ripple through the ice beneath him. It felt like he was skiing across the skin of a drum that someone had started to beat a tattoo on. It could only mean the horsemen were on the ice already.

Even though he was over halfway to the far shore, Einar knew he would never make it before the horsemen caught up with him and the others. They would have to turn and fight. Up ahead he saw that Ulrich and the rest had come to the same conclusion, as they had already turned around again to face back the way they had come.

Einar's heart sank. They were badly outnumbered this time and would have to fight men on horseback. On top of that there was no time to get rid of their skis. They would now be at the same disadvantage in terms of lack of mobility that the Wolf Coats had used to their advantage against the warriors they had ambushed on the hill summit.

Then he heard a tremendous crack. The ice beneath his skis ceased to vibrate. A great wail of many men and horses in distress and dismay rose into the winter air behind him. Then came the sound of splashing and more shouts.

Einar turned to see the ice had given way under the column of horsemen. The beasts and their riders had plunged into the freezing waters of the lake beneath. As he watched he saw the long sledge upend on a broken shard of ice and slide into the lake below, spilling the men on it into the freezing water. For a few moments the stag banner on its long pole remained above the water, then it too was gone. That told Einar that the lake was deep, as well as cold.

Their pursuers thrashed and churned in the water, desperate to stay above the surface. Some scrabbled for handholds on the edge of the broken ice but just slid off the smooth surface, or more of the ice cracked, tipped up into the air and sent the unfortunate warriors sliding back into the water again. The thick furs the men were clad in to protect them from the cold drank deep of the lake and became heavy, pulling their wearers down into the cold darkness below.

The shouting became less and less and, one after the other, the warriors disappeared beneath the surface. Some managed to stay afloat despite their sodden garments but the intense cold of the water soon began to take its toll. As the Wolf Coats watched, their cries faded like those of a tired madman falling asleep, and then the last of the warriors too slipped under. Some of the horses managed to blunder across to the shore and make it out but, as far as Einar could tell, none of the men did.

Silence once more descended across the winter landscape. The Wolf Coats and Surt watched the broken ice for any sign of survivors as Wulfhelm skied on to catch up with them.

'The Norns are with us today,' Einar said, referring to the great uncanny women who ruled the fates of men. 'That was really lucky. It's the middle of winter. I'd have thought the ice would have been thick enough to support them, on horseback or not.'

'It looks like they thought that too,' Affreca said.

Ulrich shook his head. 'You two clearly know as much of the lore of our folk as Gerpir's men did,' he said. 'Did you not see the cows on the lake? This is exactly how Halfdan the Black met his end.'

Einar shot a questioning glance at Affreca, who shrugged.

Einar knew Halfdan the Black was the father of King Harald Fairhair, who in turn was father of Eirik Bloody Axe and the present King Hakon. How Halfdan had died, on the other hand, he had no idea.

'I forget. Neither of you are from Norway,' Ulrich said. 'Once Halfdan was driving from a feast in Hadeland and his road lay over the Rand lake. But some holes had been broken in the ice by farmers for their cattle to drink at. Where the warm cow shit and their piss fell on the ice it ate holes in it, weakening the ice further. When Halfdan drove over it the ice broke, and he and many with him perished. When I saw those cows drinking at the lake I thought to myself, perhaps we can lead Gerpir and his men to the same fate.'

'What if Gerpir had remembered Halfdan the Black?' Einar said. 'If they'd ridden around the lake instead of straight over it they'd be killing us by now.'

Ulrich shrugged. 'Perhaps,' he said. 'But I looked in Gerpir's eyes when we talked to him last night and knew he did not have the imagination to look ahead. He's a stupid man who is full of his own importance. I knew if I offered him obvious bait in the form of us going across the lake he would follow like a bull led by a ring through its nose.'

Einar looked at him for a long moment. With regards to someone being full of himself, Einar mused that Ulrich had just gambled all their lives on a conviction that he was correct about how Gerpir would act.

'What now?' Affreca said. 'I'm freezing.'

'Well now there is no one following us anymore,' Ulrich said, 'the first thing we should do is climb back up that hill and get our heavy furs back.'

'Perhaps we shouldn't be so sure,' Kari said. He was looking towards the other end of the lake.

Einar's heart sank once again. The far end of the ice was crowded by a horde of many warriors. There were even more of them than there had been in the company of riders who had chased them onto the lake. They had round shields held before them and their spears, held upright, stood above them like a forest of bare trees.

'Shit,' Starkad said. 'If we were outnumbered before then we're really in trouble now.'

'Perhaps we're not all dead yet,' Skar said. 'I recognise that banner from Frodisborg.'

They all looked at the warriors gathered on the lakeshore ahead. One of them was a *merkismaðr*, a standard bearer, and he held a tall pole that stood higher than the spear points around it. From it fluttered a green banner on which was emblazoned the white head of a stag.

'That's the banner of Jarl Sigurd of Hlader,' Einar said. 'What's he doing here?'

The ominous sound of creaking ice made them all glance over their shoulders.

'I don't know,' Ulrich said, 'but we should probably get off this ice before the rest of it cracks and we all go for a swim.'

The Wolf Coats, Surt and Wulfhelm trekked on their skis across the rest of the lake to the far shore where the crowd of warriors waited.

In their midst was a stout, barrel-chested man with long blond hair tied behind his head, mounted on a horse near the standard. Despite the heavy fur hat on his head, Einar recognised Jarl Sigurd. Mounted on a horse beside him was another man. As the Wolf Coats drew near he pulled down his fur hood and unlaced an expensive, silver-ornamented helmet beneath.

'Who's this, do you think?' Affreca said.

'He looks like one of your lot,' Skar said to Wulfhelm from the corner of his mouth.

'My lot?' Wulfhelm said.

'That's a Saxon helmet if I'm not mistaken,' Skar said.

The man on the horse pulled his helmet off, revealing brown hair that was cut in a stylish fashion. His young, good-looking face bore a long, well-groomed moustache and he smiled when he spotted Einar. Einar narrowed his eyes. He looked familiar but he could not quite remember where from.

'Einar!' the young man said. He spoke in the Norse tongue but with the strange lilting accent it had acquired where it had taken root in the north-east of Britain. 'Good to see you're still alive.'

Einar realised who he was.

'It's Sweyn the Northumbrian,' Einar said to the others, nodding at the young man on the horse. 'He was Hakon's chief bodyguard back in Jorvik. He was the man who led us on that raid in the land of the Scots when we sought the Raven Banner.'

'What's he doing here?' Kari said in a quiet tone.

'I don't know,' Einar said. 'But it must have something to do with King Aethelstan.'

'Lord Sigurd,' Ulrich addressed the squat jarl in a loud voice. 'I'm glad, though surprised, to see you. What brings you here? I thought you sent us to quietly find out what your lendermann was up to, but here you are with what looks like most of your war band?'

The jarl grinned. 'Ulrich,' he said. 'We thought that if Gerpir turned out to be bad after all, you might need a bit of help dealing with him and his own war band. However, it looks like you've already sorted out the problem by yourselves. Thank you for that.'

Ulrich did not reply. Even Einar could tell there was much more to this than met the eye.

'Come,' Jarl Sigurd said. 'Gerpir's mead hall is prepared for the feast. He will have no need for it now, and there is no sense in all that meat and drink going to waste. Let's go there and see if we can salvage something of this Jól festival.'

5

Einar relished the warm glow of contentment that wrapped around him. Gerpir's feasting hall was very comfortable, his ale was good, and the amount of meat and bread piled on its tables was more than acceptable.

The hall was long and narrow, like an upturned ship sitting in the midst of the snowy landscape. Two long firepits stretched in parallel down the floor for most of its length, running from the entrance almost to the far end. The heat from the glowing wood and charcoal drove away the chill of outside. The light from the fires was added to by many torches that burned in brackets along the low walls.

The air was filled with the aroma of roasting meat, fresh bread and the tang of ale. Long tables ran up the hall lengthways between the firepits. Benches flanked the tables and they were filled with feasters, the warriors of Jarl Sigurd and a contingent of men who had come with Sweyn from Britain. Two rows of wooden pillars flanked the firepits for the length of the hall, rising from the floor to the roof they supported. Each one was hand carved to look either like the trunks of mighty trees, twisting serpents or *jötnar* giants. Long tapestries were hung from one pillar to the next, embroidered with scenes of ships, warriors and battles. There was fresh straw on the floor and the benches were strewn with many furs both for comfort and warmth.

Thralls moved around the tables, heads obsequiously bowed, replenishing ale horns from jugs of frothing ale or passing out platters of meat or bread.

At the far end of the hall, the one opposite to the entrance, was a raised dais on which sat the high seat of the lendermann, Gerpir. Tonight it was empty as its owner was at the bottom of a frozen lake.

'If he hadn't drowned I would have blood-eagled that treacherous bastard,' Jarl Sigurd said, casting a regretful look at the empty high seat.

The jarl, who could have by rights taken the high seat, was instead ensconced in the midst of the long table alongside the Wolf Coat company. On the bench on the other side of the table sat Sweyn. They had all stripped off the thick furs they had worn outside and while no one had brought their best clothes with them, were dressed in more comfortable garments.

'I'm glad you are a man of tradition, Jarl Sigurd,' Ulrich said. 'The blood eagle would deter any others like him who might have thought of betraying you.'

Like most of those at the table, Einar's cheeks were flushed red, the effect of moving from the cold outside to the heat of the hall, combined with the influence of the strong Jól ale.

'The blood eagle is just a punishment from legend, surely?' he said, a bemused expression on his face. 'No one would be so cruel as to cut a man's back open and haul his lungs out while he still lived.'

'I've seen it done several times,' Ulrich said in a matter-of-fact voice.

'I've done it twice myself,' Jarl Sigurd said. He looked directly at Einar as he spoke, and Einar could see from the faraway look in his cold, grey eyes and the flat expression on his face that the jarl was not joking. Einar felt a shiver trickle down his spine at the realisation that in the real world, not just the imaginary one of memory and tales he often sang about from the lore, there were men who carried out such brutal acts.

'Now it feels more like Jól,' Skar said, a broad grin on his face, an ale horn in his left hand and a meat-covered bone in his right fist.

Those around said *aye* or nodded their satisfied agreement. Einar was aware of a slight foolish smile creeping across his lips. This was great. Not long before they had been out in the freezing wilderness, with death a very real prospect, but now here they were in the warmth with as much meat as they could eat and enough ale and mead to keep Thor himself happy. The conversation at the tables was lively and good-natured, with cheers and shouts of laughter bursting out now and again.

Not everyone was enjoying themselves at the feast, however. Some women were helping the slaves to serve the food and drink. Their clothes – expensive soft wool embroidered with bright-coloured threads – showed they were of higher standing: noblewomen. Their eyes were red-rimmed and their faces bore scowls that had nothing to do with them being made to do serving work while the others feasted.

When Jarl Sigurd and the Wolf Coats had arrived at the hall earlier, these women had rushed out to meet them, their faces full of joy, expecting that it was their husbands – the warriors of Gerpir's chosen war band – who were returning to them so the feast could commence. Their smiles were soon replaced by tears.

'Careful!' Ulrich chided one of them as she slapped a platter of meat on the table beside him, sending splashes of juice in every direction.

The woman just sniffed and flounced off.

'Go easy on her, Ulrich,' Jarl Sigurd said. 'You probably made her a widow today.'

'I'm not the one who insisted on making these women serve us tonight, lord. That was you,' Ulrich said. 'But I would at least have expected them to bear their misfortune with a little more dignity. You have your own men guarding the cooking house, I take it?'

'I'm not stupid, Ulrich,' the jarl said, his jovial grin fading a little. 'I don't want them poisoning us or shitting in our dinner. My men are watching what goes on in there but I want these women to know their place. Their husbands followed Gerpir and planned to rebel against me. Now those men are dead and their women will be our servants. At least for tonight.'

Jarl Sigurd had declared Gerpir's wife an exile straight away. She had wandered off, sobbing, into the surrounding snow-covered forest while the rest of the noblewomen had been put to work in the cookhouse.

'About that, Lord Sigurd,' Ulrich said. 'Were we not supposed to be the ones working out if Gerpir was plotting against you and Hakon? Yet here you are, with what looks like most of your war band. Why did you need to send us at all?'

'When you're hunting a wolf, Ulrich,' Jarl Sigurd said, 'sometimes you need to send a goat first to draw him out of the forest.'

Ulrich sighed and held up his drinking horn for a refill.

'So you used us as bait?' he asked.

'Don't take it badly, Ulrich,' the jarl said. 'I knew you lads were big enough to look after yourselves. And you were! I came down here expecting to have to save you lot from Gerpir and his men, and you'd already taken care of the lot of them.'

Einar held his own horn up for a refill and one of the serving noblewomen came over with a jug of ale. She was younger than many of the others, perhaps not that much older than Einar himself. Her hair was black and bound up behind her head in the manner of a married woman. Einar found it difficult to take his eyes off her fine features as she poured golden ale into his drinking horn. He found it hard to believe she was married, never mind now a widow.

'Thank you,' Einar said as the foam reached to the mouth of his horn.

To his surprise the woman smiled at him and held his gaze for a moment longer than needed. Then she turned and walked away. Einar felt his heart start to speed up as he watched her move off down the hall.

'She likes you, lad,' Skar said, slapping Einar on the shoulder.

'Any woman so soon a widow who is looking at another man must not be worth much,' Affreca said, scowling after the ale bearer.

'Her husband was probably a bit of a bastard,' Ulrich said. 'She's maybe glad to be rid of him.'

'And maybe...' Skar said in a mock-conspiratorial tone of voice. He leaned towards Einar, a lascivious smile on his face. 'Maybe later on she'll show the lad here just how grateful she is to us for getting rid of the old bastard for her, eh?'

He elbowed Einar.

'Good luck to her with that,' Affreca said, folding her arms.

'Aye,' Ulrich said, glancing at Einar. 'That lad's so slow to realise a woman fancies him that she could be prancing naked round him and he'd still be wondering: *does she really like me, do you think?*'

The others at the table roared with laughter.

'Still,' Skar said. 'That might be some entertainment for the rest of us.'

Einar felt his face flush deeper. His tongue felt like it was made of wood.

The noblewomen of the district were not the only ones who looked like they were not enjoying the feast. Sweyn the Northumbrian sat with nothing but a platter of bread, hunks of cheese and some fish before him. His expression was downcast as he eyed the steaming piles of meat laden on everyone else's platters.

'What's the matter with you anyway?' Kari said. 'Do you not like meat?'

'Oh I love meat,' Sweyn said, casting a longing look at a particularly bloody piece of roasted horseflesh that Skar was slicing in half with his knife. 'But I can't eat any of this. It's been sacrificed to the heathen gods. I'd lose my soul if I ate it.'

'I forgot about that,' Ulrich said. 'Sweyn the Christian Viking.

You are of our folk, but living in Britain has changed you. You still speak our tongue but you forsake the gods of your forefathers for the misery of a life following the Christ God. What is he anyway? No more than a poor man's Balder.'

He shot a look of derision in the young man's direction. Sweyn frowned.

'But it's Jól!' Einar said. 'I thought you were a Norseman. Just because your grandfather settled in Britain, does that mean you can't celebrate the greatest festival of the year?'

'That's the misery of the Christian faith, lad,' Ulrich said, pointing a bone in the direction of the short-haired Sweyn. 'Anything fun, anything that looks like it might lead to folk enjoying themselves is forbidden by their God.'

'Well that's not really true,' Sweyn said, meeting Ulrich's challenging gaze.

While many were intimidated by the mere glare of an *úlfheðinn* like Ulrich, Sweyn was not. This did not surprise Einar, who knew Sweyn had a heart as fearless as any of those at the table. He recalled one of the last times they had met, when they had stormed the gates of Cathair Aile together. It looked like life had been hard for Sweyn since then. There were lines around his eyes. He was only a few winters older than Einar but there were a couple of streaks of grey through the Northumbrian's hair. Einar judged this was probably due to how much blood Sweyn had lost when they were attacked by the huge savage dogs that day in Scotland. Einar had saved his life then but now the situation between them was strange. They had fought together, side by side, and yet there was this gulf between them, caused both by their difference in faiths, and the so-far-unspoken name that hovered somewhere in the air above the feast, waiting to enter the conversation.

'I suppose Aethelstan sent you here?' Ulrich said, finally mentioning him. 'What does he want with King Hakon now?'

'King Aethelstan did indeed send my men and I to Norway,'

Sweyn said. 'But we are not here for Hakon. We are here for you.'

The Wolf Coats around the table stiffened. Skar leaned forwards on his elbows. Starkad tried to look nonchalant, but Einar saw his knuckles were white on the fist that gripped his knife. Affreca glanced around over her shoulders, as if checking for potential ways to escape. Sweyn on the other hand was smiling.

'The king wishes to employ your services,' he said. 'He has a very special job that would be perfect for men with your particular... skills.'

'Just the men?' Affreca said, one dark eyebrow arched.

'Probably,' Ulrich said. 'We know he has special plans for you, your ladyship.'

'If this is about taking Affreca to marry Hakon and ruling Jorvik, the answer is no,' Einar blurted out.

'Aw,' Ulrich said with his provoking smile. 'I didn't know you cared, lad.'

'I'm perfectly capable of giving my own answer, thank you,' Affreca said, shooting a reproachful glance at Einar.

Sweyn held up his hands. 'Please, please,' he said. 'I can assure you this is nothing to do with the lady Affreca and her marriage plans. I believe the lord Aethelstan is more than aware after his last attempt at bringing it about, that Affreca is not ready for the union yet.'

'Yet?' Affreca said. 'How about "not ever"?'

'If it's not about that, then why *are* you here?' Ulrich said.

'I will tell you, but first how about we open this?' Sweyn said, reaching under the table and pulling up a large earthenware jug. It looked like it was heavy. 'Ulrich is wrong, by the way. We Christians do celebrate at this time of year. We, however, call it Christmas, when we remember the birth of Jesus.'

'And how do you mark this special occasion?' Ulrich said with a sigh. 'Let me guess: with those mumbled pleadings you call prayers, starving yourselves and staying up all night?'

Sweyn called to one of the serving women. 'Fresh drinking horns, please,' he said, then turned back to the others at the table. 'Actually we have twelve days of feasting and game playing, and then we give each other presents.'

'It sounds just like Jól,' Starkad said.

'So my grandfather told me,' Sweyn said. 'And as it's Christmas, we may as well celebrate with this.'

He pulled a large stopper from the earthenware vessel, which came out with a loud pop. The serving woman arrived back with new drinking horns. Sweyn took one, put the jug under one arm and tilted it. A clear, deep red liquid flowed out to fill the horn. Sweyn filled the rest of the horns one by one and handed them out to those around him.

'Wine!' Ulrich said, his eyes lighting up with delight.

'The very best,' Sweyn said. He was smiling now. 'I brought it from the lands the Britons settled in north-west Francia. I may as well break it open and share it here. It is Christmas, after all.'

'From the land of the Franks, eh? They say all the best wine comes from there,' Ulrich said, taking a sip from his drinking horn. 'So Aethelstan is interfering down there too, is he? Is that why you were there?'

Kari was staring with suspicion into his wine. 'Ulrich, what if this is some sort of Christian magic?' he said. 'I've heard they can change wine into blood.'

Starkad, Jarl Sigurd, Sigurd the Wolf Coat, Einar and some of the others at the table hesitated, their drinking horns halfway to their lips.

Skar, who was already midway through chugging down a long draught from his drinking horn, paused and looked sideways at Kari. Several plump droplets of ruby liquid dribbled down his beard. For a moment he swilled the wine around his mouth, then he swallowed and let out an explosive sigh.

'Tastes like wine to me,' the big man said with a grin. 'Good stuff, too!'

The others cheered and quaffed their own wine. Einar tasted its sweetness on his tongue and felt the burning as it went down his throat. His heart raced. It was delicious.

'Odin drinks only wine,' Ulrich said, staring into his drinking horn. 'I can understand why. So this is from Brittany? That land is famous for its wines.'

'Once maybe,' Sweyn said. 'It's a wasteland now, ravaged by war. But if you like it then how would you like to drink it every day?'

Ulrich's expression soured. 'Is that what Aethelstan wants?' he asked. 'He wants us to go to Brittany? What for?'

'King Aethelstan will explain all that,' Sweyn said. 'When we meet him in Wintanceaster.'

'It will take more than the promise of good wine to make me enter the service of Aethelstan willingly,' Ulrich said.

'He will pay you in silver and gold,' Sweyn said. 'More than enough for you and all of your crew to live the rest of your lives in comfort – if you're successful, that is.'

'That's the problem,' Ulrich said. 'We are already in the service of Jarl Sigurd here. He is paying us enough to meet our needs already.'

'Ah,' the jarl said, lowering his drinking horn and sitting up straight. 'That's true, Ulrich. However, the task I wanted you for is now complete. Gerpir is dead. I have no more need of you.'

'I'm sure King Hakon will have need of our swords then,' Ulrich said, narrowing his eyes.

'I'm afraid the king feels he cannot trust you enough to take you back into his service at the moment,' Jarl Sigurd said. 'Especially after your last escapade when you told him you would take the lady Affreca to Jorvik for their marriage.'

'We did!' Ulrich said, indignant. 'It wasn't our fault she preferred not to stay there and marry him.'

'That is neither here nor there,' Jarl Sigurd said. 'The fact remains, they are not wed.'

Ulrich sighed, folded his arms and sat back. 'So that's the way it is, eh? You've arranged all this among yourselves already?'

'King Aethelstan, King Hakon and Jarl Sigurd have come to an arrangement, yes,' Sweyn said. 'So what do you say?'

'I say I'll think about it,' Ulrich said, 'while we finish the rest of your wine.'

6

The feast continued. In many ways it was like any other Jól feast Einar had attended but there were a few differences that made this one a little strange. The food was terrific: chickens, pig, beef, all types of fish and mounds of roasted and boiled vegetables – kale, turnips, carrots and parsnips – all swimming in melted butter and accompanied by lots of bread and hunks of cheese. There was plenty of special Jól ale, mead and Sweyn's wine. The good-natured chatter and laughter from the men at the tables got louder as the drink increased its influence, but it was still clear that they were eating someone else's food and not everyone was enjoying themselves. There were no children for a start and all the folk on the benches were Jarl Sigurd and Sweyn's warriors and, apart from the female slaves, the only women were the empty-eyed widows forced to hand out food and drink. The skald chanting verses from the dais at the top of the hall was Jarl Sigurd's – Gerpir's had drowned in the lake with his master – and the entire proceedings were watched by a section of the jarl's warriors who had been unlucky enough to be appointed to keep sober watch over proceedings in case there was any trouble. They were in the hall of an enemy after all, even if a vanquished one.

Despite all this, Einar's spirits soared and he began to enjoy himself. It had been so long since either he or the rest of the Wolf Coats had really had a chance to relax and have some drinks. There had been that time recently in Hedeby when he had run into his old friends from Iceland but that had ended with Einar murdering the man who'd killed his mother and all of them standing trial the next day.

As the evening wore on, the eating came to an end but the drinking did not. With the lack of noble female accompaniment to keep their behaviour restrained, the warriors' revels got ever more raucous, their jokes more coarse and the capers and games rougher. Drinking contests were followed by wrestling matches, with opponents knocking over tables and benches as they fought. There was a tug of war across the firepit, where the losers were hauled into the flames and then went dancing around the hall patting out the patches of their clothes that had caught alight while the winners guffawed and slapped each other across the back.

Music began, with the skald and his harp being joined by a man with a flute and another with a goatskin drum. Horns of ale were refilled and everyone began singing, chanting the words to old familiar tales of heroes and gods. For Einar the night merged into a blur of laughter and songs, loud banter, drunken fellowships and inebriated fights.

At one point Einar found himself staring at the black-haired young widow who had smiled at him earlier as she served ale. She was moving around the tables serving men from a jug and avoiding with graceful moves the wandering hands that sometimes reached out to stroke her thighs or grab her bottom as drink swamped the last modicums of restrained behaviour among the feasters. A bemused smile spread over Einar's lips at how beautiful she was.

She looked around and caught him staring at her. Einar froze like a dog hearing a thunderclap. He was about to look away when she smiled and winked at him, then went on her way.

A warm glow spread through Einar's chest as he turned away, only to see Affreca looking at him, one eyebrow raised, an unmistakable sneer on her lips. For some reason Einar felt his face flush red once again as she shook her head and looked away.

As the evening grew late, the noise gradually reduced as the musicians retired and folk began to go to sleep, either passing out, slumped over the table, or crawling into the straw under it. When the sound of snoring was louder than the laughter and chatter, Einar judged it was time to go to sleep himself. As he staggered around the hall to find a fur to wrap himself in, half hoping to bump into the black-haired widow, Einar realised he was very drunk but the wine had had a strange effect on him. Instead of the befuddled drowsiness brought by ale, he felt as though his heart was racing with a fierce excitement and, as he lay down in the straw, he wondered if he would be able to get to sleep at all.

Within moments of lying down, however, he was snoring.

Then he awoke. It was dark and he was lying flat on his back. His mouth felt as dry as if someone had left a salted herring in it. His head pounded and he screwed his eyes shut as a sharp pain shot through his temple. He sat up and looked around. It was the middle of the night. The torches had burned out and the firepits were now just glowing embers. All was quiet. The floor of the hall was strewn with sleepers and the only sound was heavy breathing and snoring.

Einar felt sick.

His stomach lurched and a sour liquid crawled up his throat into the back of his mouth. A moment of panic gripped him as he thought he was going to be sick over himself. Einar lurched to his feet, fighting the waves of nausea that sloshed through his guts. He started to stumble in the direction of the hall doors, which lay in the narrow gable wall at the far end. At the very least, the cold air outside might make him feel better. At worst if he was sick, at least it would be outside.

'Are you all right?' A woman's voice, speaking in a hushed tone, made him stop and turn around. Einar was both delighted and horrified to see the black-haired widow, her beautiful features picked from the dark by the orange glow of the dying embers in the firepit and a whale-oil lamp she carried in one hand. He was delighted to see her. He was horrified because he realised he was about to vomit in front of her.

Einar swallowed hard, fighting to regain control of his lurching stomach.

'Too much ale?' the woman asked, a bewitching, playful smile on her attractive lips.

Einar nodded, scared to open his mouth in case he unleashed a torrent of sick down his own chest.

'Come with me,' the woman said. 'I can make you feel better.' She turned and hurried off down the hall in the opposite direction to the one Einar had been heading.

Einar did not need to be asked twice. Like a dog, he followed her, the sight of her hips swaying in front of him already starting to quell the nausea that was making his jaw muscles itch.

The woman led the way down the hall to a small door at the end opposite the main doors. Both of them had to pick their way over sleeping men sprawled everywhere across the floor. Einar's feeling of sickness was not helped by the air in the hall, which had become a sour mixture of the acrid smell of spilled ale and farts, mixed with the cloying aroma of cooling grease from the various roasted meats. The dying fires and torches must have given out a lot of smoke as they guttered out as well, as the smell of it hung in the air, thickening it and provoking Einar to cough.

The widow bent over to open the small door. Then she looked around, smiled at Einar and went inside.

A small voice within his mind told Einar that this beautiful woman could not be attracted to him but every glance, gesture and movement from her said she was. Then again, Einar reasoned, why not? He was a fit young man with many talents. Why would she not find him attractive? Especially in the situation she found herself now.

Einar followed her into what looked like a storeroom. Wooden barrels, some full of ale, others butter no doubt, stood stacked from the floor to the ceiling. The black-haired woman set the oil lamp on top of a barrel and turned around to face him.

She locked gazes with him. Einar found himself captivated by her blue eyes. Her breathing was fast, excited, as she looked up at him.

'You are an úlfheðinn,' she said. 'Such men are blessed by Odin himself. You dedicate your lives to the service of the One-Eyed god. All other men fear you.'

As she spoke she ran her hand down the grey wolfskin cloak Einar wore around his shoulders. Her breathing quickened, as if the touch of the fur drove her excitement further.

'I am sorry for your husband's death,' Einar said. As soon as the words left his mouth he regretted them: a bloodthirsty Wolf Coat would never regret the death of an opponent. The woman, however, seemed unperturbed.

'Take this off,' the widow said, pushing Einar's wolf-pelt cloak off his shoulders so it fell down around his arms. 'You won't need it soon.'

She pulled off his shirt next then unlaced the front of her own dress. All feelings of sickness left Einar, drowned in a rush of excitement. He took the woman in his arms and pressed his mouth to hers. He closed his eyes as their hot breath mixed and he ran his hands down her back. To his surprise he felt her warm slippery tongue flick across his lips, driving his excitement further. He felt his groin tighten.

Then there was a cry.

It was a man, shouting with pain or surprise, somewhere outside the room. At almost the same instant Einar realised that though he had both arms around the woman she only embraced him with her left.

His eyes shot open. She had a knife in her right fist, point down. Her arm was raised above her head, poised to strike.

With a cry Einar tore himself away and staggered backwards. The woman struck but too late, her blade plunging through the air where Einar had been a moment before.

The woman's face contorted in a snarl. All previous allure – her flirtatious glances, her coy smile – were gone. In its place was naked hatred.

'You bastard!' she said, and spat at Einar. 'You killed my Alvir. Now you'll all die!'

She lunged with the knife, driving it towards Einar's heart. He danced sideways so she missed him, then he drove his left knee into her stomach. It was not hard enough to wind her but it pushed her further away from him.

Whenever there was spare time, Skar constantly drilled Einar and the other Wolf Coats in all types of fighting craft. Einar had learned from the big man how to attack and counter in almost any sort of situation, except one.

If you ever find yourself with no weapon faced with someone with a knife, Skar had said, *just run away. Knives are deadly and there is little you can do to stop someone with one without getting hurt yourself.*

More shouts were coming from outside in the main hall. He had to get away, but the issue for Einar was that the woman was between him and the door.

The woman regained her balance and spun round to face Einar again. Grinning, she brandished the knife.

'I'm going to cut your balls off,' she said.

'The others are awake.' Einar pointed at the door to the hall. 'You won't get away. Why not just give this up? We'll be merciful.'

'I don't care if I die,' the woman said. 'What have I to live for without my Alvir anyway?'

'I'm sure you can find another husband,' Einar said. 'You're young. Quite good-looking too.'

'Quite?!' The woman's eyes bulged. 'You arrogant little prick. Did you really think I'd see anything in an ugly half-troll like you?'

She let out a scream and ran at him, knife aloft. Einar half turned and lashed out a kick, using the full length of his leg. This time he hit her full force. Her charge halted and she went flying backwards, crashing into the stack of barrels and falling to the floor.

Einar did not wait to see if she got up again. He dipped to the floor, grabbed his wolfskin then dashed past her and out the door into the hall, slamming it behind him. He pulled the bar across to fasten it closed. Only then did he look around him.

A short distance away, lying on the floor, flat on his back, dead, was one of the warriors Jarl Sigurd had left to guard over the feasters. He had a knife buried in his chest. It must have been him who Einar heard cry out. Another of the widowed women was being restrained by two more of the jarl's men. She was laughing.

'Get up!' Einar shouted at the top of his voice. 'We're in danger!'

Disturbed by Einar's shouting or the previous commotion, all around the hall others were waking up, groggy, still half drunk, wondering what was going on.

'What are you up to, lad, wandering around in the dark?'

Einar turned to see Skar loom out of the gloom nearby.

'Those women,' Einar said, panting. 'The widows of Gerpir's men. They want to kill us.'

A rattling came from the far end of the hall.

'They've locked the doors!' someone shouted.

'I smell smoke,' Skar said.

Einar looked around. The big man was right. Earlier he had thought the air was thick with the reek left from the guttering torches and fire, but it was much too strong, too stifling for that. In the little light there was he could see a blue haze hanging in the air all around.

'Get someone up to the Wind's Eye,' Jarl Sigurd's voice boomed from the shadows. 'See what's going on outside.'

Most of the hall was now awake. Men were brushing straw from their hair or beards as they clambered to their feet and pulled on their boots.

'All the doors are locked,' another man shouted. 'We can't get out.'

Sweyn scrambled up a ladder to a short platform near the

apex of the roof on the gable wall above the main doors. There was a hole in the wall there designed to help disperse the smoke from the fire inside the feasting hall.

'They've blocked the front doors,' Sweyn called down from above. 'There is wood and hay piled up outside them. They've set fire to it.'

'I can smell whale oil,' another man shouted from the far end of the hall. 'The walls are warm! They must have set a fire down here too.'

'They're going to burn us all to death in here,' Jarl Sigurd said. His face was grim.

'No they're not,' Ulrich, who by now was standing beside the jarl, said. 'Everyone get your swords, spears, whatever you have. We're going to dig a hole in the roof. There's plenty of us in here. More than enough to do the job. We need to work fast, though, or the smoke will kill us before the flames get in.'

The roof of the great, long hall dipped at either side almost to the ground. At Ulrich's direction some men got on the shoulders of others. Hoisted aloft, they began hacking, slashing and tearing at the heavy thatch above. Einar was glad Gerpir must not have been very wealthy – or at least that he was not wealthy enough to afford a shingled roof. Cutting through that would have presented a much harder task.

He glanced around and saw that the outlines of the doors were now marked by glowing orange lines of the light from fires outside. There was thick smoke seeping in from several points around the building, making men's eyes smart and choking the breath in their throats.

Then there was a crack from overhead and Einar felt a welcome breath of cold, clear air. One of the men digging into the roof had broken through. He and the men around him hacked with renewed vigour and soon a wider hole opened. A torrent of snow that had been sitting on the roof came tumbling in, showering everyone below with its freezing dust.

Before long a large gash had been torn in the roof. Not before time either. Flames were now licking into the interior of the hall from both gable walls and at several points along the side walls as well. With the inrush of air the flames blazed brighter, their tongues licking higher and further along the walls. Einar felt the first pangs of panic squirming in his guts.

'Grab what you can and get out,' Jarl Sigurd shouted to his men.

Stacking tables and benches to create a kind of stairway to the roof, the men in the hall began clambering up and out into the cold night air beyond. Some had managed to put on their helmets and throw their shields over their backs. As Einar climbed up himself, he wondered what further danger awaited outside.

Once through the hole in the roof he looked around and saw there was little to worry about apart from the cold and the snow. The hall was ablaze but the women who had set light to it were already scurrying off into the dark of the nearby forest. A bright moon sat high in the sky overhead along with stars that were beginning to smear from view as the smoke from the burning hall rose into the sky.

The jarl's men who had already escaped were gathering a little way from the hall in the clearing just before where the forest began. Einar slid down off the roof, landing in the deep snow below, then dusted himself off and trudged over to join the others.

Skar, Ulrich, Starkad and Affreca were already there before him.

Affreca threw a bemused look in his direction.

'Do you not feel the cold or something, lad?' Ulrich said.

Einar looked down and realised just why he actually did feel so cold. He still had no shirt on.

'Without doubt,' he said, shaking his head. 'This is the worst Jól I've ever had.'

Part Two
Britain

7

The *snekkja* was a sleek warship with a long, thin body like the snake it was named after. This made it fast and versatile. A snekkja could cross an ocean with speed or penetrate deep into a land by sailing up its rivers. However, the latter required a shallow draught, which meant crossing the open North Sea to Britain was a rocky ride as they pitched and rolled across the mountainous waves.

The middle of winter was the worst time for sea travel. Constant rain hissed down from the wolf-grey sky into a sea that mirrored it in colour. Huge swells lifted and lowered the ship over and over again, sending the crew to the side, spewing their guts into the water. Einar, who hated ships at the best of times, had not felt as miserable in a long while.

Ulrich had decided to accept Aethelstan's offer. After making their way back to the coast with Jarl Sigurd and Sweyn, they had boarded their snekkja and Roan, the wizened old skipper of their longship, had set a course south across the rolling waves of the northern whale roads.

They were flanked throughout the voyage by two larger warships sailed by Sweyn and his warriors from Aethelstan's fleet.

Sometimes the freezing sea washed over the snekkja's dragon-carved prow and swamped the deck, sending the crew running for buckets to bail the ship out before they sank. The rain and waves left the deck slippery and treacherous, and most of the Wolf Coats moved around the ship with a rope tied to their waist in case they fell and were swept overboard.

They had a long way to go. Orkney lay between Norway and Britain, and with Eirik Bloody Axe ensconced there like a troll, waiting to pounce on passing goats, Ulrich wanted to give it a very wide berth lest they run into some of Eirik's vikings. So they had sailed south across the open northern sea for several days before turning south-west.

Life aboard ship swung between periods of hard work and stretches of boredom when there was nothing to do. During these times Einar tried to play as much *tafl* as he could. It was a board game where two players compete to either stop or effect the escape of a king and his warriors from surrounding enemy forces, all marked out by black or white counters on a chequered board. Einar had bought a new folding tafl board in Norway and Ulrich had told him the game was a good way to learn how to plan and out-think enemies. To Einar's pleasure he found himself getting better and better at it, regularly beating most of the others on the ship. All of them except Ulrich, that was.

On the sixth day of the voyage they spotted a dark line between the waves and the horizon that marked the coast of Britain.

A long leather cover was raised over the deck, secured to the stern, mast and prow. This provided some shelter from the relentless weather. Everyone on board wore a hooded sealskin jerkin and breeches to keep them dry, but even with that Einar felt like he was damp and cold all the time. At sea Skar had two roles: prowman if there was a fight – the first warrior to go over the side into an enemy ship – and cook for the rest of the time. He kept a fire going on the cooking stone near the mast and boiled or fried their meals, usually some form of air-dried fish seethed in seawater.

On that sixth day Skar had boiled up some barley stew along with salted fish. The smell of it was rank and the taste not much better, but Einar and the others munched it down anyway. They sat cross-legged on the deck, the weather, discomfort and boredom of the trip combining to create a sullen, subdued mood.

'Why are we going to fight for Aethelstan anyway, Ulrich?' Kari said. His brown hair was shorn very short over most of his head except for two long tails that were wound around the top of his head and tied in a knot just to the right of his crown. The expression on his rune-tattooed face suggested he was far from happy with the idea.

'Jarl Sigurd used us,' Ulrich said, stroking a hand along the grey fur of the ship's cat, Gandr. The ship had lately suffered an infestation of mice and Roan had invested in the big creature at the same market Einar had got his tafl board. Gandr had grown fat while reducing the mice population on board and had also taken a shine to the balding little leader of the crew. He now lay purring in Ulrich's lap.

'I'm not happy with that,' Ulrich went on. 'I don't know who we can trust in Norway anymore.'

'But at least Jarl Sigurd believes in our gods,' Kari said. 'Aethelstan is a Christian. How can we trust him?'

'I'm a Christian!' Wulfhelm said.

'But you're *our* Christian,' Skar said, clapping him on the back and grinning. 'We've half civilised you in the time you've spent with us.'

'King Hakon is a Christian,' Ulrich said. 'What's the difference between one Christian king and another? I don't trust Aethelstan any more than I trust Jarl Sigurd, but I'm getting tired of all these powerful men and their games. I've had enough of statecraft and double dealings. We are vikings after all. We need to get back to acting like vikings. It's time we started working for our own good. From now on we fight for ourselves. For fame and gold, not for kings and jarls. Aethelstan will pay us in silver for this work. That's all we will care about now.'

Kari nodded and the others muttered their own assent to the plan. From Ulrich's abrupt manner, however, Einar was not sure Ulrich himself was convinced by this course of action. This was unsurprising. Einar knew that Ulrich was a man of faith. All the choices he made in his life path were governed by what he believed in. Was silver and gold enough to satisfy that thirst?

Wulfhelm also had misgivings. 'I once was an oath-sworn warrior of Edwin, Aethelstan's half-brother, remember?' the Saxon said. 'He tried to kill Aethelstan and take the throne of Wessex. What if I'm recognised?'

'Keep your head down,' Skar said. 'Comb your hair, have a good wash and those filthy Saxons will think you're a Norseman just like us.'

They all laughed.

'So we're all agreed then?' Ulrich said.

The others nodded, though Kari and Sigurd still bore sceptical expressions.

'Good,' Ulrich said.

Affreca got up and walked off towards the prow.

'What's wrong with her?' Ulrich said.

'It's the cat,' Skar said, nodding at the animal curled up on Ulrich's crossed legs. 'She's sensitive to the evil in cats. It makes her sneeze.'

'There's no evil in old Gandr here,' Ulrich said, scratching behind the cat's ear, much to its obvious delight. 'It's more likely some woman thing.'

As she had got up, Einar had seen the downcast expression on Affreca's face and he was not so sure himself if it really was the cat that had bothered her. The others began discussing the voyage ahead and debating the best route to take. Such discussions, which so absorbed the others, bored Einar, so he got up and wandered after Affreca.

The rain had eased off for once and the sky above cleared, changing the colour of the ever-moving ocean once more. Affreca stood beside the carved dragon head, staring out at the endless, undulating green waves with eyes that almost matched it in hue. She had pulled the hood of her sealskin jerkin down. Her features were pale as ever and her red-gold hair had now grown back long enough to braid from when the nuns had shorn it.

'You think Ulrich is making the wrong decision?' Einar said.

Affreca shook her head. 'He's doing the right thing for the crew,' she said. 'It's time we looked out for ourselves.'

'I don't know,' Einar said, shaking his head. 'I can't make sense of things anymore. We fought for Eirik then when he betrayed us we fought just as hard for Hakon against Eirik. Then Jarl Sigurd. Now we're in the service of Aethelstan and we fight for gold. So many have died. We've killed so many. What for?'

He fingered the hammer amulet that hung on a leather thong around his neck.

'You still wear Thor's *Mjölnir*?' Affreca asked, a faint smile coming to her lips. 'Don't let Ulrich catch you with that.'

'I know, I know,' Einar said. '*Thor is the god of slaves and farmers, but Odin has the kings and nobles*. Perhaps the gods really are leading us and there is some point to all this. But our course seems so chaotic. So meaningless.'

'If you are worried about chaos, then you may be right about the gods leading us,' Affreca said. 'One of them anyway. Odin causes strife in the world. His purpose is chaos. Did he not say, himself: *Wars I raise, princes I anger, peace I never bring?*'

'Sometimes I think,' Einar said with a sigh, 'some peace – some rest – would be most welcome.'

Affreca's smile faded. She looked away towards the rolling waves again. 'At least you have the blessing that you can wonder if it's the gods who guide your path.' Her voice was hard. 'My fate is in the hands of mere mortals.'

'You're the daughter of the King Guthfrith,' Einar said, a puzzled frown on his face. 'You're the heir to the crowns of two kingdoms: Jorvik and Dublin. What do you mean?'

'Yes, I am heir to Jorvik,' Affreca said through clenched teeth. 'But I can only get what is by right mine at the behest of Aethelstan. And I can only get it if I marry Hakon. As for Dublin, my brother Olaf rules there now. Anything I could get in Ireland would be what he deigns to share with me, like the scraps he throws to his dogs. I am of the clan of Ivar the Boneless. I'm a descendant of Ragnar Loðbrók himself! Yet I have nothing if it is not given to me by these men.'

She looked down, her anger gone, replaced by what looked like sadness. Einar longed to reach out and touch her arm, but some inner fear made him hesitate. They stood in silence for a moment as the ship rode up and down.

'You're worried that Aethelstan will try again to force you to marry Hakon?' Einar said at last.

'Yes,' Affreca said with a sigh. 'Having Hakon on the throne of Jorvik and Norway is key to his plans.'

'Sweyn said he thought Aethelstan had given up on the idea,' Einar said. 'He knows you're not interested.'

'What does Aethelstan care what I want?' Bitterness had re-entered Affreca's voice. 'I'm a piece on a tafl gameboard. The winner of that game will rule all of Britain. He won't give up on *that* – I can tell you.'

Einar looked at the waves. Now he understood why she felt this way. Gods aside, they were all powerless when it came to the whims and strategies of kings and jarls. As a woman, Affreca was even more helpless.

An idea sprung into his mind. Straight away he dismissed it as crazy. He did not dare even say it. Then after a few moments he reasoned with himself that it was actually a stroke of brilliance. Perhaps they could outwit Aethelstan and all the others after all. Not just that, but he of all people could be the one who helped Affreca.

'What if you—' He stopped, somehow unable to complete the sentence.

Affreca looked at him and frowned. 'What if I what?'

'What if you told Aethelstan you were already married?' Einar said, blurting the words out in a sudden rush. 'To someone else, I mean. Then Aethelstan cannot make you marry Hakon.'

'But I'm not,' Affreca said.

'Aethelstan doesn't know that,' Einar argued.

'He's not stupid, Einar,' Affreca said. 'And he's had enough of his allies around us since that last time we were in Jorvik to know that I've not been through a marriage ceremony between then and now.'

'Not a formal one, no,' Einar said. 'But you could have been through a handfasting ceremony. That only takes a few moments. No *goði* or *galdr maðr* needs to be present. It's just two people confirming their love for each other.'

She looked at him, mouth open.

'We could say you were handfasted on this voyage,' Einar said. 'If you are already married, Aethelstan can't make you marry Hakon.'

'It might work,' Affreca said. 'But who to?'

'Well…' Einar coughed and looked down at the deck. He was aware his cheeks were burning. 'Me.'

'It's very generous of you, Einar, but Aethelstan is a Christian,' Affreca said, shaking her head. 'Don't they believe folk are not married unless it's in one of their churches, supervised by one of their wizards?'

'Wulfhelm tells me the Aenglish and Saxons have the same customs as us,' Einar said. 'They have their church weddings, but they cost silver and are for the rich. Most folk just have a handfasting – a common marriage.'

A broad grin spread across Affreca's face. 'You're a lot craftier than you look, Einar,' she said. 'I think this is the answer! You really will say you married me if Aethelstan asks?'

'Of course!' Einar agreed.

She threw her arms around him and hugged him close. Einar was surprised at the strength of her clasp, then reasoned that she spent her days drawing a Finnish bow. She probably had a stronger grip than him. The smell of her was intoxicating and a silly grin spread across his face.

'I suppose the question is,' Affreca said, letting go of Einar and stepping away, 'will Aethelstan believe it?'

'Do you think he wouldn't believe the daughter of the King of Dublin would get married in a handfasting?' Einar said, with a grin.

'What I mean,' Affreca said, 'is will Aethelstan believe I would get married to... well... you?'

'What do you mean: me?' Einar asked, his grin fading a little.

'I'm the daughter of the King of Dublin, Einar,' Affreca said. 'You're a farmer from Iceland, the son of a former Irish bed slave.'

'I'm the rightful Jarl of Orkney!' Einar said.

Affreca nodded. 'Of course you are,' she said. 'But not the *actual* Jarl of Orkney.' She reached out and patted Einar's forearm. 'Don't take my words the wrong way; I am grateful for your idea and your offer.'

She leaned over and planted a kiss on Einar's cheek.

'And who knows?' she said with a smile. 'If you ever throw Eirik off the high seat of Orkney and actually become the Jarl of Orkney, then maybe I'll actually consider you for a husband.'

Affreca walked back up the deck to join the others. Now she was smiling and her previous pensive mood was gone.

Einar, on the other hand, was indignant. He looked out at the rolling sea and, as often in times when he felt disturbed, the lines and tune of some poetry ran through his mind. In this case it was the *Haraldskvæthi*, the lay of Harald.

As he chanted the poem in his head of how King Harald Fairhair won the battle of Hafrsfjord and became the first king of all Norway, he also recalled the story of how Harald got his nickname.

Harald was born the son of a minor folk-king of Vestfold, the same Halfdan the Black who Ulrich had used the example of to bring Gerpir to his icy death. Gyda, haughty and beautiful princess of a bigger, richer kingdom, had laughed at Harald, scorning his marriage proposal by saying she would never marry him unless he became king of all Norway, a feat she had thought impossible.

On that day, Harald had vowed not to cut or comb his hair until he became high king of the whole country. It took ten years and much bloodshed, but after the final battle of Hafrsfjord Harald "the Shaggy" became known as Harald "the Fair-Haired". Then he sent for Gyda and reminded her of her promise.

Einar grasped his Mjölnir amulet between his thumb and forefinger. He looked out at the dark clouds and the rolling sea and made a vow to himself that one day he would take back the high seat of Orkney that was his by birthright. As a mark of his intent, like Harald he would not cut his beard or hair until that day. He would comb them though – he had no desire to look like a madman, and without combing he would be riddled with lice.

In the distance there was a low rumble of thunder. Then the rain started again.

8

Einar, who prided himself on the fact that despite his young years he had already visited three cities, found himself stunned by Wintanceaster.

In the end, the voyage to Britain had taken two weeks after winds and tides had had their influence on progress. They landed at the fortified southern port of Hamtun, where a bristling confrontation with the coastguard, indignant at the arrival of a viking ship in the heart of the kingdom of Wessex, had ensued. The arrival of Sweyn and the Northumbrians, with their similar ships except for the Christian crosses that replaced the dragon on their prows, had smoothed this over, though not before the Norsemen and the West Saxons had almost come to blows.

'We are going to visit the king of the Saxons,' Ulrich said to his crew. 'So we must look our best. Everyone, put on your ceremonial war gear.'

His words provoked groans among the others. Each one of them had their own war gear, adapted to both their personal needs and the practicalities of battle. As well as that, they each kept a set of equipment to wear on important social occasions. Because it was rarely worn it was mostly ill-fitting and uncomfortable, more for showing off in than fighting. Most of it was the war gear they had robbed from the *Kunungar Haugan*, the ancient burial mounds near Grimnir's house above Frodisborg. Shiny as it was, it was also very old and far from supple.

They pulled on brynjas polished to gleaming, and visored helmets, covered by silver-embossed plates with scenes of heroes and gods hammered into them. Around their shoulders they fastened their wolfskin cloaks.

Then they swapped the longships for flat-bottomed punts and carried on their journey inland, travelling up the river to Wintanceaster, the city that was the centre of power in the kingdom of the West Saxons.

As they approached Wintanceaster, Einar grew more and more impressed. The city was defended by double ditches and high walls made of white stone. The walls were solid and complete as well, not the ancient, tumble-down, half-robbed-out, patched-up defences that surrounded Jorvik or the rampart topped with a wooden palisade that protected Dublin.

They docked their skiffs and proceeded on foot to the fortified gates of the city. Unsurprisingly, the arrival of a band of wolfskin-clad Norsemen provoked suspicion from the warriors on guard there and they were halted.

'Who are you and what is your business here?' the commander of the guard said.

'Look out,' Ulrich said over his shoulder to his company, his most provoking smile on his lips. 'The barbarians are at the gates.'

He turned back to the gate guard. 'We are here to meet your king,' he said in a demanding tone and in the Norse tongue.

Ulrich had spotted how nervous the gate commander was and Ulrich, being Ulrich, was determined to exacerbate the man's discomfort as much as he could.

Sweyn grimaced at Ulrich's words then stepped forwards, pulling off his helmet. He and his men did not look that much different to Ulrich's crew but the gold and silver crosses they wore around their necks made the commander relax a little. When Sweyn showed that he knew the necessary passwords and phrases, he gained the guard's confidence and the Wolf Coats were granted entry to the city.

'I will be sending some of my men with you,' the commander said. 'Just so you don't get lost.'

'Right,' Ulrich said, sarcasm thick in his voice.

'That is fine,' Sweyn said, sliding a reproachful glance in Ulrich's direction. 'Where is the king?'

'It's the day of the hundred court,' the commander said. 'He'll be there as he always likes to be when he's in the city.'

Once through the fortified gates, Einar looked around him with awestruck eyes.

The streets were not the wooden-planked walkways Einar had seen in other cities. Wintanceaster's were cobbled with stones so carts and horses could easily move over them. Each one intersected the other like a fishing net and seemed to go on forever. Wulfhelm, a proud smile on his face despite his concerns about being recognised, announced that there was over six miles of cobbled streets in the city. Einar, who did not know what a "mile" was, was unsure if he should be impressed or not.

Channels ran alongside the streets, bringing fresh water into the town and carrying filth and detritus away. Buildings rose along the street sides sometimes as high as two and even three storeys. Merchants hawked gold and silverware, shoes, jerkins, vegetables and all sorts of tools and weapons from stalls that also lined the streets.

Everything in Wintanceaster seemed to stand in contrast to Dublin, Jorvik and even Hedeby. There were no rotting corpses of sacrificed animals hanging outside the houses to show the homeowners' devotion to the gods. Instead the faith of the city dwellers was demonstrated by the many Christian churches, their bells clanging their racket across the morning air. Monks and nuns mingled with the crowds in the streets. Everyone seemed well dressed. It was clear to Einar and the others that Wessex was a prosperous kingdom. There was little of the filth and chaos Einar had witnessed in the Norse cities. Instead Wintanceaster exuded order and wealth. Just being there among the crowds and the tall buildings sent a surge of excitement through his heart.

'This must be what being in Rome itself is like!' he said as they negotiated the busy high street towards the south-west of the city where a towering church – one of the ones called "minsters" like the one in Jorvik – loomed over the buildings around it.

Surt laughed. 'Rome is just a ruin these days, Einar,' the black-skinned man said. 'And this town? This is a mere village compared to the cities of Al-Andalus, Baghdad, Cairo or even Constantinopolis, the city you northern barbarians call Miklagard.'

Einar's head swam at the thought that a city could be even bigger, even richer than the one he stood in at that moment.

As amazed as Einar was at his surroundings, the folk of Wintanceaster regarded the Norsemen with just as much surprise. Ulrich revelled in this and told them all to pull their wolf's head hoods up, then insisted on swaggering right down the middle of the street as the locals gawped at seeing vikings – the mortal enemies of their kingdom – right in their midst. Wulfhelm kept the hood of his wool cloak up as well. He did not want to risk anyone recognising him. Surt's dark skin drew as much attention as the appearance of the vikings around him and like Ulrich he revelled in the consternation he caused, returning the startled looks of the locals with a glare of his own that was just as hostile.

This prompted Einar to notice another difference between the Norse cities he had visited before and this one. In Hedeby, Dublin or Jorvik there had been people from all over the known world. Here in Wintanceaster the folk who now glared at them looked more or less the same, being almost a uniform blond, pale-skinned and Saxon.

They continued on through the city until they came to an open space in front of the big minster that loomed overhead. It had the look of a marketplace though today it was filled with a large crowd of people rather than merchants and stalls. They were gathered around a raised mound that stood close to the minster. The Saxons were Christians but still followed similar law codes to the Norse, as they had for centuries that went back to the days when they were all one folk who spoke one tongue, so Einar knew the mound was where law cases were heard. They had arrived at the court.

There was a wooden platform erected on top of the mound. A young lad, not much more than a boy, stood on the platform. His head was bowed, his shoulders slouched and he clasped his hands before him. Beside him stood a tall man in his middle years. He stood straight, chest puffed, head high. He was lean and though his leather jerkin and woollen breeches spoke of wealth, his broken nose, scarred left cheek and muscled frame said he was someone familiar with violence. Einar guessed him to be a reeve or similar man of importance, charged with enforcing the king's laws. The man's right hand rested on the young fellow's shoulder and the hierarchy of power was obvious.

Beside them on a seat was a man dressed in the robes of a Christian wizard, the sort Einar knew they called "priests". Einar could tell that though he was a young man, he was an important one from the amount of coloured embroidery on his clothes and the gold, gem-encrusted cross he wore around his neck. A long staff with a curled head, not unlike the crook used by a shepherd, rested against his seat. He was clean-shaven and there was a stern expression on his face.

There were many people gathered around watching. Einar could tell a judgement of some importance had just been made as an air of excited conversation bubbled around him like over-fizzy ale.

Among the crowd, just in front of the mound, was a group of richly dressed noblemen and amid them Einar recognised Aethelstan, King of Wessex and Mercia, king of all the Angles and the Saxons and Emperor of Britain.

9

This was the fourth time Einar had met the king – an impressive achievement, he reasoned, for someone Affreca had described as a *farmer from Iceland, the son of a former Irish bed slave.*

Aethelstan was taller than Einar, good-looking and in his middle years of life, which were evidenced by the lines on his face and the white strands that streaked the brown of his hair and long, Aenglish-style moustache. Two of Einar's previous encounters with the king had been in Jorvik but he looked a lot different here. In Jorvik he had been dressed in rich clothing but it was the sort of garb noblemen wore when hunting or travelling, and his torso had been padded by an obvious mail shirt worn beneath his shirt. Now he wore a soft white tunic and woollen breeches. Around his shoulders was an impressive bright red cloak that reached to the ground. His sword rested in a gilded scabbard that hung from a belt studded with rubies, garnets and other glittering gemstones. In Jorvik, Aethelstan had been surrounded by armed and armoured warriors. Here he stood in the midst of the crowd, arms folded and relaxed, though those around him did leave a respectful space.

The difference was only to be expected. Jorvik, Einar reasoned – though welcoming and familiar to a Norseman like him – was a city that saw itself as occupied by Aethelstan's army. It was hostile and dangerous. Here Aethelstan was in his own kingdom, Wessex, surrounded by his own folk, who clearly respected and adored him.

Another blond-haired young lad stood beside the king. He

looked about the same age as the boy on the platform but was much less downcast by the proceedings going on around him. Like Aethelstan and the other nobles before the mound, he wore the finest of clothing. The king had his hand on the boy's shoulder, guiding him to look at what was going on before them on the platform. The boy watched the proceedings with an expression so earnest for someone of his age that Einar judged it was most likely worn due to expectations rather than real interest.

'Does Aethelstan not preside over his own courts?' Surt said in a hissed whisper.

'This is the hundred court,' Sweyn said. 'It hears cases local to the town: theft, assaults, property disputes, that sort of thing. The king is the supreme justice in the land but this is far beneath him. The shire reeve prosecutes the cases and the bishop pronounces judgements.'

He nodded to the priest in the chair and the man with the broken nose on the platform.

'Why does Aethelstan come here then?' Skar said.

'He wants to see his laws enforced,' Sweyn said. 'And he wants the people to see that he cares about justice and the law.'

The priest held up his hand for quiet. An expectant hush fell on the watching crowd.

'This boy has now been judged guilty of theft,' he said. 'Shire reeve, what is the value of the goods the lad stole?'

'He stole two beehives, my lord,' the man in the leather jerkin said. 'At four pence each that comes to eight pence. He took six chickens as well, which makes a total of eight and a half pence.'

A collective gasp ran through the people watching.

'Then the law is clear,' the priest said. 'The boy will hang.'

The shire reeve nodded. His knuckles whitened as he increased his grip in the hand that rested on the shoulder of the boy before him. The lad started to cry. A woman in the crowd near the platform – who Einar assumed was his mother – wailed with despair.

'He's just a child!' the woman cried, tears streaking down her face.

'He is thirteen winters old,' the priest said. 'The law is quite clear: anyone over twelve winters caught in the act of stealing goods worth more than eight pence is to be put to death.'

Many in the crowd nodded.

'Have mercy,' the boy's mother moaned. She looked around her, desperate for any sympathetic face. She saw only stony faces.

'It's the law,' someone said.

'And it's not the first time he's been caught, either,' the shire reeve said.

The woman's eyes fell on Aethelstan. She gasped and fell to her knees, hands clasped in pleading before her.

'Lord king,' she wailed. 'You can intercede in this. You can overrule this hard-hearted priest's judgement. Please have mercy on my boy! Godwin is a good boy. He's a bit wild, yes, but he's not evil. If he has another chance he'll change his ways. I will make sure of it. I swear to the Lord Jesus.'

All eyes turned to the king and an expectant hush descended. Aethelstan's face was pale and wore an expression of consternation. His jaw muscle clenched and for a few moments his eyes flicked from the woman to the boy on the platform. He opened his mouth as if to speak, then stopped. His eyes then fell on the richly dressed young lad beside him and he straightened his back, took a deep breath and shook his head.

'The law must be upheld without fear or favour,' Aethelstan said. There was a slight crack in his voice. 'A king must not interfere unless there is an obvious injustice. This lad has had a fair trial and has been found guilty. Now the sentence must be carried out.'

The crowd shouted its agreement. Einar could see the righteous indignation on all the faces around him.

The boy's mother howled and fell forwards, flat on her face.

'Please, lord, please,' she sobbed but it was all to no avail. The boy was hauled off the platform by a couple of the shire reeve's men and then his mother was dragged away as well.

'That is all the cases for today,' the priest in the chair said in a loud voice. 'The court is now over. We shall meet again in four weeks.'

'Bishop Aethelwold,' Aethelstan said, raising his voice to be heard over the rising conversation around him, 'this affair is not over. I wish to speak more about this with you.'

The priest nodded and stood up. The king turned and began striding from the platform. The expression on his face suggested he was far from pleased. The blond-haired boy and other nobles in the king's retinue fell in behind him, trying hard to keep up.

'Lord king,' Sweyn spoke up as the king swept towards them. 'I have brought the men you requested.'

The Northumbrian bowed his head as Aethelstan halted and looked at him. It was clear he was perturbed by what had just happened and confused by this sudden change in context. He frowned as he peered at the group of Norsemen gathered around Sweyn, then understanding dawned.

'Ah!' the king said. 'Ulrich Rognisson and his company of werewolves. You found them, then, Sweyn?'

'Yes, lord,' Sweyn said. 'Do you want to speak to them now?'

Aethelstan sighed and looked around him. Then he said: 'Not here. Take them to the scriptorium and show them the books and let them meet Israel. Then bring them all to the hunting lodge.'

With that, the king turned again, his scarlet cloak swirling around in his wake as he walked off.

'An invitation to a king's hunting lodge, eh?' Skar said. 'That will be nice.'

'I hope he calms down by the time we get there,' Einar said. 'He's tried to hang us at least once before.'

IO

'You're taking us to the church?' Ulrich said as Sweyn led the way through the streets, getting ever closer to the looming bulk of the minster. 'We've all been washed before, if that is what your plan is. Some of us several times.'

Einar recalled the Christian ritual they had all been made to go through in the river near Edin's burh when they had last entered the service of Aethelstan before his invasion of the land of the Scots. The monks who had dunked the vikings in the river had called it "baptism". The Norsemen called it washing.

'I know that. I was there, remember?' Sweyn said, shaking his head. 'The king wants us to collect a certain person from the scriptorium.'

'The what?' Skar said.

'It's where the monks work to create books,' Sweyn said.

The great building of the minster towered above even the two- and three-storey tenements that surrounded it. Like the one Einar had seen in Jorvik, its gable wall and bell tower were painted in bright colours with pictures of weird creatures and gory scenes of torment and execution, no doubt to scare the locals from misbehaving.

The soaring tower seemed to touch the very clouds above. It made Einar's stomach churn a little and he wondered how such a building, being made of stone, could stand so tall and yet not collapse under the weight of itself.

They did not enter the great minster but instead went around it, continuing along a side wall until they came to another stone building set alongside. Einar recognised the same type of building as they had seen previously in Jorvik: its walls were shorter than the minster's, though they had very tall openings in them covered with the clear, hard substance known as glass.

Not for the first time Einar marvelled at how much wealth the Saxons and their churches possessed. Glass was unbelievably expensive – way beyond the means of normal households to even afford a small piece – yet here were vast boards of the stuff, reaching nearly from the ground up beyond the second storey of the stone building.

Einar had been in Britain several times before but he had spent most of his time in the north-east where the Norse had settled. It was a beautiful country with rich, fertile soil but he had seen nowhere near as much ostentatious wealth as here in the kingdom of the West Saxons and all around them in the city of Wintanceaster.

'I've never seen such wealth in my life,' Einar said in a hushed voice.

'Aethelstan's realm is the richest in the world,' Starkad said from the corner of his mouth. 'That's why we vikings love to raid it.'

Sweyn led them through the doors of the lower building. It was long and tall, like a vast feasting hall of a great lord. However, the light that gushed in through the tall, glass-covered openings illuminated the interior far more than any jarl – whose house had one opening in the wall to let smoke out – could ever hope for.

The walls were covered by shelves stacked full of round rolls of parchment and the large leather-bound boxes Einar knew from Jorvik to be called books. There were tables set beneath each of the tall windows, and at each one sat one of the Christian wizards they called monks. Einar could tell they were monks by the rough, plain wool robes they wore and their weird hairstyles where the tops of their heads had been shaved to look like they were going bald. This still puzzled Einar, and he had never got a satisfactory explanation for why they did it. Most normal men dreaded the thought of losing their hair as they got older. Yet these Christians seemed to want to hasten towards that day. Ulrich's opinion was that these monks hated life in general and perhaps this was part of their denial of it.

Each monk sat hunched over pieces of parchment pinned to the table before him. They had big feathers in their hands, which they dipped in pots of coloured liquid then scratched runes and drawings onto the parchment with it. This, he knew, was how they made copies of their sacred lore.

Sweyn led the way down the room past the tables and busy monks. Many of them were so engrossed in their work that they did not notice the company of wolfskin-clad vikings among them, but those who did paled and looked on with apprehensive expressions as Einar and the others stomped by, the mail of their brynjas clinking with each step.

They came to a large table with four monks seated around it, each one working on his own parchments. Sweyn laid a hand on the shoulder of one of them who, to the Norsemen's amusement, nearly jumped out of his skin at the touch. The man looked around, his mouth dropping open at the sight of the armed warriors gathered around him. He started to his feet, one hand clutching the front of his robe.

Einar regarded this man with curiosity. He wore the long woollen dress of a monk but it was a little different to any of the others Einar had seen before. Neither did he have the pale appearance common in monks who spent too long indoors. Instead his skin was sallow, nowhere near as dark as Surt's but different enough to be noticeable among the complexions of the folk Einar had seen so far in Wessex.

The man's features were sharp, like a hawk, and he had long black hair that was streaked with white. He wore it combed back to fall around his shoulders. Unlike other monks who tended to be clean-shaven, this fellow had a little beard on the point of his chin.

'What's your problem?' Ulrich said, sneering down at him. 'Never seen vikings before?'

'Oh I have, lord,' the man said. To Einar's surprise he spoke the Norse tongue but with a strange accent that Einar could not place. 'Unfortunately I have seen rather too much of them for my liking. I was living in Brittany but then the Norsemen came. I was their prisoner for a time...'

His voice trailed off. Einar saw a haunted look creep over his face and wondered just what horrors the little man had been forced to endure while a captive.

'Well, you must have some sort of value or they wouldn't have kept you alive,' Ulrich said. 'Is that how you learned our tongue?'

'Yes, lord,' the little man said. 'I have a bit of a talent for languages and your tongue is not too different from that of the Aenglish or the other Saxons.'

'You're not a Saxon?' Ulrich asked.

The other man smiled and shook his head. 'No. I come from a land far to the south of here. The lord Sweyn here was good enough to rescue me from the vikings.'

'Allow me to introduce Israel the Scholar,' Sweyn said, a proud grin on his face. 'King Aethelstan is anxious that you get to meet this man.'

'I've not heard of a "scholar",' Ulrich said. 'Does that mean you're not a monk like the rest of these curs?'

'I suppose I am a sort of monk, yes,' the other said. 'But a special kind. I study. I discover new learnings. I work things out.'

'He is perhaps the greatest scholar in all the known world,' Sweyn said.

'Did you say this man's name is *Israel*?' Surt asked. His tone of voice suggested surprise, or suspicion.

'Indeed he did,' Sweyn said. 'Is that important?'

'Isn't that name a little... unusual?' Surt said.

Einar could see the big black-skinned man was perturbed in some way.

'Unusual, perhaps.' Sweyn shrugged. 'But what better name for a good Christian to be called than that of the father of the Lord's own chosen people? Now come, Israel. The king wants us all to meet him at the hunting lodge. So if you wouldn't mind telling these men about the book?'

'Of course,' Israel said. Then he stopped. 'You do know what a book *is*, don't you?'

'Yes,' Ulrich said. 'It's one of these piles of very flat, very stiff material with runes and pictures on it, bound around with leather. You Christians are obsessed by them.'

'And rightly so!' Israel said. 'I was in Brittany because there was a certain book there of interest to King Aethelstan. Unfortunately when I was captured the book was taken away and I don't know where to. The king wants you to get it back.'

'Hasn't Aethelstan enough books already?' Ulrich said, waving a hand at the stacked-high shelves around them.

'This is a very special, very precious book,' the monk said, wagging a finger. It was clear this was his favourite subject and the enthusiasm he had for it was overcoming even the fear he had of the Norsemen around him.

Ulrich stepped closer to the table and looked down at the very flat, rectangular parchment that lay on it.

'What's this made of?' Ulrich asked, a fascinated expression on his face as he ran his fingers over the flat surface. 'It feels like the soft skin of a young woman?'

The scholar made a dubious expression. 'You're half right: it's calfskin,' he said.

The vikings burst into laughter.

'Thinking of some of the women you've shagged, Ulrich,' Skar said, 'I can understand how you'd make that mistake.'

'Monasteries all have large herds of cattle for the production of vellum like this,' Israel explained. 'When the calf is big enough to be a decent size but not so old the skin becomes too rough to write on it, it's slaughtered. The skin is stripped off, cleaned, bleached and stretched on a frame. Then it's repeatedly wet then dried and scraped again. Then there is a final abrasion with pumice and a treatment of lime water and it is ready. It takes time.'

'That's got to be expensive,' Ulrich said. 'The calves alone must be worth a fortune, never mind the cost of the work.'

Einar looked around the room with renewed wonder. The number of books and rolls in this room alone must have required the skins of hundreds, perhaps thousands of cattle.

'Each one of these books must have more value than all the wealth of a jarl!' he said.

Surt grunted. 'They use parchment in the civilised world,' he said, shaking his head. 'It's made from reeds. Far fewer cows died to fill the libraries of Al-Andalus.'

'So that's why these book things are so valuable?' Ulrich said.

'No,' the monk said, wagging a finger in the air once more. 'It's because of what they contain: knowledge. The wisdom of the ancients. The very words of God himself. All this is held and preserved on their pages. The value of such things is incalculable.'

Einar cast his eyes over the parchment one of the other monks was working on. He felt his jaw drop slightly. Even in its half-finished state it was astounding. He had seen books and pictures like these in Jorvik, but these were on another level of sophistication altogether. The colours were brilliant and the runes and pictures ornamented with vibrant, complex patterns. The patterns the Jorvik monks had etched on their parchments were beautiful and impressive, but still recognisable in style, at least, to what a decent Norse craftsman could create on expensive war gear or a rich man's furniture. These were very different. Much less angular and more realistic.

'Beautiful, isn't it?' Israel said, noticing Einar's engrossed stare.

The parchment depicted a rich man with a crown on his head, therefore a king. He was holding up a golden box above his head, while glowing people with wings on their backs hovered in the air above him. Some other important man sat on a throne among the flying people and the whole picture was surrounded by drawings of vegetation, recognisable as flowers and trees. The realism of the depiction was astounding and with the fine lines of the drawings Einar could see the delight on the face of the king, then stern seriousness of the man in the seat and the laughter of the winged humans.

'I've never seen anything like it,' Einar said, in a breathless voice.

'I'd be surprised if you had, Norseman,' Israel said. 'It's a style unique to this kingdom. King Aethelstan has brought Frankish monks here who taught the original way of illustration, ultimately derived from ancient Roman and Greek styles, which the king very much approves of. Now it's taken on a life of its own here in Wessex.'

'If they value Roman and Greek learning, then these Saxons must be a civilised, educated people,' Surt said. 'If only I'd been enslaved by Saxons instead of you Norse barbarians. I might not have had to spend the last fifteen winters chained like a dog and forced to fight in a ring.'

'You think you would have been treated any better here?' Ulrich said, a sneer curling his upper lip. 'A slave is a slave, with the same miserable life, regardless of who his master is.'

'Perhaps,' Surt said with a smile and a shrug. 'Perhaps not. But the conversation I would have had to listen to all this time would have been a lot more interesting.'

The Wolf Coats laughed.

'If we took a few of these books we'd all be rich men.' Skar looked around the room. The others all cast greedy glances at the parchments with their bright colours and strange contents. Some even looked like they were painted with actual silver and gold.

'So can any of you read Greek?' the scholar said.

The blank looks that the Wolf Coats returned made the expression on Israel's face fall.

'I assume you can, my friend?' he said, turning to Surt. 'You seem at least a little more civilised than your companions. You mentioned you were from Al-Andalus? Some of the finest libraries in the world are there. I've seen that of the Emir of Córdoba myself.'

Surt shrugged and looked as sheepish as was possible for him to. 'I was more of a warrior. But I might be able to spot the difference between Greek and Latin. I think the letters are different.'

Israel cast a dubious glance at Sweyn. 'This seems a little risky,' he said. 'How will they be able to find the right book if the only one of them who might be able to spot Greek letters isn't even sure?'

'Don't worry,' Sweyn said with a grin. 'The king has a plan for that. Speaking of which, we must get going to the hunting lodge. King Aethelstan is expecting us. Do you need to bring anything with you?'

'Me?' Israel's eyebrows arched high into his forehead. 'Why do I need to go?'

'The king insists,' Sweyn said. 'He will explain everything when we get there. Now come along.'

Israel lifted a leather satchel from beside the desk. As if concerned he might flee, Sweyn placed a hand on the scholar's arm and began to lead the little man towards the door.

As the Wolf Coats followed, Affreca took one more look at the books and manuscripts that surrounded them. 'Already I'm not sure I like the sound of this task Aethelstan has set for us,' she said.

Sweyn led the company from the scriptorium to another gate in the walls that ringed the town. There they waited until some of Sweyn's men brought enough horses for all of them. Then they mounted and rode out of the city gates.

A short distance away from the walls, they entered a forest. It was still deep winter and nearly all the trees had no leaves. This was strange to the eyes of the men from the north, whose forests were populated by evergreen spruces and pines, if covered in deep snow at this time of year. The cold winter sun cast long, unnerving shadows of the branches all around like skeletal fingers reaching out across the carpet of brown, rotting leaves covering the forest floor.

After a while they saw a hall looming through the trees ahead.

'King Aethelstan's hunting lodge,' Sweyn said, pointing in the direction of the building.

Skar gave a low whistle. 'I pictured a hut in the woods,' he said. 'Nothing this grand.'

The hall was easily as large as the one in Jarls Gard, the fortress in Orkney that had belonged to Einar's father but had been stolen by Eirik Bloody Axe Haraldsson. It was at least one hundred paces long, with a roof that rose from not far off the ground at the sides to high overhead at the apex. The roof was covered in shingles, painted white so they seemed to glow against the winter sky.

A group of riders rounded the back of the hall and came towards the Wolf Coats. As they rode past into the forest, Einar saw mounted on the lead horse the blond-haired lad who had stood with Aethelstan at the court earlier. Now he looked much more like any other young fellow his age. He had changed out of his formal robes and wore old, comfortable leather and wool breeches and a hooded mantle, dyed green and brown to help him hide in the forest. His previous expression of studied seriousness was gone, and he laughed from sheer pleasure at the feeling of freedom given by the speed of the horse and the taste of the cold, fresh air.

There were a few other lads about his age and they were accompanied by older men who from their woodsmen clothing Einar judged to be forest reeves or huntsmen. The younger boys shouted to each other in a tongue that Einar had never heard before.

The hunting party rode off into the trees, their shouts and laughter fading to a distant echo as they went.

'I doubt they'll catch much today,' Sigurd said in his usual laconic tone. 'They're making enough noise to scare every beast for miles into hiding.'

Sweyn led the Wolf Coats towards the gable wall of the hall, where a set of stout wooden double doors were flanked by a pair of wooden pillars. These held up a short canopy to form a porch. The doors were covered with ornate carvings of heroes and beasts that twisted around each other in an intricate fashion and were painted in bright colours. The pillars were the same, some of the decoration even being picked out in shining silver and gold.

A company of warriors guarded the doors.

'Look at these peacocks,' Ulrich said.

The guards had red cloaks like Aethelstan's around their shoulders. Their helmets were polished to gleam like silver. Crests in the shape of a boar ran from front to back across the crowns of their heads. The helmet cheek pieces were fastened, enclosing their faces behind masks of iron stamped with decoration every bit as ornate as the doors and pillars they guarded. Their sword pommels, scabbards and cloak clasps glittered with red garnets. Their hair was braided on their shoulders and they wore long mail brynjas that reached to their knees. These had been burnished in sand and oil so they glittered like their helmets.

Like the gate guards at Wintanceaster, these warriors eyed the approaching Wolf Coats with suspicion and hostility. Even Sweyn could not negotiate their entry to the hall this time, and it was not until a richly dressed nobleman who said he was the king's *hall thegn* – the steward who ran the royal household – came to the door and vouched that the Norsemen were indeed expected, that the big doors were unlatched and the guards stood aside to let them in.

'Weapons first,' one of the warriors said, holding out one hand. He was a tall man with a taller crest than the others on his helmet and presumably their leader.

'We saw the king in Wintanceaster earlier,' Ulrich said. 'He was safe from our weapons there.'

'This is the king's private hunting lodge,' the Saxon said with a practised smile. 'You have no need of weapons while here. I must insist.'

Seeing the Wolf Coats' clear reluctance to comply, Sweyn unbuckled his own sword belt and handed it over.

'Come on, Ulrich,' he said. 'It's the same at the hall of any great lord. No weapons allowed. Besides, do you really think you're so important that Aethelstan had me bring you all this way just to kill you? You won't be let in unless you hand over your blades.'

Ulrich nodded, though the startled expression of sudden concern on his face suggested to Einar that it had not in fact occurred to Ulrich that Aethelstan might have intended all their deaths. However, now that Sweyn had said it, the seed of suspicion was planted. Nevertheless he handed over his sword and knives and the rest of the company, though reluctant, followed his lead.

'Don't worry, we'll take good care of them,' the leader of the guards said, a tight smile at his lips.

The steward led them into a sort of porch or waiting chamber. It was a short room with benches on either side, then another set of double doors that led into the main hall. Once the outer doors closed behind them, the room became gloomy as there were no windows. The only light came from a couple of torches and four oil lamps that stood on tall stands in the four corners.

'Wait here,' the steward said and went on in through one of the inner doors. He closed it behind him before Einar could get a glimpse of what lay beyond.

'I don't like this,' Skar said in a quiet growl. 'This is a perfect killing trap. Those warriors outside could come in the doors behind us. More could come from the hall and we'll be caught between them. We won't stand a chance. Especially unarmed.'

They all tensed, looking around for any potential exits or makeshift weapons. Israel the Scholar looked just as nervous as the others, though his trepidation came from being confined in the small room with a company of Norsemen. He clutched the strap of his leather bag as if fearful it would be snatched away at any moment.

The click of the inner door latch opening made them all jump. The steward poked his head back round the door. The sound of raised voices could be heard in the hall behind him through the now open door.

'The king is just finishing his discussions with Bishop Aethelwold,' the steward said, speaking in a hushed voice. 'Come on through.'

He threw the door open and they all filed into the long hall behind.

The interior of the hall was like the other noblemen's feasting halls that Einar had been in; however, everything inside appeared to be a touch more grand. The hall was long and wide and filled with shadows and half-lights. Torches burned in brackets and oil lamps stood on tall stands. A long hearth ran up the middle of the floor, making the air warm and comfortable, while the smoke from the smouldering wood drifted off through openings in the roof so as not to clog the air.

The lofty roof was held up by two rows of mighty pillars

which, like the ones outside, were richly carved and painted with vivid colours. They were also decorated in places by gold and silver leaf, which glittered in the torchlight. Many woven cloths hung upon the walls and between the pillars, and over their wide lengths rode or ran figures from ancient legends: warriors, heroes and monsters. Some were dim and faded with years; the rest almost seemed alive with many bright colours.

At the far end of the hall, beyond the hearth and facing north towards the doors, was a dais with three steps; and in the middle of the dais was a great gilded chair. Aethelstan the king sat in the chair. Beside him stood the priest Einar had seen making judgements at the court. A third man sat on a folding chair nearby. Above their heads was another tapestry, this one portraying a mail-coated warrior on a rearing white horse. He was blowing a horn, which was gripped in his left hand while he raised a sword high with his right. His yellow hair flew behind him in the wind. Swirling water, outlined in green and white threads, curled around his horse's legs.

As they approached the dais, Einar saw that the floor beneath their feet was paved with countless tiny tiles. They too were many colours and had been arranged to create pictures, each scene surrounded by patterns made of symbols and runes, both Norse and the type the Christians used. The last one showed a bare-chested man with curly hair riding in a chariot behind two rearing horses. He had one hand raised and held a spear in that hand. It was not a hammer, but the chariot made Einar assume this was an image of Thor, which was odd, given that Aethelstan was a Christian.

About halfway down the hall a group of women were sitting at work embroidering more wall hangings. The long material was stretched across wooden frames and the women bent over these, threading coloured threads in and out to pick out the scenes from the lore and legend they portrayed.

As Einar and the others approached, the women looked up and stared, aghast at the sight of the vikings. When they had walked past they burst out in a babble of outraged chatter. It was neither Norse nor Saxon, and to Einar it sounded different to the unknown tongue shouted by the blond-haired boy who had ridden past them outside. Who were all these foreign people and why did Aethelstan have them around him?

When they reached the end of the hall, they found that the king and the priest were engaged in a lively conversation. The third man had a very long beard, which was braided and pushed aside by his fist, which he rested his chin on. He wore an expression on his face that suggested he was bored to the point of pain.

He was of middling years, perhaps a little younger than Aethelstan, but where the king was slightly built, this man was burly and dressed in hunting clothes like the boys who had ridden by outside.

As Einar and the others approached, the burly man sprang to his feet. All previous signs of his tedium vanished. He levelled a square forefinger at the approaching company. His eyes were alight below bushy russet eyebrows. To Einar's surprise, he saw that the man's twisted beard remained at an odd angle to his chin, even now that his fist was no longer there to push it that way.

'Nordmanni!' he cried in a loud, accusatory voice.

King Aethelstan glanced around and noticed the Wolf Coats.

'Yes, Lord Alan, they are Northmen,' he said. 'Don't worry though. These Vikings are on our side. At least I hope they will be. Now, Aethelwold, what was it you were saying?'

He turned his attention back to the priest. The big man, Lord Alan, sat down again and resumed his former, bored expression.

'They are *your* laws, lord king,' the priest said. 'You had it declared at Grately that anyone over twelve years old caught in the act of stealing goods worth more than eight pence will be put to death.'

'At the time, robbery was out of control, Aethelwold!' Aethelstan said. 'There was anarchy in the kingdom. I am supposed to keep the peace in my realm. The intent was to deter thieves, not hang children.'

'Alas, lord,' Aethelwold the priest said, 'some sinners will not be deterred.'

'That was a mere boy we condemned to death this morning,' Aethelstan said.

'Does his age matter when it comes to the sin he committed and the punishment he deserves?' Aethelwold said. 'Does the Book of Proverbs not teach us, lord king, that: *He that spares his child the rod hates the child: but he that loves him chastens him betimes?*'

'Spares the rod, Aethelwold,' Aethelstan said, shaking his head, 'not the rope. I must change this. This law must be reformed.'

'As I said, lord king,' Aethelwold said, 'they are your laws so you can do what you wish with them. Surely you do not intend to let thieves get away with robbery, however? If you were worried about lawlessness before, then declaring such a thing will guarantee that.'

'Not at all,' the king said. 'But we should no longer hang anyone under fifteen. When the Witan council of the realm meets next I will ask them to consider and approve this reform.'

The priest nodded.

Both men turned towards the newcomers. Sweyn made an ostentatious bow. Ulrich and the others, standing arms folded, nodded their heads.

'Sweyn, Ulrich,' Aethelstan said, rising from his chair. 'I am pleased to see you at last. This is Bishop Aethelwold and Lord Alan, Duke of Brittany.'

The priest made a half bow while the burly man in the hunting clothes barely nodded. His face showed nothing but disdain.

'You must forgive Lord Alan,' Aethelstan said. 'He doesn't like Norsemen. They are the reason he is here, an exile at my court, and not at home in his realm of Brittany. And you have met Israel the Scholar, I see.'

Israel bowed his head in respect to the king.

'I was just discussing this morning's court proceedings with the bishop,' Aethelstan said.

'We were at the court, lord king,' Ulrich said.

'And what do you think of this display of Aenglish justice, Ulrich?' Aethelstan said. 'Perhaps you prefer the Law of the Sword?'

Ulrich turned down the corners of his mouth. 'I was pleased to see you did not interfere,' he said. 'Nothing and no one should be above the law. Even the king. If he bends, breaks or changes a judgement then he puts himself above the law. He destroys respect for it. Why should anyone else obey the law if the king does not? The king becomes a tyrant and the land becomes lawless.'

Aethelstan nodded, a look of faint surprise on his face. 'As with our mutual foe, Eirik Haraldsson. The fellow called Bloody Axe.'

'Above all,' Ulrich said, 'I'm glad to see that though you Saxons may have forgotten your gods, at least you have not forgotten the law.'

The king looked at Ulrich for a long moment, as if trying to work out if Ulrich was niggling him or not.

'Well, I don't know about the rest of you,' the king continued. He was smiling again. 'But I've had enough of duties, work and being stuck indoors for one day. How about some fun for a change? I think Lord Alan here has waited long enough. Let us go hunting!'

'Thank the Lord!' the burly man with the odd beard said, springing to his feet again. He spoke with an odd accent, not unlike that of the embroidering women. 'I've listened to so much talk of state business today I thought I was about to die from boredom.'

'I know your love of hunting, Lord Alan,' Aethelstan said. 'What about you, Ulrich? No objections to some exercise in the fresh air?'

Ulrich shook his head.

'Excellent!' Aethelstan said. 'While we're out I will explain why I have brought you all here.'

I2

'First, though, you'll want to get changed,' Aethelstan said. 'Your war gear is magnificent but hardly practical for the hunt. The clinking of all that mail and rattle of shields will alert any game for miles that we are coming.'

Ulrich's face showed Aethelstan his reluctance to comply.

'Don't worry,' the king said, frowning. 'I'm not like Eirik Bloody Axe. I'm a man of honour. I am civilised. I don't intend to murder you in the woods, if that's what you are thinking.'

Ulrich nodded and, with some mistrust, the Wolf Coats, Surt and Wulfhelm took off their shining brynjas, helmets and the rest of their war gear. At the steward's command slaves brought hunting clothes for them all: soft deerskin boots, brown breeches and dark green, hooded mantles – all the colours of the forest so the wearer would be less visible once in the woods. Despite his wariness, Einar was glad of the comfort they brought compared to the ancient war gear.

Wulfhelm pulled the hood of his cloak up straight away.

'I know who you are,' Aethelstan said in a tetchy voice. 'You were one of my half-brother Edwin's men. Don't worry. I'm not going to punish you for your part in his rebellion against me. You swore an oath of loyalty to him and I cannot blame you for the direction chosen by your lord. Neither is loyalty a crime. As well as that, Hakon told me you played a part in bringing Edwin to justice, so in my eyes you have atoned for your sins. I forgive you.'

Wulfhelm swallowed, nodded and took his hood down again.

Einar was taken aback by the generosity of the king. He also spotted the look of contempt on Ulrich's face and knew the little Wolf Coat leader regarded such mercy as weakness.

'I will stay behind, lord king,' Israel the Scholar said. 'If you don't mind. I am more a man of the library than the forest, and I have this lineage of yours to work on.'

Aethelstan nodded. 'Very good. I am most interested to hear what you've found out about my forefathers.'

'Indeed, lord!' The scholar's face lit up. 'I've worked out a very interesting thing. Very interesting indeed!'

The king held up a hand to stop Israel's excited babble.

'Later, please,' Aethelstan said. 'Now we are off to enjoy ourselves.'

Once changed, the Wolf Coats put their wolf-pelt cloaks back on. They were their most precious possessions and symbols of their achievements, after all, and Einar for one appreciated the way they marked out their own identity in the midst of this foreign land.

'Lady Affreca,' Aethelstan said. 'I suppose there is little point in asking if you would prefer to stay with the other ladies here in the hall to help with their embroidery?'

Affreca's upper lip curled.

'I didn't think so,' the king said.

'I don't understand the Welsh tongue, anyway,' Affreca said.

'So you recognised their speech?' Aethelstan said, eyebrows raised.

'You once imprisoned me in a nunnery with a Welsh princess,' Affreca said, an icy smile revealing her white teeth. 'Remember?'

'Indeed. And I still pray for the souls of the monks and nuns murdered when these heathens stole you from it,' the king said. His jollity vanished in an instant and a serious look that was every bit as hostile as Affreca's fell across his face.

Like a cloud crossing a summer sun, however, Aethelstan's mood then switched back to a more convivial one. It was not the first time that Einar had witnessed the king's mask of sociability slip, revealing the stone-hard character that lay beneath. Aethelstan had not become king of all the Aenglish and Emperor of Britain because he was a nice man.

'Well, you are only partly correct,' the king said. 'These noblewomen speak the Welsh tongue, but as it is spoken in Lesser Britain, the land overseas formerly called Armorica, in the kingdom of the Franks. Lord Alan's domain.'

This was news to Einar, who had no idea that the Welsh tongue was spoken outside of Britain. Einar wondered again what these women were doing here in the court of the King of Wessex. And who was the blond boy who had spoken in another, different tongue?

Once changed, they trooped outside, leaving by a door at the far end of the hall rather than the one they had entered by. Outside, they found themselves in a courtyard surrounded by stables and other outbuildings. Grooms stood waiting with horses, saddled and ready for riding, while the sound of excited dogs barking from within one of the outbuildings almost drowned out all other noise. Forest rangers, huntsmen and slaves all stood ready for the hunt.

Five grand-looking men also waited, already mounted. Their hunting clothes were of the best of materials. Their hair was long at the back, their moustaches long and drooping too, and their chins were clean-shaven. The large gold brooches that fastened their cloaks at one shoulder supported Einar's deduction that they were Saxon noblemen. They ranged in age from a little older than Einar himself to a gruff-looking fellow who must have been quite old, though nevertheless sat straight in the saddle, with his shoulders back. The two swords at his belt, one short and one long, attested to his life as a warrior. Unlike the others he had a beard that was grey as a wolf and he eyed the Norsemen with an inscrutable expression that suggested either hostility or amusement, Einar could not tell which.

'What are we hunting today?' Ulrich asked.

'Wolves,' the grey-bearded Saxon lord said, his face breaking into a grin.

His fellow nobles laughed. Ulrich's face darkened.

The thought that although they were here at the behest of the king, they were nevertheless right in the heart of hostile territory had occurred to Einar several times since their arrival in Wessex. The Saxon lord's remark hammered that sentiment home.

'Don't mind Lord Uhtred there,' Sweyn said to Ulrich. 'He's a grumpy old bastard. He's from the north, like me. We have our own sense of humour there.'

'He doesn't like Norsemen then?' Ulrich said. 'Aren't most of you up there in the Danelaw the bastard sons of Vikings?'

'He's killed many Norsemen, yes,' Sweyn said. 'But I think deep down inside he has a soft spot for you lot.'

'We will be hunting deer,' Aethelstan explained in a loud voice. His smile and tone of voice showed he was relishing the prospect. 'And if we're lucky maybe a boar or two, so best get prepared.'

The king, his steward and, to the Wolf Coats' surprise, the priest as well, led the way into another building to collect hunting gear. It was a store and Einar was impressed at the number of weapons and range of equipment available. There was enough to arm a small company of warriors or a whole army of hunters. Each one of them took a bundle of light, dart spears for throwing then moved to the rack on which stood heavy boar spears. Each one of these had a long, wide blade in the shape of a leaf that was mounted on a thick wooden shaft.

Lord Alan with the crooked beard shouldered his way to the front and made an ostentatious gesture of lifting the biggest, heaviest spear with the stoutest shaft. With a grin on his face that was all threat and no humour, the big man picked up a hunting knife and prised out the nails that fastened the blade to the shaft. Then he shook the spear, letting the blade clatter to the floor. Still grinning, he pushed his way back between the vikings and went outside.

'Was that supposed to impress us?' Ulrich said. 'Why is he ruining a perfectly good boar spear?'

'I'm afraid so,' Aethelwold the bishop said, looking a little sheepish. 'When Lord Alan goes hunting he likes it to be seen that he spurns taking iron weapons into the forest. All he takes to meet the dangerous beasts is a wooden staff.'

'He must be very brave,' Einar said.

'He must be an idiot, more like,' Ulrich said. 'Have you ever seen a boar, Einar? Huge, sweating, dangerous creatures they are. Strong as an ox or a bear with tusks sharp enough to spill your guts with one slice.'

'Not unlike Lord Alan himself,' the bishop said with a smile that suggested he was delighted with his own quip. 'But you must excuse his behaviour. He's only here because Norsemen drove him into exile from his own realm and he had to seek refuge here in the household of King Aethelstan. Therefore he hates Danes.'

'Einar's never seen a boar because they don't live in Iceland, do they, lad?' Skar said, clamping a large hand on Einar's shoulder.

Einar nodded. 'I've seen one roasting on a spit though,' he said.

'Well fortunately that kind are no danger,' Skar said. 'Unlike the ones we may meet today. If you end up confronted by one, you need to kill it quick.'

He poked a meaty forefinger into the dip at the base of Einar's neck, beneath his chin where his throat met his ribcage. Einar gave an involuntary cough.

'You see that spot?' Skar said. 'It's known as "the slot". Remember I taught you that the quickest way to kill a man is to stab down through that?'

Einar nodded again.

'Well, the same applies with a boar except it would be like a man coming at you on all fours,' the big man went on. 'You need to shove your spear right down that slot so it goes straight through the beast's heart. It should be dead before it gets the chance to impale you on its tusks.'

'Isn't there one problem with that?' Einar said.

Skar raised an eyebrow.

'It would have to be charging straight at me for me to hit it there,' Einar said.

'That is why boar hunters need one more piece of essential gear, lad,' Skar said, grinning. 'Courage.'

They chose boar spears for themselves. Einar made sure he picked one with as thick a shaft and as long a blade as he could find.

Then they each took bows and a bag full of arrows. All except Affreca, that was, who scorned anything but her own powerful Finnish bow and the arrows she made herself.

By the time they went outside the hounds had been let out. They were great shaggy animals, fearsome creatures big enough to bring down a deer, though not as huge or savage as the beasts Einar and Sweyn had fought at the gates of Cathair Aile. They swarmed around the courtyard like a plague of giant rats, barking and sniffing the horses and people who stood there.

Then the hunting party – the king, his lords, the Wolf Coats and forest rangers mounted. With blasts on horns and the yapping of dogs they rode off into the forest. A few more woodsmen and a company of slaves jogged along behind.

After a while they entered a valley with a track that led alongside a meandering river. Some forest rangers had gone ahead of the party and came out of the undergrowth to meet them. Einar realised this expedition was not a spontaneous idea but must have been planned well ahead. The rangers announced that there were deer up ahead. The blond-haired boy and his friends were with them. He babbled a few words to Aethelstan who laughed and replied in the same foreign tongue.

A few of the foresters took half the slaves and all the dogs then rode on ahead, heading up the hillside that ran along the side of the valley. The remainder of the hunting party dismounted and arrayed themselves on one side of a clearing opposite the river. There they unpacked their bows from leather bags and prepared their arrows.

'Allow me to introduce my nephew, Louis,' the king said to Ulrich and the others, ruffling the straw-coloured hair of the young lad who now stood beside him. 'This young fellow is heir to the throne of Western Francia – the kingdom forged by Charlemagne himself, whose blood flows within young Louis here.'

'We know the name of Charlemagne,' Ulrich said. 'Who forced folk to abandon their gods for your Christ at the point of a sword. He gave a simple choice: convert or be beheaded. The Butcher of Verden we call him. So how is this boy of the butcher's line your nephew?'

'My half-sister Eadgifu was married to Louis's father, Charles,' Aethelstan said, ignoring Ulrich's ire.

'Ah yes,' Ulrich said with one of his most provoking smiles. 'Wasn't he known as Charles the Stupid?'

The boy scowled. This told Einar that he understood both the Saxon and Norse tongues as well as his own. Knowing many tongues appeared to be an essential craft for someone living in Aethelstan's court: the king was surrounded by folk from all over the known world, and most of them seemed to have been displaced and driven into exile by vikings.

'Charles the Straightforward, perhaps,' Aethelstan said, with a strained smile. 'But poor Charles is dead now. He died in a prison after his ungrateful subjects overthrew him.'

'Such presumption!' the bishop said. 'God sets a king above his people. It is a terrible and wicked deed to overthrow that king.'

'It is Fate that sets a king above his people, not the gods,' Ulrich said. 'And it is his luck and his wits that keep him there. If he has neither his folk will get rid of him. Look at Eirik.'

'God struck Eirik Bloody Axe down for his sins,' Bishop Aethelwold said.

'Naturally I gave Eadgifu and Louis refuge in my household,' Aethelstan explained. 'But that injustice will be set right. Soon Louis will return to take back the throne that is rightfully his.'

Ulrich grunted in derision. 'How will a mere boy take a kingdom?' he said, flexing the string of his bow.

'That, Ulrich,' Aethelstan said, drawing his own bow to its full extent, 'will very much depend on you and your crew.'

13

'On me?' Ulrich said.

'This is why I brought you here,' Aethelstan said. 'A significant number of the Frankish nobles have realised the error of their ways in rebelling against Charles. I have received a request from the most powerful of them, Hugh, Duke of the Franks, that young Louis be allowed to return to Francia and be crowned king.'

'That sounds like a trap to me,' Skar said. 'Bring the boy back. Cut his throat. Hugh proclaims himself king.'

'Louis' position is far from safe – I grant you that,' Aethelstan said. 'There are many powerful men opposed to his return as king. But I am assured Hugh is not one of them.'

'How can you be sure?' Ulrich said.

'I have my sources of information,' Aethelstan said.

Einar glanced at the bishop. He had a good idea who those sources were as he had observed it in action several times over the last few years. This was where the true power of Aethelstan and the Christian kings came from. These monks and priests were in every land, and they were loyal to their God first, before the local earthly power. If a king like Aethelstan aligned with whatever purpose they thought their Christ demanded, then they would support him. They would be his eyes and ears in another kingdom, and pass what they saw and heard back across borders through the network of religious houses dotted across the lands. Einar pitied Aethelstan's foes. He knew their every move even while they were still planning them. How could you win when fighting someone with such a great advantage?

'The key nobles are ready to support Hugh and Louis,' Aethelstan said. 'But only if one more of the powerful men of Francia declares his support as well. If he aligns himself with us, then Louis' position as the new King of West Francia should be secure.'

'We're vikings, not nursemaids,' Ulrich said, casting a dubious glance at the boy.

'I'm not asking you to look after my nephew,' Aethelstan said. 'I said there is one more powerful noble who has yet to declare whose side he is on. This is where you and your men come in. I want you to take a message from me to him, asking for his support. Ask him to support Louis as the rightful King of Francia and ask him, for my sake, to pledge not to oppose him.'

'And who is this man?' Ulrich asked.

'William Longsword,' Aethelstan said. 'Count of Rouen. Ruler of Normandy.'

'You mean *Vilhjálmr Langaspjót*,' Ulrich said with a laugh. 'To give him his name in his own Norse tongue. The Jarl of Rúðu. But why us? You must have your own emissaries who can send messages.'

'The north-west of Francia is a violent, lawless place. Largely because you Danes run wild through it,' the king said. 'So who better to roam across it without hindrance or suspicion than yet another crew of vikings? This task needs to remain secret. If Louis' enemies get wind of what we are planning they will strike first and thwart our ambitions. If I send a delegation of Saxons to Normandy, it will be like trumpeting our plans to the whole world. Your company of Wolf Coats, on the other hand, will not arouse suspicion.'

'I'm not sure I like the idea of being your messenger boy either,' Ulrich said, notching an arrow to his bow.

'You'll be very well paid,' Aethelstan said. 'I can assure you of that.'

'Good,' Ulrich said. 'So what was all that nonsense we had to go through with the monks and their books back in

Wintanceaster? And what about that coal-biter, Israel? He said you've lost a book?'

'Ah,' the king said. 'That's the second thing I need your help with while you are there.'

'Why is this book special?' Ulrich said.

At that moment the rangers, huntsmen and slaves began a huge racket: blowing horns, shouting and banging sticks. The undergrowth rustled and bucked then the deer took flight, bursting into the clearing and running for their lives up the hill.

Einar knew of reindeer but these creatures were smaller and of a different colour. Their tan-coloured hides were dappled with white and their legs seemed almost too spindly to carry their weight.

Up the hillside beyond the clearing the foresters and slaves who had broken off from the main party waited. As the deer approached they loosed the hounds. The baying pack went tearing down the hill towards the oncoming herd. When the deer saw them they wheeled around and charged back down the slope again, the dogs driving them back towards the clearing where Aethelstan and the others waited.

'Here they come,' the bishop said, notching an arrow and drawing his bow.

Einar had never been on a hunt like this. The largest wild land animal back home in Iceland was the white fox. There had been bird and walrus hunts but nothing on so grand a scale as the event he found himself part of today.

He could feel as much as hear the hooves of the deer thrumming on the forest floor as they drew nearer. He drew his bowstring to his ear, sensing a surge of excitement in his chest. His heart pounded as he waited for the dogs to drive the deer towards them.

Then the deer burst into the clearing, running from right to left across the range of their bows. The hunters loosed their arrows. As the deer fled, the arrows streaking towards them whistled and whined. Wet thumps sounded as arrows hit their mark. Several of the deer went down, thrashing and kicking, arrow shafts protruding from necks, flanks or sides. The lucky ones carried on, vanishing among the trees and undergrowth into the winter forest.

Einar knew none of the shafts stuck in the fallen deer were his. He had watched his arrow sail through clean air several paces behind the fast-moving hind he had aimed at. This was not much of a surprise and it was not something he could blame on missing a finger on his right hand. He had just always been a terrible shot.

What did surprise him though was that Ulrich appeared to be even worse. It occurred to him that this was the first time he had seen Ulrich with a bow in his hand and now he understood why. If Einar's shot was bad, the wiry little Wolf Coat leader's was awful. His arrow flew far too high, going both well above and behind the whole herd of running deer. The miss was not deliberate either. Ulrich stood beside Einar and had shot after him, and Einar had caught the look of concentration on the smaller man's face before he released the bowstring.

Ulrich was a master of all kinds of weapons, but it was clear this did not include the bow. Perhaps it was not possible to be good at everything after all.

Ulrich cursed. He scowled in anger but Einar also saw his cheeks flush with embarrassment.

'Good shot, Bishop Aethelwold,' the king said. 'You took down that large doe.'

'Not as good as yours, lord king,' the priest said. 'I believe you killed the largest hind outright.'

'Bad luck, Ulrich,' Aethelstan said, a bemused expression on his face. 'You do know it's the deer we're supposed to be shooting at, don't you?'

Ulrich's face darkened further.

Affreca had not even notched an arrow. Her bow was still over her shoulder and she was watching the proceedings with disinterest.

Aethelstan noticed. 'Perhaps you don't want to hurt the animals, Lady Affreca?' he said.

'Shooting arrows into a herd of running deer is like taking random shots into a flock of birds,' Affreca said, her face twisted in scorn. 'You're bound to hit one. Where is the challenge?'

'Exactly my thoughts,' Ulrich said.

At that moment the undergrowth on their right swayed back and forth. Then a huge stag, a magnificent pair of spreading antlers rising from its head, burst into the clearing. It stopped and for a moment it looked around, startled. The hunters, just as surprised, scrambled to notch more arrows.

The stag lumbered forwards, running in the direction of the rest of the herd. There would be only moments to get a shot at it before the majestic beast moved out of range again. Everyone was desperate to be the one to bring the great creature down and there would only be one chance.

The bishop shot first. He was too hasty and his arrow fell short, thudding into the carpet of fallen leaves a few paces from the beast's hooves. The creature appeared to sense what was happening and swerved its path, causing Starkad, Kari and Wulfhelm to also miss. Einar reasoned that a stag would not have lived long enough to grow so big if it did not possess some knowledge of the danger posed by men with bows. It picked up its pace and the change in speed caused the arrows of Skar, Surt and Aethelstan's steward to miss their mark also. The Saxon lords had no luck either.

Einar loosed but again his arrow went nowhere near where it was supposed to go. The stag was over midway across the field of their bows' range. Only the king, Ulrich and Sigurd still had arrows notched.

Sigurd let go his bowstring. He missed too but only just. The stag again seemed to sense the arrow coming and changed course, leaving Sigurd's arrow to complete a harmless course into the undergrowth.

'Clever bastard,' Sigurd said through clenched teeth.

Aethelstan closed one eye, took a deep, even breath and let his arrow fly. The stag again jinked sideways and the king too missed, though only just. Einar saw the ruff of fur along the stag's spine part as Aethelstan's arrow sped past, a mere finger's breadth from the creature's flesh.

A look of triumph flashed across Ulrich's face as he realised he was the only hunter left with an arrow still to shoot. In a few more paces the stag would reach the undergrowth where the rest of the herd had disappeared and he too would get away.

Ulrich loosed his bow. His arrow streaked across the clearing. It thudded into a tree trunk nowhere near the stag and the big creature lumbered into the undergrowth both out of sight and out of bow range.

Ulrich threw his bow down, ground his teeth and shouted a curse at the heavens above.

'I see the bow is not your weapon of choice, Ulrich,' the king said. Einar was sure he saw a smile playing across Aethelstan's lips.

Ulrich made a face. 'I take no pleasure in shooting arrows at dumb creatures.'

'You're not a hunter then?' Aethelstan asked.

'If I am going to hunt then I prefer to chase something that's more of a challenge,' Ulrich said. 'Deer flee. They don't bite back when cornered. There is no contest, no danger and therefore no excitement. In short, this is boring.'

Einar grimaced at this, yet another display of Ulrich's insolence towards the king. Here was Aethelstan sharing his favourite pastime with them and all Ulrich could show was disdain.

At that moment horns began blowing in the forest. A commotion arose among the beaters and huntsmen. There came the sound of something crashing through the undergrowth. Something big and heavy by the sound of it as branches were snapping. At first Einar thought one of the deer was returning, then a huntsman burst out of the undergrowth. He was sweating and red-faced.

'A boar, lord king!' the man shouted. 'A great giant of a beast.'

Behind him a creature, twice as big and just as sweaty as the huntsman, crashed out of the brambles. It was covered in black bristles and Einar just had time to catch sight of two fearsome tusks protruding up from its bottom jaw as it slammed into the back of the unfortunate huntsman. With a flick of its head it tossed the man, howling, into the air. He tumbled head over heels over its long back then crashed to the ground.

The hounds went crazy at the sight of the boar. They howled and growled and tore across the clearing towards the creature. All the other huntsmen blew their horns while the slaves raised a racket of shouting and clashing of sticks. The boar, a long drool of slobber hanging from its lower jaw, swiped its great head right and left, glaring at the hunters with its small, malevolent eyes. At first it looked like it might try to attack all of them, then the creature realised it was badly outnumbered. It turned tail and crashed back out of sight into the undergrowth.

Einar stood rooted to the spot in shock. The beast looked as big as a cow. It resembled a pig in form but its sheer size, black spiny bristles and razor-sharp tusks made it look like some hog that had come from a nightmare.

'At last!' Lord Alan shouted as he grabbed his wooden staff and leapt up onto the saddle of his horse. 'Some quarry worthy of me!'

A look of fierce delight replaced Aethelstan's anger with Ulrich in an instant. He grabbed the boar spear from its sheath on the saddle of his nearby horse.

'Here is some sport that might give you a better match, Ulrich,' he said. 'That creature looks like he could gut us all with those tusks if he gets the chance. Let's get after it.'

Everyone ran to their horses and grabbed their boar spears.

14

As Einar swung himself up into the saddle of his horse he could hear the crashing of the huge swine as it thrashed its way through the bracken ahead. It was the biggest pig he had ever seen. He had heard legends of such creatures that roamed the forests, but in Iceland there were few woods never mind beasts like this.

He took a moment to put on his fighting glove. The stories he had heard about hunting wild boar all agreed on one thing: it was dangerous. He drew the boar spear from the sheath on the saddle and kicked his heels. His horse started forward and he joined the others as they tore into the undergrowth after the boar.

In moments his horse was crashing through brambles and weaving its way around trees while Einar ducked and leaned to avoid being swept out of the saddle by tree branches. He had no real idea where he was going but was glad his horse at least had no inclination to charge straight into a trunk. He clung on to the reins and did his best to guide the horse to follow in the same direction as the other riders up ahead. Or at least what direction he thought they were going in from the few glimpses he got of them as they too wove their way in and out of trees.

The dogs yelped and the hunters shouted. The sound of bracken and undergrowth being crushed and snapped by the horses and the boar sounded like the crackling of a raging bonfire. The hunters rode fast. Before long Einar noticed the barking of the dogs was now coming from behind them and getting further away. They had outstripped even the dogs.

Then Einar's horse burst into the open. It dug its forelegs in, skidding to a sudden halt that sent Einar lurching forwards. He just managed to throw his arms around his mount's neck and cling on.

Raising his head, Einar saw that the horse was stopped on the edge of a precipice. The ground before him fell away in a steep, shale-covered slope before reaching more woodlands below. A short distance beyond that a river meandered through the trees. Einar just caught sight of the bristling backside of the boar as it disappeared into the undergrowth at the foot of the slope.

The other horses had all halted on the edge of the sharp slope too. The stop was too quick for one of the Saxon lords who toppled off his mount and bounced, cursing down the shale, scattering stones before him.

The slope was too steep to ride down. Lord Alan was already off his horse and scrambling down it on foot.

'Come on,' he shouted. 'We can trap the beast between us and the river!'

The others all dismounted too. Before he thought much more about it, Einar found himself swinging his leg over his horse's back as well. He took a moment to find his spear, which he had dropped in the attempt to stop himself falling off his horse, then set off down the slope.

Einar's feet skidded and slipped as the loose stones on the hillside slid away from beneath him. He went as fast as he could, knowing if he went too fast he would fall and most likely hurt himself. Several times the speed of his descent got too much and he had to take a leap to regain his balance.

The others were already entering the woods between the slope and the river when he reached the bottom and plunged in after them. Einar ducked and dipped to avoid low branches in the dense woodland. Thorns from the bramble bushes caught and tugged at his cloak and breeches.

They had not gone far when Einar saw the others stop. Lord Alan was in the lead and he was standing still, left arm raised high in what Einar guessed was a hunting signal that everyone should stand still. Einar stopped moving as well. The sound of their crashing feet dissipated among the bare branches and an intense silence settled all around.

'The swine has gone to ground,' Skar, who stood near to Einar, said in a whisper. 'He's hiding somewhere.'

Einar swallowed. The thought that the great creature with its sharp tusks was lurking somewhere in the undergrowth, ready to strike at any moment, perhaps only steps away from him, made his skin itch.

The sound of barking from the top of the slope behind them announced that the hounds had caught up. Then came the hissing of shale as they too cascaded down the slope and tore into the undergrowth where the hunters already stood.

With their sharp sense of smell, the dogs made straight for a thicket to the right of Lord Alan. As soon as they did the whole bush shook and the huge boar burst from its hiding place. It charged straight at the dogs and with a flick of its great, long head that seemed too large for the rest of its body, tossed the lead hound into the air. The dog's howl ceased as it smashed into a tree truck nearby. The second hound fared no better. With a sound like wet cloth ripping, the boar's tusks tore open the dog's side from behind its right foreleg to its haunches. The poor creature's growl turned to a high-pitched whine as its steaming guts unravelled and tumbled out of the huge wound onto the forest floor.

The boar charged forwards, scattering the rest of the dogs in all directions, their natural sense of self-preservation overcoming their instinct to attack the boar. Lord Alan let out a great bellowing cry and charged towards the creature from its flank, his wooden staff held overhead in both hands like a cudgel. He brought it down right across the pig's back in a blow so powerful it would have broken the spine of a lesser creature. This boar hardly flinched and charged on through the bracken and brambles.

The hunters ran after it. Many shouted whoops and hunting cries while Einar found himself just screaming at the top of his lungs, something he found helped to dispel the nervousness instilled by being in the woods with such a fearsome creature.

The swine burst from the undergrowth and into the open air around the river. The hunters followed behind. Einar found himself on a riverbank that ran in a gentle slope to a wide stream that twisted its way through the woods. The water was low at the edge as it trickled over stones covered in black slime, then deepened into a bend and cascaded over rocks in a little waterfall.

The pig splashed through the shallows until it came to the wider, deeper part of the river and halted, realising it could not get across. It swung around to face the hunters chasing it once more. The hunters stopped too, forming a wary semicircle around the boar. It had nowhere to go. Its only escape was through one or more of the hunters.

For a moment the creature hesitated, sweeping its head right and left. Einar felt like its little eyes were boring into each of them in turn, as if it was trying to discern which one was the weakest, the least resolute, the least capable, and it would make its escape through him. Einar glanced to his right and saw Ulrich stood that way, boar spear ready. To his left was Aethelstan, spear gripped in both hands, teeth gritted. Einar puffed out his chest and glared at the pig, hoping to look more of a threat than the others.

The beast started forwards, its trotters scrabbling across the slippery rocks. To Einar's relief it was heading to his left. He glanced around and saw Aethelstan move his feet into a ready stance, holding the spear before him. After hearing Skar's advice, Einar knew that the king had to let the boar come at him if he was to hit the "slot" and kill the creature.

The boar snorted and grunted as it trundled towards Aethelstan, lowering its head as it gathered speed. Aethelstan dropped into a crouch. He levelled the long, heavy spear before him and shoved the butt into the stones on the riverside. As it reached the end of the spear the boar tried to avoid the gleaming point but the king lunged forwards, driving the point at the base of the creature's throat.

He missed the slot.

The beast twisted at the last moment and Aethelstan's spear shot across its left shoulder instead of down into its chest. The blade tore open a red trench in the creature's flesh. It squealed and twisted away. The spear, still buried in the boar's shoulder, was wrenched from Aethelstan's grasp.

The boar was hurt, but it was far from finished.

It staggered back a few steps, shaking its great head as if in disbelief that its escape had been thwarted, however momentarily. Then it turned again. With a furious squeal, the spear still dangling from its shoulder, it charged back at Aethelstan.

The king, with no spear to protect himself, stumbled back a step. Then his foot slipped on the slimy stones and he fell, right in the path of the great tusked creature as it barrelled towards him.

Einar leapt in front of it. As he had seen Aethelstan do, he drove the bottom end of his own boar spear into the rocks and scrambled to manoeuvre the sharp end into position to stop the boar. The creature opened its mouth and grunted, flashing its long tusks but also opening up the path to the killing spot at the base of its throat.

Einar felt like he was in a dream and everything around him was moving slower than him. He guided the spear point towards the slot just as the pig ran onto it. At the same time his own feet skidded on the moss-coated stones and he too fell onto his backside, sitting down flat in the cold water.

The spear jolted as the full weight of the running creature slammed into it. Einar expected to feel the spear slide on in to skewer the boar's heart and end its life but it did not. The blade went into the boar's flesh but must have lodged on a bone of its shoulder or ribs. The spear shaft bent in the middle then with an almighty crack split in two.

The boar stumbled sideways, the top end of the spear hanging from the wound beneath its chin. It recovered itself once more, then glared at the two men before it. It grunted and charged again. Einar, sitting in the shallow water realised that the beast was now maddened with pain and neither he nor Aethelstan had a spear to fend it off with. It was coming straight at them and he for one had no time to get out of its way.

Then something shot past Einar, close enough for him to feel the disturbance it made in the air. The great boar stopped dead. Its grunting ceased as if its throat had been cut. The feathered top of an arrow shaft protruded from what was left of the swine's right eye. The creature stiffened as if trying to stand on the tips of its trotters, then collapsed onto its side in the water. It kicked once, tried to raise its head, gave one last gasp, then lay still. A torrent of blood gushed out of its ruined eye around the arrow shaft.

For a moment, quiet descended on the riverbank. All that could be heard was the trickling of the river and the heavy breathing of the hunters.

Einar looked around and saw Affreca, her loosed bow held at eye level. Her eyes still held the cold, empty look they took on when they fixed on a target.

'What a shot!' the bishop said, his bottom jaw hanging open. 'She killed it stone dead!'

Affreca lowered her bow, now looking indifferent.

The king nodded to both Einar and Affreca.

'I owe you both my life,' he said.

To Einar the king looked sheepish and less than happy with the situation. This made Einar uncomfortable too.

'I think we both owe Affreca our lives, lord,' Einar said, hoping it might mollify Aethelstan.

'Indeed,' Aethelstan said, picking himself up from the shallow water. 'Now she has finally shot an arrow I see that the lady Affreca is quite deadly with a bow. King Hakon will have to get practising if he doesn't want to be outshot by his future wife.'

Affreca lowered her bow and turned to face the king. She raised her chin and glared at him in a defiant manner. 'I thought by now I had made it quite clear,' Affreca said. 'I will *not* marry Hakon. Not now. Not ever.'

Bishop Aethelwold drew a sharp intake of breath. An awkward silence fell. Einar could hear the trickle of the running river and the chirping of a blackbird but apart from that nothing.

Affreca and Aethelstan locked eyes with each other for a long moment.

'So you must no longer have any desire to rule Jorvik either,' Aethelstan said after a time. His voice was level but Einar could sense the anger simmering beneath his calm exterior. 'You once told me that you believe that kingdom is your birthright and your fate is to reclaim it for your clan.'

'I believe the Norns have woven that into my fate, yes,' Affreca said. 'And that Jorvik belongs to my clan, the Uí Ímair. But it will be I, alone, who sits on the high seat of Jorvik. In my own right. Not as the consort to some boy.'

'That boy – Hakon – is King of Norway!' Aethelstan said.

'And my father was King of Dublin and Jorvik!' Affreca said.

'King of Jorvik for what? A week?' Aethelstan said. 'Before I sent him running back to Ireland.'

'Before you stole the city from him by trickery, you mean,' Affreca said.

Einar stared aghast as Affreca and Aethelstan shouted at each other. He had been worried enough at Ulrich's insolence but Affreca's outright opposition was enraging the usually mild-mannered king. An angry king was not something anyone wanted to be on the wrong side of. He felt panic flood his chest.

'She can't marry Hakon because she is already married,' Einar blurted out.

All eyes turned towards Einar. Everyone looked as astonished at his words as they had been at Affreca's impressive bow shot.

'She's already married?' Aethelstan said. His face was contorted in an expression of confusion.

'What?' Ulrich said. 'She can't be. No one in my crew can marry without my permission and she hasn't asked for it.'

'Well it's true,' Affreca said. 'I am married. So let's have no more talk of Hakon.'

'Who are you married to?' Skar said.

'Me,' Einar said. He could feel his cheeks flushing a deep crimson. 'We had a handfasting ceremony.'

'When?' Aethelstan said in a demanding tone.

'On the ship on the way here,' Einar said.

'Before we left Norway,' Affreca said at exactly the same time.

There was another few moments of silence. Aethelstan glared at Affreca, then Einar, his face contorted in an expression of confusion mixed with suspicion.

'Well I knew you liked each other,' Ulrich said, his astounded expression being replaced by a sly grin, 'but I thought the lad Einar would never have the balls to do anything about it.'

'Shut up, Ulrich,' Affreca said through clenched teeth. She flexed the string of her bow.

Aethelstan realised everyone else in the hunting party was looking at him. He shook his head, as if trying to dispel his displeasure, then a forced smile spread across his lips.

'This is quite a prize Lady Affreca has brought down today,' Aethelstan said, gesturing to the dead boar. 'We shall all eat well tonight.'

The party cheered.

'And drink well too,' Skar added.

The king held out his hand to help Einar get to his feet.

'We'll talk more of this matter later,' Aethelstan said in a low voice. 'I'm not done with it.'

15

Kari yawned, slouched back in his seat, then blew out his tattooed cheeks as he glared at the monk who was singing on the dais.

'What are we doing here, Ulrich?' he asked.

It was later in the evening. The hunting party had tended to the injured, butchered their game and carried it back to the king's hunting lodge. As they were plastered with muck and sweat they had all washed themselves in vats of warmed water. This was not unusual for the Norsemen who bathed so regularly that the name of the sixth day of the week in the Norse tongue was "wash day". However from the giddy whoops and laughter of the Saxons, Einar could tell it was a rarer occasion for them.

Now they sat, hair and beards combed, at the tables in the great hall. They had eaten well of roasted boar and venison and drunk deep of the rich, sweet red wine Aethelstan's slaves had poured in generous quantities. They all sat in warm, fuzzy contentment as the entertainment for the evening began.

That was when the boredom had set in for the vikings. First there were readings from Christian legends that meant nothing to them and now there was a singing monk. He was accompanied by another one on a harp who plucked a dreary, meandering tune that was as insipid as his companion's voice. Einar could appreciate the man's skill as he chanted in the most beautiful, delicate tones but this was because he was a skald himself. He knew the others wanted tales of heroes and fighting; adventures of olden times to rouse the blood that they could chant along to, not this music that hung in the air like the golden threads woven into the tapestries on the walls around them.

Israel the Scholar had been seated beside them, much to his dismay. Like a lamb among wolves, he had not spoken a word during the meal and had avoided eye contact with all those around him. The Wolf Coats in turn had ignored him and carried on as if he was not even there. Einar could not help noticing Surt, however, who every now and then sent glances in the scholar's direction that looked at best suspicious, at worst hostile. Einar made a mental note to ask Surt what his problem was with Israel when next the opportunity arose.

'What's wrong, Kari?' Ulrich said, raising an eyebrow. 'Have you no taste for the finer things in life?'

'All this, Ulrich,' the Wolf Coat replied. He made a face as he looked around him. 'It's just not... us.'

He took another glug of wine from his drinking horn and grimaced at the sweetness of it. Then he slapped it down on the table before him. In Aethelstan's hall the horns had silver rims and the bottom had been cut flat so they could be set down on the table. Thus drinking could be paused, unlike with the normal, curved drinking horns that had to be held in the fist at all times, so encouraged the drinker to keep on drinking.

'Well these Saxons must do something right,' Ulrich said. 'They managed to beat the Great Army of Halfdan, Ivar and Ubbe. Odin alone knows how.'

'Organisation,' Einar said. 'I've seen it everywhere I've been in Britain. They build burgh forts and man them with warriors. Each burgh is within easy reach of the next. Men take turns to garrison them. The monks and priests write everything down and the king knows everything that's going on everywhere, at all times.'

'That's what they call "civilisation", lad,' Skar said.

'And the price of it is freedom,' Kari said with a scoff. 'Who would want to live like that?'

The Norsemen were seated in the visitors' seats at the far

end of the long table that ran lengthways up the hall, alongside the firepit. King Aethelstan was in his high seat at the top of the table, alongside the bishop, the Saxon lords and his most trusted warriors. Given the king's earlier ire, this more than suited Einar. The Frankish women were there too, at times rapt by the music and at others casting looks down the table at the vikings sitting at the far end. Einar thought he noticed that as the slaves poured ever more wine the glances the women sent in the Norsemen's direction were less and less fearful and more curious, even interested.

As they hurried around with the pewter wine jugs that had been polished to gleam like silver, Einar noticed with surprise the quality of the thralls' clothes. It seemed even the slaves in Wessex were well dressed.

The king stood up and began walking down the table towards the Wolf Coats.

'Here comes the king,' Einar said, taking a deep breath.

'Well, Ulrich?' Aethelstan said as he took a seat on the bench beside the úlfhéðnar leader. 'What do you think of my hunting lodge?'

As the king sat down, Einar thought how unlikely a gathering this was. Here was Aethelstan, bulwark of Christianity and civilisation against all that was heathen, sitting down with men who were the very epitome of the wild pagan freedom that threatened his order. Einar surmised this must be what Ulrich called "statecraft".

'I'm glad to see it isn't just for show, King Aethelstan,' Ulrich said, nodding towards the venison bones on the table before him. 'But I have to admit, your little hut in the forest here is grander than the halls of some jarls I've been in.'

'I keep this place to entertain important guests, so it needs to be comfortable,' Aethelstan said, a smug smile on his lips. 'But yes, hunting is also a favourite pastime of mine and the lodge is one of the few places I can relax and get to do something I really enjoy. What do you make of the entertainment?'

'I'm afraid that it's boring my company to tears, lord king,' Ulrich said. 'These warriors prefer something more stirring than the caterwauling of monks.'

'I'm sure there will be something more to their taste later,' Aethelstan said. 'It seems Lord Alan of Brittany appreciates the brothers' music as much as your men.'

Einar looked around and saw the big Frank with the twisted beard sprawled in his seat, head back, mouth open, sound asleep.

'Lord Alan does love hunting,' Aethelstan said. 'However, his tastes do not stretch far beyond that.'

'I'd say his wits don't stretch too far at all,' Ulrich said.

'Like a lot of men who possess an excess of strength and bravery,' Aethelstan said, 'Lord Alan does perhaps not put a lot of time into thinking.'

'Bravery?' Ulrich scoffed. 'He went boar hunting with just a staff. A boar is a strong, vicious, violent creature. That's not bravery. That's plain stupid.'

Aethelstan scowled. Einar cringed inwardly. He did not understand why Ulrich seemed to feel the need to provoke Aethelstan with insolent comments every time they met. Aethelstan was a very powerful man and they were right in the heart of his kingdom, in the very centre of his power. They should be nothing but polite – if not obsequious. The last time Ulrich had indulged in one of these verbal duels, in Jorvik, it had not gone well.

'Well you better get used to Lord Alan,' Aethelstan said to Ulrich, 'because I want you to go to Francia with him. I'm sending my fleet to Brittany to put him back on his throne. It's the perfect cover to get you into the country. What do you say to my proposal earlier? Will you take this task on?'

Ulrich made a pained face. 'I was coming round to the idea of delivering your message to William Longsword,' he said. 'But if we have to take him with us then I'm not so sure.'

'You won't even need to be on the same ship as Alan,' Aethelstan said. 'You just need to accompany him to Brittany.

That will be your route into the lands of the Northmen in Francia.'

'And what about this book you want us to find?' Ulrich asked.

'Ah, yes.' The king sat back. 'You've met Israel already.'

'Aye,' Ulrich said, his eyes sliding towards the scholar.

'Israel of Trieste here is a renowned scholar,' Aethelstan said. 'There's no person in the known world with the wisdom of languages Israel has. I invited him here to my court and asked him to bring with him a certain very important book. He was staying at the monastery of Landévennec in Brittany on his way here when it was attacked by vikings. The monks were taken as slaves and the treasures of the monastery stolen, including the book. Sweyn and Lord Alan have been raiding Brittany in the run-up to invasion and they managed to rescue Israel on one but not the book. I want you to find where it was taken and get it back. I want that book. I *need* it. And you can help me find it.'

'How will we know it's the right book?' Ulrich said. 'None of us know these Greek runes.'

'No,' Aethelstan said with a smile. 'But Israel does. He will go with you.'

'What?!' The little scholar spoke for the first time. He rose to his feet, clutching the front of his robe with one hand again. Einar guessed it was a habit of the little man in times of terror. 'Lord, I cannot go back there. It was horrible. I beseech you—'

'I am sorry, Israel,' Aethelstan said, holding up one hand as if to stop any more words coming from Israel's mouth reaching his ears. 'It is I who must beseech you. You are the only person who can recognise both the Greek and... other letters.'

'This just gets better and better,' Ulrich said. Then he narrowed his eyes. 'What do you mean "other letters"?'

'Israel will explain all on the voyage, I'm sure,' Aethelstan said. 'Israel, you will go with them. I command it. Don't worry about your own safety. You will be travelling with some of the most dangerous men on Middle Earth. If anything it's everyone else who should be concerned.'

The scholar sank back into his seat. His face was white as snow and he looked like he might be about to throw up.

'What's so special about this particular book?' Ulrich asked.

'A Dane would not understand,' Aethelstan said, waving a hand in Ulrich's direction.

'You think I'm too stupid?' Ulrich said. 'And I'm a Norwegian, as you know.'

'Not at all,' Aethelstan said. 'But you value other things more than the treasure that lies within books. What do you say, Ulrich? I promise you real treasure – gold and silver – if you do this for me. I'll make you rich enough to get your revenge on Eirik Haraldsson, or just live the rest of your life in ease.'

Ulrich sighed and looked up into the darkness of the rafters above.

'I don't know,' he said. 'It's not just about wealth. There are other things that are important to me, regardless of what you think.'

'Like what?' Aethelstan said.

'I follow Odin,' Ulrich said. 'It is what *he* wants that is important.'

'Name your price,' the king said. 'Never mind Odin. What is it *you* want, Ulrich?'

For a moment the little Wolf Coat leader looked taken aback, confused even, as if he had never thought about it. Then his eyes narrowed and he met Aethelstan's gaze again.

'Don't try your persuasive crafts on me, oh king,' Ulrich said. 'You forget, for many years I was oath sworn to Eirik Bloody Axe, the Serpent King himself. I know all about kings, jarls and their secret plans and how they can persuade men to carry them out. Never mind what I want. What are you up to? You want us to take an idiot like Lord Alan into north-west Francia? The country there is torn apart by war. Norsemen like us rove and raid. The Franks want control of it. The Count of Rouen wants it. The Britons – the very people your forefathers drove from this land and forced to settle there – want it back. You want to put an unthinking hothead like Alan in the middle of all that? It would be like putting a boar among a pack of fighting dogs.'

Aethelstan smiled and signalled to a slave to bring more wine.

'You are a shrewd man, Ulrich,' he said. 'But let us say I have my reasons.'

'You will stir more chaos in a land already racked with it,' Affreca said. She had been sitting silent on Skar's right-hand side throughout the meal. 'Odin himself would be pleased.'

'And why would that be?' Aethelstan said, a curious smile on his lips.

'Odin once said: *Wars I raise, princes I anger, peace I never bring*,' Affreca said.

Aethelstan frowned. 'I think you will find I strive for the opposite.'

'You may strive for it,' Affreca said. 'But the outcome is the same.'

Einar noticed that Ulrich's mouth had fallen open a little. He could almost sense his leader's mind working as if mulling through what had been said. Aethelstan noticed as well. The king leaned forwards, elbows on the table, in a manner Einar had noticed men who all of a sudden spot an advantage to themselves in a game of tafl.

'You speak of Odin, Ulrich,' Aethelstan said. 'Or Woden as we Saxons call him.'

'Once you honoured him,' Ulrich said, his lips curling, 'just like us. Until you were led astray by your false God.'

'Let me get my *scop* over here,' the king said. 'I think you'll find this very interesting.'

16

Aethelstan gestured to a slave hovering nearby and said a few words to him. The man hurried off then returned, this time accompanied by a short, thin man with a long black beard. He had lines around his eyes, a bald head and his bushy eyebrows were white in contrast to his beard. Under one arm he carried a lyre.

'Allow me to introduce Widsith,' the king said. 'He is my scop, my court poet.'

Aethelstan went on to name Ulrich and the members of his crew at the table. The poet nodded to each of them in turn.

'I've heard of you, Ulrich,' Widsith said. 'You are mentioned in a praise poem of King Eirik Haraldsson I learned from a poet in the Danelaw. Or rather a *skald* as you would call him.'

'I no longer serve Eirik,' Ulrich said.

'And I've definitely heard of you,' Widsith said, looking at Einar. 'Einar Thorfinnsson is reputed to be one of the best bards in the northern world. You were taught by old Ayvind, weren't you? "Einar the warrior skald" they call you. The poet who wields an axe. Your fame is a tribute to your deeds and your talent.'

Einar's mouth fell open a little. He had no idea his reputation as a skald had spread so far. Then, he reasoned, poets were like the monks and priests he had observed earlier: they wandered from land to land, often meeting when their warring lords came together for settlement talks, and they always spoke to each other, constantly keen to learn more stories, tales and poems that they could add to their own word hoards.

Aethelstan looked at Einar as if he had just noticed him.

'You are a never-ending source of surprises, it seems Einar Thorfinnsson,' the king said. 'I recall now that you were getting lessons from Hakon's skald in Jorvik.'

'I've heard of you as well,' Einar returned the scop's compliment. 'Your reputation as keeper of a vast treasure of lore is widely known. No one knows as many tales of the olden days as Widsith, Aethelstan's scop, it is said.'

Einar was not lying to impress the older poet. He had heard this said many times during his time in Jorvik.

'Perhaps you will entertain us tonight?' Widsith said.

Einar held up his right hand, showing the missing finger and disfigured palm.

'Unfortunately I can no longer do that,' Einar said.

Einar had learned a way to play his harp even with his injury by reversing his hands but in truth he had no desire to draw any more attention to himself than he already had that evening. Aethelstan had still not said any more about his and Affreca's supposed marriage and Einar was keen to remain as invisible as he could, lest he provoke that talk from the king to happen. While they were washing before the feast his fellow Wolf Coats had all agreed not to prompt him to perform either.

'*You two keep your heads down and don't draw attention to yourselves*,' Ulrich had said to Einar and Affreca. '*Things are dangerous enough for us while we're here in the middle of Christ's kingdom on Middle Earth without you adding to it.*'

Widsith stared in horror at Einar's injury then looked down, his face flushing scarlet. Einar understood the man's shock. For a skald or a scop not to be able to play an instrument meant he was nothing.

'I am very sorry,' Aethelstan's poet said. 'I did not know this, otherwise I wouldn't have asked.'

'That's what happens when a poet is also a warrior,' Ulrich said. 'But I know which one I value more. That's why Einar is still part of my company.'

'Widsith keeps us entertained here at court,' Aethelstan said. 'But he is also the custodian of the lore of our people, the West Saxons, or the Gewissa, as we were once called. Ulrich, you accuse we Saxons of having forgotten our roots since our forefathers came to Britain but Widsith is here to remind us of who we are and where we came from. He can tell you a tale of as many of the heroes of old – Sigurd the Dragon Slayer, Gunther and the Burgundians or Hethinn and Hogni – as any skald in a Dane lord's hall.'

'Then why, lord king,' Ulrich said, 'are we sitting here being tortured by those monks wailing instead of listening to something we can all enjoy?'

'Don't worry, Ulrich,' Aethelstan said. 'Widsith will sing for us soon. The Breton ladies appreciate the music right now. But I did not bring my poet over to chat about old songs. It is not just heroic lays a king's poet guards in his mind. He can also recite the lineage of the king and his forefathers, so everyone knows the bloodline that God has set upon the throne. Widsith, tell our guests my lineage, please. Tell us the ancestry of my family.'

The poet nodded, then looked down at the floor for a moment. When he looked up again his expression had changed. His eyes seemed to be looking at something very far away and Einar, as a fellow skald, knew Widsith was putting himself into the strange trance-like state that poets entered when delving into the vast store of stories, poems, sagas and epics they held within their minds – their word hoard – to recite a piece. It was a strange state of mind he knew well, where if the poet consciously tried to remember something he would find it impossible, whereas if he just let his mind go blank it was like the correct words flowed from him without bidding or control. Where they came from no one knew, but many said it was Odin who breathed inspiration into poets as they stood up to chant to a packed feasting hall, just as he breathed fury into the berserker charging into battle.

'So begins the lineages of the Cerdicings, the kings of the West Saxons, formerly known as the *Gewissae*,' Widsith said in a voice that captured the attention of all at the table. He spoke as if he was pronouncing his words to the entire hall. 'Aethelstan, king of kings, Emperor of all Britain, was born son of Edward, king of the Angles and the Saxons. He was son of Alfred, who fought the Danes and saved the kingdom. Alfred was son of Aethelwulf son of Egbert. Beorhtric ruled before him, who ruled after Cynewulf, who was killed by Cyneheard, brother of Sigeberht, whom Cyneheard usurped to take the throne.'

'Things get complicated around this time,' Aethelstan said. 'You know how it is with families.'

There followed a bewildering list of names that meant little to Einar or any of the other Norsemen at the table, as the poet listed the kings who had ruled the kingdom going back generation upon generation and spanning what must have been hundreds of years. He chanted the lineage in a rhythmic manner, like one reciting poetry, as name after name fell from the hoard of words in his mind to his tongue.

Einar, who had grown up not knowing who his own father was, never mind who his father's father was, was astonished and for the first time began to wonder just who he was descended from. His mother was an Irish princess, but of what kingdom? His father was a jarl, but how had he come to rule Orkney? As he listened to the waterfall of names, Einar resolved that he should seek to find out more about who he was and where his forefathers came from. But what would he find? Perhaps he would not like whatever it was.

'...Cedda was son of Cuthwine, who was son to Caelwin,' Widsith continued.

'These names don't sound very... Saxon, lord king,' Ulrich said. 'They sound a little Welsh to me.'

'It was a long time ago,' Aethelstan said, waving his hand as if to bat away Ulrich's words.

'Caelwin was son of Cynric, most famous of kings who fought the Welsh king, Arthur,' Widsith chanted. 'And was son to Cerdic, the first West Saxon to come to Britain and rule this kingdom.'

'Cerdic is the man whose image hangs above us now,' King Aethelstan said, nodding towards the tapestry depicting the mail-coated, horn-blowing warrior on a rearing white horse that hung above the dais at the far end of the hall. There was evident pride in his voice, something that Ulrich could not resist having a poke at.

'Is this supposed to impress us, lord king?' the little Wolf Coat said. 'My mother was an Ingling and my father was an Ulfling, two of the greatest clans in Norway. I can chant you my forefathers back to the first children of Ash and Elm if you want. My mother's people go all the way back to Yngvi Freyr, the king who men now worship as a god. Is there anything in your bloodline that comes close to that?'

'Listen and you will find out,' Aethelstan said. He turned to his poet. 'Please continue.'

'Cerdic himself was born in the old country beyond the sea, son of Elesa, son of Esla, son of Gewis,' Widsith said, 'whose name the line was known by until Caedwalla was the first to call himself king of the West Saxons. Gewis was son of Wig, who was born of Fraewine. Friðgar his father was son of Blond who was son of Bældæg.'

Ulrich sat up at the last name. Einar frowned. Skar narrowed his eyes.

'Bældæg, who you Danes call Balder,' Aethelstan said.

'Bældæg was son of Woden,' Widsith chanted. 'And it was Woden who was the father of them all. Woden founded the line.'

The poet smiled and clasped his hands together before him, showing that his performance was done.

'Woden is the Saxon's name for Odin,' Skar said, glancing sideways at Ulrich, who looked as if he had been struck by a thunderbolt.

'So you see, Ulrich,' Aethelstan said. 'You may claim to follow Odin, but his very blood flows in me.'

Ulrich's mouth dropped open further.

'Woden was not a god, however,' Aethelstan said. 'That is

where the devil has lied to you all who still raise idols to him. Woden was a man. A great man, a skilled warrior and a noble, a respected king. He was my forefather and the founder of my bloodline. Isn't that right, Israel? You've worked on writing down my lineage.'

For the first time in a long time the scholar looked up. 'Yes, lord. I copied it all out more than once. Woden is your ancestor.'

Then, like a man waking from a dream, he brightened up.

'Which reminds me, lord,' he said, 'there is something I discovered in my reading of the royal lineages of the kings of Britain that I've been desperate to tell you. I've found out something important about Woden's lineage too. That's what I've been trying to tell you all day!'

'Hush, Israel,' Aethelstan said. 'We can talk of this later.'

'What nonsense is this?' Ulrich said. 'Everyone knows who Odin's father was: Bor.'

'No, that was not the name,' Israel said.

'Quiet, Israel,' the king said.

'But, lord king—' the scholar began to protest.

'I *said*, be quiet,' Aethelstan said.

His tone of voice was commanding, his glare intimidating. Israel closed his mouth.

'So will you take the task I have for you, Ulrich?' the king said, looking the little Wolf Coat leader in the eyes.

Ulrich pursed his lips before speaking. 'We haven't talked about a price. I'm not one of your subjects to be ordered. My crew don't come cheap.'

Aethelstan chuckled. 'I am sure they don't. I assure you, if you are successful in this task I will reward you all handsomely. You will all be very rich men – rich enough to give up this viking life of yours.'

Ulrich grunted. 'It's what we're good at,' he said. 'Why would we give it up? So we can get old and fat and die a dishonourable death in our beds? But—' He hesitated. Then said: 'I have decided that I will accept your offer.'

Aethelstan grinned in a way that reminded Einar too much of a wolf.

'Excellent!' the king said. 'Then swear an oath that you will undertake the task.'

'You don't trust me?' Ulrich said.

'No, I don't,' Aethelstan said. 'I know you of old. I need some assurance you won't just sail off with my book and keep it for yourself, or not bother to take the message to Count William.'

'Very well,' Ulrich said with a sigh. 'No doubt we will have to go to one of your churches now?'

Aethelstan shook his head. 'Normally I would ask someone to swear on holy relics or the Bible,' he said. 'But you are a pagan, Ulrich. I know you have been baptised at least once and still follow your heathen gods. Christian relics mean nothing to you. I wish you to swear on this instead.'

The king lifted a knife from the table and drew it across his palm. The flesh parted and a gout of red blood welled up from the cut.

'Swear on my blood that you will carry out the tasks I set for you,' Aethelstan said, holding his hand out to Ulrich. 'Swear on the blood of Odin.'

Ulrich glared, wide-eyed at Aethelstan for several moments. Einar swallowed, wondering how Ulrich would react. The king had manoeuvred him into the position he wanted him like a skilful game player.

Ulrich gripped Aethelstan's hand.

'I swear to carry out the tasks as you ask,' he said. The knuckles of the hand he gripped the king's with were white and he spoke through clenched teeth.

'Thank you,' Aethelstan said.

He released Ulrich's hand and sat back, a satisfied smile on his face.

For a moment there was silence among those seated at the table, then the sound of benches scraping across the tiled floor heralded the fact that the Frankish ladies were all standing up.

'Ah. The ladies are retiring,' Aethelstan said. 'I must say goodnight to them. I think we can then start some entertainment that will be more to your liking. Widsith, please chant us something that will be more suitable for the tastes of our Danish guests here.'

The king stood up and went to talk to the women who appeared delighted at his presence. They then began to file out of the hall. At the sight of them leaving, the monk on the dais finished singing and his accompanying harpist ceased to pluck the strings. They too left the hall.

Almost straight away a more relaxed atmosphere descended on the folk who remained at the tables. Laughter and loud chatter rose as Widsith climbed onto the dais and began checking the tuning of his lyre.

The conversation among the Norsemen remained subdued, however, as they looked at each other in uneasy astonishment.

'Do you believe all this?' Skar said to Ulrich, who still had not spoken. 'It could be a lie.'

Ulrich just shook his head, whether in contradiction of what Skar had said or disbelief it was impossible to say.

'*Hwaet!*' Widsith thundered in a voice both loud and forceful enough to grab the immediate attention of everyone in the hall. Einar nodded his appreciation. It was a good technique.

The scop went on to chant a stirring saga of a Geatish hero who fought jötnar and a dragon and won much fame and gold. When it was over everyone banged their horns on the table and cheered in appreciation. Einar recognised some of the characters in the tale from the lore he knew himself. The Saxon names were a little different but not too different to be unrecognisable.

The assembly then lost all formality with folk leaving their seats to form other groups where games of dice, tafl or other competitions started.

Einar noticed the grey-bearded Saxon lord who had earlier teased them about hunting wolves, coming towards where the Wolf Coats sat. The others did too and they all stiffened.

The Saxon clamped a hand on Skar's shoulder and leaned over the table.

'Now, you lot,' he said. 'There's two things I know about Norsemen. One is that they're all bastard sons of bitches. The other is that they like a proper drink. What do you say we get some real ale horns and some good old Saxon beer and have a drinking competition?'

'I'd say that's the best idea I've heard all night,' Skar said.

Everyone cheered. The Wolf Coats' astonishment was all gone now and they threw themselves into something they were very good at: enjoying themselves when the opportunity arose.

All except Ulrich that was. He remained in a pensive mood as the first drinking horns were passed around.

'Did you notice what that Saxon – Uhtred – wore around his neck?' Einar said.

'No,' Ulrich said. 'But I imagine it was a cross. Like all the others.'

'If it was, then it had a leg broken off,' Einar said. 'It looked very like an amulet of Thor's hammer to me. Maybe not all these Saxons have forgotten their gods. Perhaps if Aethelstan really is descended from Odin—'

Ulrich's bench scraped across the floor as he stood up, interrupting Einar's talk.

'I've had enough to drink tonight,' Ulrich said in response to the questioning looks the others threw at him. 'Does Odin not warn us that the more a man drinks, the more he forgets where he is, and the looser his lips become? Forgetfulness hovers above a feast, waiting to pluck his memories away like a heron taking fish from a pool. I'm going to bed.'

With that, Ulrich left. The others returned to their drinking.

Einar found himself sharing Ulrich's contrary mood. For once in his life he did not feel like drinking himself silly. The refined music, the wine and the events of the day had left him in a pensive, almost dreamy mood that he could not quite explain. Instead of taking one of the proffered drinking horns he took his folding tafl board from inside his belt bag and laid it on the table.

'Anyone for a game?' he asked.

'I will play you.'

Aethelstan's voice made him turn around to see that the king had returned.

Einar swallowed. This would mean the dangerous conversation he had been trying to avoid all night.

'Come,' Aethelstan said, gesturing towards the top of the table, away from the others. 'We will use my board. As I said earlier: you and I have much to discuss.'

17

Einar folded his own game board and stood up. As he followed the king down the hall, Einar was aware of Affreca's eyes boring into him the whole way.

She would know that Aethelstan wanted to talk about what had been said in the forest and would be burning to be part of the discussion. It was about her and her future after all. She had been reluctant enough to accept his help in the deceit and Affreca was not the sort of person who was happy leaving those sorts of actions in the hands of others.

But what could he do? Could he say to the king that Affreca should be involved? No. How would that make him look? Aethelstan had asked him to play a game. For all he was supposed to know that was what this was about.

He knew in his heart, though, that this would be the confrontation he had been avoiding all evening. Einar took a deep breath, trying to dispel what felt like a flock of moths fluttering inside his chest. He knew Aethelstan was not pleased with his actions and the king was a very powerful man. There would be more to this game than a battle of wits, he was sure.

The lords who had surrounded Aethelstan at the head of the table had all gone to join the drinking and gaming further away and that area was now empty. Lord Alan had awoken and moved to join another group of foreign-looking warriors a little way off, probably – Einar surmised – his Breton supporters. He was now downing horns of ale and no doubt boasting about deeds they had done or would do.

The king spoke orders to a slave who hurried away. He soon

returned with a game board and bag of pieces. The board was set on the table and the king gestured that Einar should sit. Aethelstan pulled his gilded chair around from the head of the table and shoved the bench on one side out of the way so he could sit opposite Einar.

Einar looked at the board on the table before him and frowned. It was similar in style to his own but different in other ways. It was much more ornate for a start. Einar's had simple squares marked out on a piece of cloth but this was wood, each square painted either black or white. Writhing beasts were carved into the edges beyond the playing area to ornament the board. It was also a lot bigger.

'You don't like my board?' the king said, noticing the expression on Einar's face.

'No, lord king. It's magnificent,' Einar said. 'But it's just that it is not what I'm used to. The tafl I learned to play has a board with eleven squares by eleven squares. This has—' He ran a finger up one side, counting the squares beneath. 'Eighteen by eighteen.'

Aethelstan smiled. 'It's just a more interesting variation of *hnefatafl*, the game you are used to. It is called *alea evangelii*. Israel taught us the game. It's how they play tafl in the southern kingdoms of the world. It's a bigger board, yes, but don't worry. The basic premise is the same as *tafl*. I admit though that the step up to the bigger board is somewhat of a test. Let's see how you get on, shall we? I think you might enjoy it.'

The slave tipped the game pieces out of the leather bag and set them up on the board, ready for the game to begin. Einar saw that despite the size of the board the game was perhaps not that different after all. Like he was used to, there were two sets of pieces: one black and one white. The slave arranged the twelve white ones in a diamond formation in the centre of the board, all grouped around one larger piece of the same colour, the king. Just as Einar was accustomed to.

'So the aim of this game is the same as hnefatafl?' Einar said. 'The white player needs to move the king to the edge of the board to win?'

Aethelstan nodded. 'I think you should play white,' he said. 'Black is a little more complicated and this is your first game.'

When the slave began arranging the black pieces Einar saw that the differences in this game went beyond just the larger size of the board. In hnefatafl, the game began with twenty-four black pieces set out in four groups of six, one along each edge of the square board. On Aethelstan's board, there were twenty-four black pieces arranged in a square that surrounded the white pieces in the centre. However a further twenty-four black pieces were added, one set of five at every corner plus one larger piece that looked like black versions of the white king.

'As you will know,' Aethelstan said, 'the player playing black wins by capturing the king before he gets to the edge. If black surrounds the king by moving two pieces to opposite sides of him, he is captured.'

'White always starts at a disadvantage,' Einar said, blowing out his cheeks. 'But this game will be much harder: there are twice as many black pieces as I'm used to.'

'White is still at a disadvantage, true,' the king said. 'But if white manages to take one of the black kings in the corner, all the black pieces in that corner are out of the game.'

The slave then reached into a second bag and withdrew four extra game pieces. These were neither black nor white, but red. He set one of these at each of the four corners of the diamond formed by the white pieces.

'And these fellows can really even things up if used well,' Aethelstan said. 'They're special pieces that can move in any direction and jump two spaces if needs be. However, if they're captured by black, they turn to his side. If that happens, the game gets significantly more difficult for white.'

The slave then poured out two cups of red wine and withdrew from the table. Aethelstan picked up one and held it up towards Einar.

'Now,' he said. 'Let's play.'

18

White always moved first. Einar lifted his own cup, took a
sip of the sweet red liquid inside, then moved one of his
pieces. It was his usual, cautious first step.

Aethelstan moved a black piece into the path of Einar's piece.

'We've met several times now, Einar,' the king said. 'But we've
never really talked. Not properly. You've been right under my
nose yet I did not pay attention to you.'

Einar looked at his pieces, trying to think what his next move
would be. 'I always assumed I am not worth the notice of a king,
lord,' Einar said. 'I'm just a farm boy from Iceland.'

'Perhaps,' Aethelstan said. 'But that was an oversight on my
behalf. Sometimes a farm boy can become a jarl when a king is
not watching. A king should be aware of everything. He never
knows when the insignificant-looking wretch might become a
dangerous rival.'

The king, who had been gazing down at the game board,
looked up, gazing straight into Einar's eyes. Einar was frozen,
not for the first time feeling like Aethelstan's dark brown eyes
were looking right into his heart.

'I never met your father,' Aethelstan went on. 'But I knew of
his reputation. Thorfinn "the Skull Splitter" – isn't that what he
was known as?'

'Skull *Cleaver*, to be more correct, lord king,' Einar said,
aware and confused by the strange feeling of pride sparked in his
heart that a king as great as Aethelstan would know of his father,
even though he had never felt anything but hatred for Thorfinn.

'Really?' the king said. 'So whose skull did he cleave?'

'I don't know,' Einar said, moving a white piece behind the one he had moved first.

'I'm sure there is some family legend about it,' Aethelstan said. 'A man doesn't get a nickname like that without there being some story behind it.'

Einar made a half-embarrassed grunt.

'My father killed many folk, lord,' he said. 'He was not a good man. I know very little about him. I was born the son of one of his bed slaves. She ran away and I grew up in Iceland far away from him.'

'Ah,' the king said, in a manner that suggested this explained a lot to him. 'Well it may interest you to know that you and I perhaps have more in common than you might think. My father was the King of Wessex, but my mother was his consort, not his wife. They lived *in more Danico*, the bishop would call it in Latin: *according to Danish Custom*. That is, not sanctioned by the church. Because of that I've been called a bastard all my life by those who hate me.'

Aethelstan caught Einar's eye again. 'Your move,' he said.

Einar looked at his red pieces. He had yet to move any and with their special abilities he knew they could be across the board to take one of the corner kings in a flash. Once there, however, they would be far from his other pieces who could protect them from getting captured. He moved one towards the bottom-left corner.

Aethelstan straight away moved one of his own pieces towards it. Einar, fearful of losing such a useful piece, moved the red piece back to the safety of the rest of his pieces.

The conversation paused as each of them made several more moves each, culminating in Aethelstan capturing one of Einar's white pieces.

'However,' the king said, setting the piece down on his side of the board, 'so often marriages among the greatest and good are soulless, arranged affairs. Brought about for reasons of statecraft: to form an alliance or bring two warring clans together. I at least can say to those who call me a bastard that my mother and father came together out of love for each other.'

'There was no *love* between my mother and father,' Einar said. 'My mother was an Irish princess enslaved by Thorfinn's vikings and forced to lie with him. She fled from him when she found she was pregnant with me. She hated him. She said he was a monster and if he had brought me up I would have become one too. She feared him. And she was right to. When he found out where she was hiding he had her murdered.'

Einar blinked, trying to still the rage that had ignited in his heart. He swallowed hard then moved another of his red pieces forward, this time to the bottom right of the board. Aethelstan countered with a piece of his own and Einar retreated his red piece once more.

'I see,' the king said. 'But now it seems you have joined with Affreca Guthfrithsdottir *in more Danico* too. This is most inconvenient for my plans for her, and for Britain. Is this because of love?'

Einar opened his mouth to answer but at first no words came out. Confusion reigned within him and the deep brown eyes of the king were once more boring into him. Did Aethelstan suspect he was lying?

The king made his move and Einar thought hard about what he would say next while pretending he was thinking about his own next move. A memory of some of the stealth craft Ulrich had taught him surfaced in Einar's mind: *If you are lying to someone, it is best to use at least some truth. That way you are more convincing.*

'Affreca does not want to marry Hakon,' Einar said, leaning forward and moving a random white piece. 'She's married to me now so that cannot happen.'

Aethelstan gave a little chuckle. The look on his face changed to one that suggested bemusement, or at least that he was unsure whether to believe Einar or not.

'Are you telling me,' the king said, moving a piece on the

board, 'that you married Affreca to save her from something she did not want? You must really love her.'

Einar glared at the game board, doing his best to avoid the searching eyes of the king.

'Such a selfless act is commendable,' Aethelstan said. 'Though a little foolish and ultimately futile.'

Einar looked up from the game board.

'*What God has joined together, let no man put apart*, we say of a marriage,' Aethelstan said. 'But that is a Christian marriage. God is not involved in a handfasting like you two went through, so it can be ended at any time. Either of you can walk away from it at any time, for example. Or one of you might die.'

Einar's stomach lurched when he saw how serious the expression on the king's face was. They locked gazes for a long moment. Then Aethelstan sighed.

'Your being married in a handfasting does not prevent me from having the bishop of Jorvik marry Affreca to Hakon, or anyone else for that matter,' he said. 'But it does make it more difficult. Her being married before means she is not a virgin. I am not sure how Hakon would take that.'

'If he loves her he won't care about that,' Einar said.

Aethelstan barked a laugh. 'Everyone is not as unselfish as you, Einar,' he said, peering at Einar again as if still trying to see if he was joking or not. 'To do something as magnanimous as this suggests you're a very different man from your father.'

'I like to think that, lord king,' Einar said, shaking his head. 'I hate all he stood for. Though I recognise that there are parts of him in me. Like an evil Norn he gave me gifts at my birth: rage. Bloody-minded determination. The fact that I seem not to care about the men I've killed.'

'Your father was Jarl of Orkney, Einar,' Aethelstan said. 'Is that what you want? To be jarl?'

'I *will* be jarl,' Einar said through clenched teeth. Anger flared in his eyes. 'I *am* jarl! Eirik Bloody Axe stole Orkney from me but someday I will take back what is mine.'

'I have no doubt a capable young man like you could do that,' the king said. 'And when you do, what sort of jarl will you be? Your father was really just a viking. A tyrant. A leader of men needs to be much more than that. Will you be the same? Will you be a jarl or a viking?'

'Why do you care?' Einar said, frowning.

'You really don't know why?' Aethelstan said. 'Come on, Einar. You can drop this guileless pretence now.'

The scepticism in the king's voice was clear, along with something else. Was it disappointment?

'I care, Einar, for the same reason I care who the lady Affreca marries,' Aethelstan said when Einar did not reply. 'I care because it is my *duty* to care. I am King of Wessex. I am Emperor of Britain. Look at where I sit: the king of the one light of civilisation and learning surrounded by heathen wolves, chaos and darkness. In the west is Ireland and Olaf King of Dublin – Affreca's brother – desperate to reclaim Jorvik and Northumbria. To the north is Constantine, that wily old Pict who rules the land of the Scots.'

'The Scots are Christians like you,' Einar said. He frowned, trying to work out which of his own pieces he should move next. He had lost a worrying amount of them and they had not been playing long.

'Not true Christians like us. Their faith has errors,' the king said. 'And they hate me and everything I stand for more than they love God. They will align with pagans if it brings them victory. The Welsh in the north and the west are the same. To the south is Francia – a land torn apart by war where the Danes run wild and will take it like they took Ireland if something isn't done. The tyrant Eirik Bloody Axe used to be to my north-west but thankfully now I have an ally in Hakon. Hakon's position on the high seat of Norway is far from secure, however. And now Eirik is in Orkney. What are his plans? What will he do next?'

The king paused. Einar looked down at the game board where the white pieces had started outnumbered and surrounded on all sides. He also saw that his white king was almost surrounded by Aethelstan's black pieces.

'And now there is you, Einar,' Aethelstan said. 'One day you may be Jarl of Orkney. And you are married to Affreca, heir to both Dublin and Jorvik. That is a significant position to be in. You have put yourself on the playing board. So I need to know which side you are on. Will you run with the wolves or hunt with the wolfhounds? Will you be a friend or a foe? Will you fight for light and civilisation or pagan darkness?'

Einar felt both astonishment and a sudden surge of panic. How could one action, taken by himself and Affreca without much forethought, have such far-reaching consequences?

'Could you ever regard someone you call a heathen,' Einar said, 'the bastard son of a Viking warlord as you called him, as a friend?'

The king gave a little chuckle.

'Einar, consider the man I am sending you to Francia to meet, William Longsword,' he said. 'He is son of Rollo – *Göngu-Hrólf* as you would call him – the pagan Viking who took the north-west of Francia and founded his own realm there. William was born a pagan too. He was not baptised into the true faith until his father finally realised where the true power in the world lies; with the side who, when the great chronicle of the world is finally written, will be seen as the winners. Hrólf was baptised, had his son baptised and changed from Viking Jarl of Rúðu to Frankish Count of Rouen. William now faces a very similar choice. Which side will he choose? Will he complete the journey his father began or will he step backwards into the darkness of the past?'

There were a few moments of silence as Einar contemplated the king's words.

'I will let you think on that,' Aethelstan said after a time.

With a smile, he moved a second black piece alongside Einar's king. With dismay Einar saw that he had lost the game. Aethelstan had barely lost a piece. The game was over already.

Forgetting he was in the company of a king, Einar cursed.

'Do you want to know where you went wrong?' A new voice made them turn around to see Israel standing nearby. They had both been so engrossed in the game, neither had any idea how long he had been watching.

'In the game, I mean,' he said, looking at Einar.

Einar nodded.

'When you are white the way to win is to take one or more of the black kings,' Israel said. 'You can only do that by using the special red pieces.'

'But won't I lose them if I do that?' Einar said. 'They are my most useful pieces. My best warriors.'

'And you protected them instead of sending them to where the greatest need was, even if it meant losing them,' the scholar said. He looked at Aethelstan with a sad sort of expression in his eyes. 'Sometimes you have to sacrifice the best pieces to win the game. Great kings do that often. Not just in silly table games either. If you'd done that then perhaps you would have won.'

Aethelstan returned Israel's glare with a cool gaze of his own.

'And as for the greater game,' the king said, 'if you decide that you stand against me, then I hope you're as poor an opponent in that as you were in this game.'

Part Three
Francia

19

Einar had been told that the further south you travel, the warmer it gets. This is because the traveller is getting nearer to *Múspelheim*, one of the other realms beyond where men dwelled. Múspelheim was a realm of fire where the land itself burned. On the last day of the world, the *Ragnarök*, Surtr the fiery giant would lead the sons of Múspelheim north and all the worlds would be destroyed in flames.

Thankfully, as the Wolf Coats' snekkja rode the waves southwards from the kingdom of the West Saxons, it seemed they were still a considerable way off from Múspelheim. Even though this was the furthest Einar had ever travelled south, the weather was as miserable and cold as it had been in Britain.

In contrast to the voyage from Norway, the trip to Francia took a little less than two days and Roan the skipper claimed to have completed the same journey in less than one with a good following wind. Einar could understand why Aethelstan was nervous if that part of Western Francia, within such easy reach to the shore of his West Saxon kingdom, had become overrun by vikings.

They saw the coast of Francia on the evening of the second day. The Wolf Coats' snekkja sailed amid a small flotilla of four larger warships that bore the banner of Wessex on their masts. The other ships were crewed by Sweyn and his Northumbrian Danes, who as in the invasion of Scotland the year before, made up the bulk of Aethelstan's navy. Lord Alan, much to Ulrich's relief, was aboard Sweyn's ship. They were invading another land, Brittany, and had much to plan. The Wolf Coats would not be directly involved in that, so there was no need for their leaders to sail together.

The relatively small number of ships gave the Wolf Coats much to think on, however. It was a much smaller force than they had been with on Aethelstan's invasion of Scotland, and the armed warriors in Sweyn's war band did not number more than two hundred men. It was nowhere near large enough a force to subdue a whole country.

'I hope Lord Alan is popular in his homeland,' Skar had said. 'Otherwise this could be a very short trip.'

As the ships neared the coast they took down the flags of Aethelstan and the emblem of Alan of Brittany – a white fox on a black background – was run up the masts instead.

'And just like that, we became Bretons,' Kari said, looking up at the fluttering standards.

'I hope Ulrich knows what he's doing,' Sigurd said. 'We could end up fighting Norsemen like ourselves here.'

'It wouldn't be the first time,' Skar said.

'It would be the first time we did it on behalf of a Christian king,' Kari said.

Ulrich had said little during the voyage. He had kept apart from most of the others, either standing at the prow gazing at the waves or taking a turn guiding the ship with the steering oar at the stern. The few times he spoke were just to bark orders. Einar could tell the wiry little man was pensive. He spent a lot of time stroking his chin, a habit he had when he was thinking about things. Ulrich had not mentioned Einar's game with Aethelstan, nor asked what they had discussed over it, but the suspicious looks the Wolf Coat leader sometimes cast in Einar's direction made him uncomfortable and he yearned for an opportunity to talk and clear the air. Ulrich was not the sort of person you could just walk up to and start a conversation with, however. He had to invite you in. If not, it was easier to have a discussion with one of the rocks on the shore.

Affreca too had not spoken much during the journey.

After Einar's talk with Aethelstan she had demanded to know what they had discussed. Einar told her but got the impression she did not fully believe him and felt angry she had not been included. The suspicious glares she shot in his direction told him she suspected he had made some sort of private deal with the king that involved her in some way. He knew he had to speak to her and straighten things out between them, but on a ship at sea, surrounded by the others, there was little opportunity.

Adding to the air of misanthropy on the ship was the scholar, Israel, who also kept himself to himself. He was far from happy to be either on the voyage or in the company of Norsemen and did not try to hide the fact. He did his best to find places he could sit or stand that were away from the others, which was difficult enough on a ship where everyone had work to do and moved around the deck all the time. Kari and Sigurd started standing close to him on purpose just for the amusement of the discomfort it caused Israel as he hurried away, trying to find somewhere else to lurk.

Now they had gathered under the leather shelter strung from the mast for a last meal before landing.

'Remember: eat when you can, lads,' Skar said as he doled out fried chicken, boiled sausage and barley boiled with herbs. 'One of the great things about short voyages is you get fresh meat instead of salted.'

Not all of the three unfortunate chickens they now ate had met a quick end with a twist of the neck from Skar. Gandr the cat had somehow got into their wooden crate and killed one before he could be chased away. The big creature now sat, purring, crunching on the bones of the carcass Skar had thrown to him once the meat was cleaned from it.

Ulrich did not join them. He remained at the steering oar, allowing Roan a break so he could eat with the others.

Hunger was too much for Israel, however. He overcame his antipathy to the others to come and get something to eat.

'What's in the sausage?' he said, poking at the pale, boiled lump with the point of his eating knife.

'I got it from the stores of Aethelstan,' Skar said. 'As I didn't make it I don't know. But I imagine it has all the usual sausage stuff in it: fat, blood, meat trimmings, maybe some lamb suet. All wrapped up in the guts of a pig.'

With a dubious expression on his face, the scholar returned his slice of sausage to the pot.

'I'll stick with the chicken and barley I think,' he said.

'What's the matter with my sausage?' Skar said. The big man always took it personally when people made any comment about his cooking.

'Nothing, I'm sure,' Israel said, fear spreading across his face at Skar's reaction. The man's timidity at angering Norsemen made Einar wonder, yet again, what sort of treatment he had experienced at the hands of the vikings who had held him prisoner.

'Surt doesn't eat it but at least he has an excuse,' Skar said in a grumble. 'His god doesn't allow him to eat pigs.'

'That's just it, isn't it?' the dark-skinned man, who was sitting cross-legged on the deck, a trencher of chicken and barley before him, said. 'His doesn't either. Isn't that right?'

The scholar's face took on a resigned expression. He heaved a sigh.

'What do you mean?' Einar said. 'The Christians eat pigs all the time. We ate boar with Aethelstan only three nights ago.'

'He's not a Christian,' Surt said, nodding at Israel. 'Are you, my friend?'

Israel looked down at the deck. He shook his head.

'Is he one of your lot, then?' Skar said. 'I thought his skin looked a bit darker than most.'

Surt frowned at the comment but continued: 'He certainly is not a Muslim,' he said. 'But he is one of the Ahl al-Kitāb, the people of the book. Our friend here is a Jew.'

'A Jew?!' Wulfhelm the Saxon said. There was outrage in his voice.

'What's that?' Einar said.

'They are a people who follow the same God as we do,' Surt said. 'But with errors.'

'They're filthy murderers!' Wulfhelm said. 'They killed Jesus!'

'Well maybe you're not so bad after all, friend,' Kari said, grinning. He leaned forwards and clapped Israel on the back.

Wulfhelm set down his trencher and began running his hand through Israel's black, curling hair.

'What are you doing?' the scholar said, batting the Saxon's hand away.

'Jews have horns on their heads,' Wulfhelm said. 'I want to see them.'

'Jews don't have horns,' Surt said.

Wulfhelm withdrew his hand but still glared at Israel, eyes full of suspicion. 'I can't believe we have a Jew on board,' he said.

'I too am surprised,' Surt said. 'Where are you from?'

'I am from Toledo, in the Emirate of Córdoba,' Israel said. 'How did you know?'

'Your name for a start,' Surt said. 'How many Saxons are called Israel? And I was once a captain in the armies of the Emir of Córdoba, in Al-Andalus, so I met others like you there. I'm surprised we haven't met before. The emir kept a close eye on the Jewish people in his realm. How did you come to this frozen northern waste?'

'About six years ago the governors of Toledo rebelled against the emir,' Israel said. 'He attacked the city and, as often happens in times of strife, my people were made the scapegoats. We were driven out. I took my books and went north, into Aragón then on into Italia and Francia. I've been travelling from place to place ever since. My skills with languages – Hebrew, Greek and Latin – made me useful to Christian monasteries and I soon got a reputation as a scholar. It turned out it was easy enough to pass myself off as a Christian.'

'I didn't know that happened in Toledo,' Surt said. 'But then again I was enslaved by vikings many winters ago. It must have happened after that. So no one suspected?'

Israel raised both his eyebrows. 'You heard him,' he said, glancing at Wulfhelm. 'They think we have horns and a tail.'

'I take it King Aethelstan doesn't know?' Wulfhelm said.

'No,' Israel said. 'He doesn't. And if possible I would like to keep it that way.'

'What's so special about this book of yours, anyway?' Einar said.

'It's written in Greek,' Israel said. 'Which I can translate. Aethelstan needs someone who can do that.'

Surt raised his eyebrows. 'In Al-Andalus there were many who could read Greek,' he said. 'But why does Aethelstan want a Greek book?'

At that moment Ulrich joined them. 'Right,' he said. 'Time to stop filling your bellies and get your war gear on. We've arrived.'

20

Night fell and a full moon arose. A storm that had been chasing them across the sea rumbled in the distance behind them, now and then lighting the horizon with a flicker of lightning. The ships were heading straight for the coast, which made Einar a little nervous. The blackness of the sea could be hiding rocks, reefs or other hazards lurking in the blackness, waiting to rip ragged holes in the hulls of the ships and send them all to their deaths in the wet, cold depths.

Lord Alan was sure of the way, however. He was on the prow of the lead ship, one arm hooked around it, hanging out over the crashing waves below. As the oars dipped, pushing the ships ever closer to the shore, the wind carried the sounds Lord Alan made back to the ears of Einar and the others whose snekkja was following behind. It was a high-pitched yipping and yelping – like the bark of a fox.

As if in response, flames sparked on the coast ahead and torches blazed into light.

'There are people waiting for us,' Einar said.

'Let's hope they are Alan's folk,' Sigurd said.

White lines of foam outlined breaking waves just ahead and they knew they were almost ashore. Beyond it the ground was pale in the moonlight and Einar could see a long, flat beach with the dark shapes of many people crowded on it.

The prow of the lead ship, with Lord Alan clinging to it, rose into the air as the ship hit the beach and ground to a halt. Moments later the hull of the Wolf Coats' snekkja began to shudder and a hissing, grinding sound came from below as they too beached on the sand. Before long all the ships in the small fleet had landed.

The men on board, clad in war gear, began clambering over the sides and into the shallows. Ulrich told everyone on the snekkja to hang back to see what happened next.

It soon became clear that the folk on the beach were there to welcome, not repel them: rather than the clash of arms and war cries, there was laughter, many smiles and much hugging and clapping on the back. Ulrich nodded and the Wolf Coats left the snekkja to join the others.

Einar and the others splashed their way through the chill water of the shallows to the throng on the beach. When they got there, Einar saw the contrast between the two groups. Sweyn's men were full-time warriors, their bodies clad in leather jerkins and metal ringed brynjas, their heads protected by conical steel helmets, their shields slung over their backs. Swords were sheathed at their waists and they bore fighting spears. The crowd of locals looked like every sort of man from the nearest village who was of fighting age, warrior or not. There were a few mail-clad warriors but most were ordinary folk: men wearing the smocks of farmers, some in hunting clothes, and most had the appearance of people who had been dragged out of bed at short notice by the news of the arrival of the ships.

They were of all ages from mere boys of perhaps fourteen winters to bald or grey-haired old men with very few teeth left. They bore every type of weapon that could be thought of from spears and hunting bows to old rusty swords, which were probably ancestral heirlooms, handed down from father to son. Many of them just bore farm implements: adzes, axes or scythes on long poles. Few had shields. Many carried blazing torches that spread their light around the throng on the sand. They all babbled away in excited tones of what sounded to Einar like the Welsh tongue. The night air was filled with an air of excitement mixed with anticipation.

Einar observed a very different Lord Alan than the oaf they had observed in Aethelstan's kingdom. Gone was the languid boredom and aggressive posturing. Instead he roamed through the crowd, back straight, an excited gleam in his eyes as he clasped hands, spoke greetings and met the gazes of the folk who it was clear adored him. Here was a leader among his own people. Einar could see the expectation in their eyes and feel the anticipation in the crowd. These people believed Alan was here to save them; to lead them to victory against their oppressors and they loved him for it.

A monk pushed his way to the front of the crowd. He was so thin he looked as though the weight of the large silver cross that hung around his neck might pull him over as it swung back and forth on a long chain. In the flickering torchlight his emaciated face looked like a skull. He wore the long flowing dress that the Christian monks wore, though his was a uniform black, which Einar had never seen before. When the monk saw Lord Alan he cried out and ran to him, throwing his arms in the air.

'This is Brother Jean, abbot of the monastery at Landévennec,' Lord Alan said to Sweyn, switching from his native tongue. 'It was he who wrote to Aethelstan, explaining that the time is now right for me to return here.'

'The Northmen are in disarray!' the monk said, also changing tongues. 'The time is right to drive them from *Lydwiccum* and now Lord Alan is back to lead us, victory is assured.'

'Where is this Lydwiccum?' Sweyn said, frowning. 'I haven't heard this place mentioned before.'

'Lydwiccum is what the land of Brittany is called in our own tongue, Sweyn,' Lord Alan said. 'Have no concerns.'

'And King Aethelstan, the Emperor of Britain, is with us too,' Lord Alan said. 'He has sent these warriors to show his support.'

The monk cast his eye over Sweyn's men in their Saxon armour. He seemed a little less enthusiastic about them.

'You are from Landévennec?' Ulrich said. 'Do you know of a man called Israel the Scholar?'

The monk's eyes widened. 'Of course I do,' he said. 'He was taken by heathens like you when they raided our monastery.'

'Do you know what happened to the book he was carrying?' Ulrich said.

'They took it, along with all our other treasures,' Brother Jean said through gritted teeth. 'Such injustice cries to the Lord above for vengeance!'

'And we will start our vengeance tonight, Brother Jean,' Lord Alan said. 'The Norsemen are still at Dol?'

'They are, lord,' the monk said. 'They are encamped beyond the town in the meadows. They suspect nothing.'

Alan turned to the gathered crowd and began speaking in his own tongue again. After a few words they all raised their hands into the air and cheered with enthusiasm.

The Wolf Coats stood a little way off from the crowd. Einar felt they were very much outsiders. If any of the Bretons noticed them they cast hostile, puzzled glares, clearly wondering why there were Norsemen among the men from the ships Aethelstan had sent.

'What's going on?' Affreca said.

'It seems we are going to war,' Ulrich said.

21

'Ihope that the enemy is either a long way off or they're very heavy sleepers,' Ulrich said. 'Otherwise this lot have just told them we're coming.'

Sweyn detached himself from the main crowd and walked over to join Ulrich and the others.

'What's the plan, Ulrich?' Sigurd said. 'Are we really going to fight our own people?'

'You're to stay out of the fighting,' Sweyn said before Ulrich could answer. 'King Aethelstan was very clear on that. He does not want you getting killed before you complete the task he gave you.'

'So we just sit back and watch, right?' Ulrich said.

'No you need to come with us,' Sweyn said. 'My task is to both support Lord Alan and get you inland to the territory controlled by the Northmen. There is an important town near here called Dol that Lord Alan intends to retake tonight.'

'I didn't think he was the type to watch his enemy first,' Ulrich said, folding his arms. 'To observe his strengths then strike where his weaknesses are. No, not Lord Alan. Charge straight in there. I hope at least he's going to take a weapon this time and not go into battle armed only with a stick?'

'Now, Ulrich,' Sweyn said, a slight smile of mock admonishment on his lips. 'Lord Alan has so far proved to be an effective warrior. And a lucky one too.'

'I'd say any of his success has more to do with the latter,' Ulrich said. 'But continue: what is our friend with the twisted beard's grand plan?'

'He's not as stupid as you think,' Sweyn said. 'If he strikes at Dol now the enemy camped there will have no time to hear we have landed. And a quick, early victory will bring more people to Lord Alan's camp. The Bretons will go cross-country and attack that way. We will row our ships up an estuary and hit them from another side. They will be caught between us like iron between the hammer and the anvil. When we've defeated them and taken Dol, Lord Alan says there is a portage there. We can carry your ship across to another river that will take you deep into the lands of the Northmen.'

'I hope you all got some sleep earlier,' Ulrich said to his crew. 'Because it looks like it's going to be a long night.'

The Breton horde set off into the darkness up the beach while Sweyn and his men shoved their ships back into the surf until they re-floated, then they clambered aboard. The Wolf Coats did the same, then they all took to the oars. The ships moved in a line along the coast, travelling parallel to the beach, until a light showed at the edge of the shore. This was a signal from some of the locals and the ships turned, heading landward once more. Sure enough, the wide mouth of a river estuary opened before them.

At last the storm caught up with them. Rain hissed down in sheets from the dark skies above and a rumble of thunder echoed through the night. Through it all the Wolf Coats rowed in silence, following the Saxon warships up the twisting river. Einar, facing backwards on his oar bench, could see nothing of where they were headed, so just kept hauling away. After a little time he saw the dark outline of Ulrich, who stood at the stern beside Roan the skipper, make a gesture with his right arm that meant they needed to slow their rowing. Roan shoved the steering oar to the side and the snekkja glided, silent as a snake, to the riverbank. There were a few bumps and a rustling as the ship ground to a halt amid bulrushes at the edge of the water.

The Wolf Coats pulled their oars in and rose from the benches. Einar turned to see that through the rain and darkness there was a glow up ahead. It looked like fires were burning, casting light from behind a rampart.

'That looks like our target,' Ulrich said. 'Let's go.' He turned to Israel. 'You stay here on the ship. Battles seldom go the way they're planned and even if Sweyn wants us to stay out of the fighting that might not be possible. You're important in finding this precious book of Aethelstan's but you don't look like you'd be much use if there's trouble. I don't want any of us getting killed keeping you alive either. So wait here.'

The scholar looked delighted at the news. He did not argue.

Sweyn's Northumbrians were disembarking from the Saxon warships that had grounded ahead. Skar and Sigurd manhandled the gangplank out over the edge of the snekkja and the Wolf Coats left their ship.

Nearby, dark walls arose against the night sky. A flicker of lightning lit the sky and Einar realised with some surprise that the walls surrounded a large town. In the brief moment of illumination he saw roofs behind them. The glow of fires appeared to be in an enclosure beyond the walled town. The settlement itself was dark and silent.

Shoulders hunched against the rain, they made their way along the riverbank until they caught up with Sweyn, who was talking to the leaders of his war band.

'Behind those walls is Dol,' Sweyn said, speaking in a hushed voice. 'It is our task to get inside and retake the town.'

'That shouldn't be too difficult,' Ulrich said. 'It looks deserted.'

'There are Norsemen camped beside it,' Sweyn said, pointing his sword in the direction of the palisaded enclosure further up the riverbank from where the glow of fires was emanating. 'The Bretons will attack from the meadow and storm their camp. Lord Alan wants it to be seen that his people win the victory so we are to hold the town and stop any vikings fleeing inside. We are only to join the fight if the Bretons get into trouble.'

'I'd say that is highly likely,' Skar said. 'They're just a band of farmers. If the folk in the camp are hardened vikings they'll make sausage meat of them.'

'Let's give the Bretons their chance, all right?' Sweyn said. 'And you lot are to stay well back and out of the fighting, as we discussed before.'

'Fine by me,' Ulrich said. 'I'm more than happy to let someone else do all the work.'

They set off towards the town walls. Another lightning flash showed what looked like a large gate near the river and the entire settlement was surrounded by a water-filled ditch.

'If there is no one in the town,' Einar said in a loud whisper, 'why are the vikings camped outside? Wouldn't they be safer behind its walls?'

'That,' Skar said, 'is a very good question. There is something strange going on here.'

'That's what we call a *longphort* in Ireland,' Affreca said, pointing at the encampment. 'It means either they haven't been here very long, or they aren't sure if they're staying yet.'

When they reached a point perhaps fifty paces from the darkened main gate of the town, the company halted.

'You wait here,' Sweyn said to Ulrich. 'We will go inside and see if there are any vikings in the town. If the coast is clear I will send someone back to get you. The watch word you will know him by will be "fox".'

Einar and the Wolf Coats crouched into the cover of the reeds that lined the river. As they watched, Sweyn and his men hurried across the last of the open ground to close the distance to the walls. Now they were closer Einar could make out that there was a short bridge across the ditch to the entrance to the town. One large wooden gate door stood closed but the other lay fallen on the bridge. In another flicker of lightning he saw the buildings of the silent, dark town beyond. There were no signs of life. The town looked deserted.

'What do you think happened here?' Einar said.

'I don't know, lad,' Skar said. 'But if that camp is full of warriors and they find out we are here before those Bretons attack then we'll be in trouble. Sweyn's men might be good but there won't be enough of them, so best be quiet, eh?'

Einar nodded. He watched as Sweyn ran across the bridge and into the town beyond. The rest of his men rushed after him. They were impressively quiet for a band of perhaps two hundred men but it was impossible for them to maintain complete silence. Every splash of a boot in a puddle, creak of the wood of the bridge as feet crossed it and the clinking of mail as the warriors ran made Ulrich and his watching crew wince lest the noise give away the unfolding attack to the folk in the encampment nearby.

When they were about halfway across, a flicker of lightning lit up the whole company. They all froze. Then it was gone and in the following crash of thunder they continued over the bridge once more. In a short time all of Sweyn's war band had crossed the bridge and disappeared into the darkness beyond the gate.

Einar felt some relief as silence descended once more, apart from the hissing of rain and the random rumble of thunder.

'Now we wait,' Skar said.

After a short while another flash of lightning lit the scene.

Affreca stiffened. 'Someone's coming,' she said, pointing her bow in the direction of the palisaded viking camp. That could only mean that whoever was approaching could not be the messenger they were expecting Sweyn to send.

'What do we do?' Sigurd said to Ulrich.

22

There was a flash of lightning and Einar saw the visored helmets and round shields of the band of five men sneaking around the ditch towards the main gate of the town.

'They're Norsemen,' Kari said in a hoarse whisper. 'Just like us.'

'What do you mean just like us?' Ulrich said. 'They could be Danes. Or Irish. Maybe even Icelanders.'

'Like me?' Einar said.

'You know what I mean, Ulrich: our own folk,' Sigurd said. 'Who speak our tongue. Who worship our gods.'

Ulrich glared at them. The whites of his eyes were clear even in the dark.

'What are you trying to say?' he said. 'We've fought other Norsemen before. It's not been a problem for any of you until now.'

'We've never done so on behalf of a Christian king,' Sigurd said.

'We're doing it for Aethelstan's gold, not his God,' Ulrich said. 'But if you're really too scared to fight tonight I'll do something else about it for you.'

To the astonishment of the others Ulrich stood up. Leaving the cover of their hiding place in the reeds, he began walking towards the approaching vikings.

'Hallo, lads,' Ulrich said, waving his right hand. 'Everything is fine here. You can go on back to the camp.'

Seeing Ulrich in his wolfskin and visored helmet, talking to them in their own tongue, the vikings halted. Einar spotted several of their jaws had dropped open.

'Who are you?' the lead one demanded. 'Are you one of Jarl Ingvi's men? And keep your voice down.'

'We can't just leave him standing there on his own like an idiot,' Skar said to the others. 'Come on.'

He too stood up and joined Ulrich. With some reluctance, the others followed. The approaching vikings stiffened, seeing they were now outnumbered.

'What are you doing out here anyway?' the leader of the vikings said, casting a wary glance across Ulrich and the others.

'I could ask you the same thing,' Ulrich said.

The viking leader frowned. Einar slid his right hand towards the hilt of his still sheathed sword. He cursed himself for not being better prepared. If there was fighting he would not have time to attach the sword to his fighting glove properly.

'The jarl sent us,' Ulrich said. 'He thought you might need some help.'

Then the viking's eyes widened as he recognised that the fur cloaks around the shoulders of Ulrich, Skar, Sigurd, Kari, Starkad, Einar and Affreca were wolfskin.

'Úlfhéðnar?' he said, his voice dropping to an awed whisper. 'We could do with more men, yes, but I know the jarl has his problems at the moment. I did not expect him to send wolf warriors! Each one of you will be worth ten men. You're most welcome, friend.'

'So what's going on?' Ulrich said.

'A watcher on the rampart thought he saw a band of men sneaking along the riverbank,' the viking said. 'We came out to see what was going on.'

At that moment a bright white fork of lightning lit the sky. For an instant Einar saw its many branches reaching like the roots of a tree from a point high in the sky to several points on the horizon. Straight after it, came a thunderous crash that made everyone flinch.

'Thor is watching over us tonight,' the viking said, touching the hammer amulet that hung from a leather strap around his neck. 'Let him keep us safe.'

At that moment a deafening roar arose to the night air. It was the sound of many men's voices all screaming at once.

'It's an attack,' Ulrich said. 'You get back to the camp. We will deal with whoever is sneaking around in the town then join you.'

The viking nodded then flicked his head at his own men and they trotted off in the direction of the palisaded rampart. In moments they were gone back into the darkness and rain.

'And that,' Ulrich said to Sigurd, a playful smile on his lips, 'is how you win a fight without fighting. Come on.'

He led the way across what was left of the bridge into Dol. As they went over, Einar noticed that the fallen gate was not the only sign of disrepair in the town. In places planks had fallen out of the bridge and he could see the rain splashing into the black water of the ditch below.

Once through the gates they found themselves surrounded by darkened, deserted buildings. There was no glimmer of light anywhere and the only sounds were the roaring of the fighting outside.

Ulrich raised his arms in the air and began repeating the word 'fox' in a loud voice. It was a good thing he did, as moments later a semicircle of armed warriors emerged from the darkness around them. They were crouched behind shields and their spears were levelled at the Norsemen approaching through the gate. Their leader recognised Ulrich.

'It's all right, lads,' he said to his men. 'It's Aethelstan's tame vikings.'

'You were nearly caught,' Ulrich said. 'The Norsemen in the camp spotted you. They were on their way in here to look for you when I talked them out of it. Where's Sweyn?'

'He went up onto the rampart,' the warrior replied, pointing with his spear towards the left.

His eyes now well attuned to the darkness, Einar peered in that direction and saw a rickety wooden ladder that led up to a rampart that ran along behind the top of the walls surrounding the town. This provided a platform for defenders to throw spears, stones, arrows or whatever it took to discourage anyone trying to assault the town from outside. Ulrich scurried up the ladder and the others followed.

Once on the walkway the Wolf Coats began following the walls. Einar glanced to his left as he went, seeing that the whole town was quiet, dark and empty. A flash of lightning showed him a glimpse of more details: many of the buildings in the town had holes in their roofs. Some had collapsed entirely. Many of the streets below were clogged with grass and brambles. Here and there the top of the wall they were travelling along had crumbled, leaving gaps. Dol was not just deserted, it had been so for some time. With every footfall the wooden walkway beneath their feet bounced and creaked, and Einar hoped with a fervent heart that it had not been neglected so long that it would break, sending him tumbling into the dark below. The walkway was several times the height of a man above the ground and any fall from it would be very painful, if not fatal.

After a short while they came to a small group of warriors huddled at another point where the wall had crumbled. Sweyn was there, like the others looking outwards.

From this position they could look down on the viking camp outside the town. The camp lay beside the river, where two longships and a couple of smaller boats were moored. The vikings had thrown up a semicircular rampart of earth around the stretch of riverbank to protect their ships from a landward attack. They had topped the rampart with a palisade of sharpened stakes. Within the earth rampart were several makeshift huts, an enclosure with sheep and a couple of cows in it and another with horses.

In contrast to the surrounding darkness of the countryside, the camp was awash with light. Torches, braziers and a bonfire blazed. The straw that covered the roof of one of the long huts was on fire. Vikings clad in mail and helmets, their round shields held before them, were on the ramparts, fighting with the horde of men swarming up and over the palisade.

The Bretons may have been mostly simple farmers but they were well prepared. They had brought many ladders, which they threw up against the palisade and multiple points around the perimeter. Men were scaling them and hurling themselves at the defenders. From the darkness all around, cascades of flaming arrows rose into the night air then fell into the encampment, setting more fires alight wherever they landed. The noise was formidable: war cries, screams of dying or injured fighters and the clash of weapons filled the air.

'The war has begun then?' Ulrich said as they joined Sweyn and his fellows.

The fighting on the ramparts was desperate. Injured men and hacked corpses were piling up behind the palisade. Where they managed to hack their way to the ladders the vikings heaved them off the palisade, sending them and the men on them screaming away into the darkness. There were many Bretons, however, and as soon as one ladder was repelled two others took its place.

A horn blew and the vikings began to disengage, pulling away from the ramparts and running down into the enclosure below. There they regrouped to form a shield wall, lined in front of their ships.

Behind the shield wall Einar was a little surprised to see women and children, bundles of what few possessions they were able to carry clutched to their chests or slung over their backs, flocking onto the ships moored in the river. One of the ships was already untied and moving off into the river, the ranks of oars on both sides looking like the undulating wings of a dragon.

'I see now why they didn't take the town,' Ulrich said. 'There's not enough of them to defend it. There aren't even enough of them to defend that camp.'

Einar did a quick count of the men in the shield wall and reckoned there were perhaps sixty or seventy of them. Nowhere near enough to defend the whole of the perimeter of the walls that ringed Dol.

A brief lull in the fighting ensued as the Bretons flooding over the palisade hesitated, unsure why the resistance to their onslaught had ceased. The shouting of angry men dissipated into a suspicious silence as the two sides regarded each other, each waiting for the other to make a move.

Einar spotted Lord Alan. He wore a Saxon helmet that shone in the firelight. It had the tail of a fox hanging down from the back. Despite the helmet visor Einar could tell it was Lord of Brittany as his strange, twisted beard hung below his chin. His polished brynja gleamed like silver and was splattered with fresh blood, as was the sword he held in one mighty fist.

Lord Alan turned to his men and began shouting at them. He spoke in his own tongue but from the gestures he sent in the direction of the vikings it was obvious Alan was haranguing his men into an assault on the shield wall.

Behind the viking defensive line more folk ran onto the remaining longship and the smaller boats. As they did, the rain slackened off and a rumble of thunder to the south announced the storm was moving on across the sky.

'Perhaps Thor has grown bored of all this,' Kari said.

'I wouldn't be surprised. The big red-haired lout probably can't pay attention to anything too long,' Ulrich said. 'And he's about to miss the best part.'

Einar, a little shocked at Ulrich's disrespect, touched the Mjölnir amulet that hung at his throat.

With a high-pitched scream, Lord Alan raised his sword and charged down the rampart. The Bretons swept down behind him in a wave that crashed into the viking shield wall. The roaring of battle cries rose once more as men hacked, slashed and shoved at each other across the line of linden wood shields. Lord Alan was in the thick of it, slashing his great sword left and right. Several of the vikings fell and the shield wall buckled a little but they recovered fast and their line held firm. Many more Bretons, with no mail and few swords, fell to the Norsemen's blades. After a time a small wall of dead bodies began to build up before the line of shields, making it more difficult for the Bretons behind to strike at the vikings.

The Norsemen's gritty resolution and superior weapons and war gear was enough to blunt the Bretons' initial attack. Despite their numbers, the Bretons' assault faltered and they began to draw back. Even Lord Alan, finding himself alone at the shield wall, was forced to retire and join the rest of his war band.

'The Norsemen are holding them,' Starkad said, clear admiration in his tone.

'Perhaps we may need to get involved in the fighting after all,' Sweyn said with a sigh.

Ulrich shook his head. 'They can't hold out forever,' he said, pointing towards the stream of Bretons that still clambered over the palisade and into the camp, replacing their dead and injured with new fighting men. 'There's too many against them.'

While the Bretons licked their wounds and prepared for another attack, the Norsemen began to rearrange their shield wall. To the surprise of everyone around Einar, watching from the walls of Dol, men began dropping out of the formation. It began to shrink as more than half its number lowered their shields, turned and began hurrying towards the last remaining ship. The remaining vikings closed their shields to seal the gaps and reform the line.

'They're making their shield wall weaker?' Einar said. 'Why?'

Then he noticed that the men left holding the line were of stouter frames, the beards that tumbled from below their helmet visors were white or grey.

'The old men are sacrificing themselves to let the others get away,' Skar said.

Lord Alan was haranguing his men again. Einar could still not understand his words but he imagined that he was urging the Bretons to attack again before more of the vikings got away.

The remaining vikings closed their shield wall with a clap of wood on wood. They began to drum spear butts and sword pommels against the backs of their shields, creating a crashing rumble to rival the thunder in the sky above. At the same time they let out a great yell, screaming their defiance at the ranks of enemies before them who now outnumbered them perhaps ten to one.

With a roar, the Bretons charged into the vikings' shield wall. Again the crash of weapons and screams of wounded men filled the air. The shield wall rippled but held. For a time the fighting continued then one of the vikings went down, quickly followed by a second. There was no time to close the breach and the shield wall broke into two. When that happened it was just a matter of time. The remaining vikings reformed into two small circles, facing outwards at the Bretons who now surrounded them.

The fighting continued for a little while more, with the old vikings dying one by one until there was only one left. He threw down his shield, cried out the name of Odin and charged straight towards Lord Alan. He did not get far as the horde of Bretons closed around him. In moments he disappeared amid a storm of blades.

There were a few moments of quiet as the Bretons caught their breath, then they turned to rush for the viking ships. It was too late. The second longship had already set off down the river and the last of the small boats was pulling away. All the Bretons could do was vent their frustration by hurling spears and firing arrows after the retreating ships.

'When it is my time to go,' Kari said with a sigh, 'I hope I go out like that.'

Sigurd looked up at the dark skies above. 'The Valkyries must have seen that,' he said. 'Surely they chose those old men to sit in Odin's Valour Hall tonight.'

'They'll be drinking with Ragnar Loðbrók before we get to our own beds tonight,' Skar said.

'Well Lord Alan has won his first battle,' Sweyn said. There was an expression on his face that suggested he was relieved he and his men had not had to get involved in the fight. 'Now we just need to move your ship across that portage and you can be on your way.'

The rain had stopped completely as they began to make their careful way back along the crumbling walkway. They had not got far when new shouting came from the darkness. Cries of surprise and pain came from some way off. It was not coming from the viking camp. In fact it seemed to be coming from the opposite direction, along the riverbank. As Einar strained his eyes against the darkness he saw flames burst to life through trees and bulrushes.

'Our ships!' he heard one of Sweyn's warriors shouting from the deserted street below. 'The vikings are attacking our ships!'

23

Despite the peril of falling in the dark, they rushed the last of the rampart and slid down the ladder to the gates. Then they dashed out and clattered over the rickety remains of the wooden bridge over the ditch.

The rest of Sweyn's war band were already ahead of them, running headlong along the riverbank back in the direction they had crept so stealthily from earlier. From the dark ahead Einar could see flames growing higher and stronger.

Rounding a bend in the river they arrived back where they had left the ships. The two viking longships that had earlier left the viking camp were now drawn up alongside them. One of Sweyn's ships was on fire and vikings were running across the decks of the others, hacking ropes, smashing oars and throwing burning torches into the sails or anything else that might burn. There were cries of pain and Einar heard Sweyn cursing, knowing that he was regretting not leaving more men behind to guard the ships.

With a lurch in his guts Einar saw the Wolf Coats' snekkja was outlined in the flames.

'Bastards!' Ulrich said, seeing the same thing. 'Come on: to the ship.'

They charged along the riverbank and splashed through the reeds until they came to the snekkja. There seemed to be vikings swarming everywhere. One of Sweyn's ships was now well ablaze; its sail burned, dropping tendrils of flaming wool onto the deck to start more fires. How it had started and spread so fast was astounding.

The Wolf Coats pounded up the gangplank onto their snekkja. Skar was in the lead, Surt behind him and then Einar. The rest followed behind. Einar had drawn his sword and now clasped it in his fighting gloved right hand. There were five vikings in various positions on the deck of the snekkja. One was slashing at the ropes that fastened the sail to the mast. Another was emptying an earthenware jar of thick, oily liquid over the deck while a third stood ready, holding a flaming torch aloft. From the stench that met his nostrils Einar knew the liquid in the jar was whale oil. The fourth hacked at the steering oar with an axe. The last one was standing over a man lying flat on his back near the prow with his sword raised. It was hard to make out amid the smoke, flames and dark but the prone man looked very like Roan their skipper. He was holding both hands up in desperate hope of warding off the blade that was about to fall.

Skar had not seen Roan and was going for the man attacking the sail. Surt had missed the skipper too as he made for the viking chopping the steering oar. Einar knew he had to deal with it. There was no time to think or argue about whether or not they should be fighting other Norsemen now.

Einar pounded down the deck. The men preparing to set alight the oil looked up, the expressions on their faces showing the surprise they felt that anyone had made it from the town so fast. The viking with the flaming torch swiped it at Einar. Einar ducked, feeling the heat of the fire pass over his head. Then he powered back up, driving his shoulder into the viking's chest. The man staggered backwards, colliding with his companion who was tipping out the contents of the jar.

Whether the torch went into the neck of the jar or the flames just leap through the air the way they sometimes do with oil, Einar did not know, but an instant later they both were engulfed in a sheet of flame. Einar flinched as a blast of hot wind swept over him. His nose wrinkled as he smelled his own hair, eyebrows and beard singe.

The two vikings, now wrapped in flames, screamed and ran

into each other, then charged for the side of the ship. Howling and trailing fire behind them, they dived over the side and into the water. Einar skirted around the pool of burning oil now blazing on the deck and kept going for the prow.

The viking standing over Roan was distracted by the commotion behind and suspended his blow. He twisted around to see what was happening. Roan, seeing at least a momentary reprieve, swung his foot up, catching the viking in the groin. The man grunted and hunched, then staggered a few steps. Einar was only a short distance away and cocked his sword arm to strike. The viking recovered fast, however, and turned and ran for the side. In one bound he leapt up to the strakes, reaching up to grab a rope that trailed from the mast of the nearest viking longship. A moment later he had swung himself off the snekkja and over to the longship.

Neither of the vikings that Skar and Surt had gone after had put up a fight either. Both jumped ship as well. Moments later the two viking longships were pulling away and setting off down river.

Einar ran to Roan who was struggling to sit up. He crouched beside the skipper but the wizened old seaman shoved his hand away.

'Never mind me!' Roan said. 'Do something about that!'

He pointed to the pool of blazing oil that was now spreading across the deck.

'Use the sail,' Ulrich shouted.

Einar and the others rushed to the mast. The sail had been hacked and slashed by the vikings, and parts of it now hung down in long rags. Kari scuttled up the mast and released the ropes that held the sail at the top. It crashed to the deck and the others gathered it up. Einar grabbed one corner, Skar another, Sigurd the third and Surt the fourth. Then they spread it over the flames on the deck. As one they dropped it, then they all ran on top, stamping their boots all around and smothering the fire beneath.

Satisfied that the blaze was out, Einar looked around. Whatever brief fighting had occurred on the other ships was finished too. The burning ship looked beyond saving but Sweyn's men had retaken the rest of their ships. The vikings had all run back to their own longships, which were already well away in the direction of the sea.

The immediate danger over, the crew checked the ship. Roan, shoulders hunched due to sore ribs Einar assumed were due to being shoved to the deck by the viking who assaulted him, hurried back and forth, crying out with dismay at each area of damage he came across. The steering oar was half chopped through and the sail was in tatters.

'They didn't put up much of a fight,' Kari said, peering after the longships retreating down the river.

'They just wanted to cause enough damage that we couldn't chase them,' Ulrich said. He looked around as if suddenly remembering something. 'Where's the scholar?'

'They took him,' Roan said, wincing as a stab of pain shot through his ribs. 'They weren't just trying to cause damage. They were trying to grab whatever final booty they could get as well. I heard one shout that Israel would get a good price in the slave market.'

Einar recalled the horrified look on the scholar's face when he had recalled his previous time of captivity among the Norsemen. Now he was a slave again. Such a thing could be enough to break the spirit of the strongest of men. Einar hoped the little man was tougher than the meagre strength of his body.

'Everyone all right?' Sweyn shouted up from the riverbank.

'Some damage that will need to be repaired before we go any further,' Ulrich said. 'Lucky we have a spare sail.'

'It's the same with our ships,' Sweyn said. 'And we've lost one completely. We won't be going anywhere tonight.'

'More's the pity,' Ulrich said. 'They took Aethelstan's scholar, Israel, too.'

'Blood of Christ!' Sweyn said, shaking his head. 'This all takes the shine off our first victory, that's for sure. There's no way we could fix things up in time to catch them though. We may as well go back to Dol and get to work on repairs in the morning. The Bretons will have started quite a party back there by now I'm sure.'

'Well don't forget to post an adequate guard on the ships this time,' Ulrich said.

'Don't worry. I will,' Sweyn said. His tone was tetchy and Einar could tell the young Northumbrian was angry enough with himself for not leaving sufficient men behind earlier. He did not need Ulrich reminding him.

'Einar,' Ulrich said, turning to the young Wolf Coat. 'Is your harp all right?'

Einar, who was surprised to hear his leader speak his name, went to his chest that sat beneath one of the rowing benches. Pulling it open he saw with some relief that the instrument had escaped the random damage inflicted by the vikings to the snekkja. It had cost him a lot of silver, something he was running short of as the days went past since they had last done anything to warrant pay.

'It's fine,' he said, sliding the instrument back into its leather bag.

'Bring it, will you?' Ulrich said.

Einar nodded and slung the bag over his shoulder, then they all left the ship once more. As they trekked back along the riverbank to the walled town, Einar hoped Ulrich did not intend to ask him to sing at whatever party the Bretons were having to celebrate their victory. The excitement of the fighting and chase to the ship had drained away now, and he felt cold and tired. It was very late into the night and all Einar could think about was crawling into his leather sleeping bag and getting some rest.

They arrived at the conquered viking camp. Several of the huts were now ablaze, sending flames and smoke roiling into the night sky. The palisade had been broken down in several places and men were dragging the sharpened stakes down to keep the large bonfire going. The vikings' livestock had been slaughtered and now were being butchered in preparation for a feast. The corpses of men were being piled high as well. The Breton dead were being laid in respectful rows. Some women and children were already weeping over their slain menfolk. The Norsemen, in contrast, had been stripped naked and tossed in a heap like rubbish.

'Woe to the defeated,' Ulrich said. 'Take a good look, lads. That's what happens to men who lose a battle.'

'If we ever go down in battle I hope we leave as high a pile of enemy dead as these men did tonight,' Kari said.

He pointed to the relatively small pile of viking dead in contrast to the many Breton corpses.

'What would you expect when men armed with farming tools and rusty old swords go up against hardened warriors in mail, helmets and full battle gear?' Einar said.

Wounded lay all around and black-robed monks moved among them, tending to their injuries as best they could. Some had mere deep cuts to deal with and sat grinning, relieved to have survived the fight with nothing worse. Others, less lucky, could only lie on their backs, moaning and waiting for death.

Einar saw there were now lights within the town as the Bretons re-entered it. The process of reclaiming Dol for themselves and bringing the deserted town back to life once more had begun.

The Bretons themselves had tired grins on their faces and many were singing jaunty songs in their own tongue. As he passed among them, Einar could also see that a lot of them had faraway, haunted looks in their eyes and reasoned that tonight had been the first taste of bloody battle for many of these simple farmers, something they may not get over for a long time. Happy as the singing was, Einar suspected it was also to help drown out the groans of the dying.

Even Lord Alan did not seem his usual boisterous self, though his subdued mood was more to do with the sobering realisation of the capabilities of his war band than sympathy for the fallen.

He stood surrounded by the Breton lords who had come with him from Wessex at one end of the viking camp. Ulrich led his crew to the gathering and they joined it at the back of the small crowd. Lord Alan had taken off his fox-tailed helmet and his hair was plastered to his head with sweat. His brynja was splattered with dried blood.

'It's been a hard-won victory, lord,' one of the Breton nobles said, glancing at the ranks of dead.

'We needed to win something quick and the news of this night will spread through Brittany like wildfire,' Lord Alan said. 'Our people will flock to my banner. So it will have been worth it in the end, but yes, the price was very high.'

'Our warriors are just ordinary folk, Lord Alan,' another nobleman said. 'They have a few old swords and the tools they farm the land with. The Northmen have iron helmets, shields, mail shirts and swords.'

'From now on until we break their strength,' Lord Alan said, 'there will be no more head-to-head battles. We know the countryside. It is our home. We will hit them hard then disappear into the forest before they can respond. We'll make life a misery for them until they get sick of it and leave Brittany. Only if we absolutely have to will we fight them in open battle.'

His nobles nodded their agreement.

'Now let's go and see if there is a tavern in the town we can reopen, eh?' Lord Alan said.

The expressions on the faces of the men around him brightened and the crowd began to break apart.

'Allow me to congratulate you on your first victory, Lord Alan,' Ulrich said, pushing himself closer to the Breton leader.

The big man sighed and nodded but did not reply. His hostile attitude towards Ulrich and his crew was evident. This was not surprising, Einar mused, given that regardless of them being in Aethelstan's pay, to Alan they were just nine more Northmen, his enemies.

'Your victory here is complete, lord,' Ulrich said. 'Apart from the vikings who got away, there appear to be no survivors at all. Not even wounded.'

Einar wondered what the little Wolf Coat was up to. He appeared to be flattering the Breton leader, a man he had so far only shown contempt for.

'We really did kick your lot's arses tonight,' Lord Alan said, a slight smile of pride creeping across his lips. 'There were some wounded but the ones who looked like they might recover we beheaded. The rest we left to die in that hut over there. We don't want their girlish whining disturbing our celebrations.'

He gestured towards a nearby thatched building.

'Now I could really do with a drink,' Lord Alan said.

He stomped off, surrounded by his oath-sworn warriors, in the direction of the town.

When they had gone, Ulrich turned to his crew.

'I think it's best you all go back to the ship after all,' he said in a low voice. 'If you can find some wine then enjoy it, but better not hang around here. I sense that if the Bretons are drunk later on and catch sight of more Norsemen like us among them, we might be in trouble. They've lost a lot of friends and family tonight, and if the mood turns ugly I doubt even Sweyn's men will be able to save us.'

The others nodded. The hostile and suspicious glances any passing Breton threw in their direction were obvious.

'Einar and I will stay here for a little,' Ulrich said. 'There is something we must do, but we'll follow on presently. If we don't return by daylight then set sail without us.'

'Me?' Einar said. 'Why me?'

'I have a special task for you,' Ulrich said. 'Come. We will visit the house of the dying. Prepare yourself. This won't be pretty.'

24

'**Y**ou've been through several battles now, Einar,' Ulrich said as they walked towards the hut Lord Alan had earlier pointed to. 'But I don't think you've ever been in one of these places.'

'What sort of place is it?' Einar said, casting an apprehensive glance at the building.

'Lucky men die quickly in war,' Ulrich said. 'Some wounds are fatal but take a long time to kill you. If you're stabbed through the guts you're a dead man but it might not be until the next day that you finally breathe your last breath. Nothing can be done for those wounded except, if you are on the winning side, make them as comfortable as you can. Perhaps if their wife or children are there they can provide some solace. For those on the losing side, it's not so easy. They are thrown somewhere like this hut and left to suffer their final agonies alone.'

Einar searched his memories. He had indeed been in many fights since leaving Iceland, as well as several pitched battles, but he had not been around to see much of the aftermath. At Cathair Aile he had been one of the wounded but they were tended to by monks. All the wounded enemy at Frodisborg were finished off by the villagers. At Viken he had been a prisoner after the battle was over.

They stopped as they reached the door of the hut.

'There is no hope for the men inside here,' Ulrich said. 'These places are not pleasant. I think the worst thing is the smell. Or perhaps the noises.'

A large Breton stood in front of the door, blocking the

entrance with his considerable bulk. Seeing Ulrich and Einar approaching, he said something in the Breton tongue neither of them understood.

'What want you, Northmen?' the guard said in a broken, accented version of the Norse tongue, seeing the puzzled expressions on Einar and Ulrich's faces. 'Come to join your fellow vikings in dying?'

'These fucking vikings are not our friends,' Ulrich said. 'We are honourable Danes, sworn to King Aethelstan who sent ships and warriors to help Lord Alan. We worship the Jesus. Lord Alan wants us to question these men to see what he can learn about the bastard heathen vikings' plans.'

Einar shot a questioning look at Ulrich. Ulrich was a Norwegian and hated Danes almost as much as Christians. Lord Alan had asked for no such thing. As well as that, he felt surprise and dislike at this disrespectful way Ulrich spoke of the men they had watched in admiration fight and die with great courage.

'Very well,' the Breton said, stepping aside so they could go in. 'You'll have to put up with listening to their cowardly whimpering and crying. They know Hell awaits them. Don't be long though. There is a celebration starting.'

Ulrich pushed open the door and he and Einar went inside, closing the door again behind them.

A torch burned in a bracket on the wall, illuminating a gruesome scene. Eleven men lay scattered on the ground among some dirty straw. They had been stripped of their weapons, war gear and clothes, and their pale flesh was streaked with dried brown and fresh red blood. Ulrich had not been exaggerating about the smell. The air in the hut was thick with a stench that was a mixture of shit, piss and rancid meat. The men had a variety of wounds, mostly stabs or slashes that looked like purple lips in their stomachs or chests that oozed blood and some sort of green and brown sludge. Einar winced at the sight of one viking who lay on his side, his belly sliced right open, one hand clasped across the wound to stop the loops of his guts from spilling out onto the floor. The man's teeth were clenched and his whole body was slick with sweat. He must have been in incredible pain; however, the only noise he made were short gasps.

The others made soft groaning noises. Einar was amazed that none of them were screaming. There was also a strange low howling, sucking noise that Einar could not identify.

'What's that noise?' he asked.

'Chest wounds,' Ulrich said. He pointed to a man lying nearby whose chest had been pierced by a blade. The edges of the wound vibrated with every hissing, sucking breath the man laboured to take.

'What are you up to, Ulrich?' Einar said in a low voice. 'Lord Alan did not ask us to come here.'

He wanted to say more, to reproach Ulrich for his disrespectful words about the vikings, but he found himself lacking the courage to criticise his leader.

'There's something not right about this whole situation,' Ulrich said. 'And I think these men might be able to tell us more. Now I brought you for a reason. Get your harp out and make sure it is in tune. I'm going to need you to play something soon.'

He began to walk up and down the hut, picking his way around the dying men on the floor, taking a close look at each one in turn. At last he stopped and knelt down beside a grey-bearded viking who was flat on his back, the flesh of his stomach ravaged by two wide stab wounds. His face was covered in dried gore but he was placid, looking up at the thatch above.

'You fought well tonight, old man,' Ulrich said. 'We saw how you stood against the Bretons to let the young folk escape.'

The dying viking's eyes flicked to Ulrich, as if noticing him for the first time. 'We elders have had our days on Middle Earth,' he said, his voice cracked and husky. 'It was only right that they had a chance. Did they get away?'

'They did,' Ulrich said with a grunt. 'And they raided the ships that brought the attackers on their way up the river.'

The viking gave a wheezing chuckle. 'So not only did they

get away,' he said. 'But they took slaves and gold too. Good for them. Odin will be pleased.'

'Odin will be pleased with you, grey beard,' Ulrich said. 'His Valkyries cannot fail to have seen the bravery you showed tonight. Soon you will drink on the ale benches of Valhalla.'

The viking's face crumpled in a pained scowl. 'I should have died in the battle,' he said. 'In all my glory. With my war gear on and my sword in my hand. Now I'll die like a dog, naked and alone in this stinking hut. The Valkyries will have flown on to other fights. We'll be forgotten.'

'You're not alone,' Ulrich said. 'You have your brave comrades all around you. I'm sure the screeching battle women will wait to claim your spirits. And I am here too, along with my skald. Einar, play something for these dying heroes. Keep it low though. If that Breton guard hears he'll be in here in a flash.'

Einar settled down, cross-legged on the floor, his harp in his lap. He thought for a moment about what he should play, then his fingers began to move across the strings. He played in the backwards manner he had learned to since losing a finger on his right hand, where he played the melody with his left hand instead of his right. The rhythm, plucked with one finger less than was required, sounded more deliberate and forceful as he dropped notes he could not pick. The effect was a unique sound. To accompany it he chanted the *Krákumál*. It seemed especially appropriate for these old warriors breathing their last.

'Thank you,' the old viking wheezed.

'What is your name?' Ulrich said.

'Thormod,' the viking said. 'And who are you men? I don't recognise you yet you speak our tongue. Those look like the pelts of wolves around your shoulders, which says to me that you are úlfhéðnar. Is that right?'

Ulrich nodded.

'If only you had been here earlier,' Thormod said. 'You would have made a difference to the battle. Maybe we could have beaten those Bretons.'

'There were too many of them,' Ulrich said. 'An army of Wolf Coats would not have made a difference.'

'What are you doing here?' Thormod said. 'Are you prisoners?'

'No,' Ulrich said. 'We came here in search of a great treasure that belonged to Aethelstan of Wessex. We saw your final stand and thought we couldn't let such brave men die without paying our compliments.'

'Well, don't let that Breton guard catch you,' Thormod said. 'He's a right bastard. He kicked one of the lads in his wound earlier. Poor bastard then bled out.'

The old man chuckled, a sound that turned into convulsive coughing. When he managed to regain control of his breathing there were flecks of blood on his lips.

'So you came here for fame and gold, eh?' Thormod said. 'The old lure of treasure. Is that not what drove Fafnir to kill his father and Regin to betray his brother? Yes. And we've learned nothing since. We keep on running after gold like hounds after deer. I was once like you: eager for wealth and glory. It did not work out as I planned though. I had some fine times, following the whale roads as a viking. Living from battle to battle, raid to raid. I've known many women and killed many men.'

'A man your age must have seen many things,' Ulrich said. 'Done many great deeds. If there were more time, I'm sure you would have some amazing tales to tell.'

'Oh he has,' a new voice interrupted the conversation before Thormod could reply. 'He's a legend in his own saga, that one.'

Einar and Ulrich turned and saw the words had come from another viking who lay on his side beside Thormod. He was a similar age to Thormod but his hair was all white and he was completely bald on his crown. His beard was flecked with blood. Like Thormod he had been stripped naked. His torso was swollen to an impressive extent by years of beer and butter. Despite its considerable girth, however, a spear had still pierced him from front to back, going into the left of his belly button and coming out to the left of his spine. The man also had a deep slash across his left shoulder and he had rolled onto his right side to give himself some sort of respite from the injuries.

'He's dogged me for years, old Thormod,' the man said, his voice not much more than a gasp. 'Always trying to outdo me.'

'What do you mean, "trying", Harek?' Thormod said, attempting to turn his head towards the other. 'I always did. And you followed me. You're still following me now, when we wait for death.'

'We were equals,' the other, Harek, said. 'I matched every deed you did over the years.'

With a lot of effort, Thormod turned back towards Ulrich. 'He's right,' he said, his face turning to a grin. Einar noticed there was fresh blood around his teeth. 'I was always first to the fight. Harek here was first to the feast.'

They all laughed.

'You know, we both once courted the same girl?' Harek said. 'I married her though.'

'Fuck off, Harek,' Thormod said. 'I beat you in everything else.'

'You can both die with no regrets, I'm sure,' Einar said.

The old viking did not reply. He lay silent and still for a time and had it not been for his shallow breathing, Einar would have thought the man had died.

'Perhaps,' Thormod said at length. 'Perhaps not. Before I knew it, I was an old man with no land or hoard of silver to pass on to my family.'

'This is no time to get into one of your maudlin moods,' Harek said. 'There hasn't even been any wine taken tonight.'

'They may have promised us much more but the wine was good here, eh?' Thormod said, a smile shaking across his lips. 'If nothing else.'

'We were kicked out of Ireland,' Harek said, for the benefit of Ulrich and Einar. 'We moved to Britain and they ran us out of there too.'

'So you came here?' Ulrich said.

'I was told tales, my friend,' Thormod said. 'Stories of wealth and land available here in Francia. It was true, plentiful, fertile land, with warm summers far removed from the ice and snow of the north. That was my new dream: to settle down, find a nice farm where I could live out my last winters in comfort. That is not to be, it seems. The Norns have woven a different fate for me.'

'Did you come here with Göngu-Hrólf?' Ulrich said.

Again the dying viking went into a little spasm of chuckles and Einar marvelled that the man could retain his sense of humour even in such dire circumstances. All of a sudden the idea that heroes like Ragnar Loðbrók could chant a song as he lay dying in the snake pit of a Saxon king – the story behind the Krákumál Einar had just performed – or that Gunnar the Burgundian could play a harp in the same situation, right at the door of death – did not seem so far-fetched.

'We must look older than we are, eh Harek?' Thormod said when his chuckles had subsided. 'Hrólf settled here over twenty-five winters ago.'

'It's not that long ago,' Ulrich said.

'It's long enough,' Thormod said. He lay back on the straw, looking at the roof above. Einar noticed that his face had become very serious, his eyes hard. 'Long enough for men to forget the gods of their own people, forsake the tongue of their forefathers and treat their own folk as foreigners.'

There was a bitter edge to the dying man's voice. Ulrich exchanged a look with Einar that did as much to tell the younger man *now we are getting somewhere*, than if Ulrich had spoken the words.

25

'**D**o you mean Hrólf?' Ulrich said. 'His fame is great. I've never heard he betrayed his own folk.'

'Hrólf was baptised a Christian!' Thormod said. He started to sit up, then winced and lay back down again. 'He forgot the old ways. He had his son turned as well.'

The old viking turned his head to the side and spat bloody phlegm into the straw.

'The sons of all those first settlers here forgot their gods, forsook their tongue, took to fighting on horses,' Harek said.

'On horses?' Einar said. 'Would that work against a shield wall?'

'It's the way the Franks fight,' Thormod said. 'They beat Hrólf that way once so he thought it was a much better way to fight. Everything the Franks did in his eyes was much better. So it was all horseback fighting from then on. Horseback fighting, speaking in the tongue of the Franks and grovelling before the nailed Christ God. Typical Danes.'

'Then we arrived: a new generation of Norsemen,' Harek said. 'This time Norwegians. We were lured here by promises of land. We honour Thor and speak in our own tongue. We were nothing but an embarrassment to them. They helped us when it suited them but now we need them they're nowhere to be seen.'

'You don't think much of William Longsword then?' Ulrich asked.

'He's his father's son,' Thormod said. 'Hrólf became "Rollo". His head was turned by pretty Frankish women and strong red wine. But Harek is unfair: not all the Norsemen who settled here have forgotten their roots.'

'Thank Thor for Heriwolf,' Harek said. 'The Jarl of Cotentin. If he were here we'd not have lost tonight.'

'Where is he?' Ulrich said.

'He's gone to teach Jarl William a lesson,' Thormod said. 'Heriwolf knows how to keep the Bretons in their place. And he's a true Norseman. He was born here but has not forgotten the tree from which he sprung.'

'So why is he not here to help you?' Ulrich said. 'You abandoned a walled town. The only reason for that could be because you didn't have enough men to defend it.'

'Jarl Heriwolf raised an army of Northmen and rose in rebellion against William,' Thormod said. 'Half our fighting men – the youngest, fittest and best of them – went with him. Last I heard they had William at their mercy. If we'd been united, the Bretons would never have dared attack.'

'Why did you not go with Heriwolf as well?' Ulrich said.

'Our own jarl, Ingvi, needed warriors to stay behind to keep the Bretons from rising,' Thormod said. 'He's stuck in Nomsborg – Nantes as the Bretons call it – surrounded by the bastards. If we all left, the Bretons would flood back in and take back what we fought so hard to gain. There weren't enough of us though – we always knew that. But we were gambling on the Bretons' usual cowardice. Normally the sight of a Norseman's helmet is enough to send the natives running for the forests. I don't know where they got the backbone to attack us tonight.'

'Their leader has returned,' Ulrich said. 'Lord Alan. He made the difference.'

'Ah!' Thormod said. 'Another thing we can blame Jarl William for: Alan raised a rebellion here a few winters ago and William punished him with exile. It was too merciful. He should have blood-eagled the bastard. That would have shown who was in charge. So now Alan is back, eh? His return will be like throwing whale oil on an open fire.'

Harek gave a loud gasp, closing his eyes shut as a wave of pain gripped him.

'Thormod, here is one race you won't beat me in,' he said in a wheezing voice, a trickle of dark red blood gurgling from the side of his mouth. 'I will be first to the doors of Valhalla. I'll tell Odin you're coming behind me and we'll both bar the door so you don't get in.'

He started to laugh at his own joke, then coughed instead, ejecting a wad of bloody phlegm from his lips. He rolled over onto his back, his face relaxed, and a short, gurgling rattle came from his throat. His chest went still and the old viking breathed no more.

'That old bastard,' Thormod said. 'This is the first thing he's beaten me at, you mark my words. So you see, my friends, this is a land of war, divided among powerful men, each vying to rule and with no one to enforce any laws. If you are true vikings, then there is much opportunity here. You'll win much booty.'

'I hope you're right,' Ulrich said. 'If we do, where would a viking go to sell any loot or slaves he might win? Silver would be easier to sail home with.'

'Mikla Fjall is the place to go, lad,' Thormod said, through the midst of a pained cough. 'It's an island off the coast towards Rúðu. There's a market there. You can buy or sell anything you want at it.'

'I thank you, my friend,' Ulrich said. He started to rise. 'You can die with no regrets.'

'My only regret is that I did not die with my sword in my hand in the battle,' Thormod said. 'Instead I must endure this lingering naked, ignoble end.'

Ulrich chewed his bottom lip in the way Einar knew he did when thinking about something. Then he crouched down again and spoke in a quiet voice that Einar could not make out. Thormod nodded then Ulrich seemed to shove something – Einar could not see what – into the straw beneath the dying viking.

'Let's entertain these brave men a little more,' Ulrich said, rising once more and turning to face Einar. 'Play something else, but go to the far end of the hut to do it this time. And play loud this time. Let the Valkyries hear you and be summoned back to collect the spirits of these dying heroes.'

'But the Breton guard outside—' Einar began to say.

Ulrich held up a hand to stop Einar talking.

'Never mind him,' he said. 'Just do as I say.'

Einar shrugged and walked to the back wall of the hut. He readied his harp then began to play once more. This time he sang the death song of Gunnar. As the words flowed from his lips he quite forgot himself, and before he knew it he was chanting the rousing words at the top of his voice.

The door of the hut burst open and the large Breton rushed in, eyes glaring around the interior.

'What's going on?' he shouted. 'There is to be no comforting of these bastards! You lied to me. Stop that right now.'

He swiped a heavy stick through the air in a threatening gesture.

'Play on,' Ulrich, who now stood beside Einar, said to him.

Shouting a word in his own tongue that Einar guessed was a curse, the Breton raised his cudgel and stomped forwards, coming down the hut at Einar. Einar found it very hard to concentrate on playing as the big man got nearer and hoped fervently that Ulrich had some sort of plan.

As the Breton passed Thormod, the dying man, sat up. His right arm struck out. The Breton stopped dead in his tracks, eyes wide as full moons, mouth open in astonishment. Thormod dropped back to the ground like a sack of grain as the Breton first dropped to his knees then toppled onto his left side. His mouth began moving but only a little squeaking sound came out. He reached around himself with his right arm. Einar saw the hilt of Ulrich's seax sticking out of the man's back. Thormod had driven it right through the man's spine about halfway down.

Ulrich went over and looked down at the Breton. 'You said these men were whimpering and crying like cowards,' he said.

'But all I can see here is a man who hasn't even the backbone to stand up.'

Thormod gave a heavy sigh and went limp.

'Good work, old man,' Ulrich said, even though Thormod was now dead.

The Breton gasped a couple more times, then he too died.

'I think we learned as much as we can tonight,' Ulrich said. 'Let's get out of here before someone misses our large Breton friend.'

26

The morning light revealed a surprise in the meadow beyond the conquered viking camp. A huge standing stone towered in the field. It was slender and tapered from a wide base to a rounded tip perhaps five or six times the height of a man from the ground. Einar had seen stones like it in Orkney and Norway, and it was the common belief that Odin had placed them in the ground using magic, at some ancient time when the world was still young.

When they awoke, Einar and the others – unencumbered by the hangovers that kept the Bretons and their Aenglish allies in their beds – had wandered out to look at the stone while Roan made some final repairs to the ship that he insisted only he could carry out.

Einar looked up at the enormous stone and wondered if Odin really had put it there. It was not natural – that was for sure. Someone had cut it from the ground and carved it into its shape. The idea that there could have been one single slender column of rock standing in this field alone, when there were no other stones like it anywhere around, was just impossible, which meant someone had brought it to this place. The weight of it was unthinkable. Surely only a god or powerful wizard could have done that. Then he thought of the minster in Wintanceaster with its sky-scraping bell tower, and wondered if perhaps men could have put the stone there after all.

As with the standing stones in Orkney, the splatters of dried blood on this one showed that while they had been there, the Norsemen had used it as a place of *blōt*: sacrifice to the gods, the Norns, and the *dísir* or the land spirits. There had been a recent sacrifice and it had been a large one, as there had clearly been so much blood the night before's rain had not yet washed it all away.

The vikings had also erected three god posts nearby: wooden poles carved into the likeness of Thor, Odin and Frey. The Bretons had already uprooted them, perhaps before they had even attacked the Norse camp or straight after, and they now lay, broken and disfigured, among the grass of the meadow.

'They honoured the gods,' Kari said, looking down at the toppled idols and shaking his head. 'Yet Odin still did not grant them victory last night. Instead he let Christians defeat them. What message is there in that?'

'They were brave men,' Ulrich said. 'Tough old warriors who had come to the end of their days anyway. Odin granted them one last favour: a glorious death. He needs such men for his *Einherjar* and he gathered them to him. They will feast in Odin's Valour Hall until the final day of the world, the Ragnarök, when they will form Odin's army. They will march out against the forces of chaos: the terrible Surt, the monstrous children of Loki and Hel's army of the dead.'

'And they will lose,' Einar said. There was bitterness in his voice. 'Just like those men last night. Odin is gathering this great army – an army made up of all the greatest heroes who ever lived – and they still won't win! The Einherjar will be defeated, the gods themselves will die. The world will be destroyed in fire by the sword of Surtr the Jötunn and sink into the ocean. All the killing and the dying. The heroism and cowardice? What's it all for? What is the point?'

The others all stared, open-mouthed at Einar. He felt his cheeks flush. He saw Ulrich's upper lip curl into a sneer. The disdain in the little Wolf Coat's eyes was strong enough to make Einar swallow.

'Do not speak to me of *for*? Or *why*?' Ulrich said. 'Those are the words of cowards and shirkers. Are you now so presumptuous that you want to know the plans of the Norns themselves? Who knows what pattern those great magic women are weaving on the loom of Fate, a web so strong that not even the gods can escape it. It was enough that when they had to make their stand, those men last night did and did not shirk the challenge. Nor will the Einherjar on the final day. Who would want to live on knowing they had?' He turned on his heel and strode off.

'Enough standing around looking at the scenery,' Ulrich said over his shoulder. 'Roan should be done by now. Back to the ship.'

Einar cursed himself for letting the words that were churning in his own heart come tumbling out of his mouth yet again. This feeling was deepened as the other Wolf Coats followed their leader, one by one casting disappointed or angry looks in his direction. Last of them was Affreca, who shook her head.

'Like I always say, Einar,' she said, 'you think too much.'

Einar trudged after them, keeping a little distance behind as he neither wanted nor believed he would be welcome to join any further conversation.

When they got back to the snekkja they found a bleary-eyed Sweyn waiting for them. Lord Alan stood beside him, looking like he too was out of his bed a lot earlier than he would have hoped. At first Einar was concerned that someone had discovered the dead Breton guard in the hut full of dying vikings and they were there to question the Wolf Coats about it but, as it turned out, there was a different reason for them being there.

'I heard you were preparing to leave,' Sweyn said. 'My men were still sleeping off last night's wine when word came. They won't be happy to move the ship through the portage to the other river for you.'

'There's a change of plan,' Ulrich said. 'We need to go to Mikla Fjall instead, which might mean sailing back to sea. Have you heard of this place?'

Sweyn at first looked puzzled, then said:

'Fjall – Fell. It's the word for a mountain? Mikla is great, so a large mountain?'

'You haven't forgotten all of the tongue of your forefathers,' Ulrich said. 'Yes.'

'I think you might mean *Michael's* Fjall,' Sweyn said. 'Michael's Mountain. Or rather Saint Michael's Mountain.'

Ulrich rolled his eyes. 'It's named after a Christian saint?' he asked. 'They're like small gods or Christian heroes aren't they?'

'You might like Saint Michael,' Sweyn said. 'He slew a dragon, just like Sigurd.'

'We call it *Menez Mikael* in our tongue,' Lord Alan said. 'It's a rocky outcrop in a bay at the mouth of the river that leads to Rouen. When the tide comes in it becomes an island. There was a monastery on it, and it used to belong to Brittany, then the cowardly king of the Franks gave it to the damned Northmen. The impudence.' Lord Alan turned his head and spat.

'It was not his to give away,' he continued. 'He was scared of them. Of course the Nordmanni threw the monks out and turned it into a market. Now human misery – viking loot and slaves – is bought and sold where once monks sang praises to God.'

'Vikings will be vikings,' Ulrich said. 'But that's why we need to go there. I think we can find where Aethelstan's scholar and maybe even his book have ended up.'

'Well you can stick to the original plan then,' Lord Alan said. 'The same river will get you where you want to go. How did you hear about Saint Michael's Mountain?'

'All Northmen have heard of it. It's famous across the whale roads,' Ulrich said.

'Yet you don't know where it is?' Lord Alan said, his eyes narrowing.

'I've heard of Rome too,' Ulrich said. 'But I don't know where that is either.'

Lord Alan nodded but the suspicious expression did not leave his face. Ulrich was wearing his insolent smile, and Einar hoped with all his heart that if someone was going to find that big dead Breton, it was not going to be now.

'You don't trust any Norsemen, do you, Lord Alan?' Ulrich asked.

'No, I don't,' the Breton lord said, glaring down at the

diminutive Wolf Coat leader. 'The Nordmanni are treacherous, heathen curs, every one of them. And they are trying to steal my homeland, just as they stole the land ruled by the Count of Rouen. They should all go back to their own lands and if they don't they should be put to the sword.'

'The success of our venture here, Lord Alan,' Sweyn said, 'could well depend on the success of the task King Aethelstan has set these particular Northmen.'

'You do realise, don't you,' Ulrich said, 'that the grandfather of Sweyn here, who you rely on for ships and warriors, was a Norseman who settled in Britain, just as the fathers of those Nordmanni you talk about did here?'

Lord Alan's mouth gaped open and he swung his glare onto Sweyn. Sweyn in turn grunted and pursed his lips.

'Is making trouble how you have fun, Ulrich?' he said. 'You just can't help yourself can you?'

'*Wars I raise, princes I anger, peace I never bring,*' Ulrich quoted. 'As Odin said. Now can we get moving? Where do you want the ship?'

They all boarded the snekkja and the Wolf Coats, Surt and Wulfhelm settled down on their oar benches. They shoved off and started rowing upstream. Lord Alan directed them to a point further along the river with a sloping bank where a large company of Sweyn's men waited. As Roan grounded the ship amid the reeds, Einar could see the men waiting were as hungover as Sweyn was.

Sweyn's men attached ropes to the Wolf Coats' snekkja. They hauled it out of the river and began pushing and heaving it up a short hillside. The shallow draught of the keelless vessel meant it slid over the grass almost as easily as it cut through the water.

'When you have the right kind of ship you can go anywhere,' Skar said as they walked along beside it. 'Even if there is no water to ride on.'

'The right ship,' Ulrich said, 'and enough men to make pushing it easy work.'

It was not as easy work as Ulrich made it out to be, however. As the late winter sun peered down from above and Sweyn's men hauled and strained to move the boat across the land, the morning air was filled with the smell of sour wine and ale they sweated from their skin.

'We should travel everywhere with an army, Ulrich,' Skar said. 'I'd hate to be trying to do this on our own.'

Once over the summit of the hill, the going did not get easier as the men had to expend just as much effort to stop the ship sliding out of control down the other side. Einar saw that another river lay ahead, this one narrower than the one they had left behind. Sweyn's men heaved the ship into the new river with a collective grunt of relief. As it rocked back and forth, the Wolf Coats clambered aboard and took their places at the oars again.

'Ulrich, one thing before you go,' Sweyn said from the riverbank. 'Just in case you think about disappearing into the countryside instead of following Aethelstan's task. Just so you know, Aethelstan sent a chest of silver with me here to Francia. It's only a portion of the final amount but, even at that, there is enough to make you rich. That is waiting for you here when you come back with the message delivered and the book.'

'I look forward to it,' Ulrich said. 'When will I get the rest?'

'When you deliver the book to Aethelstan in Wintanceaster,' Sweyn said.

'Follow this river until it joins a much larger one,' Lord Alan said. 'Upstream that one takes you to Rouen or Rúðu as you Nordmanni call it. Downstream goes to Saint Michael's Mount.'

'Lord Alan, farewell,' Ulrich said as the ship began to drift with the river flow. 'It has been... an experience to meet you. Sweyn: good luck. May Odin bless you as one of his own folk. You may have forgotten about him, but he will never forget about you.'

Ulrich winked at him then went to join Roan at the stern.

'Good luck, Ulrich,' Sweyn said as the ship slid away. 'Do not betray King Aethelstan's trust. He never forgets either.'

27

Unlike the night before, as it was daylight they were able to appreciate the countryside they passed through. It was winter but the fields were green and the riverbanks covered by trees and bushes. The weather was pleasant and far from cold. In the summer it would be lush and rich, the fields fertile and the sun warm. Einar could understand the attraction in this countryside for folk like him from the northern realms, where the winters were bitter and clawing a crop from the iron-hard earth was nothing but hard work. Life here must be good.

As Lord Alan had told them, after a while the river merged with a much larger one. Roan steered the longship out into the new confluence, trying to keep them as far away from either shore as he could manage. The wind caught the sail and it snapped taut. Combined with the downstream flow of the river, it meant the crew could pull the oars in and take it easy.

Most lounged around the deck, glad of the chance to catch up on some more sleep. Einar still sensed an uncomfortable air of disapproval from the others over the words he had spoken earlier, and he decided to find somewhere away from the others. Seeing the prow unoccupied, he got up and started walking towards it.

'Einar, start watching those riverbanks while you're up there doing nothing,' Ulrich said from behind him.

Einar turned, frowning, as he looked at the pleasant countryside they were sliding past.

'What for?' Einar said, making a face.

'Anything threatening,' Ulrich said. 'This is a hostile land and the last thing we need is some locals, emboldened by the news of Lord Alan's return, deciding to take a few arrow shots when they see a longship sailing past. You may be Aethelstan's little pet now, Einar, but you're still one of my crew. And while you are, you'll work like everyone else.'

Einar sighed again and wandered to the dragon-carved prow.

So there it was. He had suspected Ulrich was not happy with his personal talk with Aethelstan but as the Wolf Coat leader had not yet mentioned it, he could not be sure. Ulrich had been very standoffish with everyone since leaving Wessex, so it was hard to tell if he was annoyed with Einar in particular, Aethelstan's claims about Odin or if he was just pissed off with everyone and the situation they had found themselves in, mere lordless sellswords sailing the whale road for gold. Now Ulrich's words made at least one of those options clear.

It seemed everyone was angry with Einar right now and with them all being on the one ship this situation could become intolerable.

Perhaps it would not be such a bad thing to leave this life, Einar mused. To find himself a nice piece of land around here like those dying vikings the night before had hoped for. Marry a local girl and live the rest of his life enjoying the sunshine and the sweet red wine.

Looking at the countryside he noticed that here and there columns of smoke drifted up from the trees. Some were wisps, the output of the fires of ordinary people. Others were thick and meant something more than a cooking fire was ablaze.

After a while, Skar joined Einar at the prow.

'See anything?' the big man asked.

'Not much,' Einar said. 'But what do you think those are?'

He pointed at one of the dense columns of rising smoke.

'This is a land of war, lad,' Skar said. 'There is chaos; folk are fighting all over it. There is no law, no order. In such places certain people take advantage of that and take what they want. Bringing an end to that is now Lord Alan's problem.'

They both scanned the banks again for any sign of trouble. Up ahead the estuary was opening into the sea.

'What were you doing going up here on your own anyway?' Skar said. 'You don't want to get the reputation of being an *eingangr maðr*, do you?'

Einar swallowed. An eingangr maðr was a man who went through life alone. They were men who got the reputation of being inherently unlucky: they may be great warriors, good company and good-looking, but bad things just kept on happening to them. Whatever they tried tended to go wrong, for no perceivable fault of their own but just through bad luck. For that reason it was better not to associate with someone like that in case the bad luck rubbed off on you. Were the others starting to look at him that way?

'I just wanted to get away from everyone for a bit,' Einar said. 'I seem to have annoyed all of them without even trying. Ulrich especially.'

Skar glowered at him and Einar took the hint. The big man did not like anyone saying anything bad about his leader.

'How do we know they took Israel to this place Michael's Mountain anyway?' Einar said, trying to change the subject.

'We don't, lad,' Skar said. 'But it's the nearest market and we need to find him fast. If they take him to Dublin or Hedeby he could be sold on anywhere in the world and then we'll never find him. If I was trying to get rid of loot quickly I'd sell it on as fast as I could at the nearest market and turn my stolen goods to silver. Ulrich's gambling that those vikings on the run from Dol would do the same.'

'Ulrich knows it all, doesn't he?' Einar said, risking one more bitter barb.

'Don't take Ulrich's words too personally, lad,' Skar said. 'He's been in a funny mood recently.'

Einar spat over the side. 'Why is he so hard on me, Skar?' Einar said. 'I didn't ask Aethelstan to have a private talk with me and if it annoys him that much all he needs to do is ask what it was about. And it's not just that, is it? I can't believe he's still angry at what I said at the standing stones this morning.'

'Ulrich is annoyed precisely because it was *you* who said it, Einar,' Skar said.

'Why does he hate me so much?' Einar said. 'I can't do anything right in his eyes.'

Skar looked at Einar for a long moment, turning down the corners of his mouth as he did so. 'Ulrich doesn't hate you, lad. Far from it. He thinks you're special. He looks at the gifts Odin has given you – poetry, divine rage, luck – and sees you as someone blessed by the gods. He doesn't see you as an eingangr maðr. We've talked about it several times, me and him. Would it surprise you to know that when Ulrich finally decides to give this all up – or more likely, he is killed – he sees you as the man to lead his úlfhéðnar?'

'Me?!' Einar said, incredulous.

'You, Einar,' Skar said.

'But you are his prowman,' Einar said. 'His right-hand man. It's you who leads us into battle.'

Skar made a face. 'I can do that, Einar,' he said. 'But I'm like a big wooden club. Good for smashing things up but not much else. To lead a company of úlfhéðnar it takes wisdom, cunning and to be able to think ahead. Ulrich sees that in you. So he has a much higher expectation of you than the others. When you say something stupid like you did today, it makes him question himself and his own judgement, and I feel that the words Aethelstan said about Woden have already given Ulrich much trouble. He may not *like* you, Einar. But he sees you as the next Ulrich.'

'Why are you telling me this?' Einar questioned.

'Because I don't want you making any stupid mistakes just because folk are unhappy with you,' Skar said. 'It's my job to lead us into battle, yes. But it's also my job to make sure the company stays together. Now come back to the others and we will straighten out any ill feeling. There's nothing worse on a ship than discord. It can be more dangerous on a voyage than fire. Someone else will take their turn on lookout.'

With that, the big man turned and walked back down the deck.

Einar hesitated for a moment then followed him, shaking his head in complete astonishment.

28

The mountain of Michael turned out to be more of a hill, but when Einar first saw it, he was still impressed.

They spotted it from quite a distance away. They had sailed down the river for a time as the sun rose high into the sky. Eventually the banks had got further and further away and the river broadened into a very wide estuary, surrounded on both sides by flat marshland that seemed to go as far as the eye could see. Rising on the horizon was a conical-shaped hill that stood in stark contrast to its level surroundings.

'I'm pretty sure that's it,' Roan said, pointing at the island. 'I sailed along this coast years ago when I voyaged with a trader from Frisia. I was just a deckhand then. The skipper pointed out the Mount of Michael and that looks very like it.'

'So you've been here before?' Ulrich said. 'You could have said earlier.'

'There's very few places I haven't been at one time or another,' the wizened old skipper said. 'It would be easier to give you a list of them than where I have been. We never landed there though. There were monks there when we came before.'

As they sailed closer, they could make out that the mount was very steep, indeed like a mountain. Smoke drifted from a collection of buildings on the summit. The steep slopes were covered by trees.

'Those buildings look like they're made of stone,' Einar said, using his hand to shade his eyes from the winter sun. 'I wonder if the Romans were here too?'

'Why are you always going on about the Romans, lad?' Ulrich said, his face screwed up in annoyance.

'Their deeds impress me,' Einar said. 'I saw the stone buildings they made in Jorvik. They towered up to three storeys tall. And the roads in Britain were laid by them too. Miles and miles of straight, flat pathways you can ride horses and wagons along, not the mud-clogged dirt tracks we have back in Iceland. Their wizards must have been very powerful to have created all that so long ago and for it still to be standing.'

'It was not witchcraft that allowed the Romans to build all that,' Surt said. 'It was wisdom. They knew a great deal that has since been forgotten. Now it only exists in books, hidden in places like the Great Library of the Emir of Córdoba, or even Aethelstan's library back in Wintanceaster.'

'Well, all you need to know about the Romans,' Ulrich said, 'is that Hermann of the Cherusci ambushed them in the Teutoburg Forest, slaughtered their whole army and sent them running south of the Rhine. After that they were too scared to go north of the Rhine. They never conquered any of our folk. What is there to admire in that?'

'Ulrich, we have a bit of a problem,' Roan said from the stern. 'We're running out of water.'

As if to emphasise the skipper's words, a low grinding noise came from the bottom of the ship.

They all looked around and saw that the estuary opened into a very wide bay filled with an enormous beach. Sand flats stretched as far as the eye could see and the sea itself was so far out, it could not be seen. The sand was wet, though, which meant it had been here recently, and would no doubt return. At high tide the river they were travelling on would gush straight into the sea but now it dissipated itself into countless little rivulets running across the sands. The Mount of Saint Michael sat out in the bay, like an island in a sea of sand. After a few more moments the water around the ship became too shallow to float it, and the snekkja ground completely to a halt.

'What now?' Kari said.

'It looks like we aren't the only ones here,' Skar said.

Several other longships were stuck in the sand. They sat, leaning to one side or the other at the point they had run aground. Their sails were furled and oars taken in. There was no one on any of the ships but a group of men were gathered around a small fire on a dry patch of sand round about the middle of the ships. They were wrapped in heavy woollen cloaks and had spears, shields and helmets. The style of their war gear – round shields and visored helmets – showed they were Norsemen. The fact that they had war gear suggested to Einar they were guarding the ships.

'Let's ask them,' Ulrich said.

They scrambled down off the ship and went to join the men around the fire. As they walked past one of the ships, Skar made a surreptitious gesture at the fresh scorch marks and cuts on its wood.

'It looks like some of our friends from last night might be here,' he said to the others from the corner of his mouth. 'Be careful what you say.'

'Hallo, lads,' Ulrich said as they arrived at the group near the fire. The men there swept appraising looks at the approaching Wolf Coats and saw men like themselves, so did not stiffen into readiness for a fight.

'Good day,' one of them, a stout man with a shock of ginger hair braided around his shoulders, said. 'Come to sell your loot at the market?'

The men spoke in the Norse tongue but with a slightly strange accent. Einar surmised that this must be a local accent, the tongue changed a little by its time here in Francia, just as he had heard it changed by those descended from Norsemen in Ireland, and again with Sweyn's accent for the north-east of Britain.

'We're buying today,' Ulrich said. 'I'm on the lookout for slaves. If I can get them at a decent price, I'll ship them over to Dublin and make a healthy profit in the market there.'

'Nah,' another of the ship guards said, a blond-haired man with a long beard. His tongue sounded more like Ulrich and Skar's. 'It's a fool's game that. I tried it once. A few of them died on the voyage, then those bastards in Dublin swindled me. I never even made back the silver I put into it, never mind make profit!'

'Still, I think I'll take my chances,' Ulrich said.

'Well, you'll need to see old Bersi Tree-foot out there on the island,' the ginger man said. 'He's the main slave trader there.'

'Watch yourselves though,' his blond companion said. 'He's an evil bastard: used to be a notorious viking. He'll rip you off as soon as do a fair deal.'

'Why do they call him "Tree-foot"?' Einar said.

'That will be obvious when you meet him,' the blond man said with a chuckle.

'I need to get there first,' Ulrich said. 'We didn't expect this.'

He swept an arm around the beach and the grounded longships.

'You've not been to Michael's Fjall before?' the ginger man asked.

'No, we came down from Norway before Jól,' Ulrich said. 'We heard this part of Francia has rich pickings for enterprising men.'

'I heard that legend too,' the blond-haired man said with a grunt. 'It's not true. Any of the good land has already been taken by the fucking Danes who came here thirty winters ago. Now they don't want to share it. I'm done with the place. Last night was the final straw. When the skipper comes back with the silver he gets from selling our loot, I'm taking my cut and going home.'

'What happened last night?' Ulrich said, trying to sound as innocent as possible.

'A bunch of Breton bastards attacked our camp,' the viking said. 'They found some backbone from somewhere and overwhelmed us. There were thousands of them. We were lucky to get away alive.'

'And where is home?' Ulrich asked.

'It's back to Norway for me,' the blond-haired viking said.

'You're lucky,' his ginger companion said. '*Where is home*, you say? My father was born in Ireland. The Gaels threw us out, and my family settled in Britain. Then the Saxons threw us out and we came here to settle. I grew up here. This *is* my home.'

'Your skipper is at the mountain?' Ulrich said.

'Yes, all our crews are. The lucky bastards,' the blond man said. 'We got stuck with guarding the ships while they're over there having the time of their lives.'

'At a market?' Skar said, making a puzzled face.

'Oh it's not just any market, friend,' the ginger man said. 'You can buy anything your heart desires there. And there's a tavern with ale, wine, the finest of food. There are girls too. If you have the silver to pay for them.'

'So how do we get there?' Ulrich said. 'Do we walk?'

The ginger viking nodded.

'It's the only way they'll let you in,' he said. 'When the tide comes in the mountain becomes an island. There's a small harbour on it, but they won't let you land a boat there, unless it's just to unload goods to sell; but they want you away again as soon as possible.'

'And who are *they*?' Skar said.

'The jarl's men,' the blond-haired viking said. 'They run the place for him. They keep it tighter than a fortress. And for good reason: there's more wealth stashed on that island than in the hoard of the Níflungs.'

'Jarl William must make a fortune in tax from it,' Ulrich said.

'Jarl William?' the ginger man scoffed. 'You're behind the times, my friend. Jarl Heriwolf runs it now. Jarl William is too busy trying to save his own arse.'

'So the tide does come in then?' Einar said. 'It's retreated so far I was starting to wonder if it ever comes all the way back in to here.'

'Oh it does, make no mistake about that, lad,' the ginger viking said. 'It comes in all right. And at this time of year it starts to come as a *bara*: a tidal bore. Sounds like thunder it does. A great wave comes crashing in and goes right up the river, against the current, flooding the marshes on both banks. You don't want to get caught out on the sands when that comes in. You'll be swept away and good as dead.'

'It can't be that strong!' Einar said with a scoff.

'It can be,' Skar said, impassive. 'There are places in the world where the tide returns with the speed of a galloping horse and the power of a battering ram, especially around this time of year.'

'And if the tide doesn't get you, the quicksands might,' his blond friend said. 'That beach is treacherous. Put a foot wrong and you'll sink all the way down to Hel's kingdom.'

'I'm beginning to see why Jarl Heriwolf keeps his hoard there,' Ulrich said. 'It must be the strongest fortress on Middle Earth. It seems you can't get in or out of it. So how do we get to this market without dying?'

'You see that ridge of sand?' The ginger viking pointed to a long, narrow raised section of beach that stretched in a slightly curved arc from just before where they stood all the way to the conical mount that sat out in the drained bay. 'That's a causeway. It's dry enough to walk across and will get you there. When the tide comes in it floods in moments, mind you, so don't dawdle on your way across it.'

Ulrich shaded his eyes and looked to the horizon.

'It looks like we have a bit of time yet until the sea returns,' he said. 'We'd better get on our way if we don't want to drown.'

29

Ulrich ordered Skar, Wulfhelm, Starkad, Kari and Sigurd to stay with Roan and guard the ship, much to their chagrin.

'We'll look pretty stupid if we come back and find the Bretons have burned our only way home,' Ulrich said in response to their protests. 'And don't worry. We're not going drinking and enjoying ourselves. We have a task to do, so there will be no messing around.'

The rest of the company – Ulrich, Surt, Affreca and Einar – set off across the sandy causeway towards the citadel in the distance.

Einar noticed that even on the supposed causeway the sand was wet and heavy, though solid enough for them to walk over. The beach all around them, however, was flat with many wide, shallow pools of seawater lying across its surface. A blustery wind buffeted them as they trudged along, sending countless ripples over the water and lifting curling sheets of sand into the air.

'What did that fellow mean by quicksand?' he said, raising his voice to be heard over the wind. 'How can sand be fast?'

'There are places in the world, lad,' Ulrich explained, 'where patches of sand that look like any other part of a beach are like traps. The sand is more like liquid than sand, or rather heavy, sticky mud. And once you step in it, it drags you down. It's so strong you can't get out and you just keep on sinking, down and down. Once you slip under the surface you drown and they are so deep your body is never found. It seems that this happens here.'

'Like a bog?' Einar said.

'Exactly like a bog,' Affreca said. 'There are many bogs in Ireland with pools of mire like quicksand.'

Einar looked around at the sand, feeling a twist of dread in his stomach at the thought that at any moment he could, without knowing, step into one of these quicksands and begin a slow, inexorable slide down to his death.

They trudged on, most of the way solid with patches of watery sand. The further they got into the bay, the stronger the wind got. Sand whipped across their faces as did sprays of salty water, raised by the winds from the pools. After some time the company finally arrived at the base of the mount.

Einar looked up at the conical mound that rose from the sand before them. There was a gate facing the land and someone had built a fence of sharpened stakes that led away in both directions around the perimeter of the bottom of the island. When the tide came in, the base of the fence would be almost in the water, making it very difficult for someone to land a ship. Beyond that a steep slope swept upwards, which was dotted with huts and other buildings and also covered by bushes and trees. At the summit of the hill, another palisade wrapped around a group of buildings. Grey smoke rose from the buildings on the summit.

A line of warriors in helmets, their shields slung over their shoulders and spears in their hands, formed a nonchalant line behind the gate in the lower palisade.

'It looks like we have a welcoming party,' Surt said. 'I think we could easily take them if we have to.'

'We don't need any trouble right now,' Ulrich said. 'This could be our only chance to pick up the trail of that monk and his book. We only fight if we have to and only if I give the order. Understand?'

The others nodded.

Another man came strolling down to join the warriors. He was dressed in a richly coloured woollen cloak and green britches.

'Welcome to Michael's Mountain, friends,' the man said. 'Are you buying or selling today?'

He stood, hands on hips, scanning the faces before him, each one in turn. Einar could tell he was assessing each one of them, as if to see whether they were patrons or prey. He also did not cast a second glance at either Surt's dark skin or the fact that Affreca was a woman, which told Einar that Michael's Mount was used to seeing people from all over the known world. It was one of those rare places that exist outside the conventions and expectations of everyday society. The markets in Hedeby and Dublin were the same.

'Buying, hopefully,' Ulrich said. 'Slaves.'

'Well you've come to the right place,' the man in the green britches said. 'Talk to my friend Bersi Tree-foot. He'll have what you need. But you're arriving late, my friends. The tide will soon return and at this time of the year it can be dangerous when it comes roaring back.'

'If the tide comes in,' Ulrich said, 'can't I just have my skipper pick us up? There must be a harbour here somewhere.'

The man in charge of the gate warriors smiled and shook his head.

'Those are the rules, I'm afraid,' he said. 'Everyone walks in and out. It helps keep the place secure. If the tide returns you'll be stuck here. There's a tavern but I'll warn you it's expensive. The landlord takes full advantage of the fact that when folk get stuck here they have no choice but to pay his prices. You leave any long weapons here as well. This is a viking market and the folk we get here are dangerous enough without letting them bring in swords, axes and spears as well.'

Ulrich spread his hands to show he bore no sword, spear or other war gear, and Einar and the others did the same. Even at that the guards took their personal seaxes and knives, before standing aside to let them enter the interior of the island.

They climbed up a steep track that ran upwards, curving around the side of the island. It was the only walkway there was. As they walked they passed by houses and buildings that perhaps had once been part of a fishing settlement. Now their roofs had caved in and open doorways revealed dark, empty interiors. Whoever had lived here had no doubt been expelled by the Norsemen when they had kicked out the monks as well.

As they climbed higher Ulrich talked to them in a low, conspiratorial voice.

'I brought you all along for a reason,' he said. 'I need this slave trader to tell me as much as possible and the best way to do that will be to make him think he has a chance of making a great deal of silver through me. That way he'll be too busy thinking about the wealth to wonder why I'm asking these questions and who we are. Affreca?'

Affreca raised an eyebrow.

'I need you just to be yourself,' Ulrich said.

'That shouldn't be too hard,' Affreca said.

'I need you to be the princess of the Ivarssons that you are,' Ulrich said. 'Sister of King Olaf of Dublin, the biggest slave market in the world. I'm going to spin the slaver a yarn about a deal you are here to make that could make him, in turn, a very rich man, if he can supply the slaves for it. You, Surt, will be the main customer. Who was it you used to work for? Someone called Ymir?'

'The Emir of Córdoba,' Surt said, rolling his eyes. 'He's a very powerful, very wealthy man.'

'And he wants more slaves,' Ulrich said. 'Very specific ones. You are his agent, sent here from whatever terrible, savage place you came from to buy fair-haired women and boys for your master. You've done a deal with Olaf of Dublin, but he couldn't supply all you needed. There were too many black-haired Irish and redheads there. So we've come here on the lookout for more. Got it?'

'Why would the Emir want fair-haired women and boys?' Surt said.

'Because they are beautiful,' Ulrich said. 'You know?'

'I don't,' Surt said. 'And I don't like what you seem to be suggesting.'

'Look, just go along with this, will you?' Ulrich said, rolling his eyes.

'Has anyone got a kerchief or other piece of cloth?' Surt said. 'I should at least try to look right.'

'I have this headscarf,' Affreca said, pulling a coloured square of cloth from her leather pouch.

Surt took it then said to Einar: 'Give me your amulet. I need the thong to tie this.'

Einar unclasped the leather thong of his hammer amulet from his neck and passed it over to Surt. The black-skinned man put the scarf on his head, then tied the thong around his forehead so it looked like some sort of headdress Einar surmised must be common in foreign places. Surt tucked the silver Mjölnir into a flap of material behind his head.

Catching sight of it, Ulrich shook his head. 'How long have you been one of Odin's wolves now?' he said. 'One winter? Two? Yet you still wear that symbol of the god of farmers and slaves.'

Einar made a face. 'So why am I here?' he asked.

Ulrich looked at him for a moment.

'Skar insists you're lucky,' Ulrich then said. 'And we'll need all the luck we can get if we're going to get away with this.'

30

On the summit of the island was a cluster of buildings surrounded by a wall. They went through a gate and found themselves in the marketplace, which had been set up in what remained of the former monastery. The biggest building was made of stone and it reminded Einar of the churches in Wintanceaster, though in a much worse state of repair. There were large, ragged gaps in the roof. The holes in the wall that in other Christian buildings Einar had seen filled with glass of many colours were all gone, either smashed or removed and sold. There was what looked like had once been a garden, probably where the monks used to grow their herbs and vegetables, now clogged with weeds and brambles.

There were several other buildings scattered around a large courtyard that was paved but now had many broken flagstones and grass sprouting through. From the large former church the sound of raucous laughter came, along with voices raised in volume by strong ale. Einar guessed that the church was now being used for the tavern they had been told about.

Around the courtyard were many stalls, each one with a table at the front advertising goods for sale, a leather tent behind for housing stock and a canopy over all of it to keep the table dry if it rained. Sets of metal weighing scales sat on the tables, which meant that everything here had a price, and that price would be paid in silver: either in the form of coins or clipped from the rings worn around the arms of the market's clients.

Those clients by and large looked like dangerous men. A motley collection of burly fellows milled around the stalls, looking at the goods on sale or bartering with the merchants to sell them things they had brought themselves. They had skin tanned to the colour of leather by the sun and wind, which spoke of years spent on the open waves of the whale roads. Many had tattoos etched on their arms, necks or faces; black lines that either swirled like whirlpools across their arms or branched like twigs or the imprint of birds' feet. They were of all ages from young lads to men in their midlife, but no matter how many winters they had lived, all of them were lean and fit. Their muscled bodies told of long days spent at the oars of ships or hacking with weapons either in the training yard or in battle. They bore signs of a violent life: scars, bent noses, swollen ears or missing teeth. They were rough, but not poor men. Most wore thick rings of silver or gold around their bulging arms. Their fingers clinked with rings and their beards and hair were braided through little toggles made of silver or ivory.

Around the edges of the market, standing at intervals, were twelve heavy-set men in leather jerkins and while everyone else was unarmed, these fellows had clubs, long knives and other handheld weapons. Their faces and meaty arms bore scars and tattoos. They all looked like men of violence, the sort of dangerous fellows you get together if you want to go raiding or cause other trouble. They scanned the crowd in the market with half-closed, watchful eyes.

'How come they still have weapons?' Einar asked.

'They look like watchmen employed by whoever runs this market to keep order,' Ulrich said. 'Especially if folk aren't happy with the prices. They must be a hard enough bunch if they can keep the peace in a viking market – weapons or not – so let's keep clear of them, all right?'

Einar and the others wandered around the stalls, trying to look as nonchalant as possible. In other markets Einar had visited either in Jorvik, Dublin, Hedeby or even Wintanceaster, the merchants who ran each stall tended to specialise in one thing: leatherwork, weapons, silverware or cloth and other materials. Here it was much more chaotic. Each stall was heaped with random collections of goods: jewellery, piles of hacked silver and gold, lumps of ivory and amber, carvings of the gods and also Christian crosses, some bales of cloth and many items of clothing – cloaks, furs, hats, shirts – were stacked alongside weapons, ring-mail shirts and even farm implements. It all spoke to how these goods had come to be here. They were the loot of viking raids. They were whatever a band of raiders could carry away in their arms back to their beached longships from a village they had put to the sword and flame.

Several stalls were an exception, selling only wine and nothing else. These were stocked with barrels, goatskins and clay flagons. Their owners were doing a roaring trade and many of their customers did not wait to unplug the vessels they had bought. All around men were sloshing ruby-red wine into their grinning mouths.

A large group of people were gathered around a roped-off pen near the derelict monastery. It was not horses that were corralled inside. A group of thralls – slaves – stood huddled together, shackled in iron collars, their legs fettered. Their clothes were dirty and torn; all wore expressions of abject desolation. Their eyes held empty gazes. Their heads hung low as potential buyers poked and prodded them, roughly squeezing muscles to determine men's strength, patting women's backsides and grasping breasts to judge their worth as bed slaves and pushing children's heads back to check teeth and gums to assess if they were healthy enough to survive a voyage or even just a year's work.

'He's not here,' Einar said, pointing out that Israel was not among the thralls on sale.

'Not right here,' Ulrich said. 'But that must be Bersi Tree-foot. Maybe he has some more slaves somewhere.'

Einar looked and without needing to have him pointed out, recognised Bersi Tree-foot.

Before them, bantering with his would-be customers, was the

man who was trading in this human flesh. His right leg ended at the knee where it was replaced by a wide stump of wood. His barrel chest was packed with heavy muscles while his head was completely bald. A long, ragged scar ran over his crown, down his forehead and crossed where his left eye should have been but was now just a mass of healed-over flesh. Einar surmised that he must have led an interesting though violent life. His skin was tanned the colour of leather and his arms were sheathed by many rings of silver and gold, which rattled and clinked with every movement. This showed he was a very rich man. The source of that wealth was the human beings he sold like cattle from his pen. The wide grin on his face showed teeth filed with zigzag patterns and one tooth in the middle that seemed to be entirely made of gold.

'That must be our man,' Ulrich said and he led the way across the market.

Bersi's grin grew even wider as he caught sight of Ulrich, Surt, Affreca and Einar approaching.

'Ah!' the slave trader said. 'Now here is a company who look like they could do some real business. Good day and welcome.'

Bersi reached out and patted the heavy pack of muscle that padded Surt's chest.

'This is a prime lump of beef,' he said, speaking to Ulrich. 'I could give you a nice price for this fellow. Jarls and kings pay good silver for *blámaðr*, especially big strong ones like this. They use them as ring fighters and like to outdo each other with who has the most exotic wrestler.'

Surt swatted the slave trader's hand away with a swipe of his own right hand.

'I am not for sale, dog,' he said in a growl.

Bersi's smile faded and his face clouded with confusion as he looked to Ulrich once more.

'This man is the agent of the Emir of Córdoba,' Ulrich said. 'Who is a very important and powerful King of Serkland. And, as he has just informed you, he is here to buy, not be sold.'

The slave trader's eyes widened but he nodded, nonetheless.

'And allow me to introduce the Affreca Guthfrithsdottir,' Ulrich said, placing a hand on Affreca's shoulder. 'Sister of King Olaf of Dublin and proud daughter of the Ivarsson clan.'

'It's an honour to meet a descendant of Ragnar Loðbrók,' Bersi said, raising one eyebrow as he cast his eyes over Affreca's leather jerkin, smeared with oil from ring mail and the wolf pelt that she wore as a cloak around her neck. 'But if you don't mind me saying so, lady, you're dressed more like him than a princess.'

Einar could see the scepticism in his eyes. He looked at Surt's makeshift headdress too and knew this tale would be a hard one to swallow. Einar realised that the success of Ulrich's gamble now depended on how Affreca responded.

Affreca curled her upper lip and tilted her head back so that even though the slave trader was taller than her, she was looking down her nose at him.

'Do you think I would travel through a land as infested with vikings as this one in my best clothes?' she said. 'That would be asking to be kidnapped and held for ransom. Do you think me that stupid?'

Her eyes flashed with a glare so haughty that Einar almost felt he should apologise on behalf of the one-legged man. He had been on the wrong end of Affreca's condescension himself in the past and knew well just how withering it could be. The fact that in this instance it was feigned was of no consequence to its effect.

'Of course not, my lady,' Bersi Tree-foot said, looking at least a little cowed. 'A lass as beautiful as you could be nothing but the daughter of a king.'

Ulrich launched into his tale.

'And I thought that if there would be anywhere I would find more slaves it would be here,' Ulrich said, concluding his exposition of the reason for their being there. 'It was recommended that if anyone could get us what we're looking for, it would be Bersi Tree-foot at this market. If you can help us out, friend, we could make you a very rich man.'

'I am already a very rich man, friend,' Bersi said, his previous grin returning. 'However, like good ale and beautiful women, I don't believe silver is something a man can ever have too much of.'

He winked at Affreca. Einar frowned.

'So how come you got such an important piece of this deal, friend?' Bersi said to Ulrich. 'You never said who you are.'

'I am Ulrich and I run a crew of vikings,' Ulrich said. 'Powerful men hire us for special tasks. King Olaf asked me to help the emir's agent on his quest.'

'A crew of vikings, eh?' Bersi said, reaching out to run his hand through the grey fur of the wolfskin cloak around Ulrich's neck. 'More like úlfhéðnar perhaps? I was once a viking like you until... well.'

He swung his wooden leg back and forth.

'...I found more profitable ways to spend my time,' he said. 'So where is this crew of yours?'

'They are...' Ulrich stopped as if all of a sudden catching himself about to reveal something he did not intend to '... around.'

'Are they now?' Bersi said in a tone that suggested he was not convinced by this answer. 'What are you looking for in particular? Surely the markets of Dublin have slaves aplenty?'

Ulrich made a face. 'They're all black-haired Irish and redheads,' he said. 'The emir wants blondes. They look better around his palace. Or monks. Got any of those?'

'Why would a king of Serkland want monks?' Bersi said.

'He likes the feel of their soft skin and white flesh,' Ulrich said with a shrug.

Surt took in a sharp breath. 'The Emir of Córdoba—' he began to say but Ulrich silenced him with a stern look.

'I heard there were slaves taken last night near Dol,' he said. 'Have any made their way here yet?'

Bersi narrowed his eyes. 'Maybe,' he said.

'What about the monks at Landévennec?' Ulrich said. 'They

were taken by vikings recently. Did you end up with any of them?'

'I had all of them,' Bersi said. 'One of them is over there, talking to his friends.'

They all looked round and to Einar's surprise he saw a small group of Christian monks huddled together in a nervous bunch. They were not slaves, however. They stood on the outside of the roped pen. Another monk who looked much the worse for wear stood inside. His grey robe was tattered around his legs and arms, and it was streaked with dirt. The other monks were not overweight but the enslaved monk looked emaciated. His left eye was black and his lips were swollen and split from a beating.

'That's not him,' Einar said.

Ulrich shot a sharp glance at Einar.

The enslaved monk had grasped the left hand of the leader of the other monks in both his own. This other monk was a tall, gaunt, gangling man in a long grey robe who Einar judged to be the leader because the wooden cross he wore around his neck was much bigger than those of his companions. The enslaved monk was speaking to the others in his own tongue. Einar could not understand what they said but the insistent, beseeching tone in his voice and the tears that streaked his face suggested he was pleading with them for something.

Whatever he was asking for, he was denied. With an emphatic shake of his head, the leader of the other monks wrenched his hand away from the other's grasp. A look of stern horror on his face, he said something to the enslaved monk then turned and walked away with quick steps. His companion monks turned and walked away from the rope too, most casting disturbed and guilty looks over their shoulders as they went.

The monk behind the rope made as if to run after them. The chain connected to the iron collar around his throat snapped tight and he fell backwards, landing on the flagstones of the courtyard with a strangled yelp. The other slaves winced while all the Norse around them fell into gales of laughter.

'Fucking wankers,' Bersi said. 'They value their books more than the lives of their brother monks. You're sure you want one of those?'

'What do you mean books?' Einar said, his ears pricking up. 'Is that what they were talking about?'

'Aye,' Bersi said. 'The one I'm selling was pleading with the others to buy his freedom.'

'Is that why the Christians are here?' Einar said. 'I wouldn't have expected monks at a viking market. They have some nerve showing their faces here.'

'Oh we let them come,' Bersi said, his unpleasant grin spreading across his face. 'In fact we encourage it. We rob their monasteries then they come here and buy their own stuff back. Then we rob them again. It's very good business. They're so soft it's pathetic. That lot—'

He pointed at the group of monks withdrawing across the marketplace in the direction of another stall.

'Are here to try to buy back some of the books we robbed from them. They were telling their friend there that they had only collected enough silver to buy the manuscripts back. There wouldn't be enough left to buy his freedom as well. So they left him in slavery. Can you believe that?'

Ulrich shook his head. 'I can see why he was so distraught. They call themselves "brothers" you know? What man would leave his brother in slavery if he could do something about it?'

'I don't know what magic is in those pieces of parchment,' Bersi said, 'but it must be very powerful. Still, all the more silver for us, eh?'

'Of course,' Ulrich said.

'Listen, I'll tell you what,' the slave trader said, 'this deal you are talking about sounds interesting but it needs my full attention. I've some other business to get out of the way here, then I can talk to you properly. Why don't you go over to the tavern there? Tell them Bersi sent you and they'll look after you as honoured guests. I'll meet you there and we can talk serious business later. All right?'

Ulrich nodded. It was obvious that they were all being dismissed.

Ulrich, Surt, Affreca and Einar walked away from the slave-trading pen. Einar thought of the rich, sweet taste of the local wine and could not help licking his lips.

'Bersi said we'd be looked after like honoured guests,' Einar said. 'We may as well go for a drink then?'

'Agreed,' Ulrich said. 'But not you.'

He placed his forefinger on Einar's chest. Einar's face fell.

'He thinks we're important to his deal,' Ulrich said. 'But you are just one of my crew. I want to know more about these manuscripts those monks are here to buy. Who knows? Maybe Aethelstan's book is among them? Go and see what you can find out, eh? Then come and meet us in the tavern. Try not to let them know we're looking for that particular book or they'll hitch the price up.'

Einar nodded, meeting the smaller man's gaze for a moment.

'So this is nothing to do with me being lucky,' he said. 'You just needed someone not remarkable who can nose around and find out things?'

Ulrich smiled. 'Perhaps that's what I meant by lucky,' he said. 'If so then you'll find out something useful.'

Einar watched the others go in the direction of the tavern, anger and confusion competing for supremacy in his heart. Had Ulrich just said he was nothing special, unlike the rest of the úlfhéðnar, or had he said Einar's unremarkable-ness was an advantage?

He shook his head. As always with Ulrich, it was a mystery as to what he actually meant.

Trying to look as nonchalant as possible he pushed his way through the milling crowd until he arrived beside the monks now gathered at a stall on which sat a large leather-bound book.

'It's all the wealth we have!' the tall, gaunt monk Einar had guessed was their leader said in a complaining tone. He now spoke in the Norse tongue but with an accent like Lord Alan.

'Well it's not enough,' the stallholder, a fat man with a gold ring through one ear, said. 'I can make ten times that amount for a piece like this.'

On the stall counter before them was a manuscript – one of the books like Einar had seen in Wintanceaster. It was opened at a page of exquisite drawings of strange beasts twisting around one another while criss-cross patterns wove their way around Christian runes, all picked out in vibrant colours as well as gold and silver.

'Can't you make an exception?' the monk wailed. 'That is a holy book. It needs to be back in our monastery where it belongs.'

'I'm not trading here for the good of my health,' the stallholder said. The expression on his face suggested he was annoyed almost beyond patience by the monk's words. 'I need to make a living, you know. If I made exceptions for folk, how long do you think I'd stay in business? If you want the book so badly then go and get more silver. Then you can buy it.'

'This is all the wealth left to our monastery,' the lead monk said. His face darkened to a puce colour and it looked to Einar like if he pricked the monk's face, his head might burst. 'The vikings stole everything. We have scraped together this – more than adequate – hoard of silver through the generosity and piety of some noblewomen. It's all we have and all we *will* have.'

The stallholder just sat back, folded his arms and raised one eyebrow.

'It's our book!' the monk thundered. His indignation provoked a wave of scornful chuckling from the vikings close enough to witness it. 'Stolen from our monastery by devils like you! Brother Cadoc here created that very page himself. Now you expect us to pay you silver to get it back? This is criminal!'

The stallholder grinned and leaned on his elbows. 'It's good business craft,' he said. 'Now I'll tell you what, how about I say you actually do have enough silver?'

The monk looked confused.

'For one page,' the stallholder continued. 'If your brother is so fond of this particular page he can have it back. Or choose another page. But you can only have one. Take it or leave it.'

The monk looked like he was going to cry. He bit his lip then made a sharp nod.

'Sensible choice,' the stallholder said. 'Kettil, give the man his page.'

The man beside him on the stall, Kettil, drew a long-bladed knife. Einar felt an almost visceral flinch as he watched the sharp blade slice through the calfskin of the beautiful book, parting the page from the others. The manuscript was so pleasing to the eye it seemed a crime to damage it so wilfully.

The monks looked just as appalled as Kettil handed them their page while the stallholder scooped their little pile of silver into his pouch.

'Now clear off,' the stallholder said. 'I have other customers waiting.'

The monks shuffled off, their faces masks of despair.

'Can I help you, friend?' The stallholder turned to Einar.

'Have you any more like that?' Einar said, gesturing to the manuscript.

'What's wrong with that one?' the stallholder asked. 'They're all the same aren't they?'

'I'm looking for something very particular,' Einar said. 'Have you any from Landévennec?'

Einar spotted the stallholder's eyes narrow.

'I might,' he said. 'Why?'

Einar blanched, remembering Ulrich's warning.

'I, eh, heard the ones from Landévennec are particularly good,' he said. 'Have you any with different runes on them than this one?'

'You ask some strange questions, friend,' the stallholder said. 'Why is a Norseman so interested in Christian books anyway?'

'I've heard they're very valuable,' Einar said, perhaps a little too fast. 'If I buy one I was thinking maybe I can sell it on and make some silver.'

'And you're telling me that, son?' the stallholder said, an expression of scepticism mixed with pity on his face. 'Not much of a dealer are you?'

Einar thought fast. He was getting nowhere and needed to come up with a plan fast.

'Look: never mind,' he said, pretending offence. 'If you've nothing else I'll go and spend my silver elsewhere.'

Einar held up his leather purse, jingling it so the stallholder could hear the clink of metal from within. The purse was actually a weapon. It was filled with lumps of lead rather than silver. It was a trick Skar had taught him. A purse could be carried anywhere without arousing suspicion and if swung with enough force could crack a man's skull with ease. The stallholder, of course, did not know that. All he saw was a naïve young man with a fat purse.

The man looked at Einar for a moment more.

'All right, friend,' he said. 'I'll tell you what. I have more books but they're in my store. Kettil here will take you to see the rest. If there's anything there that interests you we can talk business. Kettil?'

His assistant came over to join them.

'This young man is looking for manuscripts,' the stallholder said. 'There are more in the store. Take care of him, will you?'

There was something about the way the man said *take care of him* and fixed his assistant with a knowing look that Einar did not like. However, he nodded and let Kettil lead him across the market square back through the crowd and then out the gate Einar had entered by earlier.

'I don't know what the fuss is with these bits of parchment,' Kettil said over his shoulder as he led the way down a path paved with old stones worn smooth by centuries of footsteps. 'But the Christians are obsessed with them.'

After a short while they came to a set of steps cut into the rock of the island that led downwards to a door of what must be some sort of underground room.

'It's an old cave,' Kettil explained. 'We all use it as our storeroom.'

He led the way down the steps and came to an iron-bound door set into the rock. It was barred and a huge lock fastened the bolts shut. Kettil fumbled with a set of keys then clicked open the lock and drew the bolts back. The door opened with a screech of protest from its hinges and he gestured that Einar should enter first.

'After you,' Kettil said with a smile.

Einar went ahead, entering the cool darkness of the cave. Kettil came in after him. The door closed and for a few moments they stood in complete darkness. Then with a scratching of flint and kindling, Kettil ignited a whale-oil lamp. The warm, yellow-orange glow of the lamp illuminated the surroundings and Einar looked around.

He found himself in a veritable treasure trove. There were gold cups, silver crosses, jewelled ornaments and barrels of wine. To Einar's excitement there were also piles of manuscripts and books, scattered over several tables.

'It's you! Thank the Lord! Have you come to rescue me?'

Einar flinched at the sound of Israel's voice. He turned around and saw there were three slaves at the far end of the cave. They were bound in iron collars and chains and had been cowering in the shadows, which was why he had missed them. One of them was the scholar.

'So you know each other?' Kettil said. His voice suggested he had been expecting something like this. 'Well no matter. It doesn't change things.'

Einar looked around and saw that Kettil was now holding a long-bladed knife. The point was directed towards Einar. It was close enough that in one quick move it would be through Einar's heart.

'Hand over the purse for a start,' Kettil said, an unpleasant grin on his face. 'I don't know what you're up to, friend, but the master isn't happy with it.'

'You're making a mistake,' Einar said.

'Just hand over the purse and don't try anything stupid,' Kettil said. 'This isn't the first time I've done this.'

'I'm sure it isn't,' Einar said.

They probably did this all the time, Einar thought. Entice unwary travellers down to this hideaway then relieve them of their silver. That way they got to keep their own goods as well. Good business craft indeed. He glanced around again and realised that since Kettil had shown him where they kept their hoard, there was little chance he would be allowed to walk away alive. When he handed over his purse, Kettil would kill him and no doubt his corpse would be thrown in the sea when the tide swept in around the island later. Kettil might not even wait until he handed the purse over.

Einar took a deep breath, running through the training Skar had drummed into him and the other Wolf Coats, preparing them for how to react in all sorts of situations, including one like this. His next move was risky; however, to do nothing would also mean certain death.

Einar's right hand flashed forward. The inside of his wrist slapped against the inside of Kettil's right wrist, the hand that held the knife. Then Einar swiped his left hand, grasping the back of Kettil's knife hand and forcing it to the right. The hand twisted at the wrist and Einar forced it on without mercy so his own hands crossed over.

There was a loud crack as Kettil's wrist snapped. The man shouted, at first more in surprise than pain. His hand opened, dropping the blade, which rattled onto the stone floor below.

Going so far as to break the bones was an unnecessary cruelty perhaps, but Einar, with a sense of slight amazement that he could feel so detached in what was, after all, a life-threatening situation, recalled Skar's words as he had taught them how to deal with an attacker with a knife. *You don't need to break his wrist but if some bastard is trying to kill you with a knife, best to make sure he can't finish the job.*

Einar kept a remorseless grip on Kettil's knife hand, turning and pushing it towards the floor. There was a gut-churning crunch as the broken bones ground across each other. Compelled by the pain, his face a grimace of agony, Kettil was forced to move in the direction Einar wanted him to: back and down. When he was half-kneeling and leaning slightly backwards, Einar lifted his right boot and delivered a hard kick to Kettil's jaw. It was a good shot. Einar saw Kettil's eyes roll up into his head and felt the man's full body weight come onto the hands he was holding as Kettil lost consciousness. Einar kicked him again, to be sure.

Kettil collapsed onto the floor. Einar picked up his knife.

Recalling Skar's advice again, he crouched down and slashed it across Kettil's throat. A torrent of crimson blood gushed out to flood into a sticky, wide, copper-smelling puddle around the fast-dying man.

Panting, Einar rose again and looked around. Israel and the other two slaves were looking at him with wide eyes.

'Did you have to kill him?' the scholar said in a trembling voice.

Einar looked down at the dead man at his feet and asked himself the same question. He had dispatched Kettil almost without thought – an instinctive reaction to days and weeks of training.

How many men had he killed now? There were many, and if he added the ones he knew about – the slaughters carried out close enough that he could smell the stench of their last breath – to the men who had fallen in battle before a shield wall he was part of, the bodies were starting to pile up. Once he had looked on his fellow Wolf Coats as men apart; vikings and born killers who dispatched men, women and even children to Hel without a second thought. He had always thought he would never be like them, not completely. Every person he would kill would deserve their fate.

As he looked down at the bleeding corpse of Kettil he wondered if that was true of this, his latest victim. Had he now become just the same as the others?

Einar took another deep breath through his nose and blinked hard. This was not the time to question his path through the world. They had to get out of here.

He lifted the lamp and crossed to where the slaves were bound. The light showed Israel was bound alongside what looked like another monk and a young peasant girl. Using Kettil's knife he managed to prise open Israel's collar and fetters. The blade broke when he tried to do the same to the other two, however. Using the hilt of the broken knife, he was able to smash the chains off where they were fastened to the rock wall.

'Sorry, that's the best I can do,' he said. 'You can run away but you'll be yoked together until you find a way to get that off.'

The slaves looked at him wide-eyed, clearly unable to understand what he had said and unsure what to do.

Israel spoke to them in another tongue and expressions of relief dawned on their faces.

'Go,' Einar said, cocking his head towards the door.

They did not need to be told twice. Babbling what Einar assumed was thanks, the monk and the girl scurried across the cave and out the door.

'Thanks to the Lord – blessed be His name – that you came to save me,' Israel said. 'But I have much to tell you! There is another monk taken from Landévennec here. We must rescue him as well. They took him to the market this morning. I just hope he is not already sold.'

Einar made a face. 'We can't save everyone from slavery,' he said. 'It will be risky enough getting you out of here without trying to take someone from the slave market as well.'

'You don't understand,' Israel said. 'We *must* save him. He knows what happened to my book!'

'How do we know it isn't one of these ones?' Einar said, pointing to the stolen manuscripts and books scattered around the cave.

'I think I'd know my own manuscript,' Israel said, giving Einar a disparaging look.

'You're sure?' Einar said. 'Why didn't you ask him where it was?'

'They brought me here during the night and I was chained up with the other slaves,' the scholar said. 'We recognised each other but the Norsemen beat us whenever anyone tried to talk. All I got from him was that he knew where the book had gone before they were kicking and punching us. Then they took him to the market this morning. I hope he wasn't sold.'

Einar looked around. There were some piles of expensive-looking cloth stacked nearby, no doubt stolen from a monastery or some rich man's house. He picked them up and draped a few around the shoulders of Israel.

'What are you doing?' the scholar said.

'Creating a disguise for you,' Einar said. 'We're going to have to go back to the market so you can point out who this monk is. If he's still there. You can't be walking around in your own clothes. You look too much like a monk yourself. You need a hood too.'

Once Israel was swathed in enough rich material to obscure his identity, they hurried out the door and up the steps outside.

Both jogged back to the gate and into the marketplace. Einar noticed straight away that there appeared to be fewer people milling around. This gave them a clear view across the marketplace to Bersi Tree-foot's slave pen.

'That's him,' Israel said, pointing to the monk Einar had seen earlier, pleading with the other monks to help him.

'Be careful,' he chided in a low voice, pulling Israel's outstretched finger down again. 'We don't want them noticing us. I've met your friend earlier as it happens.'

He looked around to see if Bersi had spotted them, but saw the slave trader was otherwise engaged.

Eight of the burly watchmen were gathered in a semicircle around Bersi. They were listening with intent to him as he talked in an animated manner. He gestured towards the tavern where Ulrich, Affreca and Surt had gone previously. The others nodded and hefted their clubs, cudgels and other weapons.

Given what he had just experienced with Kettil, Einar did not like the look of what was happening. He knew he had to get to the others before Bersi's crew did.

32

Ulrich, Affreca and Surt stood before the serving bench in the tavern.

It was a busy place. The air was filled with drunken chatter, laughter and the fug of ale fumes, boiling meat and the smell of damp clothes drying out in the smoky warm air from the huge fire that blazed in a hearth built into the middle of the floor.

The church was now in a sorry state. Its tall windows were now almost completely bereft of their coloured glass. The tiled roof above was falling in and the new Norse owners, lacking knowledge for how to fix it, had filled in the gaps with wood and straw.

The tavern was packed and very noisy. There were tables crowded with men on their benches or standing around, talking and drinking from ale horns. Slaves rushed around, serving the customers with ale and wine from big wooden jugs, as well as seethed meat and fish from wooden platters. Some musicians did their best to be heard from a small, raised section of the floor. The whole scene was watched over by a burly man who looked like he was the tavern keeper. He stood behind the serving bench, his face marked by several long scars, two meaty arms folded over his chest.

'This wine is delicious,' Affreca said, holding up her empty drinking horn. 'Shall we get another?'

Ulrich made a face. His horn remained half full and Surt, always wary of strong drink for religious reasons, had not touched his.

'Perhaps you should slow down,' Ulrich said. 'We're on a task in dangerous lands, remember?'

'Yes but if we stand around in a tavern and don't drink,' Affreca said, 'don't you think we'll draw suspicion to ourselves? People will start wondering why we're really here.'

'Very well,' Ulrich said with a sigh. 'You are right. Three more?'

He turned and waved towards the tavern master who seemed oblivious, remaining standing stock-still, arms folded.

'Some service please?' Ulrich said, raising his voice to be heard over the racket around him.

'That's what the serving thralls are for,' the tavern master said, pointing to one of the young girls struggling around the room, laden with a jug of wine.

Ulrich rolled his eyes and turned around again, raising one hand to try to attract the attention of the sweating thralls.

'You'll not get much by way of service from that bastard,' a new voice made them all turn around again. A ruddy-faced, bleary-eyed man of middling years stood nearby, a half-empty drinking horn grasped in one fist. He swayed back and forth and it was unclear if he was leaning on the serving table or whether the serving table was holding him up.

'It looks like you've managed to get served enough anyway, friend,' Ulrich said.

'Yes well I won't be getting much more,' the red-faced fellow slurred. 'I sold my raiding loot in the market. The bastards knew I was keen to sell, so wouldn't give me a decent price. Then I came in here for a drink and have been paying that bastard's inflated prices. This whole island is a den of thieves and robbers.'

'Frequented by thieves and robbers,' Ulrich said. 'But I know what you mean. It's like that tavern keeper doesn't want anyone here. He seems to regard customers as an inconvenience. I'd have thought he might understand that he depends on drinkers to stay in business.'

'Not that one – Danish bastard. He doesn't depend on

anything. He knows there will be a new batch of people tomorrow and that if they want a drink they've nowhere else to go on this island. Those Danes have the whole thing sewn up, the bastards. It's the only market in north-west Francia and they run it. They run the tavern too and they control who does and doesn't get onto the island. All Danes, every one of them.'

'Well their merchant craft is impressive, I must say,' Ulrich said. 'You get vikings to bring their booty here to sell, then get them to hand the silver you paid them right back to you over the bar of this tavern. You end up with both their loot and their silver. These Danes are no fools.'

'They're bastards, that's what they are,' the drunk man said. 'I'm Flosi, by the way.'

'And I am Ulrich,' Ulrich said. 'This is Affreca Guthfrithsdottir of Dublin and this is the agent of the Emir of Córdoba. Ah—'

At that moment, one of the hard-pressed serving girls finally made her way over to them.

'Refills please,' Ulrich said. 'I take it you will join us, Flosi? I'm buying.'

'I don't mind if I do,' the drunk viking said, grinning and holding his horn out to be replenished.

The slave girl told Ulrich the price and his eyes widened.

'A den of thieves and robbers indeed,' he said as he fumbled in his purse then laid the necessary amount of silver on the serving table. The tavern keeper unfolded his arms, crossed to where they stood and picked up the silver.

'Ah so he can move after all,' Ulrich said.

The tavern keeper just gave an unpleasant smile, poured the silver into his own bulging purse and walked away again.

'Friendly fellow,' Surt said.

'They're all the same,' Flosi said. 'Fucking Danes.' He jolted as if kicked by an invisible foot. 'Oh,' he said. 'I hope you're not Danes. No offence.'

'None taken,' Ulrich said. 'As I've already said, Affreca here is Irish. Surt is clearly not a Dane and I am from Norway.'

Flosi chuckled, mostly from relief, and clapped Ulrich on the shoulder.

'Good man!' he said. 'A Norwegian like myself. Like most of the poor vikings in this place. The Danes have this whole country sewn up. I don't know why we stay. And now they say Lord Alan of Brittany is back. I tell you, if that's the case then I for one am off. It's nice here but not worth dying for. I'm taking my family and sailing away. The fucking Danes can keep this place. They're welcome to it.'

'Back to Norway?' Ulrich said.

Flosi made a pained face. 'I don't know,' he said. 'Hakon is king there now. They say he's just a lapdog of Aethelstan of Wessex. Perhaps Norway isn't the place it used to be anymore either.'

'Are most of our folk here Danes, then?' Ulrich said.

'The rich ones are,' Flosi said, taking a swig of wine from his drinking horn. 'They arrived long before us and took control of everything. Then they settled down and started getting into all these fancy Francia ways. They say that Jarl Vilhjálmr of Rúðu has now completely forsaken the gods. Which isn't a surprise. They say he's just another lapdog of Aethelstan.'

'"They" say a lot, my friend,' Affreca said.

'Look round here.' Flosi made a sweeping gesture around the room, ignoring Affreca's comment. 'You can tell who's a Dane and who isn't. They're the ones in the rich clothes and their arms dripping with gold and silver rings.'

They looked around and indeed there did seem to be several tables where the clothes of the men who sat drinking at them were of more expensive material and more varied colours. There also appeared to be a strict demarcation between those richly dressed men and the other drinkers in the hall.

'Not much mixing I see,' Ulrich said.

'They don't like us,' Flosi said. 'Since we Norwegians arrived, they've done nothing but look down their noses at us.'

'What about this Jarl Heriwolf I've heard so much about?'

Ulrich said. 'These folk you know – *they* – say he is a decent Norseman. He hasn't forsaken our ways at least.'

The drunken viking's chest swelled and he straightened his back. He made a face. 'He's another Dane,' he said, finishing his horn with one more draught. 'But at least his heart seems to be in the right place. You never know with noblemen though. They say anything to get your support. We'll see soon enough if he really meant what he said or if it was just more empty words.'

'What do you mean?' Ulrich said.

'He has Jarl Vilhjálmr surrounded in Rúðu,' Flosi said. 'Heriwolf's army besieges the town while Vilhjálmr cowers behind its walls. It's only a matter of time before the town falls.'

Ulrich exchanged glances with Affreca.

'If Heriwolf wins he has sworn he will subject Vilhjálmr to the blood eagle,' Flosi said. 'If he does that, we'll know he is still one of us at heart: a Norseman. If he pushes back all this Christian nonsense and brings back worship of the gods, then we know he is a man of his word. Perhaps I might even stay here after all.'

At that moment the doors of the tavern banged open. Two figures stumbled in and looked around. One was Einar, the other was what looked like a very rich foreign man swathed in multicoloured cloth of several different patterns.

Spotting Ulrich, Affreca and Surt, Einar strode across to them, hauling the other man along by the arm.

'We have to go. Now,' Einar said.

'Is that who I think it is?' Ulrich said, pushing aside the makeshift hood of Einar's companion to reveal the pale, frightened face of Israel. 'It is indeed! Good work, lad. You deserve a drink.'

'There's no time,' Einar said.

The doors of the tavern crashed open again. This time Bersi Tree-foot stomped in, followed by his band of eight hardmen.

'Too late,' Einar said.

33

'Bersi,' Ulrich said as the slave trader and his entourage arrived at the serving table. 'At last. You've come to discuss our deal?'

'There's been a change to the proposition, Ulrich,' Bersi said. His gold tooth flashed as he grinned. 'You see, you are no longer required. I've decided to deal directly with the princess and the emir's agent.'

He turned to Affreca.

'Cutting out this middleman, your highness,' he said, an expression of mock seriousness on his face, 'will end up in a better deal for your brother and the emir.'

Affreca frowned. 'We commissioned Ulrich here to work for us,' she said, lying through her teeth. 'I'm not sure—'

'I can get you the slaves you need, lady,' Bersi said. 'At a much better price if we don't have to pay him his cut as well.'

Ulrich glanced at Flosi who was watching, aghast.

'A den of thieves and robbers,' he said. 'You were right, my friend.'

'Get out of here, Ulrich,' Bersi said. 'You're no longer required. I'm cutting you out of this deal.'

'And what if I don't want to be cut out?' Ulrich said.

'That's why I've brought my friends here,' Bersi said, cocking his head towards the ten men gathered behind him. They grinned too. Some pulled sticks and others cudgels from their belts. Several of them had knives. Bersi himself pulled a long-bladed seax from a sheath. Its blade gleamed. Then he spotted Israel.

'Isn't that one of my slaves?' he asked.

'We're taking him with us,' Ulrich said.

'What's wrong with you, Ulrich?' Bersi said, a look of genuine annoyance screwing up his features. 'Don't you understand me and my friends are about to make sure you don't take anyone anywhere again? You're about to lose your teeth, have your bones broken, maybe even lose your life.'

'I don't think so,' Ulrich said.

'And who is going to stop us?' Bersi said, spittle flying from between his teeth. 'Your mysterious crew? These supposed Wolf Coats? They don't seem to be here. Where are they anyway?'

'Right here,' Affreca said.

She pivoted on her left foot, lashing out sideways with her right. It was the most powerful way to kick with the strength of all the big muscles at the top of the thigh behind it. The flat of her foot connected with Bersi's wooden leg, driving it from under him. The straps that held it to him snapped as it flew backwards. With a cry of surprise Bersi toppled over.

'Danish bastards!' Ulrich shouted at the top of his voice. 'They're trying to rob us.'

Several men at the tables around them started to their feet, expressions of drunken righteous indignation on their faces. Others – obviously of Danish origin – leapt to their feet to confront them.

Bersi's men charged forward, yelling, and all the forces of chaos erupted in the tavern. As if they had been waiting for this excuse, the poorer dressed Norwegians fell upon their Danish companions and began punching them. The Danes hit back and in moments the room was a maelstrom of men grappling with each other. Two of Bersi's men were tackled by drunken vikings before they even got to Einar and the others. Benches clattered as they were knocked over. The serving girls screamed and there was a crashing of shattering pottery as two of them dropped their wine jugs in panic.

Surt grasped the edge of a nearby table and wrenched it upwards, throwing up a barrier that two of Bersi's onrushing men would have to deal with. A third rushed at Einar, brandishing a thick wooden cudgel that had been capped with iron. Einar dropped into a ready stance: hands forward preparing to grasp or hit, feet just over shoulder width apart, knees soft, ready to spring either right or left. He knew if the end of the cudgel stuck him, it would break bones. If it caught him round the head, it could kill him.

Bersi's man flailed at him with the club. Einar dropped to a crouch. He felt his hair move as the cudgel just missed the top of his skull. Without hesitation, he came up again, driving his left fist into the now exposed right side of his opponent, thumping him right in the kidneys.

The man gasped from the pain. Before he could recover Einar lashed out with his foot, delivering a kick that connected somewhere around the other man's knee. This time he yelled, dropping the club on instinct as both his hands moved without thought to protect his injured kneecap. As he bent forward Einar reached out, grabbed a handful of the man's hair on each side of his head and wrenched it downwards. At the same time he brought his knee up, smashing it into the other's face. His opponent's yell turned to a muffled grunt and he collapsed to the floor.

A man behind Affreca snaked his right arm around her throat and left around her chest. He lifted her backwards and off her feet.

'Time for some fun, lads!' he shouted to no one in particular as his left hand mashed her right breast with rough fingers.

Affreca drove her head backwards, connecting hard with his face. There was a sound like a raw egg cracking as her skull smashed into his nose. The man cried out and let her go. She whirled and saw him staggering away, both hands to his face, blood dribbling through his fingers.

Another of Bersi's men advanced on Ulrich, waving his knife before him. Ulrich grabbed a nearby stool and held it by the seat, legs towards his attacker. The man lunged at him with his knife but Ulrich countered with the stool. The blade punched through the seat of the stool, its point stopping just short of Ulrich's face.

Ulrich rotated the stool, twisting the knife out of the other man's grasp. Ulrich tossed the stool, the knife still embedded in it, to the side. He clenched his fists and prepared for hand-to-hand fighting. The knife owner, however, proved not keen to be a hero and, bereft of his weapon, turned and ran away.

'We need to get out of here,' Surt said, shouting to be heard over the confusion.

They looked around. The way to the door was clogged with grappling men as the Norwegians and Danes vented their mutual animosity on each other. While they had dealt with a few of them, Bersi's crew were recovering from the surprise, shoving aside the table Surt had overturned and regrouping for another assault. One of them was helping Bersi himself to stand.

'There must be another way out,' Affreca said.

Einar swept his eyes around the room and spotted another smaller door in the wall behind the serving table. 'Over there,' he said to the others.

They all turned only to see the tavern keeper was lifting a long-handled axe from under the serving table. He hefted it into both hands then and stepped between the table and the door. The tavern keeper shook his head.

'If Bersi has a problem with you, then I'm not letting you run away,' he said.

They turned back towards the main door once again. Bersi's remaining men had now regrouped and were starting to advance.

'The only way out is through them,' Ulrich said. He turned to Affreca. 'Princess: your task is to get our friend the scholar out of here in one piece.'

Affreca nodded and grasped Israel's upper arm, who was standing, mouth agape, staring aghast at the brawl that was happening all around them.

'What are the rest of us going to do?' Einar said.

'We're going to make a path out of here,' Ulrich said. 'Einar, you know the way Skar and I have taught you that the difference between an úlfhéðnar and a berserker is that we can control the divine rage that Odin sends on us? That we can channel it, and don't simply fly off into a frenzy, as much a danger to our own side as the enemy?'

Einar nodded.

'You say that's why we are better than them,' he said.

'Well, now is one of the few occasions I will tell you to ignore that,' Ulrich said. 'I need you to unleash the wild wolf that lives inside you.'

'I don't think I can,' Einar said. 'I've spent so long concentrating, striving for the very opposite...' He trailed off as he saw the look of scorn on Ulrich's face.

'I knew you were no use,' Ulrich said. 'I should have brought Skar or one of the others.'

Einar felt a stab of shame at his leader's disappointment in him, then it flared fast into anger.

'You taught me that the rage is a gift from Odin, not to be taken for granted but nurtured,' he said. 'You laugh at berserkers who can't control it, and now you show this disdain for me when I can? Fuck you, Ulrich.'

'No fuck you, Einar,' Ulrich said. 'You're a useless half-Irish bastard. For all I know Odin has taken his gift away from you and you're no longer fit to be an úlfhéðnar in my crew. I should have brought Starkad. At least he's good in a fight.'

'What?!'

Spittle flew from Einar's mouth. His eyes bulged and he felt like his chest was going to burst. He was paralysed by rage.

'If you're not going to help us, then get out of the way,' Ulrich said, and cuffed Einar around the ear with his open hand.

The blow was not hard, but it unleashed what felt like a torrent of lava in Einar's guts. The clamour around him seemed to grow quiet and the brawling men, the scattered tables and benches, the whole scene in the tavern looked like it was slowing down. A strange dream-like sensation took hold of him and everything around him appeared to be bathed in a weird red hue.

The last vestiges of his rational mind, the part Skar and Ulrich had trained to channel the insane rage that visited him in times of battle, recognised it was too strong this time and he was about to lose all control. He wanted to punch the supercilious smile from the smaller man's face and keep punching until all that was left was a bloody mess.

To his surprise, however, he saw himself glaring straight into a face he had no doubt mirrored his own. Ulrich's visage was pale as death, his lips were drawn back in a snarl, his nostrils flared wide and his eyes glared back at Einar, fierce as two glowing coals. The rage was taking Ulrich too.

At that moment Surt laid a hand on each of their shoulders and forced them away from each other, twisting both so they faced Bersi and his men instead.

'That way,' he bellowed.

The last of Einar's reason left him. He charged headlong into the crowd before him. He could hear a wild, high-pitched screaming and a detached part of him realised that it was coming from him. It felt like ice was flowing through his veins. Every muscle burned to lash out, to hit and kick. His gums itched to sink his teeth into flesh.

One of Bersi's men stepped forward to meet Einar, a broken-backed seax brandished in one hand. To Einar it seemed that the man before him was moving slowly, like someone trying to run in deep water. Somehow he knew already what the man was going to do even before he began to strike with his blade. As well as that, Einar also somehow noticed other inconsequential details like the man's missing front teeth, visible because of the snarl that twisted his lips.

As he ran forward Einar grabbed a stool that lay overturned on the floor. He did not need to look at it but somehow his outstretched hand found it and he scooped it up. In one movement he grasped it with his other hand as well and swung it upwards in a vicious arc that smashed it into the other man's face. At the same time Einar twisted to the side.

The action was so swift his opponent had no time to react. The man was still driving his seax forward but now only at thin air as the stool shattered into pieces around his skull. His head snapped backwards with the force of the blow. His nose, jaw and several more of his teeth smashed under the impact. He dropped like a stone to the tavern floor, the knife falling from his now insensitive hand.

Einar barrelled into the man coming behind him, knocking him sprawling backwards. As he hit the ground, Einar trampled him beneath his feet as he ran on.

Ulrich was alongside Einar. The smaller man made a wolf-like howling as he charged. Another of Bersi's men swung a mighty two-handed blow with a heavy club at him. Had it connected it would have knocked his head from his shoulders. Ulrich simply skipped sideways, letting the club pass by him. Then he punched his opponent in his now exposed kidneys. The man gasped in pain. Shock loosened his grip on his club and he dropped it. Ulrich caught it before it hit the ground. He grasped it in both hands, raised it and brought it down on the top of the other man's head. There was a hollow-sounding crack and the man's legs sagged then he staggered backwards. Ulrich advanced after him, remorseless, striking him on the right shoulder, breaking his collarbone, then hitting his left knee. The man collapsed and Ulrich charged on.

Bersi was back up to his one foot again. He now leaned heavily on a table, trying to regain his balance without the aid of his wooden stump.

'They're stealing one of my slaves!' he shouted, raising one hand to point at Affreca, who was hurrying towards the gap in the crowd Einar and Ulrich had battered open, dragging Israel along behind her.

Affreca stopped and let go of Israel for a moment. She grabbed a jug of ale from a nearby table and threw it. It shattered around

Bersi's upper body in an explosion of amber ale and white froth, making him stagger. Affreca swept her left leg around in a kick that took Bersi's good leg from under him and the slave trader tumbled back to the floor once more.

Surt lifted another table and held it before him, grasping it by the legs. Using it like a massive shield, he barged his way through the crowd before him sending the men, slaves and furniture in his path scattering in every direction.

Einar's teeth rattled as a man tackled him, driving his shoulder into Einar's back and sending him flying forwards onto the floor. His face ploughed into the filthy straw that covered the ground and he smelt and tasted the stale ale, wine and vomit it had been strewn to mop up.

Einar felt a weight on his back as the man who had knocked him over jumped on top of him. He should have been worried – Einar was now at his opponent's mercy – but instead all he felt was fury. He let out a roar and pushed himself up with his hands. He pulled his legs beneath him and powered back up to his feet. There was a startled cry as the man who had been on his back tumbled off.

Einar spun around to see the man who had been on him now sprawled on his own back. The look of terror on his face at the sight of Einar now towering over him sent a thrill of sheer delight through Einar. He jumped into the air, landing with both feet on his chest. He felt bones crack and collapse under his weight. Blood spurted from the man's mouth.

Einar fell onto his knees on the man and started punching him. He was well out of the fight, but all Einar wanted was to keep hitting him.

A wave of cold liquid sloshed around his head. Einar blinked, like a man waking from a deep sleep, his reason returned to his mind in a rush, bringing confusion with it. He looked up and saw Affreca, another jug of ale – this one now empty – in her hands.

'Leave him,' she shouted. 'We can get away.'

Einar looked and saw the way out was now clear. The fighting continued around them but at that moment there was no one between them and the door of the tavern.

Ulrich was fighting with another man nearby. They were both struggling on the ground. Ulrich grabbed handfuls of the man's hair and smashed his head off the floor once, twice, three times then let go. The now unconscious man lay like a rag doll as Surt dropped his table, grabbed Ulrich by the wolfskin cloak and hauled him to his feet. He shoved the smaller man in the direction of the door while Einar got to his feet as well. Then they all ran for the door.

Stumbling out into the marketplace, Einar could see some of the fighting had spilled out there. Other market-goers looked on aghast, listening in consternation to the roars of anger, cries of pain, the crack of shattering furniture and smash of breaking pottery that came from the tavern.

For a moment they stood, holding on to each other for support, panting and trying to recover their breath. As the rage drained away from him Einar felt an overwhelming tiredness oppress him as if all the strength was gone from his body. It was not a warm day but he felt chilled to the bone – way beyond anything that the weather could be responsible for.

Ulrich stood, hands on his knees, blinking hard and taking deep breaths as he struggled to bring his own rage under control. After a moment he looked up, his more usual slightly sardonic expression replacing the snarling mask that had been there.

'Come on,' he said. 'Now we need to get off this island.'

34

'Wait!' Einar said. 'We have to get another slave. He knows where the book is.'

'One of the monks from Landévennec is for sale on the slave stall over there,' Israel said, seeing the looks of incomprehension on the faces of the others. 'I was with him in that monastery when it got raided by the vikings. He said he knows where my book was taken but I didn't get time to hear where.'

'Well, we need to get him, then,' Ulrich said.

'What's going on in there?'

The remaining two watchmen, seeing Einar and the others spill out of the tavern, jogged over to them. It was one of them who had spoken.

'It's those fucking Norwegians!' Ulrich said. 'They've kicked off a riot in there over the price of ale. Bersi and your mates are all getting their arses kicked.'

The watchmen looked at each other, then hefted their clubs and ran in through the tavern door.

'Come on,' Ulrich said. 'We don't have much time.'

They crossed the marketplace to Bersi's stall then went straight behind it.

'Allow me to introduce Brother Malo,' Israel said, pointing to the enslaved monk they had seen earlier. 'Hopefully he can lead us to that book.'

'Israel!' the monk said, his face a mask of astonishment. 'You came back!' He held up his arms, showing the chains that bound them. 'In the name of God,' he said. 'Set me free and I will indeed take you to the book.'

'Find something to break those fetters,' Ulrich said and they began rummaging under a table and in some of the trunks full of goods that lay around. Einar found a knife and Surt found an iron bar and they set to work on the monk's chains.

'What are you doing?'

Another voice made them turn around again and they saw some of the market-goers were looking at them.

'The watchmen are gone, lads,' Ulrich said over his shoulder. 'We can take what we want. They're too busy with that fight in the tavern to do anything about it. I'm getting myself another slave.'

The other vikings looked at each other, excited grins breaking out on their faces. Then they started lifting handfuls of goods off the nearest stall. Others quickly joined them and mass looting broke out across the market. The stallholders protested and soon there was as much fighting in the marketplace as there was inside the tavern.

After some work, the fetters burst open and the monk was free.

'What about the others?' he asked.

They looked around at the other slaves in the pen. The pleading looks in their hollow eyes was heartbreaking.

'We don't have time,' Ulrich said. 'Let's go.'

He grabbed the monk's arm and pushed him towards the gate of the market. Ulrich, Surt and Israel started jogging along behind him.

Einar hesitated.

'What are you doing?' Affreca said.

'I can't just leave them,' Einar argued.

He found the end of the chain that the slaves were bound to and shoved the knife blade between one of the links. He twisted it with all his might, which was diminished due to the weakness he felt and the fact that he was not wearing his fighting glove. It was enough, however. There was a crack as the knife blade broke and the chain link shattered at the same time.

'You're all still bound together but you can now at least run away,' Einar said to the slaves. He did not know if they understood his words but the looks of gratitude on their faces showed they could see what was happening.

'Come on,' Affreca said. 'We've wasted enough time.'

They ran after the others, pushing and shoving their way through the milling crowd. Once through the gate of the market, they charged down the steep track that curved around the side of the island and through the now deserted fishing settlement. As they approached the bottom they all slowed to a walk before they came in sight of the group of armed warriors who guarded the gate in the palisade that led back to the beach.

They tried to look as nonchalant as possible as they sidled up to the gate.

'Hello again,' said the same richly dressed man in the coloured woollen cloak and green britches who had greeted them earlier. 'I trust you got what you were looking for?'

'I did,' Ulrich said, delivering a shove to the shoulders of Israel and the monk. 'Two good slaves who will turn a tidy profit in the markets of Dublin.'

'You're leaving?' the man in green britches asked. 'I'm not sure I would recommend that right now.'

'Why not?' Ulrich said.

'The tide's due in soon,' the gate warden said. 'Most people left earlier to give them enough time to get across the strand. If the bore catches you out on the sands it will wash you halfway to Serkland.'

'We'll take our chances,' Ulrich said.

'Don't say you weren't warned,' the man in the green britches said. 'Gunnar, get the weapons that belong to these folk.'

Einar, Surt, Ulrich and Affreca tried to look as relaxed as they could while one of the warriors, presumably Gunnar, went into a nearby hut. Inside their hearts were racing and every nerve was stretched to snapping point as they expected at any moment one of Bersi's men would come running down from the market and the game would be up.

Gunnar returned with their weapons and handed them over.

'You're sure you don't want to wait until the tide has turned again?' the gate warden checked. 'I'm not joking. If you're caught out there when the water returns, you're dead.'

Ulrich shook his head. 'We need to get going,' he said.

'Well it's your funeral,' the gate warden said, swinging open the gate. 'I'd run if I were you.'

Einar and the others filed out through the gate. As they went down the steps that led onto the beach a great crash came from the market on the top of the island. It was followed by the sound of many men's voices raised in anger.

'What's going on up there?' the gate warden said. 'Eigi, maybe you should go up to the market and take a look.'

'Come on,' Ulrich said out of the corner of his mouth. 'He said we should run anyway.'

They set off at a jog across the long stretch of sodden sand between the island of Saint Michael and the mouth of the river where the ship was. They splashed through puddles and skirted around deeper inlets, plodding over the flats or climbing up and over where the swirling tides had moulded the sand into sweeping low berms. It was on the top of one of these that Ulrich stopped and turned around for a moment.

'It looks like someone's coming after us,' he said.

They all turned and saw in the distance behind them that small dark figures were swarming down the steps they had just descended onto the sand. As they watched the distant company started jogging towards Einar and the others.

'Do you think it's Bersi and his men?' Einar said.

'Let's not hang around and find out,' Ulrich said. 'Keep going.'

They set off again, trotting their way through solid and not so firm patches of watery sand. As usual after he had been visited by the divine rage, Einar felt dog-tired and cold to the bone. His legs felt like lead as he struggled to keep them moving across the sand, the softness making every footstep twice the effort it should have been. The wind buffeted their ears while from above them came the mournful cries of seabirds circling in the sky. As before, the wind whipped the sand and sprays of salty water from nearby pools across their faces.

'Wait, please,' Israel called out when they had reached about halfway. 'I need to rest a moment.'

Ulrich did not look pleased but stopped nevertheless. While Israel and the monk bent over, hands on knees, struggling to control their gasping lungs, the Wolf Coats and Surt looked behind them again.

'They're still following us,' Surt said.

'Enough standing around,' Ulrich said. 'Get going.'

They set off again. They ran in a line, the monk on the right, then Israel, Einar, Affreca, Surt and Ulrich. Einar knew he had to dig deep if he was going to make it back to the ship. His best chance to get through the exhausting slog was to let his mind drift onto some topic. He began to chant the *Glymdrápa* in his mind, the task of recalling the lines of the poem about the deeds of Harald Fairhair drawing his attention away from his aching leg muscles and panting lungs.

They reached perhaps three-quarters of the way to the ships when a cry from nearby startled him from his reverie. The monk was shouting in his own tongue. Einar could not understand what he was saying but he recognised the high-pitched note of panic in the man's voice. Israel shouted something as well. Then Einar felt himself drop, sliding downwards in a strange motion, as if the sand beneath his feet had of a sudden turned to liquid. For a moment he thought he had run into a deep pool of water then with a lurch of horror he realised he had sunk nearly to midway up his thighs in wet sand. His initial rapid descent slowed but there was no doubt he was still sinking, the sand sucking him down with a slow, inexorable pull.

He looked around and saw the monk, who had been running ahead of the rest of them, had sunk right up to his waist. The man was shouting now, his face a mask of terror. Israel was almost as deep as Einar, a look of consternation on his face.

'It's the quicksand!' Ulrich said.

35

Einar felt his stomach lurch. He tried to move his legs but they felt like they were surrounded by stone. The effort made the sand around them turn to liquid again and he began to sink faster. He froze, and his downward slide slowed once more. It did not stop, however. He felt panic rising in his chest. His heart was racing as he tried to work out what to do. If he struggled he sank faster but if he didn't move he still sank, only slower.

'We need to help them,' Surt said.

Neither he, Ulrich nor Affreca had been caught. They now stood a little way away, expressions on their faces showing both pity for Einar, Israel and the monk, but also unmistakable relief.

'Stay back,' Ulrich said. 'We don't know where it starts. We could walk straight into it, then we'll all die.'

'Can't we throw them a rope?' Surt said.

'Have you got a rope?' Ulrich asked.

'Of course I don't,' Surt said. He gasped in frustration, an anxious expression of helplessness on his face.

The thought of what a horrific fate awaited only a short time in the future made tears spring to Einar's eyes. He could feel the soft, slimy cold of the sand around his legs and imagined what his last moments would be like as his head was sucked under the surface, the suffocating, wet sand rushing in to fill his mouth, his nose, his eyes.

'Einar!'

Affreca's voice made him turn again.

'I can get you out,' she said. 'But you must listen to me. There isn't much time.'

She began to walk towards him.

'What are you doing?' Einar said. 'You'll get caught too!'

'Trust me,' she said. 'I know what I'm doing. Remember when I told you my father's huntsman used to take me out hunting? He taught me how to shoot a bow, and the craft of the heath and forests?'

'I don't think this is time for reminiscing, princess,' Ulrich said.

The monk had sunk in over his waist now. He was howling, crying and thrashing around.

'Be still,' Ulrich shouted to him. 'You're only making it worse.'

To Einar's further horror he saw Affreca's legs begin to sink as she entered the patch of quicksand. What on earth was she doing?

'There are bogs and meres on the heaths around Dublin,' Affreca said, as if unaware that she was descending with the rest of them. 'Those bogs are as deep and as deadly as these sands if you fall into them. Turcail – the huntsman – taught me what to do if you get sucked into one. Watch.'

She had sunk in above her knees now. Affreca put her arms straight out on either side of her.

'You need to put all your weight on one leg,' she said.

Einar realised her strange stance was so she could balance.

'Then you will be able to move your other leg,' Affreca said. 'The sand only clamps around it when your weight is bearing down on it. Because there is no weight on it now, it will be easier to move. Move it around so the water and sand surrounding it mix and you can free it.'

She did just that. Einar saw the sand around her left leg liquify with the movement and she pulled her leg up and out of the sloppy mire, planting her foot on the surface.

'Now you do it,' she said. 'Hurry. You're almost too deep for this to work.'

Einar closed his eyes and tried the same manoeuvre. Arms outstretched, with all his weight on his right leg, he rotated his left leg, feeling the sand around it loosen as the water flooded in to mix with it. In a few moments it was free enough to pull up and out of the sand.

Amazement and relief flooded his heart. Perhaps he was not going to die after all.

'Now comes the hard part,' Affreca said. 'You have to get the other leg out without getting stuck again. You need to lean on your knee this time. Put all your weight over it.'

She pulled her left foot back so her knee now rested on the surface of the sand. Then she leaned forward and to the left for a few moments, moving her right leg at the same time to free it up a little. Her left knee began sinking into the mire and she rocked back, putting her weight back on the other leg. Then she leaned forward again, this time going right over onto her front. Her trailing leg came up behind her and was free once more.

Einar wasted no time. He placed his free knee on the sand as she had. As his weight moved off his right leg he rotated it as much as he could, feeling the water rushing in to mix and loosen the sand that gripped it. Then he fell forwards onto his face with little grace and his right leg came up, pulling away from the sand with a sucking noise.

'You have to crawl away,' Affreca said. 'If you stand up you just sink again.'

'We can't do that yet,' Einar said. 'We need to help the others as well.'

'Ah! So it's all about spreading your weight across the surface,' the voice of Israel made them both look round to see the scholar had just freed himself using the same technique. 'It makes sense. I believe I read something similar to this in the works of Archimedes. Or was it Pythagoras?'

The monk was not so lucky. The furthest out, he was now sunk almost to his chest. To make matters worse he continued to flail around as he wailed and shouted.

'He's too far down,' Affreca said. 'Once you are in past your waist it's too hard to escape. And the more he thrashes about like that the faster he'll sink.'

'We have to do something,' Einar said. 'We can't just leave him.'

Israel spoke to the monk in his own tongue but it had little effect. The man continued his frantic yelling and desperate thrashing.

Einar began to crawl forwards, moving further out into the patch of quicksand towards the sinking monk. He did his best to spread himself out as much as possible, keeping his belly in contact with the sand so he was half wriggling, half swimming across the surface. This meant his progress was slow. Seeing the monk was almost down to his shoulders, he tried to go faster. However, when he pushed with his arms they sunk straight down. His gut lurched at the thought of that cold, cloying death that awaited below, eager to suck him down as he pulled his hands back out of the mire and resumed his former, slower sliding along, a tiny piece at a time.

Israel was doing the same, though was still talking as he did so. He spoke to the monk who now replied to him. His voice was high-pitched and full of desolation. His face was pure white, a terrified mask.

By the time Einar got close to him he was up to his shoulders. Einar threw out his hand. The monk grabbed it. Einar felt his cold flesh coated by the sliminess of the quicksand. For someone so slight the man's grip was like iron.

Einar hauled with all his might but the monk did not budge. The grip of the sand was so tight that it felt to Einar like he was trying to pull an elk out rather than a slightly built man. To his own consternation Einar felt his own upper body begin to sink into the wet sand. The monk was dragging him down with him.

'I'm sorry,' Einar said, wrenching his hand free of the monk's grasp. 'I can't get you out.'

The monk did not understand his words but the meaning was

clear. His face contorted with dismay and tears burst from his eyes. He tried to grab Einar's hand again but Einar snatched his hand away, knowing they would both die if he held on to him. Guilt and horror seized his heart as he looked at the monk, the sand coming up around his chin now, with his wide, anguished eyes. Einar had killed men in cold blood. He had sneaked up behind them in the night and taken their lives with a stab in the throat, or watched their last breaths as he cut them down face to face in the heart of battle. The fate he now abandoned this monk to was by far the most appalling.

Israel now lay alongside Einar. He began speaking to the monk, using a calm but insistent tone. Whatever he said, it had some effect, as the monk turned his eyes towards Israel. He hesitated, then nodded and said something back. They exchanged a few more words, then Einar saw seawater was running into the monk's mouth. He spat out a mouthful of sand and began to wail again. Einar saw the last of the man's reason leave his eyes as he sank further. Sand and water rushed in to fill his open mouth, silencing his cries with a final short gurgle.

Einar turned away, not wanting to look at the monk's eyes as he slid down the last bit to disappear under the surface but knowing the man's face would haunt him for years to come.

He and Israel crawled back to the others, who reached down and hauled them out of the mire when they got close.

'What did you say to him?' Einar said.

'I told him he was about to meet his God and that he should prepare himself,' Israel said. He once more had his hands on his knees as he panted to recover his breath. 'In my experience there are no unbelievers when death is near.'

Ulrich cursed. 'Now we'll never find that book,' he said. 'Wherever it is went down in the sand with that monk.'

'You're all heart, Ulrich,' Einar said.

'Actually no,' Israel said. 'I asked him where it went as well.'

'And he answered you?' Affreca said, a look of astonishment

on her face. 'I'd have thought he had more pressing matters on his mind.'

'I told him he would save many souls if he told us where it was,' Israel said. 'And God would look favourably on his soul for that when he met him.'

'You don't even believe in the same God as him,' Surt said with a sardonic grunt.

'Actually I do,' the scholar said. 'It's the same one you follow as well, by the way. Anyway, our friend says the book was bought by a bishop and company of monks on their way to Fish Gard. That's along the coast north-west of here.'

Surt looked back towards Michael's Mount. He frowned. 'Those men who were following us,' he said. 'They've gone.'

'What do you mean, "gone"?' Ulrich said.

They all turned and indeed the sand behind them was empty all the way back to the island.

'Do you think quicksand got them too?' Einar said.

'No,' Ulrich said. 'I think they turned and went back.'

'Why?' Affreca said.

Surt looked at all of them in turn. His mouth was open and his eyes wide.

'The tide is coming!' Surt said. 'That can only be it.'

Einar strained his ears. Above the rumble of the wind and the cries of the gulls there was a distant rumbling, booming sound.

36

For a moment Einar was unsure if he had the energy to start running once again. Then the thought of the sea rushing towards them to reclaim the beach spurred him forwards and he was charging as fast as he was able over the sand.

He could still scarcely believe a tide could have the power described by the vikings earlier, though he had once seen huge waves caused on a beach at home in Iceland by a glacier that collapsed into the sea. It had taken everyone by surprise. An old man fishing from the beach was killed just by the power of the wave. His daughter was swept out to sea and drowned. Her son was washed inland and smashed against rocks. The boy never walked properly again. So Einar realised such things were possible, and the fact that Skar had confirmed it when they first heard about the similar tide here reinforced the belief in his mind.

The roaring behind them got ever louder. Einar glanced over his shoulder and saw what looked like a white wall of surf rushing in from beyond the island. Above it hovered a white mist – sand and spray thrown up by the wave as it advanced.

Up ahead the mast of only one ship – their own snekkja – rose above the mouth of the river. The others from earlier, their crews returned from the island in time before the tide returned, must have managed to float themselves and row back up the river.

To his right Affreca pounded across the sand. Beyond her was Ulrich and then Surt. The scholar was trailing behind all of them.

While the roar of the approaching tide spurred Einar on to sprint ever faster, a nagging terror that he could run straight into another patch of quicksand also gnawed at his already taut nerves.

He glanced over his shoulder again. The water was rushing ever closer. It's rumbling now drowned the cries of the seabirds and the roaring of the wind. All Einar could hear was the thumping of his feet on the sand and the sound of his own heavy breathing in his chest.

He looked at Israel and saw the exhaustion and concern on the scholar's face. He was dropping ever further behind. Einar's mind was in turmoil. If the little man was lost in the water then their whole enterprise was over. If he waited for him, however, he too could be lost.

'Not far now,' he shouted. 'Keep going.'

He was right. They had almost made it to the end of the beach.

Then Einar saw water flooding all around him. He turned around and saw the wave had caught up with them. Behind him Israel's eyes widened and he cried out as a wall of water as tall as him engulfed him. Then it rushed over Einar.

He felt as though a huge hand had picked him up. He was no longer running but rising up, his feet lifting off the sand. He gasped at the shock of the cold water that enveloped him all around. He felt the wave propelling him forwards. The salt water stung his eyes and turned everything around him to a green blur. Then he was tumbling, head over heels, arms and legs flailing. He had no idea which way was up and which way was down.

His mind reeled with panic. If there were any rocks or stones ahead he would be smashed into them like a rag and his bones would shatter like dry twigs. He tried to remember what the shoreline was like where they had left their ship but all he could recall was sand.

Einar's chest burned. He had not had time to take a decent breath before the wave took him. He could not stop himself breathing out, unleashing a torrent of bubbles into the surrounding water. He just managed to control himself and stop the instinctive intake of breath that followed. He clamped his lips shut again, knowing that sucking in a lungful of salt water would lead straight to death.

He had to do something. If he let himself be pushed along by the wave, sooner or later it would drive him into something hard, injuring, crippling or killing him. If he did not get air he would drown.

Einar kicked with his legs and dug at the water with his arms. Within a moment he had controlled his wild tumbling. His hands touched sand and he knew he was near the bottom and which way was up and down.

Lungs burning for air, he kicked his legs and beat his arms, driving himself towards the surface. His head burst into the air and he gasped in desperate mouthfuls. For a few moments he allowed the wave of the tidal bore to carry him along as he fought to control his frantic breathing and assess where he was. His ears pounded with a wild sound that he realised was his own heart.

As his breathing calmed down Einar looked around him, seeing that he had been carried right into the mouth of the river. Just up ahead the Wolf Coats' longship was lifted by the wave. Its stern rose up into the air as the water floated the vessel.

For a moment Einar's panic returned, thinking he was going to be smashed into the ship. Then he realised it too was being driven along ahead of him. As they had run aground earlier there had been no need to throw down an anchor stone that would now have held it stationary.

On the stern he saw Roan, for once his implacable expression replaced by consternation as he battled with the steering oar to gain some control of his ship. Skar, Wulfhelm, Starkad, Kari and Sigurd were all gathered at the stern, their eyes wide with surprise at the tide that had returned with such speed and power.

As they moved further into the river mouth, Einar felt himself slowing down. The incoming water of the sea was now hitting the outgoing flow of the river, which was diminishing its momentum a little. His progress became less hectic. He saw Skar pointing at him and shouting something to the others. Then Starkad threw a rope into the water towards Einar.

Catching it, he let the others pull him in. He bumped against the hull of the snekkja, then he felt the hands of the others grabbing him and hauling him up out of the water and into the ship to dump him without ceremony onto the deck. Einar lay on his front, water streaming out of his clothes, his hair, his beard, utterly exhausted and panting for breath.

He was aware of the others shouting and the sound of banging on the sides of the ship, then Israel the scholar was hauled by his legs from the water and dumped on the deck beside Einar. Einar rolled onto his back and saw Ulrich clambering over the side of the ship. Then Surt was heaved on board by Skar and Wulfhelm. Starkad and Kari were pulling the rope in hand over hand. In a few moments Affreca appeared on the end of it above the side of the ship. Skar grabbed her and lifted her on board. He turned to the others, the dribbling Affreca cradled across his huge arms.

'Looks like I got the catch of the day, lads,' Skar said, grinning.

Affreca cuffed him around the head and he set her down on the deck.

37

Ulrich crouched on his haunches, water streaming all around him like the others. He was silent, staring at the deck, his breathing heavy. As the water running from him slowed from a torrent to a dribble, he rose to his feet.

'To the oars,' Ulrich said. 'We need to get out of here.'

Einar, still lying on his back, let out a loud groan. He knew Ulrich was right, however. The chaos on the island may have already abated and the Danes who ran the market there might already be launching ships to search for them. He took a deep breath, clenched his teeth and searched his heart for whatever last scraps of strength remained there.

'You heard Ulrich, you lazy dogs,' Skar said. 'Get to the oar benches.'

With a heavy sigh Einar rolled onto his side, pushed himself up onto all fours, then rose to his feet. With all his muscles feeling as heavy and useless as if they were made of rock, he staggered over to his place beside Skar and slumped down onto the bench. As if in a dream he saw the others slide their oars into position. He laid his hands on his own.

Skar began singing a rowing song. It was a rhythmic chant, marked by regular grunted responses from the rest of the crew and designed to get them all pulling on the oars in unison. Soon the longship was sliding up the river. Einar was so tired he felt like he was rowing in his sleep. The endless training Skar and Ulrich had made him and the others do, however, meant he kept going without thought, oblivious now he was moving again, to the pain in his muscles and the tiredness in his bones.

Later, as darkness fell, Ulrich judged they had got away and allowed Roan to run the ship into a thick swathe of bulrushes at the side of the river. The Wolf Coats rolled out their leather sleeping bags on the deck and began to prepare to get some rest. Skar got the fire on the cooking stone near the mast going and soon had water boiling and dried fish and beef seething in a pot. The rest of the crew began gathering around the fire to eat something before sleep.

At first Einar thought he was too tired to eat but then heard the rumble of his stomach and knew if he went straight to sleep hunger would only waken him a short time later anyway. He joined the others.

'Ulrich told me you did well on that island, lad,' Skar said to Einar as he sat down, cross-legged on the deck. 'Good work.'

Ulrich still stood at the steering oar talking to Roan at the stern of the ship.

Einar grunted. 'Not that he would ever say that to me.'

'What do you expect him to do, lad?' Skar said with a laugh. 'Pat you on the back? Embrace you? Come on. It's Ulrich.'

'Simply recognising it was me who found Israel, and found the monk, would suffice,' Einar said. 'It was my rage that battered a way out of that tavern. Just before that he said I was useless. He actually slapped me! I was furious.'

Skar shot a sideways, bemused glance in Einar's direction. 'Looks like he did just the right thing,' he said.

Einar's jaw dropped open a little. 'You mean he made me...' He trailed off, noticing Ulrich and Roan were coming over to join the rest of them.

'Do you know where this Fish Gard is?' Ulrich said to Israel. 'The place where your friend said the book was taken?'

'It's further up the coast,' Roan said before Israel could answer. 'There's a big fortress up on the headland there. I've sailed by it a few times.'

'It's the fortress of the counts of Rouen,' Israel said.

'You mean the Jarls of Rúðu,' Ulrich said.

'It depends which tongue you speak, I suppose,' Israel said with a shrug.

'So that is Jarl Vilhjálmr's fortress,' Ulrich said. 'It's not at Rúðu?'

Roan shook his head. 'They are some distance apart,' the skipper said. 'The fortress is beside the sea. Rouen – Rúðu – is some way inland, going upriver.'

'Well it's a pity Jarl Vilhjálmr's not there,' Ulrich said, making an annoyed face. 'We could have got all of Aethelstan's tasks completed in one place.'

'Poor Brother Malo – the monk who sank in the sand,' Israel began, 'said that the bishop of Bayeux himself came to the market and bought the book at the orders of Jarl Vilhjálmr. I'm sure they paid a pretty price for it. He was then to take it to Fish Gard.'

'A bishop is an important Christian wizard, right?' Ulrich said. Israel nodded. 'I wonder what he is doing visiting a jarl's fortress.'

'And why he's taking a Christian book there?' Skar said.

'What's even more interesting,' Israel said, knitting his fingers together before his chest. 'Is that Brother Malo said it was a "farewell pay-off to his whore".'

Most of the men round the fire smirked. Starkad gave a little cheer.

'So the jarl has been dallying away from his wife, eh?' Ulrich said. 'Maybe he is still a Norseman after all.'

'Maybe they don't call him Langaspjót – Longsword – for nothing,' Kari said with a giggle.

'I'm not sure I like the sound of all this, Ulrich,' Sigurd said. 'Getting mixed up in marriage affairs of powerful people is never a good thing.'

'What do you mean Vilhjálmr's not there?' Skar asked.

'I learned on the island that the jarl is besieged by rebels in the city of Rúðu,' Ulrich said. 'He's outnumbered and the city could fall at any time.'

'What's the point in us delivering Aethelstan's message to

him if he's no longer jarl here?' Einar said. 'Isn't that the whole point of us being here? To make sure the Frankish prince has the support of the most powerful men in this realm? If Vilhjálmr is about to lose this siege then he's no longer that.'

'Why do we care?' Ulrich said. 'We're just being paid to deliver a message and find a book. Who cares who wins or loses?'

'Or who dies along the way?' Israel said.

'As long as it's not one of us, eh?' Skar said with a wink.

'So what's more important?' Einar said. 'The book or the message? We can't do both.'

'We could if we split up,' Affreca said. 'Half of us go to get the book and the other half go to Rúðu. That way we could kill two birds with one stone.'

'Like Daedalus,' Israel said.

'Who?' Einar said.

'From the Greek legend,' Israel said. 'Daedalus and Icarus. They flew too close to the sun.'

Surt chuckled, pointing at the mystified expressions of those around the fire.

'You're wasting your time with these barbarians, my friend,' he said.

'Besides...' Ulrich shot a sideways glance at Affreca '...if we split up we'd be killing two birds with two stones.'

He rose to his feet.

'No,' he said. 'We stick together. We sail for Fish Gard to get that book. I'm curious to find out just what the Jarl of Rúðu has been up to. Then, if he's still alive, we shall go and visit him in person.'

38

Skar rolled over onto his back and looked up at the sky.

'If I was Jarl Vilhjálmr,' he said, 'I'd much rather be tucked away behind the defences of a fortress like that than the rickety walls of some town.'

'It's certainly formidable,' Ulrich said.

Ulrich had allowed the crew of the snekkja to sleep but they did not get the whole night. He woke them while it was still dark and announced that they were going back the way they had come. Despite their groans of protest, the Wolf Coats and the others had taken their places on the oar benches and the ship was once more underway towards the sea. The wind was behind them and they were rowing downstream so their progress was swift and they made it back to the coast before dawn. The tide was as high as when they had left, and Roan was able to steer the ship straight out into the bay.

'I haven't lost my touch,' Roan said, pointing towards the setting moon in the lightening sky. 'I knew the second high tide of the day should be around now.'

Ulrich's plan was that they would sail around the edge of the bay, giving the island mountain of Michael a wide berth, just in case there were folk there looking out for them.

Then, as an unseen sun crept over the horizon obscured by grey clouds, they had sailed north-east up the coast.

The grey-green sea was choppy and the ship rolled and yawed past countryside that was green despite the season and lined by tall cliffs of stone so white they appeared to glow regardless of the gloomy weather.

They rounded headlands and passed sandy beaches and coastal settlements, travelling all day. A little while after they crossed a wide estuary that Roan said led to the town of Rúðu, the skipper announced that he believed they were almost there.

Ulrich ordered the ship beached. He had no intention to sail straight up to a fortress where he had no idea how they would be received, so wanted to take a look at Fish Gard before getting too close to it.

It was a tactic Ulrich drummed into all of them and Einar knew it well.

Watch first, then strike, the little leader of the Wolf Coats would often say. *Never attack until you know as much as you can about your enemy. When the time comes to attack, you should know him better than you do your own wife.*

Leaving Roan with the ship beached on a lonely strand of yellow sand, the Wolf Coats, Surt, Wulfhelm and Israel set off on foot along the coast. Crossing the next headland they came upon another inlet, this one a small, natural harbour at the mouth of a river. Behind it rose a long, low bluff like the back of a huge whale, breaching the surface of the sea. Built near the top of the rise was a fortress.

It was an elongated oval in shape and dominated the headland. The whole fortress was ringed by a ditch flooded with water and behind that rose a high bank surmounted by a wooden palisade of sharpened stakes. There was a platform behind the palisade patrolled by warriors, the sun glinting on the iron of their helmets, spear points and the mail rings of their brynjas. There were a lot of them. From their position they could stab downwards at anyone trying to scale the defences below. There was one stout gate with a wooden tower above it. Behind the first ring of defences there was a second, and another bank ran in a tighter ring around the interior of the fortress. It too was topped by a palisade guarded by warriors. The thatch of several buildings, including what looked like a feasting hall, could just be seen above the inner wall. Smoke from cooking fires drifted into the air and formed a blue-grey haze above the whole fortress. For one hundred paces around the ditch all undergrowth, bushes, trees and rocks had been cleared away, allowing no cover or hiding place for anyone trying to sneak up to the walls unseen.

'The jarl certainly knows what he is doing,' Skar said. 'Or at least whoever built this place knew how to keep unwanted guests out.'

Undeterred, Ulrich had led them in a wide half-circuit of the fortress, staying far enough away that they would not be spotted but close enough to see if there might be any points of ingress or anything they could take advantage of to get inside the walls. None were obvious.

'What do we do now?' Skar said.

'We find a position where we can watch the place,' Ulrich said. 'Then we wait until nightfall. We can get closer in the dark.'

Around the back of the fortress they found a little lake formed by a bend in the river estuary that had silted up. On the far side of that was an area of bulrushes and undergrowth with a small bowl-shaped depression in the earth that they could hide themselves in. The company settled down there and waited for the sun to set.

The darkness did not bring what they wanted, however. At twilight, warriors streamed out of the heavily guarded gate carrying burning torches. They used these to set alight beacons, watchfires and braziers that had been set around the cleared area that surrounded Fish Gard. The flames chased away all darkness within a hundred paces of the walls. Anyone who tried to approach would be spotted straight away. As well as the fires, companies of warriors on watch duty patrolled the lighted area beyond the ramparts.

'He really does know what he's doing,' Ulrich said with a sigh. 'I couldn't have organised the defences better myself.'

'The jarl must be expecting this place to be attacked,' Skar said. 'Otherwise he wouldn't have warriors on alert like this.'

'He'd be a fool not to,' Ulrich said. 'His realm is in rebellion. It's only a matter of time before someone attacks here.'

'What now?' Starkad said.

'Now, we get some sleep,' Ulrich said. 'You take the first watch while we rest up in the undergrowth. Skar will take the next watch, then Kari, Sigurd, Wulfhelm, Surt, Einar then Affreca.'

'What am I watching for?' Starkad said, a puzzled look on his face.

'Keep an eye on what's going on around that fortress,' Ulrich said. 'Who comes out and who goes in and when. Just in case any weak points come to light.'

Einar did not need telling more than once. He pulled together a makeshift bed of bracken and ferns, pulled the hood of his wolfskin cloak up, wrapped the rest of the pelt around his body and fell fast asleep.

Later, when Surt poked him awake, Einar was in the midst of a rather pleasant dream where he was wrapped in warm wool beside the hearth in his mother's farmstead back in Iceland.

'Your turn on watch,' Surt said in a hissed whisper, dispelling Einar's reverie in a moment. With a sigh he dragged himself out of the warm comfort of the undergrowth into the damp chill of the night air.

Einar climbed up out of the depression the Wolf Coats slept in then crawled forwards through the bracken and bulrushes until he had a clear view of the gard. Then he settled down to watch.

It soon became clear that staying awake would be a struggle. Some of the warriors on guard wandered back and forth in the firelight but apart from that nothing happened beyond some ducks splashing across the little pond that lay not far away, between him and the ramparts, surrounded by a small ring of trees.

The night was dark and the sky above black. No stars or moon were visible. Now and again warriors on watch outside the ramparts changed positions but apart from that nothing happened. The most exciting event was a fox barking in the small copse of trees that surrounded the little lake that lay between Einar's position and the fortress. His eyelids felt heavy. The thought of what Ulrich and the others would do to him if he was caught asleep while on watch stopped him from nodding off.

The braziers and watchfires outside the rampart burned low, almost low enough that Einar wondered if he might be able to scurry further forward in the shadows that were forming. Then he reasoned that even if he did get closer, what would he be able to accomplish alone? So he stayed where he was, though resolving to tell Ulrich about this fact in case it could help his leader form a plan.

It looked like it would not be long before dawn arrived. The sky was lightening and a mist rose from the little lake. The beacons and bonfires had almost burned out and with the arrival of the sun the warriors patrolling outside retreated back through the gate.

'Lucky bastards,' he whispered to himself, imagining the warmth and food that waited for them inside.

Time passed. The sun rose a little higher and the mist hanging above the small lake and the moist ground grew thicker.

Movement caught Einar's eye and he thought for a moment perhaps he had indeed fallen asleep again and was dreaming. Through the mist three women in long light blue hooded cloaks were walking. They approached the lake like wraiths, ghosts that had risen with the fog of the morning. A fourth woman walked behind them. She too wore a hooded cloak but hers was a very dark blue or perhaps black. She bore a staff that looked like a spinning distaff with an open elongated orb at one end, but the colour of it showed it was made of metal.

Einar blinked then narrowed his eyes. It looked like there were tiny points of light that sparkled and shimmered amid the material of her robe. Surely this was a dream? His mind knew that if Ulrich found him asleep on watch he would be in real trouble, but there was something so captivating and strange about the scene he watched that he felt he had to continue a little longer rather than force himself awake.

The three women in light blue cloaks pulled their hoods down, releasing torrents of long blonde hair that fell around their shoulders. They then unclasped and took off their cloaks. Einar's mouth dropped open as he saw they were totally naked beneath. His eyes fell on their full breasts, white bellies and rounded hips, and he saw these women were both young and beautiful.

This convinced him he must be dreaming. He bit his lip, but the pain he felt and the coppery taste were very real. He only had moments to gaze at them, however, as to his disappointment they waded into the pond and soon were up to their necks in the water.

He glanced to the ramparts of the fort and realised that the copse of trees around the pond hid the women from view of those in the fortress. The woman in the dark cloak dropped her cloak and he saw that she too was naked. Unlike the others her hair was grey, her breasts shrunken and drooping and her belly and thighs scrawny. She began to follow the others into the water. The other women laughed as they splashed around.

'So this is why you didn't wake me!'

Einar heard Affreca's voice in his ear. In his fascination with what was going on at the lake he had not noticed her crawling through the rushes to join him. It was no more than a hissed whisper but her disapproval was evident.

'What are you doing? Spying on an old woman washing herself!' she said. 'You're disgusting.'

'It's not just an old woman,' Einar said, turning on his side to look at Affreca. 'There are three beautiful young women there too.'

The look on Affreca's face told Einar he had not made anything better with these words.

'And she is a *volva*, too,' Affreca said, lying down beside Einar. 'Shame on you for looking on the naked body of a wise woman!'

'Ulrich told me to watch. So I watched,' Einar said. 'Besides, how do you know she is a witch?'

'That metal wand she put down before she took her cloak off shows she is one,' Affreca said. 'Wait.'

She laid a hand on Einar's forearm. He could tell straight away from the strength of her grip and the tone of her whisper that something was up. With her other hand she was pointing towards the other side of the trees that ringed the lake. Einar looked and saw there were a group of twelve men slinking through the trees towards the water. They wore leather jerkins, helmets and carried unsheathed swords and knives.

'This doesn't look good,' Einar said. 'Who do you think they are?'

'I don't know,' Affreca said. 'I'm going to get the others.'

'Shouldn't we warn those women?' Einar said.

'And what would the two of us do against ten?' Affreca said. 'Have you learned nothing from Ulrich?'

She crawled off. Einar turned his eyes back to the lake. To his dismay he saw the men surge forward, bursting through the undergrowth around the lake. The women in the water screamed and began to wade out of the water. They did not get far before the armed men fell upon them. Laughing, they hauled the women out of the lake. The women did not share their enthusiasm. Their screams grew hysterical and they kicked and hit as the men dragged them onto the muddy shore.

'How dare you do this!' the older woman cried. She spoke in the Norse tongue, though with the local accent. 'How dare you look upon me naked. I am a vǫlva. I am blessed by the gods.'

'Shut up, heathen bitch,' one of the armed men said. 'The bishop sent us to stop your meddling.'

'Can't we have a little fun first?' another of the men said. 'These young three are nice.'

'I don't see why not?' the other man, who appeared to be their leader, said. 'It would be a shame to waste such pretty flesh while it was still warm.'

'Help, help,' the older woman shouted towards the ramparts of the gard.

'They won't help you,' the leader of the attackers said. 'The bishop paid the watch to not be around while we dealt with you. Right, lads: let's kill the old trout then get on with enjoying the young ones.'

Einar realised that if he was going to do anything about this situation then he would need to do it now. He glanced over his shoulder. There was no sign of Affreca or the others. So whatever he was going to do, he would have to do it on his own.

39

Einar pulled on his fighting glove, fastening its laces with the help of his teeth.

'These are holy virgins,' the vǫlva screeched. 'They are not for your pleasure. You must not defile their flesh.'

'They're heathen whores,' the black-bearded warrior said. 'And we'll defile them whatever way we please.'

Another of the warriors threw one of the younger women to the ground and began fumbling to undo the laces that tied up his britches.

'I will curse you if any of you go any further,' the wise woman said through gritted teeth. 'Your pricks will shrivel and drop off. Your women will be barren.'

The other warriors froze at her words but their leader drew a long-bladed knife and walked towards her.

'Don't worry, lads,' he said, grinning. 'I'll kill her before she chants any more of her spells.'

The naked woman who had been thrown to the ground, now free of her captor's grasp, rolled over and scrambled to her feet. She grabbed the vǫlva's fallen staff and swung it. It connected with the side of the black-bearded warrior's head with a resounding clang. He staggered sideways then turned around, a look of surprise on his face. A bright red cut was open across his left cheekbone where the metal bulb at the end of the vǫlva's wand had split his skin.

'You bitch,' he said in a growl, his lips twisting into a snarl. He drove his knife into the woman's naked belly. She screamed as he ripped the blade upwards, unleashing her guts that curled out like an obscene snake to tumble onto the ground. Einar winced as he watched the woman drop to her knees, her hands grasping her own innards in a forlorn attempt to stop them spilling out. With a loud groan she then fell sideways and died.

Before he knew it Einar was on his feet and pounding towards the lake. He had no clear plan what he was going to do but could not watch what was happening any longer. Hoping that the others were not far behind him, Einar slid the metal hooks at the bottom of his fighting glove over the bottom of the hilt of his sword and grasped the rest with the remaining fingers of his right hand. Then he ripped the blade from its sheath.

The men before him were too engaged with preparing to molest the women, and Einar made it to the lakeshore before they noticed him. The vǫlva did see him, however. The black-bearded warrior who was about to run his sword through her saw the expression on her face change and turned around to see what she was looking at. He was still half turned when Einar, now holding his sword two-handed, brought his blade down. The warrior's reactions were fast and out of instinct he moved his head aside. Einar had aimed at the top of the man's crown but caught him at the base of his neck instead. The pure steel of his Inglerii sword bit through the black-bearded man's shoulder. He felt the blade buck and jolt as it skidded down the man's backbone then halt midway down his chest, embedded in his ribs. Blood welled up around the huge wound and gushed down the man's chest. His eyes widened in shock and his mouth opened and closed without any sound coming out.

Einar raised his foot and kicked him backwards, pulling his sword out of the man's chest. He collapsed with a gurgling sound as his companions let out cries of anger and surprise.

Two of them overcame their shock faster than the others and ran at Einar. Both had swords.

Skar had taught Einar how to confront two opponents but usually it was with the aid of a shield, protecting himself from the blow of one attacker while striking at the second. Now he did not have that luxury.

Einar spotted the vǫlva's iron distaff lying near his feet. He dipped and grabbed it just before the two warriors got within striking distance. He was still rising back to his feet when the man on his left swung his sword at him. Einar swept the witch's wand up above his head. With a clang it met the descending blade and halted it. Almost at the same time, Einar lunged forward, closing the gap between himself and the other attacker. The man, who had been expecting the outnumbered Einar to retreat rather than advance, was taken by surprise. He was still raising his own sword to strike when Einar drove his blade into the man's throat. The broad-bladed sword was designed for slashing rather than stabbing, but there was enough of a point when combined with the power of Einar's thrust to open the warrior's neck. He made a strange wheezing sound as his windpipe was cut then filled with the blood that gushed into it and spilled down his chest. He dropped his sword and both hands went to his throat to try to stem the bleeding.

The man was either in the process of dying or very badly wounded. Either way he was out of the fight. Einar turned to his companion who was raising his sword for another attack. Einar kicked him in the groin and he doubled over, attack abandoned. Then Einar clubbed him across the back of the skull with the iron distaff and he went down like a scarecrow when the rope that holds it to a cross pole is cut.

Three down, Einar thought.

Before he could start feeling smug, however, Einar saw that the advantage surprise had given him was now over. The remaining nine warriors had regrouped, formed a line and were advancing towards him in a measured pace. At any moment, he knew, they would all rush forward at once, overwhelming him with their numbers.

Einar glanced over his shoulder back the way he had come.

There was no one behind him. Where were Affreca and the others?

The two remaining young women, still naked, jumped on the backs of two of the advancing men. Screeching like cats they clawed at the men's eyes and faces. The warriors swore, dipped and thrashed to try to dislodge the women on their backs but they clung on, no doubt well aware that if they fell to the ground a swift death would follow.

'Give me that!' the vǫlva said, snatching her distaff from Einar's grasp. He had not been expecting this and she had it off him before he could close his fingers tighter.

'Stop where you are,' the witch said, holding the distaff high in the air and pointing a long, bony finger in the direction of the line of armed men. 'Do not come closer or I will call down the curses of the Aesir on you. You will feel the wrath of the dísir and the Norns. The *landvaettir* will blight you.'

The seven men not struggling with women hesitated, exchanging nervous looks. Then one said: 'The bishop warned us of this. He said we should pay no heed to heathen magic. It cannot harm Christians like us. All we need to do is put our faith in the Lord.'

Their expressions became resolute once more and they advanced again. Though two of them still looked a little dubious, making Einar wonder just how strong their faith in their God really was.

Regardless of the quality of their belief, however, Einar was in trouble and he knew it. There were still seven men against him, all with metal and leather body protection, swords, and – judging from the way they advanced in line – had been trained in battle tactics. And when they'd dealt with the naked women attacking them, they would add two more to their number.

The warrior on the right of the line let out a strangled cry. He staggered sideways, an arrow transfixing his throat from left to right.

Einar saw a flurry of movement from the corner of his eye. Ulrich, Skar and the others rushed in from the left and just behind the advancing warriors. Einar realised that was why they'd only arrived now. They had taken the time to go round the lake and outflank his opponents. They attacked in silence but with deadly, unswerving intent.

Starkad and Wulfhelm cut down the two warriors who still struggled with the women on their backs. Ulrich ran up behind another warrior, snaked an arm around his throat, pulling his head back as he drove his sword into the man's back. The blade erupted from his chest in a spray of crimson.

Skar swung his axe in a great blow aimed at cutting the next warrior along in two. He spotted the attack at the last moment and tried to swerve away from the descending blade. He almost got away, but Skar's axe struck him halfway down his left thigh. With a sound that reminded Einar of his mother chopping an unripe cabbage, the heavy crescent-shaped blade chopped the man's leg in two. The bottom of the leg dropped to the ground. Off balance all of a sudden, the man spun round in a semicircle, hot, iron-smelling blood spraying from his severed thigh to splatter those around him. Skar kicked his remaining leg from under him then finished him with a chop to the chest.

Surt ran the next man along through as he was still turning to meet the new threat. The seventh man had time to turn and run but did not get more than three steps before Sigurd's blade cut through his backbone.

The last two remaining warriors, seeing their comrades cut down in moments, decided the better part of valour was to flee. They turned and ran off.

It was all over in moments and the strong metallic smell of spilled blood filled the air. Affreca came loping over to join them, another arrow notched to her bow but the two running men had already dodged through the trees beside the lake. She sent an arrow after them anyway but it thudded harmlessly into a tree trunk.

'Let them go,' Skar said. 'We don't know how many more of them could be waiting beyond the trees.'

The remaining seven men were all dead and the only sound that had marked their passing had been their short, agonised shouts as they died. Then an anguished wail came from the two naked women. They were crouching beside their murdered companion who lay in a pile of her own guts on the lakeshore.

'What did you think you were doing?' Ulrich said, glaring at Einar. His voice was angry and his lip curled. 'One man against twelve? Who do you think you are? Sinfjotli Volsung?'

Einar shrugged.

'I had to do something,' he said. 'I couldn't just let them kill these women.'

'Who are these women to us?' Ulrich said. 'Have you learned nothing from me?'

Skar was looking up at the ramparts of the fort.

'Someone is bound to come soon,' Skar said. 'With all that shouting and screaming they'll come out to see what's going on. What do we do, Ulrich?'

'Don't worry about them,' the old wise woman said. Her voice was laden with bitterness. 'You heard that one with the black beard: the bishop paid him and his friends to kill us. He will have paid whoever was on guard at this time to look the other way as well. No one will be riding to our rescue from in there. The gods protect me. They gave your young friend here the courage to come and save us. For that I thank Odin.'

Ulrich pursed his lips and shot a sidewise glance at Einar.

'Perhaps I will never understand the ways of the All Father,' he said, though in a tone of voice that matched the sceptical expression on his face. He turned to the wise woman. 'You are a vǫlva?'

'I am.' She clasped her hands before her, seemingly oblivious to the crying of the two other women over their dead friend. 'And these are my handmaidens. Sprota sent for us to help in her pains of labour. She knows the old ways. She respects the gods.

She knows the Norns should be called down at the birth of a noble child.'

'Sprota?' Skar said.

'The jarl's wife,' the vǫlva said, looking at Skar like she wondered if only half his mind worked. Ulrich and Skar exchanged glances. 'She is heavy with child. It will be born soon. Perhaps today. Then the jarl will have to choose.'

She let out a cackle that sent shivers running down Einar's spine.

'*That's* why the bishop is so scared,' she continued. 'Sprota honours the gods. That's why she sent for me. Men are strange when a child is born to them. They become soft. When this child is born Jarl Vilhjálmr won't be able to hide Sprota away anymore. And if it is a son...' She waggled her finger and chuckled to herself in evident delight.

'Who is this bishop?' Einar said.

'The bishop of Bayeux, he is a wizened-up half-man. A Christian wizard. An important one,' the vǫlva said, scowling once more. 'He is jealous that the lady Sprota sent for me and worried of the influence I have on her. And through her, the jarl. He knows my handmaidens and I come here every morning to wash and sent those men to get rid of us.'

'But these men were Danes,' Einar said, looking at the corpses around him. 'They spoke our tongue. Yet they would have killed a vǫlva? They dared kill one of her handmaidens?'

'There are many here like them,' the witch said, spittle flying from the gaps in her teeth. 'Danes and Norwegians who have become corrupted by the wine and the sunshine here. Men who so quickly forget the gods, the customs, sometimes even the tongue of their forefathers. They dress like Franks, they get their hair cut like them, they talk like them. It disgusts me.'

'And this bishop is one of them?'

'Aye,' the vǫlva said. 'And he has his claws in the jarl. He whispers in Vilhjálmr's ear, twisting his heart and making him forget the gods. All for promises of gold and power. *Forsake*

Odin. Love Jesus, he says. *Then all the other kings and dukes of Francia will love you. They will be on your side. They will ride to support you and keep you in power. You will rule in his name and be as rich and powerful as Charlemagne. Or Aethelstan, the King Beyond the Sea.'*

She spat. 'What does Odin care for power? All he judges us on is the courage in our hearts. *That* is enough for Old One-Eye.' She ran both hands down the front of her cloak, head bowed, as if trying to gather her thoughts. 'But we must be away,' she said. 'Back to Fish Gard. The lady Sprota's time of birth draws near.'

'Aren't you worried this bishop will try and kill you again once you're back inside?' Einar said.

'He is a coward,' the vǫlva said, shaking her head. 'And he lacks power, as yet. The jarl has still to decide if he will stay a Norseman or become a Frank, which is what the bishop wants. The bishop may try to murder us when the opportunity arises like this morning, but he dare not try something in plain sight. Not yet. Besides, Lady Sprota needs us.'

Her face fell. It was as if she had all of a sudden remembered something. Her gaze fell on her dead handmaiden.

'Perhaps the bishop has had his way after all,' she said in a much quieter tone. 'There must be three maidens at a birth. To match the three Norns. I now have only two.'

Ulrich looked at Einar and grinned. To Einar he looked more like a wolf than the pelt he wore around his neck.

'Perhaps the gods actually did devise this situation after all,' Ulrich said. 'It just so happens we have a maiden among my crew who is also a wise woman. Affreca here was spae-wife to an Irish witch for many years. She can take the place of your fallen companion.'

He pointed to Affreca. Affreca frowned.

The vǫlva peered at Affreca.

'Do you know the *Varðlokkur?*' she asked. 'Can you chant the spells to bring the spirits?'

Affreca frowned. 'Of course I know the Varðlokkur,' she said, 'but—'

'Very well,' the wise woman said. 'Then you can wear her robes.' She pointed to the dead woman. 'Luckily she took them off before she was killed,' she said. 'There is no blood on them. The men in the fort won't know the difference between you and her. Come on.'

She clapped her hands. 'No more dawdling. The lady Sprota could already be in labour!'

'Ulrich,' Affreca said from the corner of her mouth. 'A word, please.'

They moved a little bit further away. Einar joined them.

'What are you up to?' Affreca said through clenched teeth. She whispered so the witch would not hear.

'What are you worried about?' Ulrich said. 'Perhaps you aren't a maiden?'

Affreca glanced at Einar then glared at Ulrich.

'I'm not a spae-wife!' she said. 'I don't know *galdr*. I really don't know *seiðr*. I am not a witch like them.'

'But you are a woman,' Ulrich said in a quiet voice. 'And that is what this vǫlva needs right now. And we need a way into that fortress. You can get in there and find that book we need, or at least find a way we can get in. Odin has given us this opportunity; let's not waste it.'

Affreca sighed and looked away. Then she returned her gaze to Ulrich.

'All right,' she said. 'I know the Varðlokkur. I sang it as a child. But what about when she finds out I don't know the rest of their spells?'

'Have I taught you nothing?' Ulrich asked. 'Adapt to the situation you find yourself in. Use your instincts and your wits. But whatever you do, find that book so we can all get paid.'

40

If Affreca was supposed to be a witch she could not be dressed like a viking. She pulled off her brynja and the leather jerkin she wore beneath. She put on the long white robe of the dead handmaiden. Then she handed her bow and arrow bag to Einar.

He flexed the string, feeling the incredible pent-up power in the combined wood and bone of the Finnish weapon.

'It's not a toy,' Affreca said, with a reproachful look. 'Look after it. It means more to me than a child.'

'Good luck,' he said. For a moment they met gazes, then she nodded and pulled up the hood of her white robe.

'What about our sister, Gormla?' one of the handmaidens asked. 'We cannot just leave her lying here like a butchered sow. She was a priestess of the gods.'

'We will make sure she has a proper burial,' Ulrich said. 'Who better to sing a spae-wife of the Aesir to her rest than a company of Odin's own wolf warriors?'

The others seemed mollified by this.

'We will take her away now,' Ulrich said. 'No matter what the vǫlva thinks about this bishop, sooner or later someone will come out of that fortress and when they find these bodies I don't want them realising there is now one witch too many.'

The other two handmaidens got dressed as well. The faces of the men who stood around them changed from wolf-like leers to disappointment.

Then the little company parted ways. The Wolf Coats took a hooded cloak from one of the dead men and wrapped the dead handmaiden in it. Then they lugged the corpse off through the bulrushes and away to a safe distance from the fortress where they could watch without being discovered.

'Come. We shall go inside to help the lady Sprota in her pangs,' the vǫlva said. 'My name is Heimlaug, by the way. And these two are Thordis and Freydis.'

The vǫlva walked towards the gate of the fortress. Affreca fell in with the other two handmaidens who walked a short distance behind her.

They came to the stout wooden gate and Heimlaug rapped on it with her metal staff. Faces appeared on the rampart above, warriors looking down to see who had come. Recognising the vǫlva, one of them nodded and the sound of rattling bolts heralded the opening of the gate. They walked in and Affreca saw there was indeed a double rampart. Beyond the entrance gate they entered a gap between the two ramparts, the bottom of which was lined with wooden stakes, potholes and skewers designed to slow down any attacker who managed to breach the outer walls. Affreca could imagine the despair that would greet any band of warriors who had fought their way over the outer rampart, only to find they would have to do it all again on the inner one. All this while negotiating the deadly impediments in the ground while defenders rained down arrows, stones and missiles from above. How Ulrich and the others would get through this, probably in the dark, she had no idea. She would have to look for other ways in for them.

There was a second gate in the inner rampart just as formidable as the outer one. This opened onto an enclosure with many buildings as well as pens for horses, pigs and sheep. The largest building was an enormous feasting hall, perhaps as long as three ships and with a high, pointed roof that came down almost to the ground at the sides. There were people everywhere: warriors in armour rushing to posts or guard duties, slaves, servants and others carrying pails and other burdens as they hurried around, completing the chores required to keep a large estate like this one going. Most nodded in respect as the vǫlva and her handmaidens walked by, but others looked away with studied intent.

At the far end of the compound was an area of even more activity than the rest. Timber batons stood, creating the skeleton of a new building. Men were working all around it, carrying wood, stone and other building materials as they worked on raising its walls.

They had not gone far when Affreca spotted a man hurrying in their direction from the building site. He was slender and of middle height and a little more than middle years, with very little cropped grey hair left on his freckled head. He wore the long black robes of a Christian monk and a gold cross hung from his neck on a silver chain. When she first saw him, he looked very like he was on his way to the gate behind them, but then he spotted the vǫlva and came towards her instead. Affreca was not sure, but she thought she saw a look of consternation on the man's thin, pinched features on first catching sight of Heimlaug, before he quickly changed it to one of welcome.

'Heimlaug!' he said. He spoke the Norse tongue but with a pronounced Frankish accent. 'You have finished your wash for the day?'

'I have, Bishop Henricus,' the vǫlva said, peering down her nose at him. 'No thanks to you.'

'And what is that supposed to mean?' the monk said. His smile looked obsequious and very fake.

'Bishop Henricus, if you want me dead,' Heimlaug said, 'you should at least have the balls to try to do it yourself.'

'I don't know what you mean,' the bishop said.

'You know exactly what I mean,' Heimlaug said. 'The lapdogs you sent met some wolves. I still live. Sprota and the jarl will have the rites of the Aesir sung over the birth of their child. He will be welcomed into our faith.'

The bishop sighed and the smile slipped from his face like wax melting down the outside of a candle. He looked right and left, as if to see whether there was anyone within hearing distance, then stepped a little closer to Heimlaug.

'You see that, witch?' he said in a low voice, pointing towards the building being constructed at the far end of the gard. 'That's a church of God. The jarl is having it built. That is the future. Your devils are all going to burn in hell and you with them. When Jarl Vilhjálmr deals with the rebellion he will return here and declare that from now on all his realm will be Christian.'

'Sprota will never allow that,' Heimlaug said. 'She loves the gods and their child will be brought up in our ways. The bloodline of Hrólf will continue to rule here.'

'Sprota will have no part in it,' the bishop said. 'The jarl has already abandoned her. She is a whore he was never properly married to. I am arranging a better, Christian marriage for the jarl and then your meddling will be over. Sprota, you and all the heathens will have a simple choice: convert or die.'

For a few moments the bishop and the witch glared at each other. Then Heimlaug shook her head.

'We must go,' she said. 'My lady is in need of us.'

They moved off, crossing the enclosure and walking along the side of the massive feasting hall. They passed a pen filled with some of the most magnificent horses Affreca had seen since leaving Ireland.

'Those horses are beautiful,' she said. 'They must take good care of them here.'

To her surprise Heimlaug tutted and shook her head. 'The jarl has learned to fight on them, like the Franks,' she said. 'It's not proper.'

They arrived at the door of a large daub-and-wattle building near the back of the hall. Heimlaug grasped the door handle and pushed it in.

From inside came a long, agonised, piercing scream.

41

A young woman came running to meet the witch at the door. Her face was pale and her eyes wide. From her dress, which was of higher quality than most but not of the best, Affreca judged her to be the maidservant of a noblewoman.

'Thank the gods you're here,' she said, panting. 'I was just about to try to find you. The lady Sprota's time is very near. The child is coming.'

As if in response, another long, drawn-out screech came from within the building. The maidservant turned and they hurried after her into the building. They went down a short hallway and into a room that reminded Affreca of the living quarters she had once had in her father's fortress in the heart of Dublin. Most denizens of the gard slept in the hall or other communal buildings, but the select few of the nobility had their own bowers to sleep in. This was a broad, round room with a fire in a hearth in the centre of the room. Its smoke rose to dissipate into the thatch above. Oil lamps chased away the gloom, though the stink of the whale oil that burned within them caught in Affreca's throat.

On one side of the room was a large loom with a half-woven tapestry stretched on it. Various chests, trunks and two chairs were scattered around the floor. The other side of the room contained a wooden bed that was filled with straw. On it lay a young woman who Affreca judged to be younger than herself; perhaps sixteen or seventeen winters. She was small and of slight build. Affreca thought that she may normally have been beautiful but at that moment her face was sheened with sweat, which stuck her hair to her forehead, and her teeth were clenched in a grimace of pain. She was dressed in a long white nightdress, which like her hair was stuck to her body by sweat. Her belly was swollen to the point of bursting, which told Affreca that she was in the final stages of pregnancy. She gasped for breath as another wave of pain washed over her.

This could only be the lady Sprota.

The vǫlva crossed the room and laid a hand on the pregnant woman's forehead. She examined her face with hawk-like intent, then hoisted the woman's skirt and examined between her legs. Pulling her skirt back down Heimlaug stood up.

'Her time is near,' she said. 'Go. Make sure there are no men in this building. We must start our prayers and call down the dísir and the Norns to bless this birth.'

'Heimlaug,' the pregnant woman said through gritted teeth. 'The pain is dreadful. Is there no potion you can give me to ease this?'

'It is too late for that,' the vǫlva replied. 'By the time it took effect the baby will be born. You must endure the suffering until the end now.'

She looked down on the girl, her expression stern and unsympathetic. Affreca had seen that look on the faces of older women before when younger girls were crying about the pains of childbirth. It seemed to say: *We've all been through it, girl. Now it's your time. Grin and bear it.* The vǫlva and wise women who officiated at births always seemed to be the most unpitying of all. Perhaps because they had seen so many babies born, it was not something special to them. Or perhaps they thought that by appearing unconcerned, judgemental even, it would spur the woman giving birth on to be more stolid.

Affreca could not imagine the pain the woman was in but it looked awful. Then there was the very real possibility that something would go wrong. The child, the mother or perhaps both might die.

'Bring warm water and cloths,' the vǫlva said to the maidservant in a commanding tone. 'And close all the doors. Make sure there are no men anywhere in the building. Their presence will stop the spirits coming and bring bad luck.'

The maid hurried off out of the room, closing the door behind her.

'See to the lady Sprota,' Heimlaug said to her handmaidens and Affreca. 'I must prepare.'

She sat down cross-legged beside the fire, pulled her hood over her head so it hung down over her face, held her hands out to either side and began to chant. The galdr she sang was low and rhythmical and chanted in a harsh, growling voice that came from deep in the very back of her throat.

Thordis, Freydis and Affreca went to the woman on the bed. There was a bowl of cold water on the bed with clothes floating in it. The handmaidens lifted these, wrung them out then used them to wipe Sprota's brow and cheeks. Another pang of birth pains gripped Sprota and she cried out, writhing on the bed. Affreca stared, unsure what to do.

'Get her other hand,' Thordis said, grasping Sprota's left hand herself and wrapping her forearm around it. 'Grab on to me, my lady. It will help you push.'

Affreca sat down on the bed beside the pregnant woman. Almost straight away she jumped back up again. The straw was soaking wet and there was a sweet, mould-like odour coming from them.

'My waters broke there,' Sprota said, her expression apologetic despite the pain she was in.

Affreca sat down again. If this little girl could endure such evident agony then she could tolerate sitting in some wet straw. She wrapped her arm around Sprota's right arm as she had seen Thordis do. As she did so Sprota grasped her hand in return. Her hands were warm and sweaty and Affreca was surprised by the iron-like strength of the little woman's grip.

Grunting, Sprota grasped both their hands and sat up, her face a mask of pain and effort as she bore down, heels dug deep into the straw of the bed, pushing the child within her towards its ultimate exit from her body.

Freydis took a bunch of dried herbs from a leather bag lying on the ground. She lit it in the fire and began wafting it around, spreading sweet-smelling smoke throughout the room. As she did so she too began singing along with Heimlaug. In contrast to the vǫlva, her voice was high-pitched and ethereal.

Sprota continued pushing and crying out for some time, then the pain seemed to pass away and she flopped back onto the straw, panting. After a few moments her breathing returned to normal and she looked around her.

'You're different,' she said, looking up at Affreca.

'What do you mean?' Affreca said, freezing.

'You're not the same woman who was here last night,' Sprota said.

Affreca looked down at her and saw that despite her current predicament, the woman's eyes were sharp and intelligent. She did not look like the type who was easily fooled. She did not know what to say next.

'The bishop tried to kill us,' Heimlaug said, breaking off her chanting to Affreca's relief. 'Odin sent his úlfhéðnar to protect us but they still got poor Gormla. This woman is their witch. She will stand in for Gormla during the birth ritual.'

'You know the ritual don't you?' Sprota said. Affreca felt her grip tighten and an anxious look crept onto the smaller woman's face. 'You know the Varðlokkur don't you? The Norns must be here at the birth of my son!'

'Of course I do,' Affreca said, with a confidence she did not feel. Sprota looked relieved.

'How do you know your baby will be a son?' Affreca said.

'Because Heimlaug has foreseen it,' Sprota said, smiling towards the witch who had settled down by the fire once more. 'I will give birth to a son and then Vilhjálmr will take me back. He will forget all this nonsense and Frankish ways. He will come back to his own folk. We shall rule side by side, with the blessing of the gods.'

Affreca glanced at the witch who was now muttering to herself, hoping that the old woman had not substituted her own wishful thinking for a true vision of what was to be.

There was much more going on here than met the eye. Sprota was a lady. She was clearly not a mere concubine, a jarl's bed slave made pregnant then cast aside.

'So who are you anyway?' Sprota said.

'I am Affreca Guthfrithsdottir of the Uí Ímair clan,' Affreca said. 'The Ivarssons of Dublin.'

Sprota raised her eyebrows. 'So you are a descendant of Ragnar Loðbrók himself?' she said.

Affreca nodded.

'Then I am indeed blessed to have you attend the birth of my child,' Sprota said. 'He will grow to be a great hero like Ragnar.'

'You said the jarl will take you back?' Affreca said. 'What do you mean?'

Sprota's face fell, then screwed up as a wave of agony gripped her. Whatever she was about to say was lost in an anguished wail.

Heimlaug got up and approached the bed.

'Her time draws near,' she said. 'The pains are coming close together. When these ones pass, we must get her into the birthing position quickly before the next arrive. And we must begin the ritual.'

Affreca had seen women give birth while growing up in Dublin. Some girls had romantic notions of the day when they would have children of their own, but Affreca had no such delusions. She knew it was painful, messy, sometimes deadly work and as she gripped Sprota as tightly as the other woman held on to her she felt a nervous pang. This was made worse by the knowledge she would soon have to sing spells she was not sure she really knew.

After a time Sprota's pain subsided again. Affreca, Thordis and Freydis helped her up out of the bed and onto the floor at the end of it. There she knelt with Affreca supporting her left arm and Thordis supporting her right. Freydis wafted the smoking herbs around once more. Heimlaug held both arms aloft.

'Now; the Varðlokkur,' she said.

Freydis and Thordis began to chant the words of the spell, which created an invisible holy fence around those in the room, keeping out evil spirits and malevolent Norns while at the same time invoking the benevolent Norns who would bless the coming child with gifts such as strength, courage and good luck. Affreca joined in. She had heard the song chanted many times as a girl in situations just like this, but that was now long ago. Could she remember all the words, or at least enough that those around her would not realise she was not what she claimed to be?

At that moment more birth pangs seized Sprota and she cried out. Affreca and Thordis did their best to support her as wave after wave of cramps went through her lower body. They continued singing but Affreca found to her relief that all she really needed to do was chant in the correct rhythm and tone to get away with it. None of the others had time to listen to her actual words, if they could be heard at all over Sprota's screams.

When this period of pain passed, Sprota fell forward. Affreca caught her in her arms and held her up. The intense pain and pushing had taken its toll, and the woman was exhausted. If the baby did not come soon, Affreca wondered if Sprota would be able to continue.

'We were married to seal a peace agreement,' she said, in a quiet voice after she had recovered her breath a little. 'Vilhjálmr was at war with my father over who ruled eastern Brittany and I was part of the price for peace. But it was not just statecraft. Vilhjálmr loved me. And I love him. We were happy together.'

'So you are actually married to the jarl?' Affreca said, recalling Israel's words about "jarl's heathen whore".

'I am his wife. His true wife. Though not in *their* eyes. *In more Danicum* the bishop and the Franks call it. Vilhjálmr and I were married "in the Danish manner" and not in one of their churches, so they say we are not truly married. That I am just a whore. A bed slave to be hidden away when decent folk come to visit.'

Tears began to run down Sprota's cheeks. Affreca could tell

this was a strong woman but she had been through a lot and the pangs of labour had sapped the last of her strength.

'Is that why you are here and not with Vilhjálmr in Rúðu?' Affreca said.

'He said I would be safe here,' Sprota said, her words laden with bitterness. 'But really he wanted me out of the way. He has become very powerful, one of the great noblemen of Francia. And so statecraft has entered our life again. Everyone wants his support. Even Aethelstan the Emperor of Britain has sent envoys to him. And they want him to be like them. They want him to forget the gods of his forefathers and his people. They want him to marry a Christian bitch instead of me.'

Affreca felt a pang of pity for the woman. Had she not left Dublin she could well be in the same position: married off to some Irish king to seal a peace deal, then cast aside when the balance of power shifted or her husband grew bored of her.

'I feel so hot,' Sprota said, pushing herself away from Affreca and pulling her nightdress off over her head. 'I need water.'

Affreca went to another bucket of fresh water and dipped a wooden cup into it. Returning to the end of the bed she passed the cup to the now naked Sprota who drank it down in one go.

'This time, when the pain comes you must go down on your hands and knees,' Heimlaug said. 'The child is nearly here and it will ease its passage.'

Sprota nodded. At that moment another bout of pains took her and she fell to the floor, grunting and crying as she worked to push the child from her body. The others did the best they could to support her but there was now little practical they could do. They continued chanting in between shouts of *push, girl, push*.

'The baby is coming,' Heimlaug, who squatted behind Sprota, said. 'I can see its head. Not long now.'

There were several more rounds of pushing and crying. Sprota looked utterly worn out and Affreca wondered if she would be able to last much longer.

'Hold her arms,' Heimlaug said. 'And call upon the Norns.'

Affreca and Thordis resumed their previous positions, holding Sprota slightly upright. Then they began chanting the names of the Great Norns who governed the Fate of all. They chanted one name each. Freydis chanted *Urðr* – what has happened. Thordis sang *Verðandi* – what is happening. Affreca intoned the name of *Skuld* – what should happen.

As she did so, Affreca looked up into the gloom above where the smoke from the fire dissipated through the thatch of the roof. Were there really great supernatural women gathering there, each with her own gift to give the new child, gifts and qualities that would determine its fate? And beyond them the three Great Norns who wove the tapestry of life on which every living thing was a thread. What Fate were they weaving for this child and how would its threads intertwine with her own?

Sprota's ordeal continued for some time. Affreca, who had seen strong men driven to the very edge of their strength by extreme endurance or violence, was impressed at how the little woman somehow managed to keep going through the pain and effort. Just when she seemed to be beyond exhaustion Sprota somehow managed to pick herself up and carry on. All dignity was gone, however. She was naked and had both shit and pissed herself. Affreca mused that ritual and tradition aside, there were practical reasons why men could not and should not be present during the ritual of birth.

Then Sprota let out one, final extended bellow that reminded Affreca of a cow in distress. There was a toe-curling, wet ripping sound followed by a slobbering, sloshing then Heimlaug cried, 'It's here! The child is born.'

Sprota gasped and fell flat to the floor. Affreca thought at first she had fainted but realised the woman was just utterly worn out.

For a few moments Heimlaug crouched over the child, then she held it aloft like a prize.

Despite her exhaustion, Sprota rolled over onto her back. The expression of agony on her face was replaced by one of anxious perturbation.

'Is it all right?' she said.

'You have a son,' Heimlaug said.

The witch slapped the child across the backside and it began to cry. 'And he's absolutely fine,' Heimlaug said, a rare smile crossing her lips.

She passed the baby over to his mother, who took the slimy, blood- and mucus-covered bundle to her breast. Sprota gazed down at him with loving eyes, a broad grin on her face. The other women gathered round, cooing and smiling.

'He is beautiful,' Thordis said.

Affreca looked down at the filth-covered, mewling, red-faced creature squealing in its mother's arms and wondered why she did not feel the same admiration that the other women felt. Was there something wrong with her? Had two winters spent in the company of a crew of úlfhéðnar killed all her natural sensitivities?

'We have much to do,' Heimlaug said. 'I must take him back for a moment.'

Sprota handed the baby back to the vǫlva, passing it across as carefully as if she were handling a basket of raw eggs. Heimlaug lifted a pair of shears and cut the child's birth cord.

At that moment the doors of the room crashed open. In rushed two warriors in leather jerkins with swords drawn.

Affreca recognised them as the two who had survived the confrontation at the lake earlier. She cursed herself for not having shot at least one of them then.

Behind them came the bishop of Bayeux.

'You must not be here!' Heimlaug said, an expression of outrage on her face. 'No man must be in the birthing room.'

'I take it from that squealing that the bastard child has finally been born,' he said. 'Good. Drown it in that bucket, men.'

42

'No!' Sprota said, reaching for her baby on instinct.

Heimlaug clutched the child to herself. 'You cannot touch him,' she said. 'This is the jarl's son.'

'No it isn't,' the bishop said. 'It's nothing. It has no name. It can be killed as a sickly child.'

The women all gasped. They all knew he was right. When a child was born it had to be presented to its father or another famous man who would sprinkle water on it and give it its name. Once that happened it became a lawful person. Up until that happened it was *níð* – a nothing. It could be left out to die in the cold or discarded like rubbish.

'Those are your heathen laws,' the bishop said with a sneer. 'Your so-called "customs". You insist on living by them so that child will die by them.'

'If you do such a thing,' Sprota said, her eyes blazing with anger and fear, 'when I tell Jarl Vilhjálmr his revenge will be terrible.'

'I will make sure you don't,' the bishop said. 'When the brat is dead you will be next to die. Childbirth is such a dangerous practice for a woman and unfortunately for you we will make sure you did not survive it. It will be very sad, but when you are both gone it will finally mean the jarl can make a proper Christian marriage and there will be no bastard child around to meddle with my plans in the future either.'

'What of us?' Heimlaug said. 'Do you think we will stand by and let you do this?'

'Your wolf warrior friends are not here to help you now,' the bishop said. 'Nor can they get inside this fortress. You will die too. I will make sure of it this time. We will smuggle your bodies out of here and say you simply vanished. You wandered off to the next rich man's house, as witches tend to do. Now: we deal with the child first. You, get that bucket and you get the baby.'

The two warriors advanced, brandishing their swords.

As one was bent to reach for the bucket of water with his free hand, Affreca, standing on the opposite side of it, grasped its rope handle in both her hands. With all her might, she swung it straight up. The bucket's momentum was increased by the swing and the weight of the water in it. It smashed straight into the reaching warrior's face in an explosion of splintering wood, broken teeth and spilling water. Knocked backwards by the blow, he dropped his sword as he reached with both hands for his shattered face. Affreca released the now unattached rope handle and caught the weapon by the blade before it hit the ground. She tossed it into the air so it rotated, then caught it again by the hilt.

The second warrior, who had been on his way to take the baby, saw this and spun around. With a roar he chased at Affreca, sword raised above his head.

Affreca had been knocked around enough in training with the Wolf Coats to know that head-on combat was a matter of weight and power rather than skill. Skar and Ulrich had taught her that, being smaller and lighter than most men, if she could move around her best advantage came from using her opponent's own weight against him.

She made a stance as if she was preparing to counter his blow, holding the injured man's sword up to protect her head. Then, just as the warrior brought his blade down, she stepped sideways out of the way. Missing her, the warrior's swing put him off balance and Affreca shoved her right shoulder into his side, making him stumble sideways. As he did so she kicked the back of his knee, doubling it so he twisted and fell onto his back with a cry.

Affreca reversed her sword, grabbed the hilt in both hands and drove the blade down through his right eye. The man coughed a great gout of blood from his mouth. He twitched, flailed then went limp.

Wrenching the sword free, Affreca strode over to where the first warrior lay moaning, face down on the ground and executed him with a chop to the back of the neck.

'Gah!'

The sound of the bishop's exasperated cry made everyone turn around. He was already running and halfway out the door.

'Don't think this is over,' he shouted as he went. 'I'll get you yet. You and your bastard child.'

Affreca grabbed the shears off Heimlaug and threw them after the retreating bishop. They struck him on the right shoulder and he cried out and stumbled forwards but kept on running. A moment later they heard the outer door of the building bang and knew he was gone.

Affreca, sword in hand, moved to chase him.

'Leave it,' Heimlaug said. 'He's outside in the compound. He's an important man. If you kill him in front of everyone you'll be the one in trouble.'

'But he just tried to kill us all!' Affreca said.

'He's still the bishop,' the vǫlva said. 'A good Christian. Who would believe he would try to kill anyone?'

'What about these two?' Affreca said, pointing with the sword at the bodies of the warriors. 'When someone comes do we just say we found them like this?'

'We can say they attacked us and we defended ourselves,' Heimlaug said. 'Don't worry, we won't leave you to carry the blame. But that is for the future. Now we have work to do here. The lady Sprota needs attending to. She needs stitches if she is not to bleed to death. Her afterbirth is still to come. The ritual of childbirth is not complete.'

To Affreca's incredulity, the women went back to washing

the baby and tending to the mother as if nothing had happened and there were not two dead bodies on the floor.

'We still need your help,' Heimlaug said. 'Don't just stand there gawping.'

Shaking her head, Affreca joined them and began helping as best she could.

'I only hope the Norns have not forsaken the child,' the vǫlva said. 'To have men enter during the ritual is very bad luck. Very bad luck indeed.'

Sprota winced as Freydis wove a stitch through her torn private parts. Despite the fact that she had just slaughtered two men moments before, the idea of it made Affreca queasy in a way the killing had not.

'You cannot stay here,' Affreca said. 'It's madness. You heard what that bishop said. He won't give up until you're dead.'

'What does it all matter anyway?' Sprota said, a sudden sadness in her voice. 'The bishop was right. If a child is not named by his father within nine nights of birth then he will be nothing for life. It is the custom. And Vilhjálmr is besieged in Rúðu, surrounded by his enemies. How can he get to see his newborn son in time? If he even survives at all!'

Affreca thought for a moment. An idea came to her but it seemed ridiculous. She looked down at the baby. It had stopped crying. He opened his eyes for a moment. Affreca stared straight into his blue eyes and something inside her heart melted a little.

'It just so happens my friends are on their way to see your jarl in Rúðu,' Affreca said to Sprota. 'You and the baby must come with us. That way the jarl may get to see his child before the nine days pass.'

All the others stopped what they were doing and looked at Affreca.

Heimlaug pursed her lips. 'Perhaps she is right,' she said. 'At least you may be safer away from here. Though how we will get you and the child out of the fortress right under the nose of the bishop I don't know.'

'We can use our wagon,' Freydis said. Affreca recalled how holy folk often travelled in a wagon, with a covered part containing statues of the gods. 'They can ride in the back. The guards still have enough respect for the gods not to look inside.'

'It will be risky, my lady,' Heimlaug said. 'Rúðu is surrounded by your husband's enemies. If you or the child fall into their hands, they will show no mercy.'

'If it means getting the chance for Vilhjálmr to see his son in time to name him, then I will take it,' Sprota said. She looked at Affreca. 'You are truly sent by the gods. You saved the lives of these women twice, and mine. And my son's. Now you say you will take us to see my Vilhjálmr. How can I ever thank you?'

'I am looking for a certain book,' Affreca said. 'Perhaps you know something about it?'

Part Four
Rúðu

43

'My book!' Israel's eyes lit up when Affreca handed the leather-bound manuscript to him. With eager fingers he opened it and began turning over the vellum leaves within. 'This is definitely it. How did you find it?'

'The lady Sprota had it hidden in a trunk in her chambers,' Affreca said. 'Apparently these things are worth a fortune. Jarl Vilhjálmr sent it to her as surety in case he is killed at Rúðu. The idea is that she could then sell it and live off the earnings. At least that is what she believes, anyway.'

She glanced sideways to check neither Sprota nor any of the witches had heard her. They stood a little way away, eyeing the Wolf Coats with a wary eye.

'On the other hand I also heard the jarl may be making plans to marry someone else,' Affreca continued. 'So maybe the book was just what the monk heard it was: her divorce settlement.'

Sprota looked pale and very tired now. Though she held her baby tight to her chest, Affreca wondered how much longer the small woman would be able to carry on before exhaustion overcame her completely.

Earlier, after Sprota had sworn the rest of her maidservants to secrecy, Affreca and the other women had smuggled her and the baby into the back of the volva's holy wagon. They had ridden out of the fortress gate and, as Freydis had predicted, the guards there had not looked into the covered back of the wagon for fear of disturbing whatever gods or spirits may have been inside. Ulrich and the others, who had been watching the entrance to the fortress, saw the witches leaving and intercepted the wagon a little further down the road, in the hope of learning from them what Affreca was up to.

Now they all stood on the deck of the beached snekkja and there was time to explain everything.

Ulrich, unlike Israel, was less than excited by the turn of events.

'A baby?' he said. 'It's bad enough luck to take a woman on a voyage but now a baby as well? What were you thinking, Affreca?'

'I couldn't just leave them there,' Affreca said, jutting out her bottom lip. 'Besides, if the jarl gets to name his child it could mean the continuation of our customs and way of life. He will not turn to the side of the Franks and their Christ God. Odin will be pleased with that.'

Ulrich tutted. 'Let's get underway,' he said.

Heimlaug, Freydis and Thordis said goodbye and returned to their wagon to travel on across the countryside and whatever ritual they would attend next. The Wolf Coats shoved the snekkja off the beach and set sail back along the coast.

A little later, as it grew dark, they gathered around the cooking stone to eat a meal of barley boiled in seawater along with the fried flesh of a few ducks the Wolf Coats had shot with Affreca's bow while waiting by the lake. The Finnish weapon was very powerful and had proved hard to master for them. Affreca was annoyed at how many of her arrows had been lost or broken in the hunt for their supper.

Sprota sat with them, nursing the now sleeping baby in her arms. She looked ghastly tired. The vikings around her looked at the child with expressions that ranged from indifference to curiosity to downright consternation.

'What are you men like?' Affreca said. 'It's as if you've never seen a baby before.'

'I've seen a few,' Starkad said. 'When I was younger. Just starting out as a warrior. I was on a viking raid on the eastern sea and we stormed a village. The lads played *börn á spjótaoddum* with the youngest children.'

'They played with the children?' Einar said with a scoff. 'What sort of vikings did you sail with?'

'You didn't sail with vikings before you met us, did you?' Ulrich said. 'Börn á spjótaoddum is a contest where men toss the children into the air and the other vikings try to catch them on their spear and sword points. It's fun. Not for the children, obviously.'

Einar's mouth dropped open a little. 'You played that game?' he said to Starkad.

'I did,' Starkad said. 'I was part of a crew. You have to go along with what the rest of the lads do, don't you?' His face was flat and he looked like he was staring at something a thousand leagues in the distance.

Sprota, who had been nervous enough already of the Wolf-Coated vikings she was sailing with, clutched her baby close to her chest and regarded the men around her with new fear in her eyes.

'I made that mistake,' Skar said. 'The first viking raid I was on I didn't join in. They called me Skarphedinn *barnakarl* for years after that. Skarphedinn the child man.'

'You got over it though,' Ulrich said.

'I did,' Skar confirmed.

'Well I've killed two men already to keep this baby alive,' Affreca said, glaring at the others. 'And I'll kill more if they try to harm it.'

Einar felt a chill run down his back. She meant it.

'Easy, princess,' Ulrich said with a smile. 'The lads are just reminiscing about the old times. We need this child alive as well. He could be important leverage with the jarl. Besides, if a Christian bishop wants this child dead, then I'll do all I can to keep it alive.'

'That worries me, Ulrich,' Kari said. 'From what Affreca tells us this bishop seems to want Jarl Vilhjálmr in power. Are you sure we're not just helping the Christians against our own gods?'

'When have you ever known me to do that, Kari?' Ulrich asked.

'Isn't that what this whole voyage has been about?' Sigurd said.

Ulrich scowled.

Israel sat beside Einar. He was cross-legged with his book open on his lap. He was running his finger along the strange runes written on its pages. With the fading light he was almost doubled over as he peered down with fascinated intent.

'What does it say?' Einar asked.

'This?' Israel said, looking up. He had the same expression of animated excitement on his face that Einar had seen when he was talking about books in Aethelstan's scriptorium. 'It's a version of the New Testament.'

'What's that?' Einar said.

'It's part of the Christian Bible,' the scholar said. 'It contains the words of Jesus himself. His wisdom, sayings and teachings.'

'You mean like the Hávamál? The Words of the High One?' Ulrich said, looking at the book with new suspicion.

'I don't know what that is,' Israel said.

'It's a collection of wisdom and lore passed down from Odin himself,' Einar said. 'Except it's been passed down from mouth to ear since the world began. It's not set down in runes. Ulrich has been teaching me and the others from it.'

'Then I suppose yes, it is,' Israel said. 'It contains much wisdom.'

'You sound like you admire what it contains,' Wulfhelm the Saxon said. 'I thought you Jews didn't believe in Jesus. What do you care? Didn't you put him to death?'

'For one thing, my friend, your Jesus was a Jew,' Israel said. His eyes flashed with a defiant fire Einar had not seen before. Then he sighed. 'And I have to admit, the more I read of what he said, and the more I see of the sort of kingdom King Aethelstan is building, the more I wonder if perhaps I should join Aethelstan and be baptised. I want to be part of the civilisation Aethelstan is creating. There is much to admire in it.'

'What is there to admire?' Ulrich asked with a look on his face like he had just smelled something unpleasant.

'The treasury of knowledge. The rule of law,' Israel said. 'Commerce and prosperity. Aethelstan's kingdom stands like a light in darkness. An island of peace in a sea of chaos, darkness, barbarity and ignorance. They don't amuse themselves by throwing babies onto spears in Wessex.'

'Then you and I are forever on different sides, my friend,' Ulrich said. 'As Odin said: *wars I raise, princes I anger, peace I never bring.*'

'There are many bibles and books with the words of Jesus in them,' Wulfhelm said. 'What's so special about this one?'

'Look at this,' Israel said, running his finger along a line of runes. 'This is written in the Greek tongue. Now look below, the same text is written again.'

Einar, now fascinated, looked at the rows of runes. They were very different. The lower row was much more angular and tree-like than the top. In many ways it resembled Norse runes, though Einar still could not make out what they said.

'The second version is written in Hebrew, the tongue Jesus himself wrote in and spoke,' Israel said. 'It's much older than any of the versions written in Latin. It's from a very long time ago, perhaps even the time of Jesus himself. Perhaps even in his own words.'

Surt made a low whistle through his teeth. 'So that's why Aethelstan needs a Jew who can read Greek,' he said. 'I knew there were scholars who could read Greek but they are rare here in the barbarian north. As for Hebrew? There must be none at all. And someone who reads *both*? My friend, you are indeed a very special person.'

'But what is Aethelstan going to do with this book if you are the only person who can read it?' Einar said.

'He wants me to translate it into the tongue of the Saxons,' the scholar said. 'His people will hear the words of their God in their own language. No other king's folk have such a treasure.'

'So by carrying out this task for Aethelstan, we are helping spread the words of his God?' Kari asked. His voice was hoarse. 'And from what we've heard so far it sounds like we should be fighting for this Heriwolf, not rescuing Jarl Vilhjálmr from him. He sounds more like us. Like one of our own folk. Ulrich, what are we doing? Where are you leading us?'

He glared at Ulrich. All eyes turned to the Wolf Coat leader.

'Our own folk?' Ulrich said. 'What are these second-generation Frank-Danes to us? They treat our Norwegian brothers like dirt. They worship our gods, yes, but was not Eirik Bloody Axe a most devout man for sacrifices as well? All these jarls and kings are nothing but liars and self-seeking bastards with their own games and their own goals. We've served enough of them to know that. It's time to get something for ourselves now. We fight for silver and Aethelstan is paying. That should be enough.'

Kari scowled and spat on the deck.

'And if it isn't,' Ulrich said, 'then consider this. Jarl Vilhjálmr has to make a choice: between his gods and his folk or the Franks and their Jesus. Everywhere in the world this is happening, and it always goes one way. Christ wins. It sounds like if we reunite Vilhjálmr with his wife and newborn son we could tip him in the other direction. For once, things will go our way.'

'If you believe the girl,' Kari said.

'It's a risk, yes,' Ulrich said. 'But say we side with Heriwolf? We help him kill Vilhjálmr. Aethelstan does not pay us. What then?'

Ulrich's eyes were alight and danced from face to face. Everyone in the crew knew how volatile the little man could be and it was easy to see that he was on the edge. Despite their own anger, Einar could see that the other Wolf Coats, even Kari who seemed most angered, had become wary of their leader.

'We go home?' Sigurd said in a sheepish voice.

'Home?' Ulrich said with a sneer. 'And where is that now?'

A cold chill settled around Einar's heart as the meaning of Ulrich's words sank in. Where indeed was home? His mother's homestead in Iceland was just a burned-out ruin. Orkney, his birthright, was taken by Eirik Bloody Axe.

The others fell silent too and he knew they were thinking the same thing. Most of them had lived in King Eirik's hall in Norway most of their lives but now he was gone and Hakon did not trust them. Eirik would blood eagle every one of them rather than take them back to service. Affreca had left Ireland behind. Returning there would mean submitting to an arranged marriage. Surt's home lay a vast distance to the south and he had left it many years before. What would he find if he returned? None of them had wives or children waiting for them or farms waiting to be tended. They were landless, lordless warriors – vikings – whose only home was the endless rolling waves of the whale roads.

Ulrich took a deep breath through his nose. He stared into the bowl of barley before him as if trying to see the future. Then he looked up.

'Besides all that, I swore an oath to Aethelstan,' he said. 'I will not be an oath breaker. Especially to someone who may have the blood of Odin flowing inside him. Do not worry. These Christian books are all lies and tales for children. Our gods are stronger. We have nothing to fear from books. Swords, spears and the iron will of men are what rule the world. Not words and ideas. When Aethelstan pays us for this voyage we will all be rich men.'

The others seemed mollified by his words but Einar felt an unsettling emotion in his own heart and could not help feeling that Ulrich was making a brave face of it.

'So where is this Rúðu, then?' Sigurd said.

'It's the main town in this part of Francia,' Ulrich said. 'Roan tells me we must sail to another estuary then go inland up a great river.'

The others all groaned. Unless there was a strong wind

pushing them upstream, going inland by river meant a lot of rowing against the flow.

'You need the exercise, you lazy bastards,' Ulrich said. 'And when we get there all we will have to do is find a way to break into a town that's besieged by an army.'

44

Rúðu lay on the plane below them. The Wolf Coat company were perched on the side of a mountain that overlooked the city. The broad river they had rowed up from the sea ranged across the wide, flat countryside. A wide meander curled around the town like a serpent wrapping itself around a treasure hoard, surrounding it on two sides by water. The rest of the town faced a wide meadow, which was filled by the tents of an encamped army.

Seeing the mountain that rose before the town and the vantage point it would give them, Ulrich had ordered the ship stopped so he could climb the hill and assess the situation before they rowed straight into it. Leaving Roan and Sprota with her baby on board and Wulfhelm, Kari and Surt to guard the ship, the rest of them had jumped onto the riverbank then trekked up the hillside to reach the point where they had a good view of the town and plane below.

'The river goes all the way to Paris, the main city of the Francian realm,' Ulrich said. 'The King of Francia gave Rúðu to Jarl Vilhjálmr's father, Hrólf so he would guard the way to Paris and stop vikings attacking it.'

'Isn't that like asking a wolf to guard a sheep pen?' Starkad said. 'By all accounts Göngu-Hrólf was one of the baddest viking to sail the seas.'

'Who better to stop vikings than a viking?' Skar said. 'The king of the Greeks often tasks the Varangian Guard with fighting pirates in the Great Middle Sea. The Varangians are all Norsemen like us.'

'Now Vilhjálmr guards the way to Paris in the name of the Frankish king,' Sigurd said. 'But for how long?'

Dragon-prowed longships were lashed together, blocking the river both up and downstream of the town. The meadow before the town thronged with tents and men camped a little way from the walls of the town, just beyond the range of an arrow. A blue haze from countless cooking fires smeared the air above it. They could see banners fluttering in the wind and the glint of sun on iron: weapons and armour.

'This Heriwolf has quite an army,' Ulrich said. 'They have that town surrounded and locked up tighter than the gates of Hel's kingdom. I wonder how many Danes this Jarl Vilhjálmr has left on his side?'

'It looks like that bishop fellow has bet on the wrong horse,' Einar said. 'I don't see how Vilhjálmr can escape from this siege. The bishop would be better changing his allegiance to Heriwolf.'

'Except Heriwolf is a heathen,' Affreca said. 'Unashamedly so. The bishop thinks he can influence Jarl Vilhjálmr to side with the Christians. Sprota says that Heriwolf would never do that.'

'Isn't she following the wrong star too then?' Einar asked. 'You said she respects the gods and follows our customs?'

'She believes she too can sway the jarl in the opposite direction,' Affreca replied. 'And he will reject the bishop's plans and stay in the traditions of his own folk.'

Skar gave a low whistle. 'This Jarl Vilhjálmr must be quite the man,' he said. 'Everyone wants him on their side: a bishop. That noblewoman. The Frankish kings and Aethelstan.'

'I wouldn't count the jarl out yet,' Starkad said. 'That town is strong. Look at those walls. There is a reason he has taken refuge there.'

They all looked and indeed the town was surrounded by stout stone walls. Unlike the ones at Jorvik these were not crumbling either. Here and there they were scorched or a few stones had been knocked out during assaults from Heriwolf's warriors, but they were otherwise strong and solid.

'That is Roman work,' Einar said, appreciating the straight lines, their impressive height and the now lost craftsmanship that had created them. Once he had thought the Romans were wizards to be able to build such mighty creations in stone. Now he knew they just had knowledge modern folk no longer possessed.

'There he goes again about the Romans,' Ulrich said with a tut. 'Every time you see something impressive, you say it must be Roman.'

'The lad is right,' Israel said. 'I visited this place before the war began between Heriwolf and the jarl. When I was studying in Landévennec. This place you call Rúðu was called Rotomagus by the Romans. It was a great city and capitol of one of their provinces. It has an amazing amphitheatre and the thermae are still in working order...' He trailed off, seeing the blank looks around him. 'You've no idea what I'm talking about, do you?' he questioned.

'Don't know, don't care,' Ulrich said. 'Nor does it matter who built them. Strong walls are no defence against hunger. There's no sign of any attacks happening, so I'd say that is what Heriwolf is planning to use to win victory. He will besiege the town until starvation brings Vilhjálmr's men to their knees.'

'How in Odin's name will we get inside, Ulrich?' Skar said. 'The town is totally surrounded by Heriwolf's army. Those Roman walls have kept them out so they'll keep us out too.'

Ulrich was silent. He stood, staring at the town below like it was someone who had just insulted him.

'You say you do not care about Roman building,' Israel said. 'But it seems our friend Heriwolf is also ignorant of what a thermae is.'

'And what, pray tell, is a thermae?' Ulrich said, his voice dripping with sarcasm.

'What *are* thermae, to be correct,' Israel said. 'They are baths. Warm baths to be precise. The Romans were very keen on them. They washed a lot. They had large buildings that housed the baths and everyone in the town could use them, provided they weren't slaves of course. There is one of these in Rúðu. I've seen it myself. It's near the walls.'

Einar shrugged. 'What's so special about that?'

'Ah, you are an Icelander, I believe?' Israel said. 'I hear that is a most wonderful country. Rivers of fire flow from mountains and hot water bubbles up from the ground all over. There are no need for thermae there.'

'That's right,' Einar said. 'Most settlements have a hole in the ground or a pond filled with natural warm water.'

'That is a mystery of the earth,' Israel said. 'But Roman baths were manmade. The water was heated by great fires and funnelled in deep bathing pools.'

'Is there a point of all this teaching?' Ulrich said.

'There is,' Israel said. 'A bath needs a supply of water. The source here would be the river, so somehow water must be funnelled inside the walls to the bathhouse. By aqueduct most likely. It's a sort of pipe down which water travels.'

'And if the water goes in,' Skar said, looking at Ulrich, 'we can get in that way too!'

Ulrich smiled and looked at the scholar with new admiration. 'So we may have a way in,' he said. 'Finally you prove useful to us, little man.'

Israel frowned. Ulrich was not much bigger than him.

Skar's face fell again. 'We still have Heriwolf's army to get through though,' he said. 'What will we do? We can't just walk through it.'

'Why not?' Ulrich said. 'It's what we usually do.'

45

Einar had been among several encamped armies before and walking through Heriwolf's – outside the walls of Rúðu – brought the memories of those times flooding back. The worst thing was the smell. The fug of the army camp enveloped them like an unpleasant blanket, an uncanny mixture of woodsmoke, rotting garbage, fresh baking bread, piss and shit. It was the odour of many men gathered together in tents in one small area.

The meadow thronged with the countless tents of the army, which got larger and more expensive the closer to the middle they were. The breeze drummed on the leather of the tents, whipping their guide ropes and making the many war banners and pennants dance on their poles. Men of all ages sat on stools or reclined on the ground, gathered around their cooking fires. The camp was filled with every rank of man able to hold a weapon. There were swords, spears, axes and shields everywhere. Shining brynjas, coats made of countless interlinked metal rings, stood like scarecrows on T-shaped poles outside the tents of the wealthier men. Thralls and younger boys cleaned weapons, sharpened blades or painted shields. Outside less grand tents, more humble protection made of thick, toughened leather was being washed and prepared by freemen farmers.

The air above was smeared grey with the smoke of their cooking fires. Clouds of annoying midges drifted in from the river to add to the annoyance of the smoke and the smell.

The banners of lendermenn, lords and hersirs fluttered in the wind. One flagpole rose above all others. At its top was a banner showing a red wolf on a green background.

Einar noticed some differences between this war band and the armies of kings he had seen in Norway. He was surprised just how many times they passed men brawling or arguing with each other. From the snatches of shouting they heard, it was about trivial things like who had eaten what or someone's tent space encroaching on that of another. Instead of one midden there appeared to be piles of rubbish everywhere. In a similar way, instead of communal pits dug for the purpose of shitting in, it looked like almost every tent had dug their own.

'It looks like this Heriwolf is more viking than jarl,' Ulrich said.

Einar understood what he meant. The encampment had more of the chaotic air of the viking camp of Soti off the coast of the land of the Scots they had visited the year before than the disciplined army of the brother kings at Tunsberg in Norway he had been with before that.

From the height of the piles of refuse and the hum of the overflowing latrine pits, Einar could guess that the army had been here some time. The usual palpable excited tension in the air that rises when men prepare for battle was not there either.

'There is nothing as boring as a siege, lad,' Skar said as they tramped through the encampment. 'You spend days, weeks, sometimes months sitting around twiddling your thumbs. You can't relax in case the defenders try to break out. So you just sit, ready. Waiting for the few brief bouts of action that happen every now and again. Usually when you least expect it.'

As usual when trying to infiltrate a large army or war band, Ulrich's plan was just to walk straight into Heriwolf's camp.

'Are we not vikings, just like them?' he had said. 'Who's to say we are not part of Heriwolf's army?'

Earlier they had returned to the snekkja from the mountain. The ship was grounded in some bulrushes downriver and out of sight of the army. They had picked up Wulfhelm, Kari and Surt. Ulrich had told Roan, Sprota and her child to stay behind while the rest of them went to see if they could find a way into the town. Much to her chagrin, Ulrich had also ordered Affreca to stay behind and watch over them.

'You brought them here,' he said when Affreca protested. 'So you look after them. I'm not walking through a camp of vikings with the wife of their enemy and his infant child in tow. If you want a fast way to get us all killed, that would be it.'

Affreca was at last mollified by Ulrich's assurance that once they worked out a way into the town, then they would come back for her and work out a way to get Sprota and the baby inside as well.

Einar was not sure how serious Ulrich was in this intent. A small company of men sneaking into a besieged town would be difficult enough without adding a crying baby as well.

Wulfhelm and Israel were left behind as well. As Israel had pointed out, their probable entrance into the city would be through a water course, and neither of them could swim.

Ulrich's plan was simple enough. So simple it just might work. The Wolf Coats would mingle with the army, then when it got dark try to sneak out to the walls of the town. Having seen how Jarl Vilhjálmr defended his fortress at Fish Gard, they knew they should expect similar solid defence, but there was no besieging army outside the gard, which meant patrols could go outside the walls. The only thing the Wolf Coats would have to worry about should be Heriwolf's warriors and how to explain to them what they were up to if caught by them.

Ulrich decided he would work that out if or when it happened.

It was late in the afternoon and most of the folk in the camp were settling down to cook something to eat. Einar and the others moved through their ranks, trying to look disinterested while still wary of any possible attack. When they got nearer to the middle of the encampment, a great shout arose from not far away. It was the sound of many men's voices raised in excitement. It built to a crescendo, then ended in a great cheer.

Skar looked at Ulrich and raised an eyebrow.

'Let's go and see what's going on,' Ulrich said. 'Perhaps we'll learn something useful.'

46

They moved between the tents until they neared the large ones in the middle, the tents of the most important noblemen with the banner of the red wolf flying above them. A great crowd was gathered around a large wooden-fenced pen, the sort often used to corral horses, except it was much longer than it was wide, almost like a little roadway between the fences. The crowd lined either side.

As Einar and the others walked around they could see many of the people there exchanging pieces of hacksilver. From the disappointed looks on the faces of those handing the silver over and the delight on those taking it, Einar resolved that there was some sort of betting going on.

The ground within the pen was indeed churned and worked over by hooves. There were several horses rearing and kicking at one end of the pen. Eight men stood guard around them with long spears. A ninth was clad in leather jerkin and britches and bore a long, thick horsewhip.

'A horse race?' Skar said, making a guess at what was going on.

'If it is,' Ulrich said, 'those horses don't look like they enjoy racing too much.'

The horses looked distressed. Their eyes rolled in their heads and foam and spittle streaked their flanks.

'Maybe a horse fight then?' Skar said.

Einar hoped it was not. Horse fighting was regarded as a manly sport back home in Iceland but personally he found the sight of two majestic animals kicking and biting each other, often until one was dead, unpleasant.

'There are five horses,' Ulrich said. 'Too many for a fight. Let's get ourselves a better view, lads.'

They walked round the pen until they found a spot where the crowd was a little thinner then shouldered their way to the front.

Then they saw the crushed remains of a man lying face down in the mud of the pen. His head had caved in and red crescent-shaped marks – hoof prints – were evident on his back. From the unnatural angles of his right arm and both legs, it was clear the bones in them were smashed. He was not long dead as steam still rose from his cooling sweat and his limbs twitched and jerked in an unnerving fashion.

About the mid-point on the long side of the pen, a raised platform had been built and a seat placed on it. It was a high seat with pillars like would be seen in the feasting hall of a jarl or nobleman. On it sat a man of middling years. He had long black hair tied back behind his head and a close-cropped beard. His clothes spoke of wealth and were of different colours, with red britches and green tunic. In one hand he grasped a gold cup and there was a broad smile on his face. A row of warriors in brynjas, helmets and holding shields guarded his platform.

'Is that Lord Heriwolf?' Ulrich said to one of the men standing nearby.

'Of course,' the viking said, turning to Ulrich with a puzzled expression on his face. He spoke the Norse tongue with the local accent. 'Don't you know him?'

'We are newly arrived from Denmark,' Ulrich said. 'We heard about Heriwolf's war and came to join his army.'

'News of success travels fast, eh?' the other man said with a grin. 'We'll soon take that town and get rid of that treacherous bastard Vilhjálmr. Heriwolf will be Jarl of Rúðu and lord of all the Northmen in Francia. And there is no better man. He's a true Dane. He honours the gods and keeps our customs. And look at all this. He looks after us as well. I see you brought your ring fighter with you?'

He looked at Surt and patted him on one of his burly arms.

'He looks like a good one,' he said. 'If you stay you might see some entertainment you'll really like.'

'What makes you think he's a ring fighter?' Ulrich said.

'Aren't all blámaðr?' the viking said. 'I mean, you don't see many black-skinned men in this part of the world, and every one I have seen fought in the wrestling ring.'

'Well Surt here is one of my viking crew,' Ulrich said.

For a moment the viking looked at him, mouth hanging open. Then his lips twisted in a grin and he let out a laugh. 'Good one!' he said, between chortles. 'A black-skinned man who is a viking! Good joke.'

Unseen by the other man, Surt's hand dropped to the hilt of the knife at his waist. Ulrich laid his own hand on top of Surt's to stop him drawing the weapon.

A great shout turned everyone's attention back to the inside of the pen. An unfortunate-looking man had been shoved in through a gate in the fence at one end of the long rectangular run, just in front of the horses. His eyes were blackened, his nose bent and bloody, and his flesh that was visible through the rips and tears in his dirty clothes was scratched in places and bleeding. He looked around the watching ring of faces with wild, terrified eyes as if searching for some form of solace, mercy or help. He found none.

'This one looks like a bit of a fat bastard,' the watching viking beside Ulrich said. 'I'll give you two pieces of silver if he makes it a quarter of the distance.'

'I'd rather see what's going on before I start laying bets, friend,' Ulrich said. 'We've just arrived, remember? Who is he anyway?'

'Prisoner,' the viking said. 'One of Jarl Vilhjálmr's men. We caught him and a few others trying to break out from behind the walls last night. Those are their horses too. Our lads formed a shield wall and they tried to break through it. Idiots. Everyone knows horses won't charge a fence of shields with men with spears behind them. They're not stupid.'

'That's what you get for following fancy Frankish ways,' another man standing nearby commented. 'They beat Jarl Vilhjálmr's father Hrólf on horseback and he's been obsessed with them ever since.'

One of the men with the long spears prodded the battered man with the sharp end and he began to run. At first he made for the nearest side but the watching crowd there, putting their arms through the fence, shoved him back into the main thoroughfare again. The only option for him was to start running down the long, narrow pathway between the fences.

Men blew horns and others cheered and the men with the spears prodded the unfortunate horses in their flanks. The man with the whip cracked it across their backs and the horses took off, galloping in the same direction the prisoner had taken off in.

He heard them coming – or perhaps felt the thump of their hooves on the ground beneath him – and looked around. Terror masked his face as he doubled his efforts, sprinting with all his might. The men with the spears and whip charged behind the horses, yelling, cracking the whip and goading the horses on.

The prisoner had almost made it halfway when the horses caught up with him. The frightened creatures, with fences and shouting crowds on either side and men with whips and spears behind them, had no choice but to keep going. The man before them let out a cry that was silenced a moment later as he was knocked to the ground by the lead horse and the pounding hooves of the others smashed his body to a pulp.

Another great cheer erupted from the crowd. Hacksilver began changing hands again.

'He got further than I thought he would,' the viking beside Ulrich said. 'I bet you're kicking yourself you didn't take my bet now. Heriwolf really knows how to give the lads a bit of sport, eh?'

'If you'd call murder sport, yes,' Ulrich said. 'Is it over now?'

The viking looked at Ulrich with surprise, as if he thought he had misheard him.

The men with the whip and spears drove the horses from the pen. Then the crowd parted near the platform Heriwolf sat on and a giant of a man vaulted over the fence into the pen. He was taller even than Skar, with shoulders like the yard beam of a longship and legs like the trunks of an oak tree. He was stripped to the waist and his body rippled with packed muscles. At the sight of him the crowd cheered.

'That's Beli, Heriwolf's champion. He's his ring fighter too,' the viking beside them explained. 'Tell your blámaðr to watch this. He might learn some new moves.'

'Tell him yourself,' Ulrich said. 'He understands our tongue.'

The other man's eyebrows shot up once more.

Another two prisoners were shoved into the pen.

'I'll bet you three pieces of silver Beli beats both of them,' the viking said, holding out his hand to Ulrich.

'No thanks,' Ulrich said. 'Somehow I think that's what's supposed to happen.'

The big man bared his teeth and the prisoners, realising that beating him in a fight could be a way for them to escape, looked at each other then ran at him. Beli swatted the first one away with a slap from the back of his hand like he was an annoying fly. The prisoner staggered sideways and landed with a thump in the dirt. The giant held the second man at arm's length with his left hand grasping the man's forehead. The prisoner kicked and punched but the big man's arms were much longer than his and none of the blows landed. This provoked much laughter in the watching crowd.

As the man on the ground was struggling to get up, Beli planted a big foot on his thigh. The bone shattered with a crack like a dry branch breaking off a tree. The prisoner screamed and writhed in agony. The giant then pulled the other prisoner close to him, spinning him around as if he was a toy until he was gripped under his left arm. Then Beli caught the other man's right wrist and, with a swift twist, broke it.

At length the big man killed both the prisoners but it was not pretty and it took much longer than it should. He broke each of their limbs one at a time, then eventually finished them off, one by twisting his head around the wrong way and the other by crushing his throat with one huge fist.

Einar watched in horror. He did not fear death but the manner in which these men had died – killed without hope of escape or survival, their deaths accompanied by the bloodthirsty laughter and cheers of those it was supposed to entertain – made his stomach churn.

'Beli is quite the ring fighter isn't he?' the viking beside them said. 'What does your blámaðr think of that display?'

Surt folded his arms and made a face. 'I thought that man is nothing more than a bully,' he said. 'A cruel bastard who takes too much pleasure in the pain of others. Perhaps it makes him feel more of a man?'

'What?' The viking looked at Surt, a look of astonishment on his face. He turned to Ulrich, as if expecting him to chastise Surt in some way. When Ulrich did nothing the viking looked outraged.

'Who are you lot really?' he asked. 'I don't think I like your words. And your slave here acts above his station.'

'I told you,' Ulrich said with a sigh, 'he's not my slave.'

At that moment Heriwolf stood up. The cheering, laughter and chatter fell to an expectant hush. Einar thought he swayed a little as he stood and the cup he held was at a slight angle.

'Are you having fun?' Heriwolf said, shouting. His face went red with the effort.

More cheers greeted his words.

'You deserve it,' Heriwolf said when the cheering died down again. 'You have pledged your allegiance to me and I will look after you. You know that. Not like *him*.'

He pointed a finger in the direction of the walled town. The crowd around him growled their hostility.

'The so-called "Jarl" Vilhjálmr, or – as he calls himself – William,' Heriwolf said. His face was puce now and blobs of spit flew from his lips as he shouted the words. 'A man who has forgotten his forefathers. His gods. Who has even sent his own wife away in shame, embarrassed by the fact that they were married *in more Danicum*. "In the Danish manner" his Christian friends call it. In *our* manner. Our traditions, our customs, now even our women are not good enough for "Jarl" William.'

The warriors lining the pen hissed, jeered and showed their general disapproval.

'Well, I will show him how dearly we hold our customs,' Heriwolf continued. 'I will show him how much I honour our traditions. He cannot cower behind those walls forever. Soon we will drag him kicking and screaming from behind them and when we do, I swear this oath to you, my people...'

He paused, allowing an expectant silence so quiet the chatter from the rest of the camp could be heard.

'I will carve the blood eagle on Jarl William's back,' Heriwolf said. 'I will break his bones and draw out his lungs. Then he will know how we folk respect our customs!'

Thunderous cheers erupted all around. Men clapped while others beat the fence with their hands. When the tumult was beginning to subside, Heriwolf held up his hands to hasten its quieting.

'The world knows William is finished,' Heriwolf said. 'Only days ago I was visited by emissaries of Olaf of Ireland, King of Dublin.'

Ulrich looked sideways at Skar. 'What's Affreca's brother up to now?' he said from the corner of his mouth.

'Olaf is going to war in Ireland and he had asked for my support,' Heriwolf said. 'Me. He knows William is now nothing. Friends, let me promise you this. You will be well rewarded for your support. When we are done here, when William is dead and we have secured this realm, then we will sail a great viking fleet to Ireland. We will join Olaf and rape and pillage that land from end to end. There will be more plunder, loot, women and glory than any of you can imagine!'

The crowd went wild. Bloodthirsty cheers, yells and more drumming echoed all around for long moments. When it eventually quieted down again, Heriwolf spread his hands and addressed the crowd again.

'Now, my friends,' he said when it was once more quiet enough to be heard. 'I'm afraid that is all the fun for today. Unless someone else wants to challenge my ring fighter: Beli?'

Laughter echoed around the crowd. Heriwolf himself was smiling, knowing no one would be so stupid.

Then the viking beside Ulrich held up his hand and began to wave it back and forth.

'Lord Heriwolf!' he shouted. 'There is a man here who could fight him.'

He clapped a hand on Surt's shoulder.

47

All eyes turned on Surt.

Ulrich glared at the viking who had drawn attention to him.

'What do you think you're doing?' he said through gritted teeth.

'You think you're so smart,' the other man said. 'Let's see how your slave gets on against big Beli shall we?'

'What is this?' Heriwolf said from his platform. 'Who owns this blámaðr? Does his owner really want to put him in the ring with Beli?'

'No one owns me,' Surt said in a loud voice.

A gasp ran around the gathered men but Heriwolf just cracked a wry smile.

'I see,' he said. 'Perhaps there has been some sort of mistake then. It's a pity though. You look like you would have put up a good fight. Beli would still have won though.'

Laughter rippled through the crowd.

'I'll fight him,' Surt said.

Excited babble began all around.

'You don't need to,' Ulrich said. 'We're drawing too much attention to ourselves as it is. And that man is a monster. You can't really want to take him on?'

'You forget, Ulrich,' Surt said as he pulled off his brynja and the shirt underneath, revealing a body stacked with rippling muscles every bit as formidable as Beli's. 'I've done this before and I was never beaten.'

Einar was going to point out that he had in fact beaten Surt but decided this was not the time.

Surt jumped over the fence and into the pen. Rolling his neck then shoulders, he skipped across towards the centre. The huge man opposite him regarded him with curiosity, as if he was unsure if this was a joke or not.

'Lord Heriwolf,' he said. 'This man has black skin. I have heard of such but never fought one yet. How can I be sure this is not a troll or other strange being?'

'Don't worry, Beli,' Heriwolf said. 'He is a human being; I can assure you. He is a blámaðr. One of the folk who comes from the lands far to the south. He will break just the same as any other men you have fought before.'

The big man chuckled and turned back toward Surt. He swung his arms to and fro, preparing for whatever was to come. Then his lips cracked into an unpleasant grin, revealing teeth that had patterns filed into them.

'Come on, blámaðr,' he said, gesturing to Surt. 'Come and meet your end.'

Surt, did not move.

'Are you scared?' Beli said. 'Come on. Have a go. Let's see what you can do.'

Surt remained standing beyond reach of the big man.

'Come on.' The giant dropped both hands to his sides. 'I'll even let you have a free hit. What's the matter with you?'

Still Surt did not attack.

'You *are* scared, aren't you?' Beli said with a sneer. 'You jump in the ring like the jumped-up shit you are, but you don't actually have the balls to attack me?'

'Oh I have balls all right,' Surt said, now grinning. 'As your mother knows very well. She's very fond of playing with them.'

Beli's eyes widened but he did not respond.

'And I heard you can fit the ball bags of three men in that big mouth of yours at once,' Surt said. 'A trick you learned from her.'

The big man made an inarticulate grunt and charged forwards at Surt. Surt dropped his right foot behind him, bracing himself to meet the impact of Beli's charge. Beli was bent forward, both arms outstretched, fingers claw-like, ready to grasp Surt by whatever hold he could get on him.

Just as Beli reached him Surt jumped sideways. The big man, propelled by his own power and weight, went stumbling past. Surt, who was not small himself, smashed a fist into Beli's kidneys. He bellowed and stumbled sideways.

With a roar of pain and anger, Beli spun and lumbered back towards Surt again. This time Surt caught the outstretched fingers of Beli's right hand with his own left and twisted them. Surt stepped close to Beli's body, rotating Beli's hand then his whole arm around the wrong way. Surt then delivered a swift but powerful punch to the back of the bigger man's arm, just where it met the shoulder.

With a wrenching, popping sound, Beli's arm dislocated. Surt let go of it and danced away from him. The big man howled with pain and staggered away, his right arm dangling useless at his side.

'I'll kill you with one arm, you bastard,' Beli cried and ran at Surt once more. Surt jumped out of his way again but this time swept his left foot forward as he did so, taking the legs from under Beli so he went sprawling face first into the dirt.

Before he could move, Surt jumped on the back of his head, landing with all his weight on the back of Beli's skull, driving his face into the dirt and breaking his neck with a loud crack.

For a few moments there was a stunned silence all around. All that could be heard was Surt's panting as he regained his breath. Then he looked around. 'Are you still having fun?' he said in a loud voice.

Uncomfortable murmurs went through the crowd.

'Who are you, blámaðr?' Heriwolf said. 'You did not learn to fight like that in the slave market. You have fought in the ring before.'

'I'm afraid that is true, lord,' Surt said with a smile. 'Once I was the ring fighter of King Eirik Bloody Axe. And for many years before that I was King Harald's blámaðr.'

'I have heard of you,' Heriwolf said. 'Men used to live in fear of offending against King Harald lest he send them to fight his blámaðr in the ring. It seems my own champion Beli chose the wrong man to pick a fight with.'

Seeing that Heriwolf was not enraged, the crowd relaxed. Einar felt the tension draining from the air all around.

'How did you come to be here in Francia, blámaðr?' Heriwolf said.

'He is part of my crew, Lord Heriwolf,' Ulrich said in a loud voice. 'We have come here to join your army.'

Heriwolf looked at Ulrich, then at Surt.

'Come here,' he said. 'Let us talk. Bring this crew of yours.'

Ulrich cocked his head to the others in the direction of Heriwolf. Seeing their dubious looks he said: 'This has not quite turned out as I planned, but this could be to our advantage.'

He hopped over the fence and the others followed. After crossing the corpse-strewn horse pen they lined up before the platform Heriwolf stood on.

'Who are you?' Heriwolf said.

'I am Ulrich Rognisson, lord,' Ulrich said. He swept his right hand in the direction of the others. 'This is my company of úlfhéðnar. Formerly we fought for Eirik Bloody Axe and his father Harald before him. Since he lost the throne of Norway, the only masters we now serve are silver and gold. We heard there were rich picking here in west Francia and that you were the greatest lord of vikings. So we are here to pledge our swords and our skills to your struggle. Provided there will be plenty of loot?'

'There will be plenty of loot, don't you worry,' Heriwolf said with a smile. 'And when we go to Ireland there will be even more. So you are úlfhéðnar, eh? I could certainly use some men like you. Many brave men have joined my army but we have few special warriors. We have a few berserkers but most of my men are settlers, men who should be farming not fighting to oust a jarl who has betrayed them.'

'We have many special skills, lord,' Ulrich said. 'We can fight at night, in all weathers, in all type of countryside. We can slip in and out of places like ghosts. We can fight in fixed battles, in lightning raids or carry out secret, silent killings.'

'The skills of the úlfhéðnar are famous across Middle Earth,' Heriwolf said. 'And I can use you. I accept your offer of service.'

'I am sorry about your ring fighter,' Ulrich said. 'But it was not our idea to challenge him.'

'I have lost a ring-fighting champion, true,' Heriwolf said. 'But I have gained a company of wolf warriors who might help me win this war. That is something to drink to.'

He took a swig from his golden cup.

'And your blámaðr there can replace Beli and fight as my champion now,' he said. 'Come to my tent later so you can swear an oath of allegiance.'

With that he turned and left the platform. His line of bodyguards followed him. Realising the entertainment for the day was over, the crowd began to disperse as well.

'Well that worked out even better than I planned,' Ulrich said as they clambered back out of the pen.

'You didn't plan any of this, Ulrich,' Einar said. 'You've just ridden your luck.'

'Luck. The fate the Norns have chosen. The path Odin has pushed me down,' Ulrich said. 'Call it what you will. It's working.'

'So will we swear an oath now to this Heriwolf?' Kari said. 'At least he follows our gods.'

'I have sworn enough oaths,' Ulrich said. 'That one I swore to Aethelstan has caused enough problems. We have plenty of folk here who witnessed his offer though. To them we may as well have already sworn to serve him. Let's use that.'

They walked back out towards the rest of the camp. Just as they were leaving they spotted the viking who had pointed out Surt earlier. He looked horrified to see them again.

'I am sorry, friend,' he said with a sheepish smile. 'I did not know you were úlfhéðnar earlier when I spoke up. I did not know that the black-skinned man was King Harald's blámaðr. I would not have been so impertinent had I known.'

Skar walked over to the man and slid his long left arm around his shoulders. 'My friend,' Skar said, 'as Odin teaches us: *No one knows if a man is a fool until he opens his mouth and proves it.*'

With that he smashed his right fist into the man's mouth. His eyes rolled up into his head and a gout of blood and several broken teeth tumbled from his mouth. Skar laid the man, unconscious, on the ground.

'Let's try to find a way into that town,' Ulrich said. 'Time is short.'

48

Einar eased himself into the water, careful not to make any splashes that could alert guards on the walls of the town. The river was cold but not unbearable. He had most of his clothes on but like the rest of the Wolf Coats he had taken off his brynja and left it carefully stowed near the river's edge. Being in a hostile place without the protection of its metal rings made him feel half naked. As they had to approach the town by the river, however, the weight of the brynja would have pulled him under.

Some men could swim wearing a brynja – some of the men slinking into the water with him that night could do it – but the effort required would leave them unfit to do anything else when they got out of the water again. Einar knew there was no choice except to leave it, but he still felt a degree of perturbation at the thought of leaving something so expensive as a brynja behind, hidden just by leaves and grass.

Ulrich's plan had worked out well. When darkness fell the Wolf Coats had made their way to the front of Heriwolf's army. The warriors watching the walls of the town at that time had been at the horse pen earlier and watched the fight between Surt and Beli. They recognised Surt and Ulrich and believed Ulrich when he spun them a yarn about how Heriwolf had tasked them with scouting the walls of the town at close range to see if they could find some way in. The warriors stood aside and let the Wolf Coats through.

Einar and the others used their stealth craft to creep around the deserted space before the walls. Unlike Fish Gard, the defenders did not control this area so there were no patrols or bonfires. There were plenty of men on the walls though, and the Wolf Coats had to use all their skill to avoid being seen as they crept from shadow to shadow and cover to cover.

They had gathered a couple of items on their way. While still making their way through the darkened camp, they passed the tents of two of the many blacksmiths who had come with Heriwolf's army and set up their forges to repair and service the weapons and armour of the warriors. At the first one the smith was still at work, hammering a sword by the light of an oil lamp. At the second one, however, the blacksmith, finishing work for the day, was sitting at the front of his tent drinking wine with a young lad who looked like he was probably his son.

Ulrich slipped around the back of the makeshift forge and crept in. A few moments later he returned, now carrying several of the blacksmith's tools, which he slipped into the leather bag he wore over his shoulder.

At another point on their circuit of the walls they had stumbled over the fallen bough of a tree that Ulrich had insisted through signs and hand signals on having Einar, Surt and Starkad pick up and bring with them. This made it much harder to move with stealth in the dark, but eventually they came to where the town walls met the riverbank.

Israel had told them that the point they were looking for would be upstream of the town.

'*It was for bringing water into the town for people to bathe in,*' the scholar had said, earlier. '*So you want clean water. Downstream is where all the refuse from the town flows out. You don't want it flowing back in again do you?*'

That was when they had stripped off their mail shirts and slid into the water.

Ulrich's intention for the tree bough then became clear. The river was broad and full, flowing in a wide loop around the town walls. Once deep enough to float, the Wolf Coats, submerged up to their faces, held on to the bough as it drifted downstream.

With no need to kick or swim there were no splashes to alert the warriors watching from the walls above that the Wolf Coats were coming. Anyone who did look down would only see a floating log drifting past.

They slid along in silence, their eyes accustomed to the dark, looking for a point at the base of the wall that Israel had told them to watch out for.

Along the river, the walls of the town came right down to the water. Now having gone around most of the city, Einar could understand why Rúðu had proven so hard to capture so far for Heriwolf. The stone-built walls here towered up from the water to several times the height of a man and the river that flowed around their base was deep. Einar could not feel the bottom beneath his feet.

Sigurd, who had the sharpest eyes of all the Wolf Coats was the first to spot the object of their quest. Where the wall ran into the water was the top of a stone-built arch. He pointed to it and the others kicked their legs, gently, under the water, to move the log and themselves towards it.

Once there they let the log go and it floated off down the dark river. The stone arch was wide enough for Starkad, Sigurd, Ulrich and Skar to fit inside it, with Einar, Kari and Surt all clinging to the edge to stop them drifting on down the river with the current. The arch led into what looked like a water-filled passageway going into the town through the walls. As it was at water level it meant it would be underneath the ground. The end of the passage was covered by iron bars that ran from the top of the arch down into the water. Beyond them the passageway led into pitch darkness. Einar felt a chill of dread at the thought that that was where they were going.

'The Romans built these pipes – aqueducts – to bring water from the river into the town,' Israel had told them earlier. *'They are an amazing piece of work. It's a pity folk have forgotten how they work, but in this case it's lucky for us – and the jarl – that Heriwolf and his men don't know about them. When you find*

the aqueduct, you should be able to get inside the walls through it.'

First, they had to get into the pipe itself.

Ulrich produced the tools he had stolen from the blacksmith – a pair of iron chisels – and passed one to Skar. They could not start hammering or the guards on the walls above would hear, so they set to work on two of the iron bars in the middle of the arch, scraping around their base to try to loosen them from the stone in which they were set.

The stones were slippery with moss and slime and Einar's fingers were cold. He wondered how long he would be able to hold on for. As it turned out the bars were very old, however, and years of flowing water, ice and other erosion had reduced them to not much more than rusted husks. Before long Ulrich and Skar had removed enough of them to create an entrance that the Wolf Coats could go through one at a time into the pipe beyond.

This was the moment Einar had been dreading. They now had to go into the darkness of that black, cold, flooded tunnel. The water level filled perhaps three-quarters of the pipe, leaving enough space above it that they would be able to breathe; however, once away from any source of ambient light – the moon, the stars and fires in the besiegers' camp and town – they would be in complete blackness. Who knew what things lurked in there, waiting for an unsuspecting hand to reach out and touch them, or worse, an unprotected face to brush against them.

They went in one at a time. Sigurd first, then Skar, Ulrich, Starkad, Kari, Einar and Surt at the end. Once inside Einar could see nothing. All was blackness. He stifled a curse as his shins bumped against stone then realised they could reach the bottom of the pipe so would be able to walk through it, their heads just above the surface. At least they did not have to swim.

They set off. The air was dank and smelled of mould and the sound of their breathing echoed against the unseen stones of the roof of the tunnel above them. When Einar's fingers touched the edges he felt cold stones, worn smooth and covered in slime from countless years of water flowing over them.

The journey felt endless. Their progress was not arduous. The inward flow of the water helped them along, but Einar felt as if every nerve in his body was stretched to snapping point. He was who knew how far underground, chin-deep in water, surrounded by complete blackness. The Romans who built it lived a long time ago so the tunnel was centuries old. Perhaps the roof, disturbed by their passing, would collapse in on them, burying them all in stone and earth forever. Or worse, blocking the tunnel ahead and behind and leaving them to a black, unseen, very slow death.

Now and again a faint squeak came from somewhere in the darkness. A new fear crept into Einar's heart. There were rats here too. He balled his fingers into fists and held them up before his face, dreading an accidental collision with one of the horrible creatures. There was nothing worse he could think of than bumping head first into one swimming by and feeling the slimy fur, thrashing claws and wormy tail whipping across his skin.

Einar felt like the tension was almost too much to bear. He longed to scream out just to relieve some of it, to provide some release for the anxiety twisting within him. He knew he could never do that. Any noise could alert defenders to where the Wolf Coats were. He knew none of the others around him would be so cowardly, and the shame he knew he would feel and the disapproval they would regard him with if he exposed his own weakness kept his mouth shut too.

After what seemed an eternity, when Einar was beginning to wonder if he really could go on, he did indeed bump into something. It was the back of Kari. The Wolf Coat had stopped. Einar realised he could make out the back of Kari's head, and also those of the others ahead of him. This could only mean there was light somewhere ahead. The others had noticed this too and this was what had made them stop.

'We must be nearly through,' Ulrich said in a whisper that in the dark of the tunnel sounded like he was yelling. 'Come on.'

Relief flooded Einar's heart as they started forward again, now moving with resolution rather than the tentative, apprehensive steps that had brought them down the tunnel so far. The light got brighter and before long the pipe ended. Beyond, Einar could make out a rectangular room made of stone blocks, which meant more Roman workmanship. The pipe emptied its water into a wide, rectangular pool that had the entrances of several smaller pipes in the far side leading off to take water to different places in the town. Stone columns lined the edge of the pool with passageways beyond. Somewhere further down, those lamps or fires were burning, the faint light from them making all this visible.

The Wolf Coats half clambered, half slid from the end of the pipe into the pool beyond. It was waist deep and they began wading towards the side.

'I hope there's another way out of this town,' Skar said in a quiet voice. 'Because I never want to go down that pipe again.'

Einar smiled to himself. He had thought he was the only one scared and here was the biggest, baddest one of their company admitting that he had been too. They had probably all had exactly the same thoughts and that was what had kept them going.

Then Einar's sight was dazzled and his ears assaulted by shouting. He looked up and saw there were men rushing into the chamber and lining the edges of the pool. They had spears and swords and carried lamps and torches. They were yelling down at the Wolf Coats and brandishing their weapons.

They had only just got into the town and had been caught already.

49

'Do you think we don't know our own town?' a voice shouted from above. 'Do you think we would not set guards at weak points?'

Einar, disorientated by the lights and sudden tumult after the silence and darkness, squinted, one hand above his head, half to shield his eyes from the light and half to ward off any blows he could not see coming because of it. As his eyes stopped smarting he made out that there were at least twenty warriors surrounding them. They were well outnumbered. The warriors were bearded and carried round shields and shouted curses and vitriol in the Danish tongue. It looked like a forest of spear points were aimed in his direction alone. Some of the men carried burning torches. The flames glittered off polished iron of mail and helmets.

'We are not Heriwolf's men,' Ulrich shouted, both his arms raised in the air to show he had no weapons in them. 'I come with a message from King Aethelstan for Jarl Vilhjálmr.'

All the Wolf Coats and Surt raised their hands in the air as well.

'Then why sneak in like thieves?' one of the warriors, a man with gold ornamentation on his helmet, demanded.

'What were we to do?' Ulrich said. 'Just walk through Heriwolf's army and knock on the front gate?'

Even though that was almost exactly what they had done, Einar was glad to see from the expressions on the faces of those above them that Ulrich's words had at least made them pause.

'There aren't any more of them up the tunnel, Lord Barni,' another of the warriors said to the man in the gilded helmet. He was holding a torch inside the aqueduct, its light shimmering across the surface and showing the empty tunnel beyond.

'There is only us, I assure you,' Ulrich said. 'If we were here to take the town don't you think we'd have brought the rest of the army? Please listen to me. We need to speak to Jarl Vilhjálmr. It's very important.'

'Are those wolf pelts around your shoulders?' the man in the gilded helmet who the warrior with the torch had called Lord Barni asked. 'You are úlfhéðnar?'

'We are, yes,' Ulrich said.

A hush fell among the warriors above. Most gripped their weapons tighter.

'Isn't this what úlfhéðnar are good at?' Barni said. 'Sneaking into places to kill folk? You think me so stupid as to bring you into the jarl's presence so you can murder him?'

'We kill folk, yes, but we don't murder them,' Ulrich said, anger in his voice despite the precarious situation they were in. 'And we aren't fanatics, willing to throw our own lives away to achieve the deaths of our enemies. If we kill Vilhjálmr you will kill us, right?'

'Of course,' Barni said. 'You wouldn't leave the room alive.'

'That's the last thing I would want,' Ulrich said. 'Look, just take us to the jarl and let us tell him the message from King Aethelstan. Then you can decide what to do with us. The jarl will not be pleased if you kill us without hearing what Aethelstan wants him to hear. Much advantage will come to him from it.'

'Tell me what this message is and I will tell it to Jarl Vilhjálmr,' Barni said.

Ulrich shook his head. 'If I was you, I'd get me to tell you the message and then kill us anyway,' he said. 'Sorry, my friend, but the secret of Aethelstan's words is all that is keeping us alive at the moment, so I will not be sharing them.'

Lord Barni looked down at Ulrich and the others for long moments. Einar saw his eyes flick from one of them to the other and knew he was trying to make up his mind whether to believe Ulrich or not.

'My heart tells me that I should just kill you all,' he said at last. 'But my head says you are right. I will take you to the jarl. Then he can decide your fate. Lads, bring them.'

His horde of warriors descended on the Wolf Coats in the pool. While some penned them with their shields, others took away their knives and swords. Then they bound the Wolf Coats' and Surt's hands with ropes. Finally Einar and the others were hauled out of the water then punched, kicked and shoved down a passageway that led away from the aqueduct.

They came to a set of steps and without ceremony were manhandled up them and through a set of doors. On the other side they found themselves in a street. Braziers burned up on the walls but the town around them was dark and quiet, almost like the abandoned Dol had been.

'Is there no one here?' Einar said.

'There are plenty of people trapped here in the town,' Lord Barni said.

'Those not on guard will be asleep, lad,' Skar said to Einar. 'They know an attack could come at any time so they need to get whatever rest they can. I doubt there is much to do in a besieged town. Every piece of fuel will have to be saved as well. They don't know how long they will have to make what they have last.'

'Indeed,' Barni said. 'The jarl has decreed no fires or lamps after dark. On pain of death.'

The Wolf Coats were led down darkened streets past buildings made of many different materials. Some were daub and wattle, some had been built with clay bricks and a few were made of stone. Einar reasoned that these must have been the oldest and built by the Romans. All were dark and silent and no light showed from within them. The streets beneath their feet were cobbled with stones like in Aethelstan's Wintanceaster and were not the wooden-planked walkways of Jorvik or Dublin.

Every street corner or meeting point had warriors stationed at it. Einar realised that Barni must be quite an important man, as at the sight of him every warrior stood up straight and touched his helmet in respect.

After a short walk they came to a wide-open space that looked like a marketplace. Most of it was now taken up by a fenced-off area that was filled with a large herd of horses. Beyond it was a building that towered over everything else around it. It was long, rectangular and built of stone. It had many doors and the ranks of windows on top of one another showed it was three storeys tall.

'I was on my way here anyway after I checked the guard on the old Roman cistern,' Barni said. 'Jarl Vilhjálmr is holding a council tonight for all his most trusted men. It's here in the Basilica.'

'In the middle of the night?' Ulrich said.

'What better time?' Barni said. 'Fewer prying eyes and ears around.'

They went up a flight of cracked and crumbling stone steps to the huge double doors that led into the building. Four warriors guarded the entrance. At the sight of Barni they bowed their heads, touched their helmets and swung the doors open.

'Let us go and meet the jarl,' Barni said.

50

Barni led the way into a vast room that reminded Einar of the minsters in Jorvik and Wintanceaster. It was very long and the roof seemed very far overhead, making him feel dizzy when he looked up. The roof was suspended on lines of stone columns that divided the interior into several long aisles and spaces. At the far end was a raised dais where a group of men, each with his own chair, sat in a semicircle. They were tough-looking, older men. In their middle years but fit, with grizzled beards and rich clothes. All their attention was on another man who sat in the middle. The whole scene was lit by oil lamps, candles and a few torches set in brackets on the columns, which gave it a slightly eerie atmosphere. At the sound of Barni and his men approaching they all looked up.

Barni's warriors manhandled Einar and the others to the space in front of the dais.

'Kneel before the jarl,' Barni said.

It was an unnecessary command as the warriors behind Einar kicked him in the back of the knees and forced him down anyway. Einar winced as his kneecaps struck the hard stone floor. He looked around and saw the others were all in the same position. The rest of the warriors stood around with their spears and swords pointed at the Wolf Coats. Starkad and Kari glowered up at the men who guarded them.

The man in the middle seat started to his feet. He was dressed in rich clothes, including a long blue cloak and green britches. His beard and moustache were trimmed short and were blond, though with a few white hairs showing. The one thing Einar could not help but notice was the man's odd haircut. The back of his head was shaved very short, right up to the crown of his head, while the hair at the top and front of his head, which was flaming red in colour, was left longer and brushed forward so it almost came over his eyes. He was a big man, probably as tall and broad as Skar, which Einar could tell even though he was sitting down. He looked at the group of prisoners with concern.

'I see you have finally decided to join us, Barni. But who is this you have brought?' he asked. He spoke the Norse tongue but with the slight lilt of the local accent. 'Has there been an attack?'

'We caught them trying to sneak in by the old Roman waterway, Jarl Vilhjálmr,' Barni said. 'There are only seven of them and their leader claims he has a message for you from Aethelstan the King Beyond the Sea.'

The jarl raised his eyebrows. 'So that's why they are all dripping wet?' he asked. 'A message from Aethelstan you say? Well if this is true perhaps we should hear it.'

Barni prodded Ulrich who, with a little difficulty due to having his hands tied, rose to his feet.

'Look, Vilhjálmr,' Ulrich said. 'I am Ulrich Rognisson and these are my company of úlfhéðnar. As well as Surt here, who could be one as well, if he ever sees sense and revokes his faith in that ridiculous God of his.'

'Well, my black-skinned friend, it seems you have a religious choice to make,' the jarl said. 'I am in the same position; you may have heard. Half my people want me to become a Christian and half want me to stick to the old gods and old ways.'

'Would you say half of them, Lord Vilhjálmr?' Ulrich said. 'It looks like Heriwolf's army outside outnumbers yours by quite a bit.'

The jarl shot a sour look in Ulrich's direction. 'The Norse of Francia are not my only people, Ulrich Rognisson,' he said. 'I am Lord of Brittany as well. They are all Christians there. There are still Franks in my realm as well who never stopped being Christians. How do I unite such different wants? How can I lead all of them?'

'You don't, lord,' Barni said. Even in the candlelight Einar could see his cheeks were flushed and his eyes bright. 'You drive them into the dirt. You *show* them you are in charge. You don't ask them.'

'That's what my father certainly would have done,' Jarl Vilhjálmr said.

'And it worked, lord!' another of the men in the seats said. 'Many of us fought with your father. He carved a realm here in Francia. He made himself a jarl. Now it's your turn to show you're strong enough to keep his realm.'

The jarl did not reply but instead turned to Ulrich.

'Well?' he asked. 'What is this message?'

Ulrich held up his bound wrists. 'It's very hard to talk with my hands tied, lord,' he protested.

'These men are dangerous killers, lord,' Barni said. 'You heard what he said. They are úlfhéðnar.'

'Yes I did hear that,' the jarl said. 'And what is an "úlfhéðnar" anyway?'

Einar started. From his earliest days as a boy he had heard tales of berserkers and úlfhéðnar. He had grown up worshipping the idea of these men blessed by Odin himself who were better than any other warriors. All Norsemen feared them and all Norsemen wanted to be one. That someone who spoke his tongue and worshipped his gods had not heard of the úlfhéðnar was inconceivable.

'They are a special type of berserker, lord,' Barni said. He sounded a little embarrassed to be explaining this in the presence of actual úlfhéðnar.

'Really? How interesting!' the jarl said, sounding like he meant it. 'That must explain those fur pelts they all wear. Cut him loose, Barni. They may be great warriors but there are more than enough of your men to deal with them if they want to try anything.'

Barni made a face to show his disagreement but nevertheless drew his knife and sliced Ulrich's bonds.

'Now tell me, wolf man,' Vilhjálmr said to Ulrich, 'what does King Aethelstan have to say to me?'

Ulrich delivered the message he had been given, telling Vilhjálmr about the boy king, Louis, and his proposed return to Francia. Requesting Vilhjálmr's support and pledge not to oppose the lad.

When Ulrich was done, Vilhjálmr did not say anything for a very long time. He stared at the floor throughout. Now and again his lips twitched as if he was conversing with himself.

Just when everyone was getting uncomfortable, the jarl took a sharp intake of breath and looked up. 'It seems I am very popular these days,' he said. 'It's not long since the King of Ireland was here asking for my support as well. In his case to support him in a war against Aethelstan.'

'Against Aethelstan?' Ulrich said. 'I heard it was for a war in Ireland.'

'That's only the first stage,' Jarl Vilhjálmr said. 'King Olaf needs to be secure in Ireland first, then he intends to challenge Aethelstan for the throne of Jorvik. But Olaf wants the whole of Britain really. Who did you hear this from?' The jarl narrowed his eyes.

'I heard it from your rival Heriwolf,' Ulrich said. 'We were in his camp yesterday. It seems King Olaf has been betting on more than one horse in this race.'

The jarl grunted. 'As is Aethelstan,' he said, folding his arms. 'I hear Lord Alan is back in Brittany. It was I who exiled that fool, you know? No doubt if I am usurped by Heriwolf the lord Alan is Aethelstan's back-up choice. This is what is called statecraft, Ulrich, and it is a dirty business.'

He sighed and sat down in his seat once more.

'Not that I could be much help to anyone right now,' he said. 'Stuck as I am behind these walls. It seems I have some portentous decisions to make and not much time to decide on the best path of action.'

'You can't be that short of time,' Ulrich said. 'You have all those horses in the market outside. If this town had reached starving point you'd have eaten them by now.'

Jarl Vilhjálmr chuckled and the others around the circle made wry smiles.

'Let me assure you, Ulrich, this town is starving,' Vilhjálmr said. 'But we will eat each other before I allow those horses to be eaten. They are central to my plans.'

The others seated in the semicircle shifted uncomfortably in their seats. Several made faces, a couple blew out their cheeks, while others made general sounds of disagreement.

'With respect, Lord Vilhjálmr, it looks as if your war leaders do not agree with whatever your plans are,' Ulrich said.

Einar swallowed. The rest of them were bound and held at sword and spear point. This was not time for Ulrich to start being impertinent.

Vilhjálmr sighed. He looked up at the gloomy shadows that gathered around the ceiling above.

'You hit the nail on the head, Ulrich,' he said. 'They don't agree with me. Heriwolf doesn't agree with me. I was being optimistic when I said half the folk were with me. They've turned against me. Perhaps I don't deserve to rule here.'

'You do, lord!' Barni said. 'You are the rightful heir of Hrólf. Heriwolf is not fit to rule. He's impulsive, intolerant and vindictive. A tyrant. We may as well invite Eirik Bloody Axe to rule us.'

'He has a point,' Ulrich said. 'We met him yesterday and he was torturing and killing prisoners for entertainment. He looked quite drunk as well.'

'So I'm not as bad as a drunken maniac – is that what you're both saying?' Jarl Vilhjálmr said, raising one eyebrow. 'That is very reassuring. You know what? I think I've had enough.'

'You're going to surrender?' Barni said.

Vilhjálmr was back on his feet in an instant. 'No! Never!' he said, speaking through clenched teeth. 'Never, never, never!'

There was fire in his eyes as he glowered at those around him. Einar reckoned they were getting a glimpse of whatever was left of the viking fire the jarl had inherited from his notorious father.

'But the people of this realm,' he said. 'My people. My realm. Have turned against me. You are right, Ulrich. I have been deluding myself. There are more outside the walls with Heriwolf than in here with me. We have barely three hundred warriors in the town – you know that?'

Einar looked at the others. That number was perhaps a quarter of what Heriwolf had mustered outside. It was not enough to defeat Heriwolf and break the siege.

'Lord, it is not through lack of love for you that the folk have gone over to Heriwolf,' one of the seated war leaders said. 'It is because Heriwolf embodies Danish values. The folk – those of Danish heritage like us, like you – are worried. In the generation they have lived here in Francia they have seen those customs, our traditions, even our tongue eroded and replaced by Frankish ones. They are scared their identity, their heritage, will vanish and we will become Franks. Heriwolf is offering a reversal of that. While you, lord...'

He trailed off, aware of the withering glare the jarl was sending in his direction.

'Go on,' Jarl Vilhjálmr said. 'You may as well finish now. I have become too much like the Franks. Is that it?'

'Your dress, lord. Your haircut,' another of the war leaders blurted out. 'Your sending away Sprota – your Danish wife – and this talk of you marrying the daughter of the Count of Vermandois instead. Well that was the final straw for most.'

'You sound like you agree with the rebels,' Jarl Vilhjálmr said.

Einar saw all the seated war leaders stiffen. Their eyes widened and some stroked their beards.

'We are all true Danes, lord,' Barni said. 'We swore an oath of allegiance to fight for you. None of us will break it.'

'Heriwolf swore the same oath,' Jarl Vilhjálmr said. 'At least the Franks want me to rule here.'

'To rule in their name, lord,' another of the war leaders said. 'With their ways.'

'So what do you propose, Lord Vilhjálmr?' Barni said. 'We are running out of food. We are surrounded and outnumbered. We have to do something.'

'I propose we leave the town when Heriwolf is least suspecting it and go east,' the jarl said. 'We could try to break out through their camp on the horses.'

'The horses won't charge a shield wall,' one of the war leaders said. 'We know that. You should abandon this dream of fighting on horseback, lord. If Heriwolf's men have time to form up we will be caught like rats in a trap.'

'It's a chance we have to take,' the jarl said. 'We could wait until just before dawn. They'll still be rubbing the sleep from their eyes when we are galloping up the mountainside beyond their camp.'

'And then, lord?' another war leader said. 'What do we do then? We will have lost the town, the capitol of the realm. We are still outnumbered and Heriwolf will have won a great victory. More of the folk will flock to his banner.'

'We will leave Normandy and its ungrateful folk,' the jarl said. 'We will go east and cross the River Epte to the Franks and ask for their help. The Count of Vermandois wants me to marry his daughter so I will agree.'

There was a sharp intake of breath from many in the room.

'You would forsake your Danish wife entirely for a Frank?' Barni said. The disappointment in his voice was obvious.

'Yes,' Jarl Vilhjálmr said. 'If it gets me what I want. What we *all* need: fighting men. I will agree with the count to marry his daughter on the condition that he grants me an army of his men. We will march back here and retake the realm. I will crush all those ungrateful rebel bastards beneath my heel and rule once more.'

'…as the lapdog of the Franks,' one of the war leaders said.

'Perhaps you would rather live as the bitches of Heriwolf?' the jarl said, a peeved expression on his face.

'Lord it's not just that,' Barni said. 'Many of us have raided east of the Epte. Some of us even fought with your father on the great raid on Paris.'

Wry smiles provoked by fond memories broke out on the faces of a couple of the older war leaders.

'We left many corpses on that side of the river,' Barni said. 'We took many slaves, burned many towns. Do you think they'll welcome us with open arms?'

'We'll end up in a dungeon,' one of the war leaders said. 'If we're lucky. More likely we'll lose our heads. We cannot go with you.'

Einar could see the hurt pride in the eyes of these old men and he felt sorry for them. They were doing the right thing but the man they had chosen to follow did not represent the things they held dear, while the man they were fighting did. Yet they were holding steadfast to the oaths they had sworn, which was an honourable and admirable course to take.

The jarl blew out his cheeks and looked at the ceiling again.

'Well, if you won't go with me then perhaps I should go alone,' he said. 'Perhaps I could sneak out the way these wolf men got in then head east by myself. I will get help and return with an army.'

Disgruntled murmurs ran around the room.

'Does anyone have a better suggestion?' the jarl said. 'We can't just sit here and starve to death. What do your wolf men think?'

'What, lord?' Barni said.

'These úlfhéðnar fellows,' the jarl said, waving a hand at Einar and the others. 'You said they are great warriors. Tell me, Ulrich Rognisson. What do you make of my plan? Doesn't it make sense?'

Ulrich looked the jarl directly in the eye.

'I think it's pathetic,' he said. '*Ergi.*'

Gasps ran around the room. Einar's heart sank. To call another man *ergi* was to say he was unmanly. At home in Iceland such an insult had caused so many fights that to use it was against the law. He felt the sharp points of the blades of the warriors guarding him poke harder into his flesh.

'Do you, now?' the jarl said, leaning forward. 'Please explain why. But choose your words with care, wolf man. I am still jarl and can order your death whenever I wish it.'

'If you run away you will be nothing,' Ulrich said. '*Níð*. A jarl in name only, living off whatever table scraps the lords of the Franks deign to throw you. An exile in another king's court – just like Lord Alan has been. And if this count gives you the warriors to take back Normandy, do you think the only price will be his daughter? No. You'll have the name of jarl but it will be he who gives the orders. Would you rather do that than rule here in your own right?'

'Of course not,' Jarl Vilhjálmr said. 'But what is the alternative?'

'I heard you have three hundred men,' Ulrich said. 'Stay and fight. Defeat this upstart Heriwolf and show you are truly the son of Göngu-Hrólf.'

The others nodded.

'Listen to him, lord,' Barni said. 'Stay with us and fight for your birthright. For all of us, your sworn folk.'

The jarl appeared to be astonished. He looked around him with wide eyes, his mouth slightly open. Einar also noted his cheeks were flushing a deep crimson.

'You are right,' he said. 'All of you. I am ashamed of myself for even thinking of leaving. Especially for suggesting I leave alone. You swore an oath of allegiance to me and I swore an oath to be your lord and jarl. I won't break that. Very well. We will fight. We will attack Heriwolf and take the fight to him. We may all die but we will die with glory.'

The seated war leaders all sprung to their feet. Their cheers echoed around the lofty stone arches of the ceiling above.

'Thank you, lord,' Barni said.

'Don't thank me, Barni,' the jarl said with a wry smile. 'All I've done is agree to die alongside you. We are still outnumbered at least three to one.'

'We can fight them on horseback, lord,' Barni said. 'In the Frankish manner. You are always saying warriors on horseback can defeat many more on foot. You saw it yourself when the Franks defeated your father at Paris.'

'True,' the jarl said, pursing his lips. 'But they took us by surprise. As Gorm there said, horses won't charge a shield wall. If Heriwolf has time to organise his men then we are simply charging into certain death.'

There was silence for a moment as all in the basilica contemplated this. Then Ulrich broke it.

'I am glad you have decided on this course of action, Lord Vilhjálmr,' he said. 'Can I make a suggestion?'

51

In the grey light of dawn the next morning, a thick mist crawled from the river and hung over the meadow between the walls of Rúðu and the encampment of the army of Heriwolf. A pair of swans took off from the water and flew off, their beating wings the only sound in the morning air. It was a scene so peaceful it was hard to believe a war was underway.

Then there came a rattling of bolts and chains from the barred gates of the town. The great oak doors swung open and ranks of horsemen began trotting out. Each rider was clad in a mail shirt and a visored iron helmet. He carried a long-shafted spear and had a shield slung over his back.

Once outside the gates they began to form up in a long battle line across the meadow. The warriors on watch from Heriwolf's army began blowing horns to alert the sleeping camp that the enemy was on the move. As the horsemen were still arranging themselves, warriors began flocking from the encampment. Rubbing sleep from their eyes, they pulled on brynjas and helmets as they ran, hurrying to ready themselves for the coming fight.

Heriwolf himself did not take long to arrive. He was dressed in his long coat of shining mail and visored helmet, polished to gleaming even in the overcast light of that early morning. His shield had his symbol of the red wolf painted on it. His merkismaðr, the standard bearer who carried the long pole with his wolf banner, came jogging behind him.

'What's going on?' he said to the warriors who had sounded the alert.

'They're coming out, lord.' One of them pointed to the

horsemen before the walls of the town. 'It looks like they are preparing for an attack.'

Heriwolf grinned. 'Good!' he said. 'I'm bored sitting out here waiting. What is Vilhjálmr playing at on those horses though? Does he think we won't form a shield wall?'

'I don't know, lord,' his warrior said. 'Perhaps he thinks he has surprised us so can charge before we are ready.'

'He would have to get up a lot earlier if he thinks he can get away with that,' Heriwolf said. 'Grimulf?'

His merkismaðr nodded.

'Plant my banner over there,' Heriwolf said. 'We will form the *Skjaldborg* before it. Vilhjálmr will try to charge and when his horses refuse to run onto our spear points we will rush forward and kill them all. Come on, lads. This is our chance to end this!'

It was not long before Heriwolf's warriors had formed a line opposite Vilhjálmr's horsemen. They hoisted their shields and with a clap of linden wood on linden wood, brought them together to form a wall. Then they raised their weapons and the shield wall became a bristling hedge of iron-tipped spear points and sword blades. They began yelling defiance at the men on the horses, shouting insults, curses and calling them on to join the fight. Many beat on their shields with sword blades or spear butts and the resulting sound was like thunder.

Heriwolf drew his sword. He stood in the space behind the third rank of his men where a little raised mound meant he could see over the heads of his warriors. His standard bearer had raised his banner beside him.

At the other end of the meadow the long line of horsemen began lumbering forward. Starting slow, they soon picked up pace to a trot. They let out a great shout as they all reached a gallop.

'They're really going to charge us,' Heriwolf said to his standard bearer. He was grinning, an expression of pure glee on his face. 'Has Vilhjálmr lost his mind? We outnumber them three to one at least! This is going to be easy. I can taste my victory toasts already.'

The horsemen sped ever closer. The men in the shield wall could feel the thrumming of the approaching horses. They tightened their grips on their shields, compacting their wall formation and making it even more solid.

'Kill them!' Heriwolf screamed at the top of his voice. 'Kill them all!'

The horsemen were perhaps a hundred paces away.

Then another shout arose from somewhere between the two armies. Men rose like wraiths from the mist and the long grass and began to charge forward at Heriwolf's shield wall. There were perhaps thirty of them. They were dressed for war and screaming battle cries and the ones in the centre were clad in wolfskin pelts.

52

After being supplied with helmets, shields and brynjas and given their pick of long weapons to carry, the Wolf Coats' numbers had been augmented, at Ulrich's request, by twenty-three of the jarl's warriors; men hand-picked by Barni to be battle-hardened and reliable. In the dead of the night and long before dawn they had slipped out one by one through a small door in the gate of the town. Under the cover of darkness they had crawled out through the long grass of the meadow until they reached a point where Ulrich judged they would be close enough to the most likely point where Heriwolf would form his shield wall. Then they waited for first light and the arrival of the jarl and his warriors on horseback.

The tension had been unbearable. Apart from the discomfort of lying in the damp grass in the cold of the night in complete silence, there was the ever-mounting fear that a patrol would stumble on them by accident, or that they had gone too far and Heriwolf would form his shield wall right on top of them. Added to that was the knowledge that when first light arrived battle would commence, and some – perhaps all of them – would not live to see noon. It was too much for a couple of the jarl's men who vomited from their nerves. Even so, they were experienced enough to do it quietly.

Then the darkness had paled into the grey light of dawn and Vilhjálmr's horse warriors had trooped out of the gate. Heriwolf had formed his shield wall just where Ulrich had judged he would, and now it was time to fight.

Einar rose from the ground, screaming like a man insane. Like the other Wolf Coats beside him he had the head of his wolfskin pulled up over his helmet so the ears of the beast stood up in two points like in life, and the snout projected over his visor. Along with the jarl's men they pounded with all their might towards the shield wall before them. Einar saw the shock and fear in the eyes of the men behind the shields and he felt the dragon's fire ignite in his heart, the bloodlust that was awoken in some in battle. All the tension and tiredness of the previous night dropped away, replaced by a strange, fierce joy. He howled and raised his sword. It was time to attack.

Skar was right in the middle of the line. He bore a long-handled axe in one hand and a shield in the other.

'*Svinfylking!*' the big man roared at the top of his lungs. 'On me. Form the boar's head.'

The svinfylking was an arrowhead-shaped battle formation shaped like the nose of a boar. Skar was at the point, then Einar and Sigurd on either side of him, one step behind, and the others following in turn. Each man had his shield to the fore. The jarl's men filled out the rest of the triangle.

They stormed towards the shield wall. Einar knew he was panting, his mail clinked with every step and his nose was filled with the smell of oiled leather, stale sweat and the tang of iron from his helmet. When they were mere steps from Heriwolf's shield wall, each man in the arrow-head formation linked shields so they overlapped along each side. At the same time each shoved the man in front with their leading shoulder, transferring momentum to the men at the point.

Einar saw the enemy crouching behind their shields, placing their feet wide to brace themselves for the impact. He felt as though time was slowing down and everyone around him looked like they were moving slowly, as if in deep water.

Then the svinfylking smashed into Heriwolf's shield wall. A great clanging of metal on metal erupted along with the thunderous crash of wood on wood as shields clashed together. The unlucky man Skar thundered into went reeling backwards, propelled out of his position by the sheer force of impact. He stumbled and fell, then a moment later was trampled under the merciless boots of the charging warriors.

Men screamed in pain or terror and Einar felt the full battle rage, the divine berserker fury given by Odin, take over his heart. He sliced left and right with his sword, cutting down men, kicking, biting, punching, ripping the hole they had punched in the shield wall even wider.

The men following in the svinfylking tore into the widening breach. In moments Heriwolf's men's formation had a hole in it as it broke like a shield split in two by a spear point.

But thirty men, even úlfhéðnar, could not fight a thousand. Ulrich's plan depended on them arriving at Heriwolf's line just before the jarl and his horsemen. Horses would not charge a solid shield wall – they were not stupid creatures – but men were. It was the job of the Wolf Coats to punch a hole in Heriwolf's defensive formation to allow the horses to charge through.

Einar felt as much as heard or saw the horses coming, pounding in behind them, their hooves drumming on the ground and their hot breath and drool spraying through the air. The horsemen tore into the gap in the shield wall opened by the men on foot and then chaos ensued.

Heriwolf's men, now finding horsemen among and behind their lines, broke formation entirely and the shield wall disintegrated. Jarl William and his men rode among them, hacking, slashing and stabbing from their saddles, lopping off heads, hands and arms, distributing death and maiming all around.

'Skjaldborg,' Skar shouted over the din.

The Wolf Coats and the others of the jarl's men on foot spread their swine array out into a line, forming their own shield wall. They began to advance towards Heriwolf's banner, cutting down any of his men who stood in their way.

Terror and panic spread through Heriwolf's army like wildfire through dry grassland in high summer. All trace of discipline fell apart. Some stood and fought, only to be killed by warriors on horseback or mowed down by the Wolf Coats' advancing shield wall. Others turned and fled. Many did not get far. The horsemen caught up with them fast, delivering killing blows from above on unprotected backs, necks or heads. Realising they could not outrun the horses, others turned and fled towards the river, seeking to escape the slaughter that way. Most of those who wore mail barely got halfway across before the weight of their armour dragged them under to a murky death in the brown waters of the river.

Men began dropping their weapons and shields and throwing up their hands in surrender. By the time the Wolf Coats' shield wall had made it to Heriwolf's banner, the battle was as good as over. As if to emphasise the point, Skar broke formation, stomped up to the cowering merkismaðr, Grimulf, and felled him with a mighty blow of his axe. He pulled the battle standard out of the ground, broke its shaft over his knee and threw the banner into the dirt.

It was finished.

53

Einar felt the battle rage drain from him, leaving tiredness and cold behind. His arms felt like they were made of stone and he dangled them by his sides. Einar could hear his own breathing, loud and rasping under his visor. Sweat was running down his cheeks, neck and back. He undid the laces of his helmet and took it off, then stood for a long moment, head bowed, trying to get his panting breath under control. He was splattered with blood but none of it was his own. The air was filled with the stench of shit from spilled entrails and the emptied bowels of the terrified, the dying and the dead, all mixed with the metallic tang of blood. Tents in the army of Heriwolf were on fire, either ignited deliberately or by accident, and smoke began drifting across the battlefield to replace the mist that the rising sun chased away.

Horses whinnied and snickered. Injured men groaned, the dying screamed out their last agonies and the dead were merely silent. The jarl's warriors were herding prisoners into ranks nearby, stripping them of weapons, armour and any valuables they had on them.

Einar sat down on the little mound where Heriwolf's standard had been set. The others did the same. No one spoke.

A horseman approached. He was clad in mail and a visored helmet was fastened around his face and head. The flanks of his horse and the blade of his sword were streaked with blood and his shield was battered and scarred from sword slashes. Dropping the shield, he slid the sword into his sheath and swung himself out of the saddle. Landing on the ground he unlaced the helmet and took if off.

It was Jarl Vilhjálmr. He too was sweating and breathless but there was a look of savage happiness on his face, aligned with a broad grin.

'Your plan worked, Ulrich,' he said. 'We beat them.'

'Perhaps there is something in this idea of fighting on horseback after all, Lord Vilhjálmr,' Ulrich said, climbing wearily to his feet. The other Wolf Coats dragged themselves up too.

Barni and the other war leaders came galloping over to join them. They all dismounted and embraced, slapped each other on the back and generally congratulated each other. Then they kneeled before the jarl.

'Lord, you have our renewed allegiance,' Barni said. 'We pledge to follow you as our jarl from this day onwards.'

'Thank you,' Vilhjálmr said. 'And I pledge to fulfil my oath as your jarl. I will protect our folk and our customs. We will be a proud realm who does not forget its forefathers and where they came from.'

All those around cheered.

'Jarl Vilhjálmr, there is someone you should meet.'

A woman's voice made them all turn around. Sprota stood a little way off. Unlike the exhausted woman Einar had last seen, she now looked radiant; beautiful and strong. In her arms she held her baby. Behind her were Affreca, Roan, Israel and Wulfhelm.

'Sprota!' Vilhjálmr said, his cheeks flushing. He held out his hands as if surrendering. 'I am sorry. Sorry for sending you away. Sorry for the way you were treated. I see I was wrong now. These are my people and I have forgotten our ways. The bishop may call it *in more Danicum* all he wants, but in my eyes now you are my wife. We are married. I love you.'

'And this is your son,' Sprota said, a broad grin spreading across her face.

The jarl's jaw dropped open. 'A son? I had no idea we have been apart so long!' he said.

Vilhjálmr rushed over to Sprota. He kissed and embraced

her, then stared in joyful amazement at the child. He raised a bloodstained, mail-clad finger and stroked the baby's nose, leaving a trail of crimson on the milk-white skin.

'I would do something about that bishop if I were you, lord,' Affreca said. 'He is a rather overzealous Christian, you might say.'

'You need not fear, Sprota,' Vilhjálmr said. 'Our baby will grow up in Fish Gard under my protection. He will learn the *Dönsk* tongue, the language of our forefathers.'

He glanced at Ulrich.

'This boy will not grow up not knowing what úlfhéðnar means,' he said with a smile.

More cheering broke out all around.

Another group of warriors arrived. They were shoving and kicking a bedraggled-looking Heriwolf before them. He had been stripped of his mail and his shirt ripped off. His hands were bound behind his back and one of his eyes was blackened.

'We caught him trying to swim across the river, lord,' one of the warriors said.

Barni looked at the warriors with narrowed eyes. 'Are you men from Rúðu?' he asked. 'If you are I don't recognise you.'

The newcomers all fell to one knee and bowed their heads.

'We are Heriwolf's men, Jarl Vilhjálmr,' one of them said. 'When we saw you attacking and him running away, we knew we could no longer follow him. Please forgive us for betraying you. We know we made a mistake.'

The jarl looked at them for a long moment. Then he looked at Sprota.

'Well we can all make mistakes sometimes,' he said. 'And I forgive you yours. As long as you swear to me now that you will follow my rule and never rebel against me or my family again.'

'We swear, lord,' the warriors said.

'And what about me?' Heriwolf said, revealing bleeding gums and a missing front tooth.

'You?' Vilhjálmr said, his face hardening. 'You are a miserable traitor. A despicable wretch who dared to rebel against me. Had you taken Rúðu I know you would have killed me, probably in a most painful way. There is no way out of this for you. I sentence you to death. Get on your knees. You will lose your head.'

The jarl drew his sword.

Barni stepped forward.

'Lord,' he said. 'This man has revolted against you. He almost drove you from your realm. He tried to replace you. Shouldn't he suffer a more traditional fate? A more Danish one?'

'What do you mean?' the jarl said.

'He should go through the blood eagle ritual, lord,' Barni said. 'The ancient sacrifice to Odin.'

Vilhjálmr winced. Einar mused that he may not have known what úlfhéðnar meant but the jarl appeared to know what the blood eagle was. The jarl looked at Heriwolf again and his face twisted in distaste and hatred.

'Very well,' he said. 'I believe you said you were the man out of the pair of us who most respected the traditions of our folk, the Danes, Heriwolf. Let's see how well you enjoy this old custom. You will suffer the blood eagle.'

Heriwolf's eyes widened but to his credit he did not cry or beg for mercy as the warriors around him hauled him over to the jarl and forced him onto his knees before him. An excited crowd gathered in a circle around them.

'Have you anything you want to say before we begin?' the jarl said.

'If I'd won I'd have done this to you, your bitch of a wife and your baby as well,' Heriwolf said. He tried to spit at Vilhjálmr but the jarl stepped out of the way and the ball of phlegm missed.

'Charming,' he said. 'Lucky for me you didn't win then.'

'You said you had never seen a blood eagle performed, lad,' Skar said to Einar. 'Well now that will change.'

The last rags of Heriwolf's shirt were torn from his back.

'It's considered a measure of a man's character if he can suffer the blood eagle without crying out in pain,' Skar said.

'Has anyone ever done that?' Einar said, astounded at the thought.

'Not that I know of,' Skar said.

The jarl drew his sword and stood behind Heriwolf. The warriors around him kicked Heriwolf to the ground so he lay face first in the dirt. They placed knees on his shoulders and thighs to hold him down.

The jarl took a few moments to gather himself. Then he thrust his sword into the flesh of Heriwolf's back, just to the right of his spine. Heriwolf grunted but to Einar's surprise did not cry out. The jarl swallowed then began slicing downwards, cutting the ribs away from Heriwolf's backbone one at a time until they were all detached.

Still Heriwolf did not cry out, though he did buck, snuffle and grunt. Einar was impressed. The man's willpower was tremendous. The pain he was under must have been enormous.

Then the jarl pulled his sword from Heriwolf's bloody flesh and returned the tip to the top of his spine. He plunged the blade in again, this time to the left of the backbone. He began to cut again.

Heriwolf finally screamed. His mouth flew open and he bellowed in agony as the jarl severed each of his ribs on the left side. His chest heaved so much it made the men holding him rise and fall with it. By the time the jarl reached the last rib Heriwolf's screams had reduced to whimpering.

The jarl stepped back and Barni and his other war leaders took his place. They pulled Heriwolf's ribs away through his flesh. Heriwolf let out one final shriek. Einar was not sure but he thought he was screaming Odin's name. Then, before Einar's horrified eyes, Barni and the others reached into the horrible wounds in Heriwolf's back and drew out his lungs, laying them out across his back like a pair of obscene wings.

By this time Heriwolf screamed no more. His eyes were fixed, gazing into a vast distance from a face still frozen in the agonised expression of his last moments.

Einar felt his gorge rise. He fought to control his stomach. Despite having seen wounds just as horrendous inflicted in the battle, there was something about the cold deliberation with which the torturous execution had been carried out that was sickening.

He looked around and saw none of the watchers appeared to share his disgust. Quite the contrary. Most of them, to his surprise even Sprota, were watching the gruesome spectacle with eager fascination and expressions of pleased righteousness.

The jarl held up the bloody sword for the crowd to see.

'It is over,' he said. 'Justice is carried out. Now let us celebrate.'

54

'He's going to call the child Richard,' Affreca said.

It was later and they were preparing to attend the feast that had already started in the meadow outside Rúðu. The dead had been moved away and piled into bloody heaps to be burned later. The dying were put into tents to suffer their last breaths and those with survivable injuries were sewn up, bandaged or splinted. Heriwolf's army camp had been looted of food, ale and wine and the folk of the town, along with the jarl's warriors were enjoying their first decent meal in weeks. Wine was flowing freely and the sound of music and laughter floated across the meadow.

Roan had sailed the snekkja upstream to the battlefields and now the Wolf Coats, Surt and Wulfhelm had returned to it. They stripped off their bloodied battledress and washed in the river, then pulled on clean shirts and britches and combed their hair and beards.

'The jarl?' Einar said. Affreca nodded.

'That doesn't sound like a very Norse name,' Einar said. 'I wonder just how long the jarl's new-found enthusiasm for our customs will last.'

'I don't think his people will accept another change of heart,' Ulrich said. 'He has learned that lesson, hopefully.'

'They're a strange sort here,' Skar mused. 'It's almost like they have an idea about what the land of the Danes is like. They think that is how they must behave. That they must preserve their customs and tongue, but what they have is an old-fashioned

349

notion. Denmark was perhaps like that when their forefathers left it but it isn't like that today.'

'And really they're half-Frankish already,' Sigurd said, nodding. 'They're scared the Danish tongue and customs will die out here but before they know it they'll be wine-drinking Christians who forget their grandfathers were Vikings.'

'What have we just done, Ulrich?' Kari said. His tone of voice sounded as if he was uncertain about something.

'Is your memory so poor these days, Kari?' Ulrich said. 'Perhaps you are getting old.'

'There is nothing wrong with my memory,' Kari said. 'I am just confused. We helped Jarl Vilhjálmr secure his realm and return to the customs of our folk and our gods, which is good. But at the same time we helped Aethelstan put a Christian boy on the throne of Francia and retrieved a book that he will use to make Christianity even stronger in Britain. What would Odin make of all this?'

'Odin would do what he always does when he sees confusion and chaos,' Ulrich said.

'What's that?' Starkad said.

'Laugh and saddle Sleipnir,' Ulrich said with a grin. 'Chaos brings war and Odin thrives in that.'

Kari made a face that suggested he was still not happy. He was not alone.

'I really hope you're right, Ulrich,' Sigurd said. 'I'd hate to think I go to all the bother of dying a heroic death only for Odin to slam the door of his Valour Hall in my face over some Christian book.'

'Well you'll be glad to know I've been thinking about that too,' Ulrich said. 'This hasn't sat comfortably on me either. So that is why we will stop with Sweyn and pick up the chest of silver he has for us. Then instead of sailing for Wessex we will sail for Ireland and we will take Aethelstan's book with us.'

'What?' Affreca said.

All eyes looked to Ulrich.

'So you now plan to join my brother's war?' Affreca asked.

'Yes,' Ulrich said. 'Olaf is a Viking king. I believe there will be plenty of golden opportunities for Vikings like us in his army.'

The Wolf Coats nodded. Smiles started to spread across the faces of Sigurd, Kari and the others.

'Aye,' Starkad said. 'That sounds more like it!'

'What about the oath you swore to Aethelstan?' Einar said.

'I have fulfilled that oath,' Ulrich said. 'I swore an oath to deliver a message to Jarl Vilhjálmr, which I did. And I swore to find that book for Aethelstan. Which I also did, with your help. I did not swear I would bring it back to him. Aethelstan has enough books already. We will keep this one.'

'All this talk of Odin,' Einar said, scowling. 'Yet you mean to double-cross the king who has Odin's blood in his veins?'

'Odin will approve,' Ulrich said. 'Is one of his many names not "Skollvaldr"? The ruler of treachery? Anyway, if Aethelstan really is a descendant of Odin, who's to say we should follow him just because of that? Every family has at least one black sheep. Odin could be very disappointed in how his great-great-grandson turned out.'

'What about me?' Israel said, his voice quivering with trepidation.

'You are now a useful hostage,' Ulrich said. 'You will come with us in case we ever need a bargaining piece with Aethelstan.'

The scholar looked like his world had just ended.

'What about the rest of the silver?' Kari said. 'Aethelstan said he would make us all very rich. What Sweyn has is only a down payment on that.'

'Do you want to be rich and fat or do you want adventure and to earn fame that will live forever?' Ulrich asked.

'I'd like all of that if possible,' Kari said.

'There will be plunder aplenty in Ireland,' Ulrich said.

Kari nodded.

'You know my brother's real aim is to challenge Aethelstan for the throne of Britain?' Affreca said.

'I do,' Ulrich said. 'War between Aethelstan and Olaf will be the greatest conflict ever seen on the island of Britain. Ragnarök is coming and Odin needs as many souls of brave men as he can harvest. Think of what a rich harvest it will bring for him.'

Wars I raise, princes I anger, peace I never bring, Einar thought to himself. How long would he continue to follow this mad god and his slaughtering followers? When would the bloodshed end?

'Come on,' Skar said. 'Let's get drunk. I think we all deserve it.'

55

Einar pressed his hand over Israel's mouth with his left hand, then shook him awake with his right.

The scholar awoke. It was the dead of night. Finding his mouth covered and seeing the dark figure above him, his eyes bulged in terror. Einar placed a finger to his lips and shook his head. Israel was no fool and understood that the gesture meant he was to make no noise. He nodded.

Einar removed his hand from Israel's mouth and pulled him to his feet. They stood on the deck of the Wolf Coats' longship. The others lay sprawled all around, snoring away in drunken slumber. With careful steps, Einar took Israel by the arm and led him down the gangplank off the ship. Gandr the cat watched them pass with his contemptuous green eyes. Then they set off along the riverbank.

The revellers from the town had retired back behind its walls. The blood-soaked meadow before it and Heriwolf's former camp were empty, dark and quiet. The ominous piles of the dead loomed like dark mounds in the night.

When they had gone a good distance Israel finally gathered enough courage to speak.

'Are you taking me to be killed?' he said. His voice was high and tight, fear almost choking it completely.

'I'm taking you back to Aethelstan,' Einar said. 'You and your book.'

Einar tapped a leather satchel hung over his shoulder. Even in the gloom Israel could make out the top end of his manuscript protruding from it.

'But that will mean leaving your friends...' Israel began to say.

'Do you want to go back to Aethelstan's Wessex or go as a hostage to Ireland?' Einar said. They were both speaking in whispers.

'Wessex,' Israel said.

'I thought so,' Einar said. 'Come on. I found a small boat and have it in the reeds beside the river. We can be well gone by daylight.'

They found the boat, a small *karfa*, and Israel clambered in. Einar waded into the river to push it out into the mainstream.

'Stop.'

Affreca's voice came from the riverbank. Einar and Israel turned to see her in the moonlight, standing a little way away.

'What are you doing?' she said.

'Isn't it obvious?' Einar said. 'I'm returning Aethelstan's property to him.'

'You're leaving us?' Affreca said. 'What about Ireland? What about Ulrich? That book is important to his plan.'

'Ulrich's plan?' Einar said. 'You think Ulrich actually has a plan and he's not just making it up as he goes along?'

'Of course he has a plan. He doesn't want Aethelstan to become too powerful,' Affreca said. 'So we will now make his enemies stronger. The balance will continue.'

'And so will war,' Einar said. 'Aethelstan overcoming all rivals will bring peace. While there are those still powerful enough to challenge him there will always be strife, conflict and killing. *Skeggold, skálmold, skildir ro klofnir. Vindold, vargold, áðr verold steypiz. Mun engi maðr ǫðrom þyrma. The time of axes, the time of swords. Shields are cloven. A time of winds and wolves, before the world falls. No man will have mercy for his fellow man.*'

Affreca nodded, recognising the ancient, prophetic poetry Einar had quoted.

'Ragnarök is coming, Einar,' she said. 'Odin needs the souls of brave men. Such wars will bring him a rich harvest. When it comes, whose side do you want to be found on? Aethelstan is a Christian.'

'You know that thing we say? *Wars I raise, princes I anger, peace I never bring*,' Einar said. 'Those fine words of Odin. I've been thinking about that a lot recently. You know that is from a poem don't you? The Hárbarðsljóð. Odin says it to mock Thor, his son. Thor has travelled far, gone out of the boundaries of the world, always to fight the jötnar. He fights those forces of chaos and darkness around the borders of the world so men within can live in peace. And Odin mocks him for it. Ulrich chides me for wearing a Mjölnir amulet, the symbol of Thor. And when we were in Wintanceaster I saw a Saxon wearing one and that's what Aethelstan is doing. He fights all around his kingdom to keep the wolves from coming in, so his people can live in peace. It made me think: whose example would I rather follow? Odin's or Thor's?'

'Like I've always said, Einar,' Affreca said, 'you think too much.'

'But anyway, Aethelstan offers the best chance for me to win my birthright back,' Einar said. 'To be Jarl of Orkney.'

'And what of Odin?' Affreca said. 'What of Ulrich? What about… the rest of us?'

'Sometimes you have to sacrifice the best pieces to win the game,' Einar said with a heavy sigh.

'What?' Affreca screwed up her face in incomprehension. 'Does becoming Jarl of Orkney really mean so much to you? If so, then this is a change of heart! There have been many times I've even had to remind you that you were heir to Thorfinn.'

'Perhaps,' Einar said, 'I've become tired of people calling me a farmer from Iceland. The son of an Irish bed slave.'

Affreca narrowed her eyes. 'You know my brother Olaf's plan is to challenge Aethelstan for the throne of Britain. If you go now, the next time we meet will be on opposite sides of a battlefield.'

Einar shook his head. He wanted to say something but his throat seemed tight all of a sudden and his eyes stung. He hung his head for a moment. Then looked up again.

Affreca now stood on the riverbank, bow drawn, arrow notched and aimed right at him.

'I can't let you leave with the book,' she said.

Einar felt a chill run through him. Affreca could hit a running hare with an arrow from over a hundred paces away. At this distance she would not miss.

He closed his eyes and took a deep breath. If the Norns did govern the fate of men then his was already woven. Whatever would happen was already ordained and there was nothing he could do about it. The only choice he had was how he would meet his fate.

Einar opened his eyes, turned away from her and shoved the boat out into the river. Then he clambered in himself. The boat began to drift downstream as Einar began working with the sails, expecting at any moment to feel the blow and fiery pain of an arrow tearing through his chest.

When the sails were set he turned around once more.

The riverbank was empty. Affreca was gone.

Author's Note

Some may note that the word *viking* is not capitalised in this book as might be expected. This is because I chose to use the word in its original sense rather than using the meaning it has been given in modern times. Today 'Viking' is commonly used as a proper noun used to denote all Scandinavian people of the early medieval period. At the time vikings actually sailed the seas, however, 'going viking' was something you did, rather than an identity. Young men 'went viking' in the Spring, then returned to harvest their crops at the end of Summer. A direct analogy would be the word 'pirate' which today holds very similar connotations to how the word 'viking' was used in the medieval sagas: both with a sense of opprobrium at what was an illegal and quite brutal activity but at the same time also having a sort of romantic, adventurous cachet attached to it.

About the Author

TIM HODKINSON grew up in Northern Ireland where the rugged coast and call of the Atlantic ocean led to a lifelong fascination with Vikings and a degree in Medieval English and Old Norse Literature. Tim's more recent writing heroes include Ben Kane, Giles Kristian, Bernard Cornwell, George R.R. Martin and Lee Child. After several years in the USA, Tim has returned to Northern Ireland, where he lives with his wife and children.

Follow Tim on @TimHodkinson
and www.timhodkinson.blogspot.com